PROTECTOR DADDY

LAYLAH ROBERTS

Laylah Roberts

Protector Daddy

© 2020, Laylah Roberts

Laylah.roberts@gmail.com

laylahroberts.com

ALL RIGHTS RESERVED. This book contains material protected under International and Federal Copyright Laws and Treaties. Any unauthorized reprint or use of this material is prohibited. No part of this book may be reproduced or transmitted in any form or by any means, electronic or mechanical, including photocopying, recording, or by any information storage and retrieval system without express written permission from the author / publisher.

Cover Design by: Allycat's Creations

Editing: Celeste Jones

❦ Created with Vellum

BOOKS BY LAYLAH ROBERTS

Doms of Decadence

Just for You, Sir

Forever Yours, Sir

For the Love of Sir

Sinfully Yours, Sir

Make me, Sir

A Taste of Sir

To Save Sir

Sir's Redemption

Reveal Me, Sir

Montana Daddies

Daddy Bear

Daddy's Little Darling

Daddy's Naughty Darling Novella

Daddy's Sweet Girl

Daddy's Lost Love

A Montana Daddies Christmas

Daring Daddy

Warrior Daddy

Daddy's Angel

Heal Me, Daddy

Daddy in Cowboy Boots

MC Daddy

Motorcycle Daddy

Hero Daddy

Protector Daddy

Haven, Texas Series

Lila's Loves

Laken's Surrender

Saving Savannah

Molly's Man

Saxon's Soul

Mastered by Malone

How West was Won

Cole's Mistake

Jardin's Gamble

Men of Orion

Worlds Apart

Cavan Gang

Rectify

Redemption

Redemption Valley

Audra's Awakening

Old-Fashioned Series

An Old-Fashioned Man

Two Old-Fashioned Men

Her Old-Fashioned Husband

Her Old-Fashioned Boss

His Old-Fashioned Love

An Old-Fashioned Christmas

Bad Boys of Wildeside

Wilde

Sinclair

Luke

Hunters

A Mate to Cherish

A Mate to Sacrifice

1

Reverend Pat always said she was going to meet a bad end.

Although never to her face, of course.

She figured he was still smarting from the time she'd accidentally freed his piglets and they'd spread mud through the church, scaring the ladies having their afternoon knitting session in one of the meeting rooms.

If he didn't want her to play with the piglets, he shouldn't have kept them in a pen out back of the church. Of course, technically that was actually his backyard since his house was right next door to the church. But, semantics.

Besides, she'd only been trying to reunite them with mama pig. How was she to know that mama pig had been destined for the spit roast that weekend for the local church chow down? And that after she'd been let free, she'd take off and cause havoc through the town along with her eight piglets?

If Mrs. Barlow had wanted to keep the pigs out of her veggie garden, then she really should have built a fence around it. And if

Mr. Jones hadn't wanted a huge pig eating her way through his pantry, well, he should have shut his back door.

Right?

Reverend Pat still held a grudge twenty-three years later, even though he was now retired.

She really thought it was time for him to forgive her. She'd only been four.

Although now it seemed he might be right.

He'd been surprisingly supportive of her mission. Instead, he'd waved her off with a big grin. And it was more than a bit suspicious that he'd offered to organize a goodbye/good luck party for her. He'd smiled the entire night, ending up rather tipsy.

Anyone would have thought he was glad to see her go.

Oh, well, when she returned home, she'd be able to tell him that he was right. No matter where she went, Millicent Margaret St. Clair could find trouble.

And right now, trouble came in the form of a dirty, glassy-eyed man who was holding a gun on her. His hand trembled as his gaze flitted around the dark alleyway they stood in. The stench of urine and body odor assaulted her nose, making it twitch.

Millie put her hands on her hips, glaring at him. "I don't have time for this."

He sneered at her. "Gimme your handbag, lady."

"I think not! This is a one-of-a-kind Kate Spain." She patted the enormous, patchwork bag.

He looked at her in puzzlement. "Huh? Don't you mean Kate Spade?"

"No. I mean Kate Spain. She made this bag especially for me and I'm not giving it to you."

"Fine. Whatever, just gimme the money in it. And hurry up, I don't like hanging around this alleyway. This is right on the edge of Steele territory."

Steele territory?

"Who are they? A gang?"

He gave a bark of laughter. "Yeah, lady. Sure, they're a gang. Fuck, where'd you come from that you haven't heard of Damon Steele?"

"Nowhere."

"Nowhere is right. Now stop fucking talking and give me your money."

"Where would I find this Mr. Steele? I have some questions for him." Perhaps a gang leader would be able to help her.

"You have questions for him? Shit, lady, you're insane. Can't you see the gun I'm aiming at you?"

"I see it. I'm just choosing to ignore it. See, I don't think you'll actually shoot me." Well, she hoped not since she had a mission to complete. Like she'd said, she really didn't have time for this.

"Oh yeah? And why is that? You don't think I'm tough enough to shoot you, huh?" He hitched up his jeans with one hand as he spoke.

"No, I don't think you can shoot me without getting shot yourself." She smoothly slid her gun from the pocket at the back of her one-of-a-kind handbag. Mrs. Spain, after hearing about her plan, had made this handbag for her. Complete with storage for her new gun.

And look at that, on her second night here she was using it.

She held the gun steady, pointing it at the man in front of her. This gun was also a gift. From Mr. Spain. He'd special ordered it for her. It was a Smith and Wesson, M&P, 9mm in pink. Yep. It was pink. And awesome.

Of course, maybe she should have actually loaded the magazine with bullets before leaving the motel. Seemed like she might be needing them.

The man gulped. "What are you doing, lady?"

"I'm pointing a gun at you." Wasn't it obvious?

"But . . . but you can't do that! You're some idiot tourist who got lost. You're not supposed to have a gun."

Anger flooded her at his words. "So just because I'm a tourist, it's okay to rob me at gunpoint? You scared the bejeezus out of me. I might have nightmares. I might need therapy. They don't have a therapist where I come from. So where would I go for that therapy, huh? I'd probably turn to drink or maybe drugs. How would I feed my habit? I'd go bankrupt, be driven out onto the streets. Do you think that's fair?"

The guy continued to stare at her.

She sighed. "You're lucky I'm feeling generous. If you leave now, I'm going to let you go without shooting you. Okay?"

"Fucking hell, bitch. I need the fucking money. What's wrong with you?"

"Quite a lot according to Reverend Pat," she admitted.

"You're fucking nuts!" He looked around, his breath coming in pants. "Fuck this shit, it's not worth it. I'll rob a fucking convenience store instead. Fucking crazy lady." To her surprise, he turned and ran off.

That was weird. She put her gun away when she was certain he was gone. Big city criminals were odd. Mind you, the only criminal she knew was old Dan, who printed counterfeit money out of his basement. He'd given her a bag full of it to bring with her, claiming she might need it for bribes.

She hadn't had the heart to tell him that nobody in their right mind would mistake his counterfeit for real money.

Millie took a deep breath in and let it out slowly. She turned to walk away when something caught her attention. What was that? Did it move? Was it a rat?

She stared down at it, trying make it out in the dark. The light from the street lit up some of the alley but down here by the dumpster it was dark.

She stepped forward and heard a small whine. Was that a dog?

Aww, poor little thing had to be terrified. Crouching down, she held out her hand. She waited patiently as it finally decided to step forward and sniff at her. Then it gave her hand a small lick.

Wait. She had an idea. Slowly reaching into her bag, she brought out a strip of beef jerky. It was some homemade. Another gift from old Dan. She hadn't had the heart to remind him that she was a vegetarian. Breaking off a piece, she set it on her hand. The dog snatched it and hungrily chewed at it.

"Poor thing, you're starving." She handed him some more. By the third piece, he had climbed on top of her, getting dirty paw prints all over her jacket and skirt.

But she didn't care.

"Come on, handsome boy. Let's get you home and dry." He was so small that he fit perfectly into her handbag.

Just as she was moving to get to her feet, she heard a door squeak open.

"Luther, what the fuck, man?" a masculine voice snapped. "What the fuck are you doing, dragging me out here? I can't fucking be seen with you."

Instinct told her to stay hidden. Well, that and the fact that she still hadn't put bullets in her gun. Sure, she had her stun gun, as well as her pepper spray. But she'd rather not use them if she could help it.

The side of her face started to tingle. No, no, no, the last thing she needed right now was a migraine. Crap. She had to get back to her room and take some medicine. It wasn't surprising. With the amount of stress and lack of sleep she'd had lately they'd become quite frequent.

But this was really bad timing.

"I needed to speak to you," another voice replied.

She peered around the corner of the dumpster. Two men stood in the alley. The one facing her was slim-built and dressed in jeans, a shirt and jacket. The other man had his back to her. He was shorter and wider. Could she sneak off without them seeing her?

Not likely.

"About what? Does the boss know you pulled me out?" the man facing her said.

"Do you see him here? He's got better things to do with his time. I'm fucking taking some initiative. Besides, I'm pissed with him. He's treating me like a fucking courier. You should see what the fuck is in the back of the van right now. It's a fucking joke."

"Jesus fucking Christ. The boss will kill you for this, Luther," the man facing her snarled.

"He will not!" Luther protested. "And he's not my fucking boss. We're equals."

"Uh-huh, how come you're doing errands for him then?"

"You listen to me, asswipe. You're nobody. I could take you out now and no one would give a fuck," Luther told him.

The other man didn't reply.

"I want to know what you've found out about Steele," Luther said. "I know he had something to do with my old man's murder."

Her heart pounded as she listened to them.

"I haven't heard anything about that."

"He was always jealous of my old man. He wanted his power and his girls. I know Steele took most of them when he killed my father."

"Steele doesn't sell pussy, Luther."

Hmm, that made her like this Mr. Steele more.

"Because he knew my old man would have taken him out if he'd tried. Why would he take his girls if he's not selling them? That's why he had my old man killed. So he could have his stable of girls."

Stable of girls? She made a face.

"Far as I know, Steele doesn't have any of your old man's girls working for him. And I've never heard anything about Steele murdering him."

"Then who the fuck did!" Luther screamed.

Seemed Luther had a bit of a temper problem. She ran her fingers through the small dog's fur, hoping he didn't give them away. But he seemed content sitting in her bag. Poor thing was probably freezing.

The man facing her held his arms out placatingly. "Look, shit, man. All I know is that Grady set up a meet with your old man the night he died."

"Who was it with?"

"You know the Iron Shadows?"

"No, who the fuck are they?" Luther snapped.

"They're an MC club."

"Oh, so a bunch of loser old men walking around in leather jackets thinking they're tough?" Luther scoffed. "Why would my dad want to meet with some old biker?"

"I don't know."

"Who is it then? Who did my old man meet with the night he died?" Luther demanded.

"They call him Spike. But from what I hear he never got his meet. Your old man was dead when he got there."

"That means nothing. He could've lied about that. He could even have been the one to kill him. Probably on Steele's order."

"You don't know that. You can't just go after Steele. The boss has a plan—"

"Listen, fuckwit. I can do whatever I like. I'm going to find out what this biker knows. Then I'm going after Steele. And you're going to fucking help me."

"Does the boss know about this?"

Luther flung his hand out and slapped the other man. She jumped at the sound of flesh meeting flesh. But thankfully, she held in her cry of surprise. She had a feeling neither of these men would be happy that she'd overheard their conversation.

"You'll do what I fucking say. I'm in charge. And when I say it's time, you're going to help me take out Spike and Steele. Nobody fucks with my family."

2

She barely made it back to her motel room before she started vomiting.

Shit. Shit. Shit. Not good.

After throwing up what little food she'd eaten that day, she managed to get back on her feet. Leaning heavily against the bathroom counter, she turned the tap on. Cupping some water in her hand, she rinsed her mouth from the taste of vomit.

Meds. She needed her meds.

Grabbing them from the top of the sink where she'd left them earlier, she was grateful that she knew the different bottles by heart since she certainly couldn't focus her eyesight to read what was written on them. In fact, her sight was nearly completely gone.

Really not good, Millie.

She managed to swallow some pills, hoping they stayed down. Then she heard a small whimper. Shoot. The dog.

"It's okay, puppy. Momma's just not feeling well."

What was she going to do with him? She wasn't sure she was

even allowed to keep a dog in the motel room but she wasn't going to ask, either.

Better to ask for forgiveness than permission, right? That was the mantra she liked to live by anyway.

This wasn't the best motel. She could have afforded something better. She really should have done more research before she booked it. Especially since she'd paid for a week in advance, sight unseen. But she didn't like to spend money on things that didn't matter. She hadn't planned on spending much time in here anyway.

Stumbling out to the small kitchen area, she found a bowl and poured some water in it. Then she grabbed a handful of the beef jerky sitting on the kitchen counter and placed it on the floor.

She needed something for him to go potty on.

Think, Millie, think.

It was nearly impossible with how ill she was. Finally, she remembered that there was a pile of fliers for fast food restaurants around here that had already been in the room. Not ideal, but it would have to do. She snatched them up, placing them on the floor by the door.

Then she stumbled her way to the bed, lying down with a whimper and reaching over to grab Chompers, her stuffed T-Rex, hugging him tight. He was the only one who could ever bring her any sort of comfort during these migraines.

She closed her eyes and tried to wipe her mind clear. Tried to forget that she was in a strange city, far away from home.

She'd never felt more alone.

∽

"Now that we're all here, let's get down to business." Reyes gave Ink a pointed look. The other man had arrived last. As usual. And as usual, he looked completely unrepentant and unimpressed at Reyes' reprimand.

Reyes liked to run things with an almost-military command. Kind of at odds with who they were. But at the same time, it worked. The MC was now back in a good financial position and had cut most criminal ties since Reyes had kicked the old president out and taken over.

Most. Because there were some ties that couldn't be severed.

"What business is that?" Ink drawled. "Some of us have better places to be you know."

"Rub it in, why don't ya, kid," Razor teased. "Some of us don't have a pretty Little waiting at home for us. We got no place better to be than hanging out here with you ugly fuckers."

Razor was a big, dark-skinned man pushing fifty. While he looked intimidating, he had a softer side.

"Actually, Betsy insisted on coming with me," Ink replied. "She's out in the main bar with Sunny and Jewel."

"That sounds like a recipe for disaster," Razor commented.

Spike agreed. There were few people he trusted and most of them were in this room. Even his other brothers in the Iron Shadows hadn't earned his full trust. And he wouldn't leave his Little out in the main bar.

Nope, she'd be right by his side. All the time. And if he couldn't be with her, he'd have someone watching over her. Not that it was an issue since he had no intentions of having a woman or a Little again.

"And Royal and Baron," Ink added.

"You brought the twins with you?" Duke asked. "Are you crazy?"

Royal and Baron were Betsy's stepsons. They were slightly wild. Until recently they'd been stuck in some boarding school in Texas. Where they'd nearly started a revolt.

Ink shrugged. "They've been wanting to come here. How much trouble can they get into?"

"Uh, this is Royal and Baron," Duke said. "They drugged Matthieu, stole his car, drove halfway across the country, then took your truck and kidnapped Betsy. First week at their new school and Baron nearly blew up the science lab while Royal got into a fight with the quarterback over a girl."

"The asshole kid was pushing his girl around and Royal stepped in to protect her," Ink defended. "And Baron said that the fire in the lab was an accident."

"Baron has a near genius IQ," Reyes pointed out.

"Yeah, well, so they're a handful. There're dozens of people in the bar watching them. They'll be fine." Ink glanced over at the door as though wishing he was on the other side of it.

"So what are we here to talk about?" Spike asked.

Everyone turned to look at him. He didn't speak much. Didn't see the point of wasting his breath on useless words. But he had places to be.

"Couple of things, Razor?" Reyes prompted.

Razor sighed, growing serious. "You've all heard of the Devil's Sinners? They run drugs out of Seattle and Washington. They're an off-shoot of Devil's Kings who're mainly in Arizona and Texas."

They all nodded.

"They're making moves into Montana," Razor told them. "Their foot soldiers have been hanging out in my neighborhood. Hassling the people that live there, selling drugs to kids. Made a few threats."

"To you?" Ink asked.

Razor shook his head. "No, but they got one of my boys on his way home. Beat him up when he refused to join the gang."

"Motherfuckers," Spike said. Razor hired young ex-cons and helped them get a trade under their belts. He built custom bikes from scratch. People from all over the country came to him to have bikes built or to get special order paint jobs.

"You need some muscle?" Jason asked from where he stood leaning against the back wall, arms crossed over his massive chest. There were few people as big as Jason.

"I'll let you know if it gets that far," Razor told him. "Just wanted to give you all a head's up to watch for these little pricks."

Reyes cleared his throat. "Right. The other thing I have to talk to you about . . . well, I'm gonna come right out with it."

Spike stared at their president in interest. He wasn't usually someone to sound so uncertain.

"We need to take out Jonathan Robins Senior."

3

Millie looked up at the name of the bar.

Reaper's.

"Well, that's not ominous or anything, Mr. Fluffy," she said to her handbag. Well, to her dog which was in her handbag. She wasn't keen on leaving Mr. Fluffy in the motel room on his own. He might get lonely. Also, she was worried he'd bark and someone would complain to the manager.

Not that the manager ever paid attention to anything but the 24/7 porn that played on the TV behind his desk. But it would be just her luck that he'd care about Mr. Fluffy.

So she'd brought the dog with her. He fit perfectly into her bag anyway. And he was no bother. Such a quiet, sweet thing. She didn't know what breed he was. He had a black face with a brown, fluffy body.

He was the perfect purse dog. Calm and small.

Pretending a bravado she really didn't feel, she stepped up to the door and opened it. The noise hit her first, followed by the smell of tobacco, beer and leather.

Reminded her of home.

She walked forward, headed towards the bar that was at the back of the room. Several men wore cuts with Iron Shadows patches on them. None of them had their name on them.

That was unfortunate.

Still, how hard could it be to find a man called Spike?

She would have come last night, but it had taken her a while to recover from her migraine. Fortunately, when she'd finally been able to move without feeling like she was going to vomit, she'd found that Mr. Fluffy was pretty well toilet trained. He'd used the fliers, making clean up easy. And while he might have chewed his way through the spare pillow and a towel he'd managed to pull out of the bathroom, all-in-all she'd thought he was pretty well behaved.

Gradually, she became aware of all the noise around her stopping as people turned to stare at her.

Uh-oh.

This didn't seem good. Despite the crowded bar, she had a small space around her. As though no one wanted to get close. Did she smell? She was certain she didn't. Maybe she had some Danish on her face? It was probably a mistake to eat one for dinner, but they'd looked so good she'd been unable to resist.

"Hello." A young man stepped in front of her. He was dressed in a nice button-down shirt and jeans. He smiled. "Are you lost?"

She studied him. He didn't look old enough to be in a bar. Where were his parents?

"What makes you think she's lost, brother?"

Another young man, his identical twin, stepped forward. He wore a ratty band t-shirt and ripped jeans and black boots.

"She's obviously lost, Baron," the first one said. "Look at the way she's dressed."

Millie had to resist the urge to stare down at herself. What was wrong with how she was dressed? Today she had a red dress that ended mid-calf. The skirt was full so when she twirled it swung around her. And she liked to twirl a lot. It was cinched in at the waist with a black belt and had a sweetheart neckline.

She'd worn a black cardigan for warmth and had black, shiny flats on her feet.

She thought she looked pretty good.

"What's wrong with the way she's dressed, Royal?" Baron asked with a frown.

"Does she look like a biker chick to you?" Royal asked.

"No, but Ma doesn't look like a biker chick," Baron stated.

"True," Royal mused. "Neither does Sunny. Jewel does, though."

This was a very strange conversation.

Both boys took a moment to study her.

"Um, hi," she said. "I'm looking for someone. Excuse me."

"Royal! Baron! Don't be so rude." A gorgeous woman with white-blonde hair, dressed in a pair of flowing black pants and a tight white top stepped up to them. She looked like she could have walked straight off the catwalk.

And they thought that Millie looked out of place in this bar?

The woman reached them and immediately Baron stepped half in front of her, blocking her.

"Baron, get out of the way," she said with exasperated affection.

"Ink said we were in charge of looking after you," Baron told the woman.

The woman groaned. "He said no such thing."

"Pretty sure he did," Royal agreed.

"We're supposed to watch out for you," Baron added.

The other woman rolled her eyes heavenward as though searching for patience. Then she aimed a smile at Millie. "I'm so sorry. I'm Betsy, these are my sons, Royal and Baron."

Wow, she didn't look old enough to be their mother. Millie wished she had her genes. And her looks. And that waistline.

"I apologize for my boys, they're a bit overprotective."

A bit?

Millie glanced around, her cheeks reddening as she noticed they still had an audience of rough looking bikers watching. Not one of them made a move towards them, though.

"That's okay. I'm Millie."

"Can I help you? Are you lost?" Two more women approached. The one who'd spoken was dressed in jeans and a bright pink hoodie with rhinestones down the arms.

"Ooh, I love your hoodie," Millie told her. "Where did you get it?"

"Oh thanks, I bought it at Walmart and then just added rhinestones."

"So cute. I must try that. My belt could totally use some rhinestones."

"All right, enough," the third woman said. Millie's gaze landed on her then couldn't look away. She was one of the most gorgeous, sexiest women that Millie had seen in her life. Long blue-black hair combined with a short denim skirt and a halter neck top that ended midriff, showcasing her small waist.

Wow.

"My goodness, you're gorgeous."

The woman blinked a few times and gave her a curious look. "What?"

"You're absolutely beautiful," Millie breathed out. She glanced around at the three woman who looked so different. From the elegant beauty of Betsy, to the second woman's warmth, to the third woman's edgy sexiness.

"Right, uh, who are you?" the sexy woman asked. "And where do you need to be, because it ain't here."

"Jewel," the second woman said with a worried look at her friend. "She's probably just lost."

"This is Reaper's bar, which is run by the Iron Shadows, yes?"

Millie asked. Around them, everyone looked on. She wished they'd just go back to their conversations.

She really wasn't that interesting.

"Uh, yes," Betsy said, from where she was sandwiched between her sons.

Millie smiled. "Then I'm in the right place."

"You are?" the woman in the pink hoodie asked.

"Yes. I'm looking for someone named Spike, do you know him?"

By the looks on everyone's faces you'd have thought that she'd asked for an audience with the Pope. They ranged from shock to disbelief to glee on one of the twins' faces. She wasn't sure which one.

"You know Spike?" Jewel asked skeptically.

"Oh no, I don't know him. I've come here to warn him. I think someone is going to try and kill him. Now, do you know where I can find him?"

4

Spike just stared at Reyes after his declaration. Along with everyone else.

"You want to take out Jonathan Robins Senior?" Ink finally spat out. "Have you gone fucking insane? He has more money and power than God."

"And he uses that money and power to hide what a monster he is," Reyes pointed out. "You're the one who wanted to take the fuckers down for what they did to Betsy."

Betsy's husband had worked for Forrest. After his death, Forrest had taken Betsy and the boys to his home. And hadn't let her leave. When she'd tried to escape with the twins, Forrest had sent the boys away as punishment.

"I wanted to take Forrest and his merry band of fuckers down," Ink said in his usual way. "But why are we going after Senior? He's no threat to us."

"He could be if he finds out we have shit on him," Spike said quietly, thinking it through. They'd stolen a file Forrest had on his father containing photos of him with a drug lord and a mob boss. Considering, the image he portrayed to the world was one of an upstanding citizen that wasn't something he'd likely want leaking out. They'd used it as leverage to keep Betsy safe from Forrest.

"How would he know that?" Ink asked, but he was starting to look worried. "Forrest wouldn't have told him."

"Someone could have," Reyes said.

"But we have no way of knowing that," Duke added. "We really going to try and take on someone like Senior? It could be suicide."

"He's evil," Reyes said. "He hides behind his money, but we know he's involved with a cartel. He could be using his shipping company and warehouses to import drugs or girls or guns. Or he's being paid to turn the other cheek. Are we going to let him get away with that?"

"We could go to the cops," Ink said, looking doubtful even as he suggested it.

"And have him pay them off?" Reyes spat.

Ink dropped his head back. "Fuck."

"How would we even take him on?" Duke asked. "There's no way we could get close to him. He doesn't even live here. And he's bound to have plenty of security. We can't get to him."

"No, but the Fox could."

They all gaped at Reyes.

"Have you lost your fucking mind?" Duke demanded, jumping to his feet.

Duke wasn't given to outbursts. Not usually, anyway. But the Fox was a sore spot with Duke. He had a thing for Sunny, Duke's woman. Spike didn't think it was sexual. But the Fox was . . . different. An assassin for hire, it was clear he had few morals. Maybe he was even a psychopath, or was it sociopath? Spike didn't know what the difference was. However, he cared about Sunny. Was protective of her. And he really enjoyed pissing Duke off.

Case in point, the pink motorcycle he'd sent Sunny for her birthday that Duke had yet to let her ride. Spike didn't think he could hold out much longer. Not with Sunny begging him. Duke was fucking putty in her hands. One only had to look at the patch she'd sewn onto his cut that he was still wearing.

The glittery patch that had the words *Property of Sunny* on it and a picture of the sun.

Yeah, he couldn't deny Sunny much.

Not that Spike blamed him. Sunny was a complete sweetheart and Duke loved her. But if she'd been Spike's, she'd have been unable to sit for a week if she'd touched his cut.

Sometime soon, Sunny would be riding her pink motorcycle, wearing her pink riding gear that she'd covered in rhinestones.

Spike couldn't wait.

"We're not fucking hiring the Fox to assassinate Senior," Duke practically hissed at Reyes. With his hands clenched into fists he leaned them on Reyes' desk, getting right in his face. Duke was a good vice-president because he didn't lose his head.

Right now, though, he looked like he'd happily rip Reyes' head from his body.

Reyes looked up at him calmly. "Why not? It would be a quick way to take care of a problem and there would be zero risk to us."

"What about how much the Fox would charge? How would we find the money for that?" Ink asked.

"He'd likely give us a discount," Razor joked. "Especially if Duke invited him to Thanksgiving."

"Fuck! This is not happening. We're not dealing with the Fox," Duke told them. "I already owe him for Sunny's life. Ink owes him for Betsy's. You don't think that one day he's going to want to cash in on those favors?"

Duke was likely right. Spike couldn't see the Fox just forgiving or forgetting those debts.

"Look, none of this matters because we're not hiring the Fox to assassinate Senior," Duke told them. "Even if that was something I could stomach, we can't afford his fee."

Spike could. But he didn't offer that tidbit. The state of his finances was something that was no one's business. Not even his brothers. And he wasn't sure that hiring the Fox to take out Senior was something he wanted to get behind. Not that Senior deserved to live. And if he did somehow find out what they knew about him . . .

Yeah, this was going to take some thinking about.

"We can't go after Senior without good reason," Duke stated firmly, ever the voice of reason. "I know he's scum, I don't like it anymore than the rest of you, but we have our own people to protect."

Reyes scowled. "Fine. We'll shelve that idea. For the moment."

Spike knew Reyes wouldn't give up. When he got an idea in his head, he couldn't let it go. Hell, Spike didn't like the idea of Senior continuing on, business as usual either. But Duke was right, it was too risky.

Reyes, for all his cold calculation, had a serious trigger when it came to women and children being abused. It made it hard for him to remain objective.

There was a knock on the door and Duke stormed over to open it. "Baron? What's going on?"

Ink jumped to his feet. "Baron? Is Betsy all right?"

"Of course she is," Baron stated, sounding offended. "Do you think we'd let anything happen to her?"

"Then what's going on? Do the girls want to go home or something?" Duke asked.

Baron stepped into the room and his intense gaze landed on Spike. He smiled. Spike swore those two boys were sixteen going on forty. And Baron had this almost dark streak to him.

"There's a hot chick out in the bar asking to talk to Spike," he said slyly.

Ink sighed. "Don't call women chicks."

Razor started laughing.

"What's so funny?" Ink demanded.

"Nothing man, just you in a father-role. It's fucking amusing."

"Tell her I'm busy," Spike said. He wasn't interested in whatever this woman had to say.

"Are you sure? She's fucking hot. Bit weird, but weird is the new sexy."

"Baron," Ink groaned.

"What? It's just the truth. I should always speak the truth, right?" Baron looked at Ink with confusion, but Spike wouldn't be shocked to find out he was playing them all. He thought Baron understood more than he let on.

"Doesn't matter what she looks like," Spike told him. "I'm not speaking to her."

"Harsh, man. Especially when she came here to warn you." There was that sly look on Baron's face again.

Seriously. What did he do to deserve this?

He sighed and crossed his arms over his wide chest.

"Don't you want to know what she wants to warn you about?" Baron asked.

Spike stared at him impassively. Baron was going to have to work harder to get a rise out of him. And he had a lot to learn about patience.

"Fine, I'll bite since Spike could stand there all day and never ask. What does she want to warn Spike about?" Ink asked him.

"She thinks someone is going to kill him."

5

Millie laughed as Sunny told her about sewing a patch onto her boyfriend's cut. She wiped a tear away from her eyes then reached for her soda water, taking a sip. Alcohol was a trigger for her migraines so she tended to steer clear.

Reaching into her bag, she gave Mr. Fluffy a pat. She was going to have to take him outside soon. He didn't seem to like it in here, he'd been hiding in her bag since they entered.

"Oh, here's Baron." Betsy frowned as she looked behind him. "Couldn't you speak to Spike?"

"Would they not let you in without the secret handshake?" Jewel asked sarcastically.

So far, she'd learned that Sunny's boyfriend, Duke, was the Vice-President of the club. Betsy was with a guy called Ink and Jewel worked here in the bar but had the night off. She didn't seem to be with any of the Iron Shadows members. In fact, Millie was starting to think she had a thing against men. And most women. Just people in general, really. Except for Sunny, Betsy and her boys.

Baron grinned down at Jewel. "Do you think they have one?"

Jewel snorted. "How would I know? I don't have a dick."

Betsy shook her head. "Baron? Could you not find Spike?"

"Oh, I spoke to him. I have got to spend more time with him. He is the king of showing zero emotion. Like, all he did was raise an eyebrow and then he stared at me like I was an annoying fly he couldn't find the energy to swat."

He sounded rather unpleasant.

"I'm so sorry—" she started to say.

"It was awesome," Baron continued on as if she'd said nothing. "I want to be him when I grow up."

He did?

Betsy ran her hand over her face. "Dear Lord, help me."

"Anyway, he's not interested in talking to you," Baron told Millie bluntly.

"Why not? Doesn't he want to hear about the possible threat?" she asked.

Why wouldn't he want to know? It didn't make much sense.

"Spike is . . ." Sunny bit her lip. "Well, let's just say he's kind of intimidating. And I have no doubts he can handle himself. He's likely not all that worried."

She still didn't understand. Even if he felt capable of dealing with the threat, he should want to know about it right? Maybe he thought that she wasn't serious. Perhaps she should leave. She'd done her bit. But she felt like she needed to do more. If she walked away and something happened to Spike, she'd never forgive herself.

"Oh, here comes Duke and Ink. Maybe you could tell them and they could pass it on to Spike?" Sunny suggested, giving her a sympathetic look.

She guessed she could do that. But how did she know they would tell him?

Oh, give it up. You just want to tell him yourself. You're being stubborn.

It was a flaw of hers. She was sad to say she had several. Perfect, she was not.

"Or maybe you could convince the man himself to listen," Jewel said, nodding over at a well-built bald man that was headed towards the front door.

All right. She now saw why he was so confident in his own abilities. He looked terrifying. A scar ran down his neck. His biceps were probably as thick as her thighs and that was saying something since her thighs were fairly thick.

She gulped. Dear. Lord.

Run, Millie, run.

They didn't make men like that back where she came from. But . . . she just couldn't leave. She stood as two men stopped at their table, the dark-haired one kissed Sunny. The blond-haired, heavily tattooed man pulled Betsy up against him.

"Nice to meet you all," she said abruptly. "Hopefully, I'll see you soon. I need to go now and catch him."

"Wait, Millie, I don't think that's a good idea." Alarm filled Betsy's face but Millie simply smiled and turned away, heading towards the door.

She was confident she could get this Spike to listen. After all, it was just a few seconds of his time and then her good deed for the night would be done.

And she could get back to her main mission.

Yes. Simple.

∽

"Excuse me!" She spotted him several feet away heading towards a row of motorcycles. She wondered how he could tell them apart;

they all looked the same to her. "Mr. Spike? Could you wait up for a moment?"

Nothing. He just kept walking away. Hmm. Nobody mentioned he was deaf.

With a sigh, she started to run.

Running was not something she liked to do. Her body was not made to run. All of her bits jiggled. Her ass. Her thighs. Her tummy.

Her boobs.

Her boobs, in particular, hated running. In fact, they often mutinied by bouncing right on out of her bra. This is why she avoided running.

Shoot. There it went. Boob popage. Really, men had it so easy. Sure, they might take the occasional hit to the balls, but really. Periods. Boobs. Childbirth. Women had it far harder.

But she managed to get close enough to reach out and grab his arm. "Mr. Spike, I—"

She startled so badly as he suddenly turned that she stumbled backwards and tripped over her own feet, landing on her ass. She managed to keep hold of her bag, cradling Mr. Fluffy on her lap. No doubt he was wondering what all the jostling was about.

She opened the bag, peering in. Mr. Fluffy gave her a look that loosely translated to *what the fuck, lady*.

Ouch, that landing was going to leave bruises.

The big biker loomed over her.

Well, he could offer to help her stand! How rude. She used one hand to try and push herself up, holding onto her handbag with her other hand. Suddenly, he reached down and grabbed her around the waist, lifting her up onto her feet.

She gaped at him. He was strong. Really strong. Nobody had picked her up in years. And he'd done it so effortlessly. Standing next to him, she got more of a sense of how big he was. At barely five feet tall, Millie was short. But she wasn't light. He had to be at least a foot taller and his shoulders were twice as wide.

Holy. Hell.

And here she was in a dark parking lot with him. Alone.

Too late now to worry about your safety, foolish girl.

Fear made her heart race and her tummy clench. So she did the only thing she could think of to get past her discomfort. She shoved it deep inside, into that box she loosely labelled as *shit she didn't want to touch*.

And she smiled at him.

He gave her a look back like he thought she was a freaking lunatic.

Hey, not the first time she'd seen that look. Not even the first time tonight she'd seen that look.

"Thank you," she told him, wishing she could put her boob back in the cup of her bra. So annoying. She shifted around.

Wait. Why was she thanking him? It was his fault she'd landed on her ass. If he hadn't turned so suddenly . . .

She frowned then shook it off. *Spilled milk, Millie.*

"Why are you running after me, yelling?"

"You mean you heard me call out to you?" She scowled up at him then pushed a finger into his chest. "Why didn't you stop?"

"Why should I?" He stared down at her finger until she dropped it, feeling silly.

Damn, he was intimidating.

"Be-because it's polite when someone is calling your name to stop and talk to them."

She nearly groaned.

Really, Millie, that's what you're going with?

"Never put much stock in being polite," he drawled.

She huffed out a breath. "I can tell." She shifted around again. Damn it. This was so uncomfortable.

"Do you need the toilet?" he snapped.

She stilled. What kind of question was that? It wasn't something you asked a stranger.

"Excuse me?"

"You're doing the pee dance."

Pee dance? She wasn't two. Well, sometimes...

"I'm having a wardrobe malfunction," she told him with false dignity. "Could you turn around?"

He gave her a look that clearly said he thought she was nuts.

"Listen, lady—"

"My name is Millie—"

"Don't care."

Wow, he was rude. And he was turning away, completely ignoring her. She took the opportunity to fix her bra then called out to him again.

"Wait! I still need to speak to you."

"Don't need to speak to you."

"Urgh. I'm beginning to see why you don't care that someone might be out to harm you!" She stomped her foot.

To her surprise, he stopped and turned. "Yeah? Why's that?"

"Because with your attitude, I'm certain you've had so many threats that you likely aren't worried about one more, right?"

She felt terrible as soon as she said that. She bit her lower lip in consternation.

She froze as he leaned in, brushing his lips against her ear. A shiver went up her spine. Holy. Hell. How could she react like that when she'd just met him? And when he was such a jerk?

"There's few that could take me on and win. Go home. You don't belong here. Understand?"

Her cheeks flamed in embarrassment and anger.

Suddenly, he jumped back and gaped down at her bag which had been between them. "Your bag bit me!"

"What? How could my bag bite you?" Had he lost his mind?

Then she remembered. Mr. Fluffy.

"Oh no, poor Mr. Fluffy, are you all right? Did he hurt you?" She drew Mr. Fluffy out of her bag, inspecting him as well as she could with the amount of lighting there was out there.

"He bit me!" Spike stared down at her incredulously.

"You obviously scared him. He's never bitten anyone before."

Well, that she knew of. She'd only known the puppy for forty-eight hours and for most of those hours she was sleeping off a migraine.

"Why is he in your handbag?"

"I couldn't leave him alone. He might get separation anxiety. Or have a panic attack. Poor baby. Did the big, mean man scare you? I bet he tastes bad too, doesn't he?"

"For fuck's sake," the big man muttered.

"There's no need to be so rude. We're leaving." She put Mr. Fluffy back in her bag and turned on her heel.

What a jerk! Why did she bother coming here? It was obvious he didn't even have the brains to be worried.

"Wait!"

She stilled. She shouldn't. She should ignore him the way he had ignored her. Thing is, she'd been raised with better manners.

"Yes?" She turned to look at him.

He gave her a once over. She stiffened, wondering what he saw. Did he find her lacking? Did he think her hips were too thick? Her boobs were too big and saggy?

What was it?

"Where's your car?"

That's what he wanted to ask her? She didn't get it.

"I don't have a car."

"How you getting home?"

"I was going to call a taxi."

He pinched the top of his nose. "At this time of night?"

"And what's wrong with that?"

"Lady, where did you come from?"

"Why do people keep asking me that?" she muttered.

"Can't believe I'm saying this."

"Saying what?" she asked. "At the moment you're not saying anything that makes sense. If anyone is speaking gibberish, it's you."

He stiffened then let out a deep breath. "Fuck. Don't come back here, okay? Ever."

Hurt flooded her. Tiny pinpricks of pain stabbed through her skin. She wasn't able to prevent the pain from filling her and it took her a long moment to push that hurt deep where it couldn't reach her anymore.

If anyone knew what it was like to feel like she didn't belong, it was Millie. But she didn't care.

Or at least she tried not to. One day that box she kept everything locked up in was going to smash open. Everything would be laid bare. And she'd be overwhelmed by the feelings she'd kept at bay for years.

But today was not that day.

"You got two choices."

"What are those? Leave town or be run out?" she snapped.

He gave her a strange look. "No. I wait with you for a taxi. Or I give you a ride home."

Those were her choices? What sort of choices were they? Spend time with him or spend more time with him?

"I'll be fine on my own."

Except it was much later now. There were fewer people around. And those that were around . . . okay, so he had a point.

"Wasn't one of your choices, lady."

"Millie. My name is Millie." She sighed. She could tell from the way he stood there that he wasn't going to budge. "I could go wait inside for the taxi."

He didn't reply. He didn't have to. That wasn't one of her choices.

"How do I know I'm any safer getting a ride home with you than I am standing around and waiting for a taxi?"

He just growled at her. She guessed that was the only answer she was going to get. Pulling out her phone, she sent off a quick text.

Spike stood there, like a silent sentry. A grouchy, rude sentry. But still . . . it was kind of sweet that he was insisting on protecting her. He didn't know her. Most men would have just walked away.

She knew that better than most.

WHY WAS HE STANDING HERE?

Why did he even care if some lunatic with less common sense than an ant roamed the streets in this neighborhood, in the dark?

Because you know you'd feel guilty if she ended up murdered or raped. And she was so damn naïve it made his back teeth ache. Why the hell were her family letting her wander around unsupervised? Christ. She was like a beacon for anyone within a mile radius.

Pure innocence stands here.

Nothing about her faded into the background or was going to let her walk around unnoticed. Not from that bright red dress to her long, dark, wavy hair and that ridiculously oversized bag with the equally ridiculous dog.

Fuck. Him.

At least she'd stopped talking. Why the hell would she try to warn him that someone might be out to kill him? It was ridiculous. They didn't know each other. They definitely didn't move in the same circles. It was obvious she wasn't from around here.

Either she was a fucking good actress and he was being messed with. Or she really was as innocent and naïve as she portrayed. In which case, he needed to stay far away from her.

Spike didn't do innocent. He wasn't ever going to have a happy-ever-after. His happy-ever-after died years ago, along with part of his soul.

Now he was content living in the shadows. That's where he belonged.

This girl here. She was pure fucking light. A star in the deep, inky night sky. Definitely not for him.

He kept his attention on his surroundings, ignoring the petite, curvy woman beside him. She rustled around in that huge, ugly bag.

"I know I had it somewhere. Where did it go? Oh yes, here we are. Want a mint?"

She held out a packet of mints. He shook his head. Where was that damn taxi? Her scent was teasing him. Bubblegum. She smelled like bubblegum.

He took a step away from her. She stiffened. "Not a mint fan, huh? Gum? I have gum. Ooh, and a pack of Twizzlers! Do you want a Twizzler? No? Huh, more for me, I guess."

How did she manage to carry all that stuff in her bag as well as a dog? And did she need sugar? She seemed hyped up enough as it was. If she was his . . .

Jesus. Fuck. Why was he having thoughts like that?

A car screeched around the corner and with a scowl, he stepped forward protectively.

"Oh, that's Manuel. He's my ride." He turned to watch her waving at the man who was half-leaning out the window.

While he was still driving.

"That's not a damn taxi," he stated. There was no signage on it.

"Yes, it is. Manuel just started his own taxi company. I think it's rather entrepreneurial of him. He's crazy cheap. I told him he needs to raise his prices."

Yeah, he'd bet he was cheap.

Millie stepped forward and he reached out to clasp her arm. "No."

"No?" She glared up at him. "Manuel drove me here. He's perfectly safe."

"Millie!" Manuel called out. He'd finally come to a stop, but he was hanging even further out of his window. "Let's go. Wheel of Fortune is on."

"Ooh, I love Wheel of Fortune."

"You're coming with me," Spike told her.

"Uh, no thank you. Manuel is already here. I can't turn him away. Besides, we're neighbors."

They were neighbors? That made him feel a bit better. Obviously, she knew him and was trying to help him in his new business venture. Fuck it. He really had other places to be right now.

She slid out of his hold and turned to look at him. "Nice to meet you."

Was she nuts?

She must have realized what she'd said was kind of ridiculous because she turned away and walked quickly towards the 'taxi' while he stood there and ground his teeth together.

Not your girl. Not your problem.

As she reached the back of the car, he found himself stepping forward and grabbing hold of the door, opening it.

"Oh, thank you."

He was an idiot. Why didn't he just walk off?

"Hey there, big man," the driver said. "You want a ride as well?"

Spike turned and glared at the guy. He sat back in his seat. "You fucking drive her home safely."

"Sure. Sure. I always drive safe."

"Safer than you were just driving?"

"Yeah, yeah, man, for sure!"

He took a step back as she wound down the back window. "Oh, wait, I forgot to tell you about…"

Turning, he strode away. Without a backward glance.

Thank God he'd never see that crazy lunatic again.

6

She paced up and down the motel room.

How the hell had tonight gone so wrong? She'd gone to Reaper's to tell Spike about the risk and she'd completely failed.

Not that it had been entirely her fault. After all, the man hadn't exactly wanted to listen to her.

"So rude," she said to Mr. Fluffy who was stretched out on the new dog bed she'd bought him.

Before going out tonight she'd gone to the pet store and bought one or two things for Mr. Fluffy. Just a bed. And those puppy pads for toilet training. Food. And some toys. A couple of outfits, because they were too irresistible to ignore.

Maybe she'd spent a bit more money than she'd intended. But they were all necessities.

Well, perhaps the blue and white onesie pajamas he was currently dressed in was overkill. But it almost matched her own onesie that she was wearing, so how could she resist?

She may also have taken a few selfies of the two of them and sent them home to Mrs. Spain.

Speaking of home . . . with a groan, she pulled out her laptop and brought up Skype. It didn't take long for them to pick up on the other end.

Millie had to smile as five people crowded into the shot. Happiness filled her, pushing aside her anxiety.

"Hi, guys. You didn't all have to stay up so late to talk to me."

She settled on the bed. Her onesie was one she'd sewn herself. It was pale blue with white stars on it and had a hood with white ears. She'd also added a detachable tail and a drop seat so she didn't have to pull the whole thing off to pee.

Overall, she thought it was damn cute.

Sewing was her stress reliever. She made most of her clothes and all of her Little outfits, like her onesies and her skirts and dresses. She rarely wore pants or shorts.

Doug had told her that she was too big to wear those outfits. That she looked ridiculous dressed up like a little girl.

But Doug isn't here anymore. And after he'd broken up with her, she'd pulled all her old outfits from storage. She didn't wear them in front of anyone else. Well, except for the onesies, but they could pass for pajamas.

And they were like a security blanket to her. They helped soothe her when she was stressed.

"Hello dear," Mrs. Spain said. She frowned slightly. "You look upset. Harold, doesn't she look worried?"

Her husband peered into the computer. He was near-sighted and almost completely deaf. "I can't hear her speaking," he yelled.

"That's because she's not saying anything, you old fart," Mrs. Spain replied.

Millie had to bite her lip as the pair of them started arguing.

Yeah, she missed this.

"Hush, you two, poor Millie can't get a word in." Mrs. Larson shushed them all. "Millie, dear, are you all right? How is your mission going?"

"Not so great," Millie told them. She explained everything that had gone on, including going to Reaper's bar to find Spike tonight. "I left without telling him about the threat."

"I am not sure it was a good idea to go to a bikers bar alone, dear," Mrs. Spain said worriedly.

"There were other women there." How nice would it be to have friends like the women she'd met tonight? "But I wish I'd been able to warn Spike."

"Sounds to me like he didn't want to hear what you had to say," Reverend Pat said. At seventy-three, he was the youngest of the group.

"Reverend Pat are you all right?"

"Why wouldn't I be?"

She'd just never seen him look so relaxed. "Have you done something different with your hair? You look younger."

"I'm stress-free for the first time in twenty-three years."

Okay. That was odd. He'd retired several years ago, why would he only be stress-free now?

"But I should have tried harder. He could be in danger." The guilt was flaying her.

"You cannot make him drink if there is no water," a heavily accented voice boomed.

"That's not even close to the saying," Mrs. Spain said to Andrey.

Andrey immigrated to the states from Russia at least a decade ago. And his accent was still as thick as when he'd first moved there. She was starting to think it was on purpose. He seemed to take great delight in annoying everyone around him.

"No?" Andrey asked.

"It's you can lead a horse to water but you can't make it drink," Mrs. Spain explained.

"But we no talk of horses."

She sighed. Too much more of this and her migraine would return.

"Hush, all of you. You'll make Millie even more stressed. And she looks pale. Have you been eating? Did you finish Dan's jerky? Do you need us to send you more? Are you taking your medication?" Mrs. Larson shot the questions at her.

She smiled at the fussing. She didn't bother to remind any of them that she was vegetarian. They all tended to forget that she didn't eat meat. "I'm fine. Thank you."

"Dan said to remember to use the cash he gave you for bribes," Mrs. Larsen reminded her.

She smiled and nodded.

"We have to go now. It's late. We're old. Good luck, dear," Mrs. Spain said.

"What?" Mr. Spain barked.

"Don't worry about that biker, he's not your problem," Mrs. Larsen told her.

Only problem was. She couldn't forget about him. Or stop worrying.

She ended up tossing and turning half the night. And she kept coming to the same conclusion. If he wouldn't listen to her, then she was just going to have to make certain nothing happened to him. How, exactly, she wasn't sure. She still had to work that part of the plan out.

She also needed to figure out where to find this Damon Steele. Then there was her mission. There was a lot to do. But Millie could accomplish it.

Failure wasn't an option. Not this time.

7

Spike nodded to the bouncer as he walked through the front door of Pinkies. As far as strip clubs went, this one was at the higher end. And Steele looked after his girls. There was a zero tolerance of any sort of abuse. He also didn't sell sex. Yeah, there was full nudity. You could also get private lap dances. But that was it.

Still, it wasn't Spike's kind of place.

He scowled as he made his way to the stairs that led up to Steele's office. Some flunky he didn't know was standing at the door at the bottom of the stairs.

He gave Spike the once over, sneering as he took in his worn jeans, scuffed motorcycle boots and leather vest.

"You can't come up here. It's private."

"Get out of my way." Spike didn't have the patience for this. That dark-haired vixen from last night was still plaguing him. This morning, he'd found himself scouring the news for any mentions of a missing or murdered woman like some crazed stalker.

When he didn't find anything, he'd actually sighed in relief. What was it about her that had gotten to him? He never should have stopped to listen to her nonsense. But then she'd tripped and he couldn't just leave her sitting on the ground.

Or on her own in a fairly rough neighborhood. She was a sexier, more naïve version of that woman from *The Sound of Music*. He swore, if she'd broken into song, he wouldn't have been shocked.

He needed to forget about her and her bubblegum scent, her handbag dog and her over-the-top optimism. He had actual shit to worry about.

Now he was late to his meeting with Steele. And he was in a damn bad mood.

This flunky stood no chance.

Spike stepped closer. "Move."

The dickhead stood his ground, although Spike saw a hint of worry enter his eyes. How the hell did this idiot get this job?

"You can't get up here without an invite. Mr. Steele is having a meeting and he doesn't want to be disturbed."

Spike would enjoy toying with him. If he wasn't already running behind.

"Move. Now."

The door behind the idiot opened. He had crap instincts considering he just stood there, glaring at Spike.

"Jerry, what are you doing?" a smooth voice asked.

Jerry jumped and turned to face the man standing behind him. Slim-built but muscular, he wore a white shirt with black pants. He had a neatly-trimmed short beard and dark green eyes. Thomas Grady was a man who could blend in when he wanted to or cause complete fear and chaos when he put his mind to it.

He wasn't a man to cross.

"Ahh, Mr. Grady. Was just telling this idiot to move on."

"Really? What were my instructions to you when I left you here?" Grady asked.

"To send up the guy Mr. Steele's meeting with when he arrived. But this isn't him."

"Why isn't it him?"

Jerry grew pale, seeming to realize his mistake. "You mean... he... but shit. He looks like..."

"Yes?" Grady asked quietly.

"Nothing. Sorry, sir," he said to Grady then Spike. "Go up please."

Spike resisted the urge to growl at him. Barely.

When the door was closed on the idiot, Grady turned to him with raised eyebrows. "Why didn't you just tell him your name?"

"He's an idiot. He made assumptions. Steele needs someone better guarding his back."

"I'll let you tell him that."

Spike would.

He followed Grady up the stairs into Steele's office. Which was actually more like a suite of rooms than just a simple office. They entered into a huge room with floor-to-ceiling windows that looked out to the club below. It had its own bar as well as a lounging area and a dining table.

A woman stood behind the bar, mixing drinks. She was wearing the tight top and short shorts that all the servers here wore. She sent him an interested, sultry look. But he ignored her. All the servers were taught to treat the patrons like that. As though they were tasty snacks to devour. It got them more tips.

He was no snack. He was barbed wire wrapped in leather.

Beyond the living room was a bathroom, a private office and a sleeping area. With how much time Steele spent here, he guessed it made sense to have a bedroom.

A tall man, shoulders thick with muscle that he'd developed as a cage fighter, stood in front of the windows. He turned around, giving Spike a bored look. There wasn't much that interested

Steele anymore. Sometimes Spike thought it was like looking into a mirror.

Maybe that's why he didn't like to spend time with the other man.

Or maybe that was due to the memories. Either way, he was already itching to get out of here.

"Spike, you're late."

Spike just grunted.

Steele, used to his ways, turned to their server. "You can go, Lucy. We'll call you back up if we need you."

Disappointment filled her face. He wondered if it was the missed tips, because Steele might own the place but he was always a generous tipper or if she'd been hoping to be the filling in a Steele-Grady sandwich.

Steele was known for that as well.

But she was too well-trained to argue. Instead, she strode across the room, with sultry, hip-swaying steps. It struck him as false. And wrong. He turned away from her, and he noticed Steele did the same.

He waved him to a seat and Grady took over getting the drinks. He brought them both glasses of scotch before grabbing one for himself. Spike set his down on the coffee table. He wasn't much of a drinker.

"What do you need?" Steele asked.

Spike raised his eyebrows.

"You only visit when you need something. Last time it was a meet with that asshole pimp, Frankie." Steele grimaced. "The city is a better place without him. Wish I could congratulate the person who got rid of him." He sent Spike a knowing look.

"It wasn't me."

"Uh-huh."

Whatever. He wasn't here to convince Steele that he didn't kill Frankie.

"Luther is back," Steele told him.

"Frankie's son?"

"Yes."

"Thought he was working for Jared Bartolli in Seattle. Isn't he married to Jared's cousin?"

"Hmm. Makes you wonder why he's here."

"Think Jared Bartolli is trying to get a foothold in the city?" Spike asked.

"It's possible he's trying to expand out. He had a link into the city with Frankie, but now that he's gone . . ."

Fuck. That was all the city needed. Luther Franklin buying and selling women. Spike felt ill at the thought.

"Jared Bartolli is smarter than his father was. But he doesn't have much interest in selling skin. Which makes him a better man than Fergus, the fucker," Steele said.

"You know much about the Devil's Sinners?" Spike asked, changing the subject.

Steele's eyes narrowed and he gazed over at Grady. Steele had most of the city tied up. His guys ran drugs. He owned chop-shops. Underground gambling clubs. This was his only strip club. But there wasn't much competition, just a couple of seedy clubs in a bad neighborhood, so it was popular. He also owned a restaurant and a nightclub.

There wasn't much that happened in the city that he didn't know about.

Steele's jaw tightened. "I know they're scum. They're bringing in a low-grade meth that's mixed with shit. They're making moves into Montana, taking over territory. They're on the outskirts of the city, trying to inch their way in. Already heard reports of several people dying from a bad batch they've cut. They like to target high school kids, get them selling in the schools and move up from there. Know you don't like what I do, but we don't target kids."

"They're not just here," Grady added. "They're moving in on

Markovich's territory. Heard from Gray, his second in charge, that he's fucking livid. Markovich doesn't run drugs, though. He's a loan shark, runs a few illegal gambling houses, but no guns, no drugs, no sex. He's practically a saint. You know, for a criminal."

"They've been hanging around Razor's neighborhood, tried to recruit some of his boys. Beat one up when he refused," Spike told them.

Steele's jaw tightened but he didn't say anything. However, Spike knew that was enough to start him thinking about what to do with these assholes.

Steele nodded, opening his mouth to say something more when there was a knock at the door. He frowned as Grady rose smoothly from his chair. He walked over to the door, opening it and speaking quietly to the man on the other side.

Then he stepped back and gestured for the idiot from downstairs to come in. "Uh, Mr. Steele?"

"Yes, Jerry?"

"There's a woman here to see you."

Steele sighed. "I don't need any company. Tell her thank you, but no."

Spike wouldn't have been so polite. Especially not with how often Steele was propositioned.

"Umm, this woman . . . she's not . . . she's not your usual type."

Steele raised his eyebrows. "I have a usual type?"

Spike snorted. Steele turned to him.

"Blonde, busty and tall," Spike told him.

"I hadn't realized I'd become so predictable. So I'm guessing she's a short brunette?"

"Well, yeah, she is, but that's not what I mean. I don't think she's here for a fuck. Umm, she seems like a lady."

Spike sat up straight. No, it couldn't be. There were plenty of short brunettes in this city. No way it would be her.

"My answer remains the same," Steele said in a low voice.

"Right, sir. Do you want to tell her yourself?"

"No, I don't want to tell her. Get rid of her."

Something didn't sit right in Spike's gut. It couldn't be her. Impossible. Why would she be here? Yet he couldn't stop himself from checking. He walked over to the windows. And caught sight of dark gleaming hair as a woman dressed in red strode towards the back room where all the strippers got ready.

Fuck. Was it her?

Spike watched until the woman disappeared. He turned to Jerry. "This woman, was she carrying an ugly, oversized purse? Maybe with a dog in it?"

"A dog?" Steele asked, looking shocked.

"I didn't see a dog, but yeah, she did have a big purse," Jerry replied.

"You know her?" Steele asked curiously. There was something in his gaze. A reminder of their shared ties. "Do you want her sent up?"

"Don't know her. May have met her. Can't understand why she'd be here. Or asking for you."

Unless she'd followed him. But why ask for Steele? Fuck.

"Send her up," Steele told Jerry.

Jerry disappeared before Spike could tell him not to bother, that she'd already wandered off.

"Tell me about this woman," Steele said, watching him with predatory eyes. Spike just stared back at him calmly.

Jerry returned, his breath coming in harsh pants. "She's disappeared."

Steele glared at him. "Then find her!"

Spike sighed. "I know where she is." Question was, did he want to go after her?

Fuck it.

If it was her then he obviously needed to give her a harsher warning about staying away from him. He strode out of the room, coming to a stop as he realized Steele was moving with him. "Stay here."

"But this woman did come here asking for me. I feel rude just turning her away."

"Didn't bother you two minutes ago," Spike pointed out with a scowl.

"Ah, but that was before I knew that you knew her. You never get involved with women."

"Not fucking involved with her."

Steele just gave him an amused look. Fuck him anyway.

∽

"Oh look at the pretty puppy!"

Millie smiled as she watched Chardonnay cuddle Mr. Fluffy. Mr. Fluffy sent a look back to Millie as though asking her why she was letting some other woman accost him. But she figured Mr. Fluffy was her way in. She'd been watching Chardonnay up on the dance floor while she'd been waiting for that nice man to find Mr. Steele.

Hm. Actually, she probably shouldn't have wandered off the way she had. She really should go back and find out if Mr. Steele would see her.

She'd just had to come back and tell Chardonnay how talented she was.

"I wish I had your talent for dancing," she told Chardonnay as she took back Mr. Fluffy before he suffocated against the other woman's impressive cleavage. "The way you twisted and turned. I'd have found myself flat on my back, probably with a twisted ankle."

Chardonnay gave her a look that was equal parts amused and cynical. "It just takes a bit of practice. And yoga. Lots of yoga."

"Back in my hometown, one of the residents started up a yoga class. Only Mrs. Larsen slipped and broke her hip and we decided it probably wasn't a good idea to keep continuing on."

"That's too bad. If you ever want me to show you some moves, you can come in here while I'm practicing."

"I can?"

Chardonnay smiled at her. "Sure."

Another girl walked through the changing room, completely naked. Chardonnay had pulled on a robe as soon as she'd left the stage. But the dark-skinned, beautiful girl who took a seat in front of a mirror to adjust her make-up didn't seem to care.

Millie sighed.

"What you staring at?" the other woman snapped. "Who's she, Chardonnay?"

"Chill, Tawny. She just came back here to tell me how good I was on stage."

"You're not supposed to have clients back here," Tawny told her.

"Relax. Not like she's some old perv come to gawk at you."

"I don't know, she seems to be doing plenty of gawking," Tawny said slyly. "Like what you see?" She wrapped a gown around her body.

Millie felt her face grow red. "I'm sorry, that was rude of me. It's just that you're beautiful and I was wishing I had hair like yours and eyes like yours and that body . . . I'm so sorry."

She stood, feeling flustered and like a complete moron. Just a country bumpkin making an idiot of herself. Spike was right. She didn't belong here.

Problem was, she didn't belong anywhere. Not back home. Much as the people cared about her, there wasn't much there for her. Not here, where she knew no one.

Loneliness assaulted her.

"Hey, don't go." Chardonnay reached out a hand to stop her as she turned away. "Don't worry about Tawny, she's snappy with everyone. It's just her nature."

"I should go anyway," she said. "I asked some nice man to see if Mr. Steele would talk to me, he's probably wondering where I've gotten off to."

"Where is she?" a loud voice demanded.

Tawny let out a gasp, looking terrified as she jumped to her feet. A skinny man pushed away a girl who'd just entered the room, shoving her against a table. She let out a pained cry and instantly, Millie slid her hand into her bag, feeling around for her stun gun.

She set her bag on a table, she didn't want to risk Mr. Fluffy getting in the way, and hid the stun gun in the folds of her skirt.

The man wore baggy jeans and a holey wife beater. His head was shaved bald and he had tattoos that went up one side of his neck and over his face.

"Yo bitch!" he said, his gaze zeroing in on Tawny. "What the fuck did I tell you about running from me? You're not fucking working here, showing off what fucking belongs to me. You want a good fucking, you'll get it from me!"

He grabbed his crotch and pumped his hips.

Ew. That was disgusting.

Thankfully it was over quickly. But then he shoved past Chardonnay and Millie towards Tawny who cowered away from him, with such a terrified look on her face that it actually made Millie's stomach hurt in fear for her.

"Come on, Tawny, I won't tell you again, bitch." He grabbed Tawny's arm. Hard if the way she cried out was any indication. Then he started dragging her from of the room. Where the hell were the bouncers? Why wasn't someone stopping him? It was obvious that Tawny didn't want anything to do with this asshole.

He was creepy and terrifying.

But that wasn't going to stop Millie from doing something. She stepped out in front of him, keeping her stun gun hidden. Her full skirt was pleated with a layer of tulle sewn between two pieces of material so it flowed out from her waist. It was one she'd made herself. And it was perfect in this situation.

Millie stood between him and the door.

"Get out of the way, bitch," he spat at her.

"Corey, please," Tawny begged.

"Let Tawny go and I will."

Chardonnay stood frozen off to the side, watching with wide eyes. Tawny just stared at the asshole, face filled with terror, her entire body trembling.

Corey grinned. It wasn't a pretty sight. His teeth were yellow and he was missing one at the front. "Listen, you fat bitch, get out of the way now and I won't mess you up. Much."

Yeah, she could see just how much he'd love to 'mess her up.'

"Let Tawny go and I won't have to hurt you. Much."

"Jesus fucking Christ, what are you doing?" Chardonnay whispered.

Corey turned to glare at her and she shied away. Millie had had enough of this asshole. "Let. Her. Go."

To her shock, he shoved Tawny away. Then he took a step towards her. There was death in his gaze. And Millie had to work hard not to run. To stand her ground.

"Oh, you're gonna regret that, bitch. I am gonna mess you the fuck up." He reached out for her and she struck, pressing the stun gun to his arm and pushing down.

He stumbled backward, looking dazed and confused. Tawny gasped as he tripped over a bag on the floor and fell onto his back.

"What the fuck!" a deep voice exclaimed.

Somebody walked through the door. A huge man that had on black pants and a black T-shirt with *Pinkies* written on it. The bouncer. About time. Following him was a calm-looking man dressed in a suit. It had to be especially made for him, considering his large build. His pale blue gaze flickered from her to the stun gun in her hand, the man groaning on the floor to the two scared women.

Another man walked in, dressed in black pants and a white shirt.

His gaze immediately took in the scene then moved down to Corey who was starting to swear up a storm as the bouncer grabbed him, picking him up and holding his arms behind him.

"You fucking bitch. You fucking tasered me. I'm gonna mess you the fuck up. I'm gonna lay you out. Fucking mess you up inside then I'll put a fucking bullet in your brain." She tuned him out before his words could truly terrify her. Well, terrify her even more than she was.

"What. The. Fuck."

She spun at those words, spoken in a voice she recognized and met a pair of furious eyes.

Uh-oh.

Spike was so angry he was nearly shaking.

At least he told himself it was pure anger. And nothing to do with fear. But he figured he might just be lying as he listened to the asshole spouting off shit at Millie. Unable to take any more without losing it, he stormed up to him, grabbed him by his ratty wife beater and smashed his fist into his face, knocking him out cold. The bouncer let go of him as he dropped to the floor, unconscious.

"Well, that was one way to take care of things," Steele drawled. To anyone who didn't know him, he likely sounded relaxed and uncaring. But Spike knew differently. He was pissed. Somebody had fucked up by letting this guy in here. And that someone was going to be subjected to Steele's wrath. It wouldn't be pretty. He turned to the bouncer. "Take him into the back room and stay with him there until we decide what to do with him. Actually, get Jerry to watch him. You go back out front."

The bouncer nodded and grabbed the asshole by the feet, dragging him out, uncaring if his head hit anything on the way out.

Steele turned to Grady. "Find Mitchell. I want to know how he got in here."

Grady nodded and disappeared. Mitchell was the club manager. He was in for a rough time from Grady and Steele. Neither accepted failure.

Steele turned to the three women. The two strippers huddled together against a table. Millie stood slightly in front of them. As though protecting them. She watched Steele with guarded eyes. Her gaze seemed assessing. It surprised him. But that look cleared from her face almost as quickly as it had come.

She smiled as she looked over at him. Was she insane? She'd just tasered some asshole who was now out for her blood. What reason could she possibly have to smile?

"Spike, I'm so glad to see you. What are you doing here?"

What was *he* doing here? He was pretty certain he should be asking her that.

"So you two do know each other?" Steele asked him.

Millie turned to Steele. "We met last night. Who are you?"

"That's Mr. Steele," one of the strippers told her. The one with bright, red hair. "He owns this place."

"Mr. Steele? Oh good. I need to talk to you. Do the two of you know each other?" Her gaze slid between him and Spike. "Because that will make things easier."

"I'll be happy to have a chat with you, Miss?" Steele said smoothly.

"Just call me Millie."

Steele smiled. And instead of looking like a shark's grin it was almost gentle. Spike found himself frowning at him. He better not get any ideas about her. She wasn't his type anyway. Then again, she wasn't Spike's type either, but that hadn't stopped him from worrying about her all night. From wishing he'd swung her over his shoulder and taken her home himself.

Fuck.

"First, though, I need to take care of this problem. Is that all right?"

"Oh yes. Of course." Millie frowned. "I'm surprised that horrible man was allowed entrance. He didn't even have a proper shirt on."

"Indeed," Steele drawled. "He did not. And be assured he won't be allowed entrance again." His sharp glance went to the two women. "Tawny? Chardonnay? Are you both all right?"

Both women nodded.

"I'm so sorry, Mr. Steele," the dark-skinned girl said, her eyes wide. She was rubbing at her arm. Where the asshole grabbed her? Had he come in here for her?

"I take it you know him?" Steele asked her.

"We used to date back in Seattle. He's a jerk. He liked to hurt me."

Millie made a pained noise and he stepped closer, ready to whip her out of here if this was all too much. But the look of anger on her face shocked him.

"I managed to get away from him with the help of my cousins. I don't know how he found me here. I haven't seen him in months." Tawny's breath started coming in sharp pants.

"Come. Sit." Steele pulled out a chair and Chardonnay helped Tawny sit. Millie moved forward but Spike reached out and gently grabbed hold of her arm.

When she gave him a questioning look, he just shook his head. He couldn't explain it, but he wanted her close to him. There was no obvious threat in the room. Well, anyone would be an idiot to discount Steele as a threat, but he wasn't a threat to Millie. Not physically. Although if the other man didn't stop giving her interested looks then Spike was going to . . .

Chill. Fuck, man. Not yours.

Steele turned to the other girl. "Chardonnay, can you tell us what happened?"

Chardonnay ran a shaking hand over her face. "Uh, we were in here talking—"

"Miss Millie too?" Steele asked.

Spike narrowed his gaze at Steele who didn't miss a beat. A slight grin twisted up the edges of his mouth.

"I came back here to talk to Chardonnay," Millie told them. "I caught the end of her act. She's so good at what she does. She was offering to show me some moves."

Spike felt his eyebrows rise. What the fuck?

"She wasn't bothering anybody." Chardonnay glanced at Steele warily as though she thought they were going to get in trouble for Millie being back here.

Steele just nodded and made a motion with his hand for her to continue on.

"Tawny came in and then that guy stormed in." Chardonnay looked at Tawny who still appeared ill. "He pushed Lily aside. He was threatening Tawny, telling her how she was going to pay for leaving him. He grabbed her hard and was dragging her out the door, when . . ." Chardonnay stopped talking, looking over at Millie. She swallowed heavily.

"I stepped in front of him," Millie told them both, shoulders back.

"You. Did. What?"

Spike's voice was a quiet whisper dripping in menace. She had to hold in a grimace. She didn't owe him an explanation. He had no say in what she did. So why did she get the sense that she was in a world of trouble?

Still, she forced herself to look at him then over to Mr. Steele. Actually, that wasn't much easier. Mr. Steele looked nearly as upset as Spike did.

"I stepped in front of him," she repeated herself. "I couldn't just let him drag her out of here. He didn't, uhh, seem very nice."

"He didn't seem very nice?" Steele repeated.

"He was hurting her," she whispered, staring at Tawny. A small shiver worked its way across her skin and she quickly suppressed it. Now was not the time to fall apart. She needed to keep herself together. Taking a deep breath in, she tried to calm herself. "I couldn't let him hurt her, right?"

"What if he fucking hurt you?" Spike ran his hand over his bald scalp as she shrugged.

"I guess I had to take that risk."

"For fuck's sake. This isn't some damn game, woman. He likely had a weapon on him. He would have gutted you and walked over your bleeding body without a second glance."

Millie grimaced. She didn't do well with blood. Especially her own. She knew she'd likely paled and Spike gave a satisfied nod. No doubt he thought he had suitably scared her.

"What would you have had me do?" she asked him.

"Run for help."

"Huh."

Spike cursed. "That never even occurred to you, did it?"

She shrugged. It hadn't. "I try to avoid running whenever I can."

"What about common sense? Do you try to avoid that too?" he snapped.

Now he was just being mean.

Mr. Steele obviously thought so too because he turned to give Spike a quelling look. "Spike."

She gave Mr. Steele a big smile.

He gave her a small one back. "Right, then what happened?"

Millie pulled out her stun gun. "I let him get close to me, then I zapped him. I thought about using the pepper spray but I didn't want it getting in anyone else's eyes."

"You used a stun gun?" Mr. Steele said slowly. "And you also have pepper spray. On you?"

"In my handbag, see?" She walked over to where she'd put her handbag on one of the tables. She reached in and drew out a sleeping Mr. Fluffy. Maybe she should take him to the vet. He seemed to sleep a lot. Then again, he was a puppy.

"Is that . . . a dog?" Mr. Steele asked, sounding incredulous.

"Isn't he so cute?" Chardonnay cooed as she reached for him, pulling him into her breasts.

Mr. Fluffy gave her a look that said, *why did you wake me for this?*

She had to bite her lip. "Ahh, yes, this is Mr. Fluffy. I'm not sure what sort of dog he is yet."

"You brought a dog into my strip club?"

"Yes. Is that a problem?" She looked over at Mr. Steele. "Oh dear, I didn't think about that. Are dogs allowed in here?"

He shook his head, appearing dumbfounded.

"I'm sorry. I won't bring him next time."

"There won't be a next time," Spike grumbled. She didn't know why he was so grumpy. She figured it was just his personality as she was certain she hadn't done anything to annoy him.

As Chardonnay cuddled a clearly disgruntled Mr. Fluffy, she drew out her pepper spray and her rape whistle and set them down by her stun gun.

"Anything else in your arsenal?" Mr. Steele asked.

"Well, there's my gun but I forgot to put bullets in it again," she explained.

"You have a gun?" Spike asked in a strange voice.

"Yes. Why? Did you want to see it?" She pulled out her Smith & Wesson.

"It's pink." There was something odd with his voice. Was he coming down with something? Maybe she should offer to make him some of her grandma's honey and lemon drink. Guaranteed to cure all ills. Then again, maybe not considering he was so rude. She only made that for people who were nice.

Oh, who was she kidding. She'd make it for him if he wanted it.

"Isn't it pretty? Mr. Spain had to special order it for me and we picked it up from the next town over since we don't have a gun shop in Nowhere."

"Nowhere?" Mr. Steele asked.

"It's where I'm from. Nowhere, Nebraska."

"Interesting name," Mr. Steele commented.

"Hmm, a few years ago some of the townspeople wanted to rename it. But nobody could agree on a name. The winning contender was Somewhere. But in the end Nowhere stayed well, Nowhere."

She noticed everyone was giving her strange looks. She started to feel flushed and self-conscious. Those looks told her they all thought she was bonkers.

It doesn't matter what other people think of you. Only what you think of yourself.

Still, she could feel her shoulders hunching. Maybe she should learn to be less. Less talkative. Less friendly. Less impetuous.

Less ridiculous.

"I owe you some thanks, Miss Millie," Mr. Steele said, moving closer to her. He reached out and touched her chin, tilting her face so she was staring up in those pale blue eyes. They reminded her of the sky on a sunny, cloudless day.

"You do?" she asked, feeling flustered at having his entire attention on her. Wow. This guy packed a punch.

"Yes, I do. You helped save one of my staff. I try to take care of everyone that works for me and it seems in this instance that I've somehow failed."

"Oh, I'm sure it wasn't your fault," she reassured him.

"I'm not so sure. You see, that man should never have been allowed entrance. Someone let him in. Someone who answers to me. And it also should have been made clear to Tawny that if she had anyone who might be a threat to her that she should have informed my manager. That didn't happen either. So it is very much my fault that you were nearly harmed."

"I'm fine. It was Tawny that was in danger."

"Hmm."

Suddenly, a looming presence appeared next to them. "Let go of her."

She turned shocked eyes to Spike. He had a muscle tic by his left eye. And he looked furious as he glared at Mr. Steele. She took a shocked step back but Mr. Steele just stared at Spike, looking almost . . . amused? But that couldn't be right.

"Tawny, Chardonnay, you're excused for the night. I'll have someone take you both home. Tawny, do you have somewhere safe you can stay? I wouldn't advise going home."

"I have a friend I can stay with," Tawny said quietly.

"Good. Tomorrow, come in early. We need to have a chat."

Tawny nodded then stopped by Millie, giving her a strange look. "Thanks. For helping me."

"You're welcome." She wanted to say more, but she didn't know what.

Chardonnay slipped past her as well, giving her a small smile as she handed over Mr. Fluffy. Millie felt a stab of disappointment. Somehow, she didn't think the other woman was going to give her those dance lessons. Her shoulders slumped.

Making friends had never been hard for Millie. But keeping them? That was a completely different thing. Oh, she had all the people back in Nowhere, but since ninety percent of the population was over seventy, that wasn't quite what she needed or desired.

She gave a soft sigh and to her shock, she felt a heavy, hot hand land on her lower back. She startled, but the hand didn't budge.

"What's wrong?" Spike asked her quietly.

"Oh, nothing." She forced a big smile onto her face.

But the look he gave her told her that he knew she was faking it.

Before he could say anything more, though, the man who'd come in earlier with Spike and Mr. Steele returned.

"Damon, need a word," he said, then his gaze caught on her. "Is that a dog?"

His eyes roamed over to the table to where she'd laid out her tools. "And a gun? A pink gun?"

"Hmm, it seems Miss Millie here carries around quite the arsenal," Mr. Steele told him. "She's fully prepared for any eventuality."

The other man gave her a somber look. "Yeah, well, she might need it."

"What is it?" Mr. Steele asked in the voice of a man who was used to reoccurring fires, but was running out of water to dampen them.

"Asshole has a very distinctive tattoo on his inner forearm."

"Oh, the devil one?" she asked. She'd noticed that.

Both Spike and Mr. Steele turned to look at her. Mr. Steele looked thoughtful; Spike looked angry. But she was starting to wonder if that was normal. Some people had resting bitch face. Spike had resting grouch face.

"Yeah, he's a member of the Devil's Sinners. And pretty sure when he wakes up, he's gonna be gunning for her blood."

Uh-oh.

8

Millie looked around the long room in interest. It wasn't at all what she'd expected. Well, she wasn't sure what to expect and really, she shouldn't make assumptions about someone without meeting them.

Just because he owned a strip club didn't make Mr. Steele a bad man. Of course that guy that tried to rob her the other night had implied he was a gang leader. Well, she'd just come to her own conclusions. But so far, he seemed nice.

At least he was talking to her. Unlike the grumpy hulk standing in the corner, glaring at her.

"This is nice. Not at all what I'd expect to find in a strip club."

She'd been trying to get Spike to speak ever since Mr. Steele had asked her to kindly wait upstairs for him.

Kindly wait.

So polite. Definitely not what she'd expected.

Spike didn't react at all. She sighed. As though sensing her mood, Mr. Fluffy looked up from where he was sitting in her arms and yawned. He really was a lazy thing.

After she'd repacked her stuff downstairs, Spike had snatched her handbag out of her hands and escorted her up here.

And when she said escort, she meant he grabbed her wrist and practically dragged her beside him. She'd had to jog to keep up.

Remember her opinion on running? It hadn't improved any. And running upstairs? Even worse.

"Not that I've been in many strip clubs, of course. Well, none actually. Still, I'm sure few are as nice as this."

You're rambling, Millie.

Well, he was making her so nervous just staring at her like that.

"Do you think Mr. Steele will mind if I let Mr. Fluffy down?"

"Mr. Steele doesn't mind at all, sweetheart." She whirled, one hand resting on her heart.

Mr. Fluffy let out another exaggerated yawn. She had a feeling he wasn't going to be much of a guard dog.

Mr. Steele gave him a slightly skeptical look which belied his words. "Is he toilet-trained?"

"Oh, he's pretty good," she said vaguely. She placed him down, hoping he didn't make a mess. "Do you have any newspapers by chance?"

Mr. Steele gave her a slightly horrified look. She swore Spike snorted but when she looked over at him, he was still glaring at her. Huh.

"Here you are." Mr. Steele handed over some newspapers.

"Thank you, Mr. Steele."

He gave her a strange look. "Please, call me Damon."

She smiled at him. He didn't smile back, though, instead he just studied her. That was slightly strange.

Spike grunted. She risked another look at him, not sure she could withstand many more of his scowls. To her surprise, he was glaring at Damon this time. Weren't they friends? If they weren't then why was Spike here?

Maybe he'd come to watch the dancers? Hm. That thought didn't sit too well with her. Why? Was she actually jealous? She didn't even know him. And what she did know wasn't that flattering. He seemed to intensely dislike her or at best, be constantly annoyed by her.

She laid the papers down on the linoleum floor by the bar area then she walked over to Spike. "Bag please."

"Why?"

"Because it's my bag."

He arched a brow. "You planning on using the stuff in it?"

"Well, yes."

"Then no."

She huffed out a breath at him, all too aware of their audience. "It's my handbag. I want it back."

"No."

He didn't even look regretful. In fact, he turned away from her to look at Damon. "What will you do with him?"

"Grady will be up in a moment. Then we can all have a chat about what to do next."

She crossed her arms over her chest and tapped her foot. "I want my bag, Spike."

His gaze flicked back to hers. His eyes were a mix of colors. Green. Hazel. Blue. They would have been quite beautiful if he wasn't such an ass.

Oh, who was she kidding? They were beautiful despite the fact he was an ass.

"Darn it, why'd you have to have beautiful eyes. Why couldn't you have mean, ugly eyes?"

"Did you just call his eyes beautiful?" Damon asked with amusement.

"Urgh. Said that out loud, did I?"

"You did." Damon looked from her to Spike. "Just how do the two of you know each other?"

"We met last night," she said at the same time Spike spoke.

"We don't."

Ouch. That shouldn't have hurt as much as it did. Technically, they didn't know each other. But he could have said it nicer.

She sighed. "Just give me my handbag and I promise, after tonight you won't ever have to see me again."

"If only I could believe that."

With a narrowed gaze, she started tapping her foot.

"Uh-oh, that's the look of a pissed off woman, man. You sure you want to keep on this path?" Damon asked.

"With what's in her bag, she's likely to shoot someone or herself."

"There's no bullets in my gun!" she exclaimed, throwing her hands into the air. "How am I going to shoot anyone! Give me my bag."

"No."

"Urgh." She stomped her foot. "You are so infuriating."

He leaned in; his mouth so close to her ear that she could feel his breath against her skin. She froze as tingles of awareness ran through her. What was that about? Was she attracted to the big meanie?

"Stomp that foot again and you'll find out what happens to naughty little girls who throw tantrums."

She stumbled back from him, would likely have tripped over her own feet if Damon hadn't materialized behind her, steadying her with his hands on her hips.

Spike looked over her shoulder at him and growled. Actually growled. Like a caveman.

Okay, so she didn't think she was well prepared to deal with him. Maybe with any man. Which was fine, since she didn't intend to ever fall in love again.

Not. Happening.

Damon didn't immediately let her go, which she thought was

odd. It felt like the three of them were in a stand-off. She was frozen, uncertain whether moving would make things better or worse.

A throat clearing startled the men out of their frozen state and she chose that moment to slip away, stepping over to the bar to search for something to put some water for Mr. Fluffy in. She found a small bowl, filled it and placed it down next to the paper.

When she rose, she was grateful to find both men standing on opposite sides of the room. The man who'd arrived downstairs with Damon earlier was now standing there, watching them with amusement on his face.

"Millie, this is Thomas Grady," Damon introduced.

"Hello," she said politely.

He gave her a regal nod back. "Please, call me Grady. Most everyone does."

"You spoke to Mitchell?" Damon asked Grady who walked over to the bar.

"Yes, of course. He's going to look into things. Our intruder is under guard for now. Can I make everyone a drink?"

She slid past him and walked towards where Mr. Fluffy was pawing at Damon's shoes. He was staring down at the dog like he'd never seen one before.

"Come here, Mr. Fluffy."

"Interesting name," Damon said as Mr. Fluffy turned and with clumsy steps, managed to make his way over to her.

She scratched him behind the ears and he settled with a big yawn.

"Maybe I should have called him Mr. Lazy." She smiled up at Damon. He gave her another curious look.

"Drink?" Grady prompted.

She grew red at her lack of manners in not answering him earlier. She tried to stand and nearly tripped over the bottom of her skirt. All three men jumped towards her. She grew even more red.

"Sorry, I can be a bit of a klutz."

She looked away. All of them were gorgeous in their own way. Grady, refined and almost genteel with a sharp edge. Damon, deadly but with a charming exterior. Then Spike, how to describe him? She couldn't even find the words. He was stubborn. Angry. There was nothing sweet or charming about him. Yet, she felt this pull towards him. Like there was an invisible string, connecting them.

You're being ridiculous, Millie.

"She'll take a soda," Spike told him.

"I'll take a strawberry daiquiri please," she replied, sending Spike a look.

She'd never had one, but it sounded nice.

Grady gave her a surprised look.

"Oh, unless you don't know how to make it."

He's not a bartender, Millie.

"I know how to make one."

Spike scowled and went to open his mouth.

"But are you able to make it without the alcohol," she added.

"So a virgin daiquiri?" Grady asked.

"Yes, please. Is that okay?"

"Of course," Grady said smoothly.

"If you're both finished, can we get onto the important stuff?" Spike barked, making her jump. Even Mr. Fluffy gave a small woof of surprise.

Damon turned away from where he'd been staring out the viewing window to the strip club below. She wondered how late it stayed open. She already felt fatigued and it wasn't even midnight.

"What are you going to do with him?" Spike asked.

Steele looked over at Grady.

"It's tricky. We let him go and he's likely a danger to her." Steele nodded to her.

"To me?" she asked.

"Yes," Steele replied. "Assholes like that don't take kindly to people getting in their way. Especially women. Plus, you tasered him."

"Spike punched him."

"Yes, but Spike is a man," Grady told her.

"Well, that's hardly fair."

All three men gave her incredulous looks.

"I'm just saying that he should hate us both equally is all," she muttered.

"So get rid of him," Spike said sharply.

"It could create issues with the rest of them," Grady commented.

"You cannot let him leave, not when he's a threat to her," Spike countered.

Steele nodded. "You're right. We'll deal with him."

Grady handed her a drink in a gorgeous glass then handed everyone else their drinks.

"So . . . umm . . . by take care of him, what exactly do you mean?" she asked.

None of them answered her. Which was an answer in itself. Oh shoot. That was what she thought.

Damon gestured for her to sit on a sofa. He sat on the one opposite while Grady took an armchair. Spike remained leaning against the wall.

"Do you know who the Devil's Sinners are, Millie?" Damon asked, leaning forward with his forearms resting on his legs.

"No, should I?"

"They're a gang. They've got a nasty name for themselves. They're trying to move in on Montana and more specifically into this city. My city."

"A man I met the second night I was here said that he didn't want to linger around because we were on the outskirts of Steele territory. He seemed scared."

"That so?" Damon drawled. "What man was that?"

"Oh, just this guy who wanted to steal my handbag. It's a one-of-a-kind. My friend made it for me."

Damon looked over at the handbag still hanging from Spike's hand. It was a patchwork of material in various shades of red and gold. "Since you're still in possession of it, he obviously wasn't successful."

"No, I suppose he thought that his gun gave him the upper hand."

"He pulled a fucking gun on you?" the voice came from right behind her and she jumped. How had Spike gotten so close and she didn't even notice? For the size of him, he should sound like a stampeding bull when he moved, not a light-footed ballerina.

She had to grin at the thought of him in a pink tutu, now that would be hilarious.

Millie always dreamed of being a ballerina. But instead of being svelte and sure on her feet, she was chubby and clumsy.

"You think it's funny that some guy held you up at gunpoint?" Spike asked incredulously as he came to sit beside her. His big thigh was pressed up against hers. She had to suppress a shiver. What was wrong with her?

She took in a steadying breath and slid her gaze over to Damon. "I didn't find it funny at all . . . it was . . ." terrifying, frightening, a sign of how unprepared and naïve she was. But she didn't let any of that show because . . . because those emotions were all too real. They were dark. Scary.

And she didn't deal with dark and scary well.

"Anyway, that's why I'm here."

"I'm sorry?" Damon asked with a confused look. "I don't

understand. How does you nearly getting robbed lead you here to Pinkies?"

"Oh, not that part." She waved her hand. "It was the bit that came next."

"What came next?" Damon inquired.

She licked her lips, looking over at Spike. Why was he sitting so close to her? Sure, he was a big guy but there was plenty of room on the sofa for the two of them to sit without being pressed up against one another.

"This is what I tried to tell you last night, but you wouldn't listen to me," she said to Spike.

"Really?" Damon drawled. "Why don't you tell me, Millie. I'll listen."

Spike grunted.

"See, the guy who tried to rob me had just run off—"

"Why did he run off?" Grady asked.

"Oh well, I might have drawn my gun out and aimed it at him."

"Your gun that has no bullets in it," Spike stated.

It wasn't a question so she didn't reply. "He ran off and I was turning to leave when I spotted Mr. Fluffy huddled by a dumpster. I was bent down, coaxing him towards me when a backdoor into the alley opened and two men walked out."

Spike groaned. She turned to look at him in concern. He sounded like he was in pain. "Are you all right?"

"Fuck. Me."

She noticed Grady watching her curiously as though she was a puzzle he couldn't quite solve. She gave him a wide smile, but she felt certain that he saw entirely too much for her liking.

But she ignored that for the moment. She'd likely never see him again, so it didn't matter what he saw or thought he had figured out about her.

Nobody knew all of her.

"Forgive me, but why were you in an alleyway to begin with, my dear?" Grady asked.

A blush filled her cheeks. "I got a bit lost. And I think the maps app on my phone is broken as it led me down that way. I'm afraid I'm not used to navigating around the city."

Spike made a strangled noise. She was starting to wonder if he had intestinal issues. Poor guy.

"Anyway, where was I? These two guys started talking and I was kind of stuck crouching behind the dumpster. I didn't want to move and risk them seeing me."

And because she was nosey as hell.

Spike gave her a look like he knew exactly what she'd been up to.

"They started talking. One of them wanted to know what the other one was doing, pulling him out here. He said something about being in trouble if one of Steele's guys spotted him. The first guy, well, he didn't seem to like you very much." She wrinkled her nose as she looked over at Damon. He seemed unperturbed. "He wanted to know if you had anything to do with his father's death. And he said he was certain that you had helped his father's girls get away. It sounded like, well, like his father had a lot of women who worked for him."

She couldn't read Damon's face. Spike had stiffened next to her. Grady took a sip of his drink. Oh, she hadn't tasted hers. She took a sip and smiled. "This is delicious."

"Thank you."

"Did they say anything else?" Damon asked.

"Oh yes, the second guy he said something like, he hadn't heard that you'd killed the other man's father or helped these girls, but that you didn't sell, umm, oh dear . . . umm, sex."

"Hmm." Damon frowned, appearing thoughtful.

"How did that lead you to Spike?" Grady asked curiously.

"Oh, he said the one thing he did know is that Grady set up a meeting between a guy named Spike from the Iron Shadows and this man, Luther's, father."

"Luther? The first man's name was Luther?" Damon asked so sharply that she sank back into the sofa in surprise.

"Careful how you speak to her," Spike said in a low, almost casual sounding voice. But one that made an impact on her. She turned wide eyes on him, watching him carefully.

"I apologize, Miss Millie. I'm not upset with you. Just at this news. It sounds like this second man is close to me. Like maybe I have a rat, someone whose loyalty lies elsewhere. It explains a lot actually."

"The shipments that have been interfered with, deals that have gone wrong," Grady muttered.

"Yes, I'm afraid it sounds like this other man is spying on you. He asked Luther if the boss knew he had contacted him. Luther basically said that he was angry at the boss because he was having to transport stuff around. And how they were equals. I'm not sure who the boss was that they both spoke of."

Damon just looked thoughtful. Grady appeared furious.

She bit her lip, worried for a moment at the darkness in Grady's gaze. She hoped that she'd done the right thing, coming to these guys. Although they'd been nothing but nice to her. Well, Grady and Damon had.

"Anything else?" Grady asked.

"Just that this Luther, he said that he was going to deal with Spike and Steele. It sounded like a threat to me."

"Why're you warning us?" Spike asked.

She didn't point out that he hadn't wanted to listen to her last night.

She shrugged. "Luther wasn't very nice and I didn't like the way he talked about . . . about women. It sounds like he's planning to rebuild what his father had."

"Luther's father was a pimp," Damon told her, cementing

what she'd already deduced. "He used to recruit young girls. Usually runaways. Or he'd buy them from guys that were even more evil than he was, often selling them to other men to be sex slaves."

She shuddered, her mind going to dark places. Her breath started to come in sharp pants.

"Millie? Millie? Are you all right? Millie?" Spike demanded.

Her body went cold then flushed hot. She glanced down at Spike who was now crouched in front of her, her hands in his.

"I need the bathroom," she managed to get out.

"This way." Grady jumped from his chair and pointed to a door. She raced towards it, barely making it to the toilet before she started heaving.

She didn't take the time to close the door behind her. But she was surprised as someone came in behind her. A hand wrapped around her hair, holding it back from her face as she heaved up the daiquiri as well as the chocolate croissant she'd had for dinner.

The heaving stopped but she remained kneeling there, shivering in reaction. She knew exactly who was behind her and she didn't want to move. Didn't want to face him.

"Here, this might help," Grady said from the doorway.

She cringed. Well, this was humiliating. And try as she might, she couldn't lock down the embarrassment coursing through her body. Shoot.

"Can you turn around, doll?" the man behind her asked. It was the gentlest she'd ever heard him speak. She wasn't sure where the nickname came from.

But she couldn't resist the coaxing in his voice, turning and sitting on her bottom with her back leaning against the cool wall. She didn't look up, didn't want to see anyone.

The toilet flushed. There was the sound of a cupboard opening and then a pair of jean clad legs appeared in front of her. A big hand reached out and gently grasped hold of her chin, raising her face.

Millie closed her eyes. A cool cloth was run over her face, wiping off the sweat. It was soothing. And sweet. And not something she'd expected from him at all.

The cloth disappeared and a cold glass was pressed to her lips.

"Open your eyes. Drink this."

She really didn't want to. Opening her eyes meant looking at him. And that meant acknowledging that this wasn't some nightmare.

"Come on, doll," he coaxed.

Shit. She opened her eyes then her mouth, gulping down the glass of water he held. She was helpless against this side of Spike. This gentleness. Caring. When was the last time someone cared for her?

"That's a good girl," he told her.

Had she banged her head? Was this some alternate universe?

With a shaking hand, she reached for the glass.

"Uh-uh," he said in a firm voice with a look that just did things to her. Why, she had no idea. She was always the one who took care of others.

And aren't you tired?

Didn't you spend countless nights wishing for some help? To not have to shoulder every responsibility?

Still, it was odd to let someone else take over.

Spike removed the glass when she'd drunk it all down. He grabbed another washcloth from the cupboard under the sink, wet it, then gently pulled her away from the wall. Twisting her hair up, he laid the washcloth on the back of her neck.

Oh. That was nice.

She must have made some sound because he drew back and gave her a knowing look. "Feels good, huh?"

"Y-yes. Thank you."

He just gave her a sharp nod. "Want to tell me what that was about?"

"Not really."

His gaze narrowed. "What was that about."

Definitely not a question this time. She still shook her head, wincing slightly as a sharp pain engulfed one side of her head. Shoot. She hoped that wasn't going to turn into a migraine.

"You need anything else?"

She glanced up into the doorway to see Grady standing there. He gave her a small smile. "Ibuprofen? Another glass of water?"

"A time machine to go back ten minutes?" she said dryly.

"Only ten?" he said with a wink. "Not further back to before you had to stun gun that asshole?"

"No, because then he might have succeeded in dragging Tawny out of here and I don't think she would have fared well."

Grady's face softened. He glanced down at Spike, his eyes narrowing. "Isn't every day that something sweet lands in your life after a lifetime of sour. Sweet things need to be guarded. To be treated for the rare treasure they are. Not thrown away and discarded."

He disappeared.

"What was that about?" she asked, thoroughly confused.

He shrugged. "Color's better. This a reaction to what happened earlier?"

As an explanation it was as good as any. Okay, it was a lie. But only a little white one. Surely Reverend Pat would understand.

She nodded her head, not actually trusting herself to answer him without giving herself away.

"Was starting to wonder if you had any common sense," he grumbled.

She frowned at him. Of course she had common sense. It was just that she didn't like to dwell on things. Once she started thinking, well, she never stopped. And she didn't have time for that. She had a mission to accomplish.

Spike suddenly stood and picked her up. But instead of setting her on her feet, he lifted her into his arms and carried her out of the bathroom into the other room.

She blushed bright red.

"Stop wiggling," he growled.

"Please put me down before you hurt yourself."

"Why the fuck would I hurt myself?"

But he did set her down on the sofa.

"You didn't injure your back, did you?"

He gave her an incredulous look.

"My dear, I hope you're not implying that you're too heavy for Spike to carry around," Grady said, leaning back with one arm along the back of the sofa opposite them. Damon sat next to him, studying her intently.

She went bright red. "Well, I'm not exactly light."

Spike made a grumbling noise of discontent. Then he leaned in, placing his hands on the back of the sofa on either side of her so she was boxed in.

"No."

No? That was all? Just no? No, what? No, he hadn't hurt his back?

What was going on with him right now? He stepped away into the kitchen.

"I think what Spike was trying to say, my dear, is that you shouldn't be disparaging yourself. You're gorgeous. Lush. Sexy. Those curves." Grady ate her up with his gaze.

She'd never been looked at like that before. Like she was a tasty snack to be eaten up.

Suddenly, Spike appeared between them and she was staring at his sexy ass. Holy hell. How was it possible for a man to have such a gorgeous ass? The longing to reach over and squeeze one cheek was almost too much for her to resist.

"Not. Yours."

Wait, what did Spike just say? She peered around to look at Grady who was gazing up at Spike, a small smirk on his face. Damon, though, was looking at her.

Holy. Crap. That was one intense look.

"Not yours, either. That means she's fair game, yes? You don't have a husband do you, Millie? A boyfriend?" Grady asked.

"N-no," she said, not understanding what was happening.

"Back off," Spike commanded. He sat beside her. Then he wrapped his huge arm around her shoulders, dragging her in close.

Spike and Grady stared at each other for a long moment.

Damon looked tired as he studied her. "Millie, could you describe the man you saw talking to Luther?"

"Sure, but he was pretty nondescript and the light wasn't great. Taller than Luther, pale skin. Brown hair, I think."

"Would you know him if you saw him?" Damon asked.

Spike stiffened as she nodded. "Yes, I'm certain I would."

"You're not using her to sniff out a rat in your ranks," Spike stated.

Damon raised his eyebrows. "I'm not proposing to use her. I was merely going to ask for her help. You don't mind, do you, Millie?"

She shook her head, not understanding why Spike suddenly leaned forward and jabbed his finger violently at Damon. "No, you'll put her at risk. If this guy finds out you're searching for him, if he knows that Millie saw him, then he could come for her."

"There's no way he'd learn about it. No one in this room would say a thing," Damon said. "I need to know who it is. And who he's working for. You're sure they didn't name him?"

She shook her head. "The other guy just called him the boss."

"Likely Jared Bartolli," Grady said. "Luther is married to his cousin."

"Millie, you never said why you came to the city? How long have you been here?" Damon asked.

Should she tell them? "I arrived here a few days ago, I'm looking for someone."

"Who?" Spike asked.

She didn't want to say. Not because it was a big secret, but because she knew that talking about it would upset her. And she wasn't ready to be that vulnerable in front of these men.

"How much longer did you plan to stay here? Do you have a job to get back to? Family waiting for you?" Damon asked.

"Oh well, I'd planned to stay as long as I needed to. Nobody is expecting me home at any time and I don't have a job anymore. The library had to let me go."

Sympathy filled the men's faces. She couldn't have that. Hastily, she changed the subject.

"Luther sounded like he wanted to rebuild what his father had. We can't let him do that. We can't let him use women like that. Hurt them. Pick on them when they're vulnerable and alone."

"You're not having anything to do with it," Spike growled.

"No," Damon agreed. "This has nothing to do with you, sweetheart. You leave Luther to me. I'll make sure he doesn't have a chance to do that."

"But what about his threats? It sounds like he was planning on hurting you both." She looked at Spike.

Spike snorted. "That dickhead doesn't scare me."

Damon gave an arrogant nod. Well, she was glad they were so confident. Because she wasn't so sure. He seemed shady.

Someone's phone buzzed. Grady stood and pulled a phone from his pocket, walking into another room to answer it.

"Millie, I—"

"Fuck!" Grady stormed into the room, his face a thundercloud.

Damon straightened. "What is it?"

"Mitchell just found Jerry unconscious. The Devil's Sinner guy is gone."

"What the fuck!" Spike snapped, making her flinch. "You lost him?"

Damon's jaw tightened at Spike's words. "I want to know how."

Grady nodded.

"We'll find him," Damon assured her.

"He's going to come for her," Spike stated angrily.

"But he doesn't know who I am," she pointed out. "Or where I'm staying."

Grady rubbed a hand over his face. "He could find out. Even though none of us would say anything, we can't guarantee that the girls won't. And guys like that, they kill people for a lot less than what you did."

"He's going to need to save face," Damon told her. "He's likely pissed at all of us, but you are the most vulnerable. Which is why I think it would be a good idea for you to stay with me."

"Stay with you?" She gaped at him.

"It would be my honor to keep you safe, Millie," he practically purred.

"And she'd be conveniently placed for you to parade your men in front of her until she points out the rat," Spike said sardonically.

Damon shrugged and sat back. "A bonus."

"She ain't staying with you."

"She's not? Where is she staying then?" Damon inquired.

"Well, I have a motel room—" she began.

"She's staying with me."

Those four words fell into the room with a sonic boom, leaving an eerie silence in its place.

9

Spike stared at the bathroom door.

Millie was on the other side. She'd excused herself after he'd laid out his offer.

Okay, it wasn't an offer. She didn't exactly have a choice. Even though Steele tried to give her one. There was no way Spike was letting her go stay with Steele in his cold, enormous mansion.

He'd never get her out.

And he cared because . . . fuck it. He wasn't going to think about that too closely now. All he knew was that she was in danger. And he couldn't stand the idea of her being out of his sight. Even knowing she was just in that bathroom was difficult for him.

He frowned, hoping that she wasn't throwing up again.

"Haven't seen you this interested in a woman since Jacqui died," Steele mused.

Spike turned his gaze to Steele. "I'm not interested in her."

Grady huffed out a laugh. "If you were a dog you would've pissed on her."

"I can keep her safe, Quillon," Steele told him.

Spike glared at him. He was one of the few people who knew Spike's name. Possibly the only one who would dare use it.

"So can I. And I don't have an ulterior motive."

"Don't you," Steele mused.

Spike narrowed his gaze. "If you're inferring I want her for sex . . ."

"Oh, I'm definitely inferring that," Steele answered.

Spike let out a breath. "I'm not after her for sex."

Steele leaned forward. "She needs a keeper. She's been here how long did she say?"

"A few days," Grady mused.

"She's been held at gunpoint, overheard a pretty damning conversation between fucking Luther Franklin and some bastard who's managed to infiltrate my ranks to spy on me," Steele stated. "Then she tracks you down to warn you. Bet you're regretting not listening to her now, huh?"

Spike just grimaced.

"And then she tracks me down, where she proceeds to charm one of my girls into offering to give her free dance lessons. Then she steps in when some asshole threatens another one of my girls and takes him down. She doesn't just need a keeper; she needs a fucking protector. She needs a Daddy."

"A protector Daddy," Grady mused. "Or Daddies."

Amusement filled the other men's face as Spike snarled at him. Oh, he knew what would happen if the two of them got her back to Steele's mansion. She'd never leave. She'd be tied to their bed. Fucked. Pleasured.

Then when they got bored, they'd release her. Usually with a nice, healthy bank balance. The two of them were picky. And they didn't pay women to be with them. No, they came willingly.

But they never kept them.

"She's not a temporary plaything," Spike bit out.

"Anyone can see that," Grady said.

"How do you intend to keep her safe?" Steele asked. "Sounds like Luther is gunning for you and you don't have the protection I do."

Spike snorted. "I'm not scared of Luther Franklin."

"Did you kill Frankie?" Grady asked him.

Spike narrowed his gaze at Grady. "I didn't."

Grady studied him. "But you know who did?"

"Lot of people hated Frankie; he was scum."

No way was he telling anyone who actually killed Frankie. He didn't want to be next on the Fox's hitlist. Besides, far as he was concerned, the Fox did the world a favor when he got rid of Frankie.

Grady looked over at the bathroom. All of them were aware of how long she'd been in there. Spike glanced down as her dog flopped itself over his boot. Heavy for something so small. What the hell kind of dog was it, anyway?

"Anybody else notice that the way she reacts to things isn't exactly right?" Grady mused.

"What the hell does that mean? What way should she react?"

"Most people, if they were held at gunpoint, would just hand over their bag, yes? Most people, if they overheard the conversation she did, wouldn't immediately search out the people who were talked about, would they? Especially not when they learn one of them owns a strip club and runs a *gang*."

Grady's lips twitched at that. Steele hated being referred to as a gang leader.

"And when a scary looking guy forces himself into a room and starts to drag someone off, most people would call the cops or run for help. Especially if that person is far smaller and more delicate than the attacker. And they don't even know the person being attacked. They definitely wouldn't pull out a stun gun and shoot him. And even if they did, then I'm certain they wouldn't brush it off and sit calmly in a room with three of the city's most dangerous men, drinking virgin daiquiris and putting down newspaper for their narcoleptic puppy."

"It took a while to catch up to her," Spike said. "She ended up vomiting in the bathroom."

"Did it? I'm not sure that's why she ended up in the bathroom. Does any of that seem normal to the two of you?" Grady asked.

Steele shrugged. "Perhaps she's simply brave."

She was a menace. She was clumsy, nosy, smart and far too reckless with her safety.

Yep, he couldn't stop thinking about her.

"There's something more going on with her. Mark my words."

Grady was right. None of it was normal behavior. The way she kept bouncing back like nothing touched her. She couldn't be as ignorant and innocent as she appeared. His suspicions stirred, wondering if she was hiding something.

And if so, what could it be?

She'd had enough time in the bathroom. The door opened as he rose and she stepped out. He narrowed his gaze. She looked pale. And was she squinting? As though she was in pain?

"Do you think I could get that ibuprofen?" she asked Grady.

"Of course, my dear." He rose smoothly and walked over to grab them from the bathroom cupboard. Spike walked into the kitchen and grabbed a bottle of water. Then he took the pills from Grady who sent Spike an amused look but let him take them. He shook two out and handed them to her along with the water.

"What's wrong? What hurts?" he barked.

She winced.

Easy, man.

"Just my head," she whispered. "I'll be fine in a moment. Just a lot has happened in the last few days. My life was rather boring before now. I think the most exciting thing to happen was when Mrs. Larsen pulled a Lady Godiva one Halloween. Of course, she was riding a bike rather than a horse. And unfortunately her hair wasn't quite long enough to cover her boobs. And . . ." she looked around at the three of them, "you probably don't want to hear that."

She rubbed at her temples tiredly. Poor baby. He felt the sudden urge to tuck her up in bed and insist that she stay there until there was color in her cheeks and the worry had faded out of her eyes.

The fact that she didn't seem to have any sense of self-preservation worried him. Her penchant for getting herself in trouble was clear.

But was that reason enough to take her home with him? He didn't know her. He could leave her to Steele. He would keep her alive.

She'd be safe, but she'd also be controlled. Kept in the lap of luxury, but only until her appeal ran out.

"Millie, who would you like to stay with while this mess gets sorted out? In the Hulk's cave? Or Bruce Wayne's mansion?" Grady asked.

Spike scowled at him.

"I'd really just like to go back to my motel room and stay there with Mr. Fluffy." There was a hint of tears in her voice and he couldn't stand it.

Reaching out, he gently tugged her into his chest. "I'm afraid that's not an option."

He saw Steele flash a look at Grady. Were those two bastards up to something? He frowned over at them suspiciously. Steele gave him an innocent look back.

Definitely up to something.

Assholes.

Millie kind of slumped against him, and he held her tight, worried about her.

"Doll? You okay?" he murmured.

"Just tired, I think. I can't . . . I can't think right now. I don't want to . . . I don't think I can . . ." her voice broke.

"Shh, you don't have to. It's okay. You can let go."

"I can't," she mumbled. "Can't ever let go. Got things I need to do. Can't ever let go."

Fuck. She was killing him.

He looked straight at Steele. "She's coming home with me."

Steele nodded. "Fine. But if you need us, you know where I am. You'll both need to be careful. We'll keep this info about Luther and the rat to ourselves, but I still need to find this guy. Luther will be coming for both of us. And the Devil's Sinners will be after Millie. Sure you can handle all that?"

Spike gave him a look. "I don't need your help."

"We'll see." Steele smirked at him. "Did you bring your bike?"

"Yeah." Spike grimaced. Fuck. "Can we use your driver?"

"Don't need my help huh?"

Asshole.

10

Millie ran her hand over the smooth leather of the seat. She'd never been in a car this luxurious before. She kept a good hold on Mr. Fluffy. She wouldn't like to think how much it would cost to replace the upholstery in something this expensive.

She felt a bit ashamed of how she'd kind of just given up in there and let Spike take over. Everything had gotten to her and she just hadn't known what to do next.

Still, she shouldn't lean on him. She didn't know him.

And yet you're going to stay with him? Shouldn't you at least put up some sort of protest?

He sat beside her, and their driver closed the car door.

Well, Damon's driver. Yikes. How rich was he? For her eighteenth birthday, her grandma had rented a limo to take them to dinner. It had been neon pink and had smelled of cigarette smoke with faux-leather seats and the driver, her grandad, had ridden the clutch the whole way.

But it had been the best night of her life.

She blinked back tears at the memory.

Spike suddenly leaned over her. She shied back.

"Seatbelt," he grumbled, pulling it over her and locking it in as the car started moving. She hadn't even heard the driver get in. There was a partition up between the back seats and the front.

"I really don't need to go home with you. I'm sure that awful man has better things to do with his time than come after me. All I did was stun him. You knocked him out."

"A woman besting him will hurt his rep. Plus, he'll go after the weakest of us. That's you."

"Won't I be putting you in danger, though? If I come to stay with you?"

"I can handle it."

"What will Damon do about Luther?"

"You don't need to worry about it."

That didn't make her feel better.

"This is silly. Nobody knows who I am or where I'm staying. I'm sure I'll be safe on my own."

He snorted. "How long you been in the city?"

"Ahh, this is my fifth night."

"And how many times you been threatened or in danger?"

Hmm. She was starting to see where he was going with this. She wisely kept her mouth closed. But he made a noise that suspiciously sounded like amusement. Although she may have misread that as she didn't think much amused him.

"Your choices are to stay with me or go home."

"I can't go home."

"Then your choice is clear."

"I don't want to put you out. I'm sure you don't really want me coming to stay with you. I don't even know you. I mean, we're strangers. Why do you even care what happens to me?"

He was silent for a long moment. "Why'd you care what happened to me?"

Shoot.

"What do you mean?"

"You searched me out to warn me. You didn't have to do that."

She sighed. "Because I wouldn't have been able to live with myself if I hadn't warned you."

"Were you going to try again?"

"Yeah, I was going to try again."

He nodded. "You're staying with me."

And that was that. She was too tired to argue anymore. At least tonight.

"You're okay with Mr. Fluffy coming to stay too?" She patted the sleeping puppy.

"Yep."

"What about my stuff? Can we go grab it?"

"Get you new stuff."

"But there are things there I need. Nobody knows where I'm staying. It can't be unsafe to go grab my things, surely?" She couldn't do without Chompers or her onesies.

Oh, and her meds were important too.

He sighed. "Fine. What's the address?"

She told him and he lowered the partition to speak quietly to the driver.

∼

Spike stared out at the cheap motel Steele's driver pulled up in front of.

Fucking hell. This was where she was staying? Seriously?

"Stay in the car," he told her. "I'll get your stuff."

"Uh, no way. It's my stuff. I'll do it. You wait in the car."

Was she serious? She reached for her belt. Christ, she was. Leaning over, he grabbed her hand. "There could be someone in there."

"There's no way he could be waiting in there for me."

Fuck it. He knew she was right. "Fine. But you do as I say. At all times."

"Why do I get the feeling you'd like that rule to apply all the time and not just while I'm getting my things?"

That would make his life much easier.

"Stay there. You get out my side. When I say."

"Righto," she said cheerfully.

Spike really didn't understand her. How could she be cheerful right now? Shouldn't she be a mess? She wasn't like any woman he'd met before.

He climbed out and stood in the open door of the car, looking around suspiciously. The lot was dark. There were hardly any working lights in the parking area. Movement off to the right caught his attention. Raul, Damon's driver, reached for his gun, holding it out at his side as he gazed over at the same spot.

A woman dressed in a barely-there, skin tight dress stepped forward. "Interest you boys in some fun?"

"No," Raul told her. "You'll have better luck somewhere else."

"How about you, big guy," she said in a husky voice. The smell of cigarettes and sweat clung to her. "You want me to join you in the back of that fancy car?"

He just gave her a look.

She huffed.

Millie stood up on the lip of the door and looked over his shoulder at the woman.

What the fuck did she think she was doing? Anger flooded him; his palm grew itchy.

If she was his...

Not yours.

Yes, but maybe they'd need to establish a few rules for while she was under his protection.

And some consequences if she broke those rules.

"Hey, Rhonda," she said cheerfully.

The woman lost that predatory look, actual warmth filling her face. "Millie! What you doing?" She frowned at Spike. "You okay? This guy bothering you?"

"Nah. He's an, um, friend. We're just here to get some of my stuff."

"Millie," he warned.

He should have known this was a bad idea. The woman didn't seem to have a clue of the possible danger she could be in. Or the fact that she shouldn't trust anyone.

Oh no, she seemed to go around trusting everyone.

"A friend huh?" Rhonda drawled. "It's all right, sweetie, you don't need to say anything more. You go have some fun with your new friend."

"Wait," Spike said sharply. He reached into his pocket and drew out his wallet. He handed her over a hundred dollar bill. "Anyone asks, we were never here."

Rhonda didn't grab the money like he assumed she would. Instead she gave him a suspicious look and then glanced up at Millie. "You in some trouble, girl?"

"Seems so," Millie sighed. "It's okay, though. I'll be all right."

"Uh-huh." Rhonda snatched up the money, turning away. "Good luck, hon."

"You too."

Spike stepped back and turned. Grabbing Millie around the waist, he lifted her down. He loomed over her, placing his hands on the top of the car. "Just what did you think you were doing?"

"Talking to Rhonda?" she asked, looking up at him in confusion. Although it was hard to read her expression in the poorly-lit parking lot.

This wasn't the best time for this conversation. He took hold of her wrist. "Come on."

"Wait, Mr. Fluffy. My bag." She tugged back against his hold.

Turning, he stared down at her again. "Don't do that. You'll hurt yourself."

"Maybe instead of just grabbing hold of me and dragging me places you could actually speak to me instead. Like a normal person."

The bite in her voice raised his eyebrows. So she did know how to snap back. Good. Because she was going to need a tough side in order to get through these next few days.

And you're gonna need a lot of cold showers or else you're going to be walking around with a permanent hard-on.

Stop thinking about your dick.

"Not the time to chat," he told her abruptly. "Inside."

"Yes, I want to get inside too. But to do that, I need my handbag. It has my keys."

Idiot.

He sighed, his irritation completely and utterly turned inward. "Grab your bag. Dog can stay in the car."

She climbed into the car, her ass wiggling around so much that he had to bite back a groan. He forced himself to concentrate on his surroundings.

Focus.

When she slid out, she held her bag in one hand and the dog in the other.

They definitely needed a chat about obedience. And listening. And who the boss was.

Newsflash. Not her.

She must have sensed his irritation. "Mr. Fluffy doesn't like to be apart from me. He gets separation anxiety."

Lord give him patience.

"Keys," he demanded, holding out his hand.

She tried to juggle the dog and her bag, but couldn't manage it. So she held out the fluffy ball of fur to him. He took the dog. It settled onto his arm. And promptly fell asleep.

This dog had issues. Weren't puppies meant to have energy?

"He likes you," she told him.

"Last night he bit me."

"You scared him. He wouldn't fall asleep on you if he didn't like you."

"When does he do anything but sleep?" Spike asked incredulously.

She didn't reply, just jangled her keys. He snatched them from her and then handed back the dog. Who nestled in against her breasts with a happy sigh.

He was not jealous of a damn puppy.

He. Was. Not.

She slid the puppy into her handbag. "I don't want the manager seeing him. I didn't exactly ask permission. Mind you, I don't suppose he's awake at this time of night. I'm sure watching porn all day tires him out."

Spike stared down at her. Was she joking or . . . fuck it. Likely not.

Christ.

"Room?" he barked, making her jump slightly but he was too irritated to care. What the hell was she thinking staying here? This wasn't the sort of place someone like Millie should be. It was a wonder she'd lasted four nights.

"Five." She pointed to a room. "It's on the ground floor, which is lucky, right? No having to traipse up and down stairs.

Lucky? Right. Lucky for any criminals that she'd made it so much easier for them to get into her room by taking a ground floor.

Someone hated him, they really did.

This was his punishment for all the bad shit he'd done in his life.

11

Spike was muttering something quietly as they walked toward the motel room she'd rented. She couldn't make out anything he was saying, but she was pretty certain it wasn't flattering.

He kept close to her and his scent kept teasing her. Rich leather and tart cherries. It was a weird mix. But damn intriguing.

When he started to unlock the door, she stiffened. Shoot! She couldn't let him into her room.

Reaching out, she grabbed his hand. He snatched his own hand back and the keys clanged to the ground. She tried not to be hurt that he obviously didn't want her to touch him.

"Shoot. Sorry." She bent down at the same time as he did, their heads clanging together.

Ow. Ouch. Owie.

Rising up, she held her hand to her throbbing head and tried to convince the tears she felt welling to disappear.

This day sucked.

Everything was a mess. It wasn't going the way she thought she would. She was tired. Her insides felt empty. She just wanted to have a hot shower, get into her onesie and watch cartoons on TV until she fell asleep.

Instead, she now had some gangster out for her blood. She had to go stay with a stranger, a stranger who didn't even like her, who seemed more than a little bit irritated by everything she said and did, where she'd have to hide everything about herself.

And now her head hurt.

"Millie? You okay?"

Nope. She wasn't okay at all.

"Look at me."

Nope. Not happening.

"Baby doll, look at me."

Why'd he have to use that ridiculous name? And speak in such a kind voice? If he was going around demanding and being all gruff then she could keep resisting him. Maybe.

As it was, she had to fight the urge to lean on him. To take from him. Just for a moment.

"I'm fine. Sorry. I need to go in by myself." She kept her head lowered.

"Still not looking at me."

She looked up at him. "I need to go in by myself. I'll be quick, I promise. Can I have the keys?"

"Can't do that." He sighed. She thought she heard a hint of regret in his voice. He unlocked the door. "Stay here. Wait for my okay."

Stay here? She gaped at him as he set her to the side of the door. The driver, she noticed, remained by the car watching their surroundings.

Spike turned on the lights quickly and she walked into the doorway, shutting the door behind her. He gave her a fierce scowl that almost had her apologizing. He prowled through the room, checking the closet and under the bed.

This was kind of over-the-top.

Yet, she didn't protest, because there was a part of her that liked it. Liked how protective he was, even if it was over-the-top. She always enjoyed reading books with those crazy, protective heroes. Maybe because she'd never had anyone worry over her. Not like this.

She glanced around, noting that Chompers was sitting on her bed, right beside her onesie.

There's no reason to be ashamed. Lots of adults have onesies, and soft toys. He'll never know.

Still, as he walked into the bathroom she strode quickly over and gathered them up, wrapping the onesie around Chompers. Then she placed the small bundle as well as her handbag carefully on the floor before climbing up onto the bed. She stretched up for her suitcase, which sat on top of the wardrobe. It had been a pain in the ass to get it up there in the first place, but she hadn't had anywhere else to put it. As she grabbed it, her foot slid out from under her on the loose covers of the bed and she started to fly backwards.

A screech of surprise escaped her before she found herself gathered into two thick, muscular arms, and pressed against a wide chest.

"Christ," he grunted.

Oh hell. Had he hurt himself? "Are you okay? You should have just let me fall!"

She tried to scramble out of his hold. He set her on the floor on her feet, giving her an incredulous look.

"Let you fall?"

"I could have hurt you! I didn't, did I?" she worried.

"How the fuck would you hurt me?"

"By falling on you!" She thought that was obvious.

"Jesus," he muttered. "You're fucking crazy."

Okay, that hurt. More than it should have. It was like thousands of needles working their way under her skin and then pushing deep. She took a breath. *Reality check, Millie.* It wasn't the worst thing anyone had ever said to her. It wouldn't be the last mean thing anyone said. In the grand scheme of things, his opinion didn't matter.

Right. She could tell herself all of that until the cows came home. Still, didn't make it hurt less.

"I'll just start packing," she muttered, side-stepping him. Or she attempted to. He reached out and wrapped an arm around her waist, turning her. A big hand tucked itself under her chin, tilting her face up.

Those kaleidoscope eyes of his studied her. He ran his thumb over her cheek. She knew she wasn't crying. But it felt like he was trying to soothe away her tears.

"Didn't mean to hurt you, baby doll."

Well, whether he'd intended to or not, he had.

He winced. "Asshole."

Her eyes widened. Why was he calling her an asshole?

"Me. Not you," he said gruffly. "I'd never let you fall."

For some reason he felt obligated to take care of her. She had no idea why. But she hadn't protested as much as she probably should have.

Yeah? Why is that, Millie? Because you actually want to be around this gruff, grumpy ass?

Maybe.

Sometimes she thought she was a glutton for punishment.

"Should have asked me to get the suitcase for you," he scolded. "Don't do that again."

With soft fingers, he pushed back her hair off her face, gently prodding at the sore spot on her head from where she'd banged it into his earlier. "Needs ice."

"I doubt it will even bruise. I've had far worse, don't worry."

He frowned but didn't say anything.

"I'll just, uhh, pack up my stuff."

"This motel is crap. And it's in a fucking bad area of town."

"It is? The people all seem so nice around here, though. I admit it's not the nicest place, but I got a good deal on it. I paid for it a week in advance without seeing it first."

He just gave her an incredulous look. "When you said your neighbor was starting a taxi service . . ."

"Oh yes, Manuel. He lives a few rooms down. Such a nice man."

Spike closed his eyes, his lips moving. He appeared to be counting. She had no idea why.

This time when she slid around him, he let her go.

And that was not disappointment she felt. It was not.

She moved around, shoving things into her suitcase while Spike picked up all the dog's toys. He glanced into the small kitchen area. "You really like jerky, huh?"

"What?" Glancing over to where he was looking, she ran a hand tiredly down her face. "No, one of my neighbors gave it to me. I'm a vegetarian."

"You didn't tell him?"

She shrugged. "I have. He didn't remember. And I didn't want to hurt his feelings by refusing. Do you want some?"

He shook his head and picked up another bag, glancing in. "Uh, doll, what the hell is this?"

"Hmm?" She glanced over and froze. "That is not what it looks like."

"No?"

"No. Honestly."

"So it's not counterfeit money."

"Okay, it is what it looks like. But I'm not going to use it."

Spike drew one note out, studying it. "What the fuck?"

"One of my neighbors makes it. The same one who makes the jerky."

He sighed, pinching the top of his nose. Did he have a headache? Should she offer him some pain relief?

"You know this is illegal?"

"Well, yes. But it's not real."

He gave her an incredulous look.

"I mean, it's not good counterfeit. It's just a hobby. He's old. I didn't like to tell him no when he insisted I bring it."

"Like the jerky."

"Umm. Yeah."

He zipped the bag back up, muttering something to himself. He seemed to do that a lot.

"I'll take this load out. Stay in here." The look he gave her told her he meant business.

"Sure."

Striding over to her, he placed the bag down then took hold of her shoulders in his hands, peering down at her. Then he placed his mouth close to her ear.

Why did he keep doing that? Did he know the way it was affecting her?

"You're clearly not very obedient, so let me make this clear. Leave this room without my permission and your ass is toast. Got it?"

Before she could reply, he was moving out the door.

Did he just threaten to spank her?

Holy. Heck.

12

Spike buckled her seatbelt before she could reach for it.

He felt her stiffen. But wasn't sure if it was because he was being bossy and crowding her or because when he slid the belt over her, he accidentally brushed his hand against her breasts.

Maybe both.

He'd given her space while she packed her personal things, but that didn't mean he hadn't noticed the stuffed dinosaur she'd attempted to hide. Or the stash of candy she drew out of one of the kitchen cupboards. He'd also spotted a pair of dinosaur slippers next to the bed.

None of that meant anything. Lots of adults had slippers and soft toys. It didn't mean she was a Little.

But it also wouldn't surprise him if she was. In fact, it might explain a few things. This overwhelming need he had to protect her, for one thing.

However, it wasn't his business, even if she was. And the red in her cheeks as she'd hastily hidden the toy dinosaur told him that she wouldn't appreciate him asking her.

What worried him were the bottles of pills in the bathroom. He wondered what they were for. And if she would tell him.

She had an independent streak. She tried to do everything herself. Who'd been looking after this girl that she thought she had to carry her own suitcase? That she was so shocked when he wanted to do things like check through her motel room to ensure it was safe? Or catch her when she slipped and fell?

He was still in a state of disbelief over that one. Had she really thought he would let her fall?

She was a menace. That was for certain. He didn't think bubble wrap would help. Hell, he wasn't even certain that locking her up in Ink's safe room would help. He had a feeling she could find trouble anywhere.

Not on his watch.

The driver pulled up outside his gate. Raul had been here a few times with Steele. Spike didn't like strangers coming up to the house, but Raul had been with Steele a long time.

The electric gates opened automatically, sensing the controller in his pocket. The car moved slowly up the driveway. Lights shone along the driveway then security lights flickered on at the house. It had six bedrooms and three bathrooms. There were two levels and a wrap-around porch. But he'd bought it because of the land. It was set on just less than five acres, on the outskirts of the city.

It was an older house he'd slowly renovated. The neighbors were far enough away that you couldn't see or hear them. It gave him the privacy he wanted but he could still get into the city in under forty minutes.

"Oh wow," Millie said, looking out at the farmhouse. She'd probably been expecting something more like where Ink lived. A big, renovated warehouse. Or maybe where Duke lived, a small house in suburbia.

Although, no one had really expected Duke to end up in a house like that. Duke was the only one out of them who regularly had everyone over to his place. Spike had been to Ink's place maybe a handful of times. Razor's place, he'd been to more often. He had no clue where Jason or Reyes lived. They were far more private.

Most of the people closest to him hadn't seen his house, yet he'd fought Steele to bring a virtual stranger here.

Yep, he wasn't going to think too closely about that one.

Raul opened her door. Shit. He'd been too slow. She tried to climb out but seemed to have forgotten about her seatbelt.

"Shoot," she muttered. Reaching over, he undid it for her and she sent him a smile. It did something strange to his insides, seeing her smile at him like that.

Easy, idiot.

After getting out, he grabbed her suitcase from where Raul had set it on the ground and nodded his thanks to the other man. He left the piles of dog things outside for the moment. How she'd managed to accumulate so much stuff for one small dog in a few short days he had no idea. This dog owned more shit than he did.

The driver turned around and left. Spike started up the steps and pressed a code into the keypad by the door. When the light went green, he pressed his finger to the pad reader.

"Whoa, that's high-tech. Back home most people don't even lock their doors when they leave the house."

Okay, he did not like the sound of that. But he bit back his reply as he led the way inside. He reset the alarm and checked the camera for the front gate to make sure that Raul had gone through.

"Are you some kind of security tech specialist?" she whispered.

"Nah, just like my privacy." Ink had put in the system himself. He was the only one of the guys who had been here. He'd teased him for a while, calling him rancher Spike, even though he didn't have near enough land for a farm nor did he own any animals. But still that asshole had continued to rib him.

At least until Spike gave him a black eye and told him to shut the fuck up before he got really mad.

Ink had just grinned.

Jerk.

"Oh," she said, staring in awe at the system. The video feed flicked continuously through the cameras around the property, letting him see it from all angles. Although the alarms would tell him if there were any intruders.

"Come."

He led her through the house. Lights flicked on as they walked, set on sensors once the sun went down.

His footsteps were silent on the hardwood floors as he walked to the stairs. "Kitchen's downstairs to the right. Help yourself." There were four bedrooms upstairs and two downstairs. He stopped outside the door to one of the spare bedrooms. He pointed across the hall. "Bathroom." He opened the door. "Your room."

The light came on, showing the fairly utilitarian room. A bed with a gray cover. A set of bedside drawers. A wardrobe. And a large window looking out on the back garden. He set her suitcase on the bed and strode to the curtains, pulling them closed.

"I'll get the dog's stuff." And the bag full of counterfeit. Which he'd stick in his safe. Fucking hell. He should probably just burn the stuff.

"O-okay. I'll help you."

"No."

She flinched and he grimaced. He wasn't used to explaining himself.

"Cold out. Stay in where it's warm."

She nodded. "Thanks."

He strode out of the house and grabbed the stuff up, trying to make it all in one go. He left the food and water bowls downstairs in the kitchen, along with the huge bag of food then made his way up with the bedding . . . and a bag of what looked to be dog clothing?

Really?

Climbing the stairs, he entered her room, surprised to see her still standing there. Her handbag was on the bed and the dog had managed to find the energy to crawl out and was currently curled up on her pillow.

Spike placed the dog bed down, putting the bag of clothing next to her suitcase on the bed. Then he shifted the dog onto his bed before turning back to her, wondering why she was so quiet. She'd barely spoken since they'd arrived.

Her arms were wrapped around herself, her eyes flicking around the room. She licked her full lips. The red lipstick she'd had on earlier was gone. She appeared pale and fragile. And he felt the urge to take her into his arms, to reassure her that everything would be all right.

Clearing his throat, he just stared at her, uncertain what to say. Words weren't his specialty. He was a hands-on sort of guy.

"It's late."

She nodded.

"You should sleep."

Her gaze shifted to the bed. She nodded again. So his attempts at reassuring her were pretty crappy.

"Want some help?"

Her forehead puckered into a frown. "With sleeping?"

"Unpacking."

"Umm, no."

"Leave it until morning. Go to bed. Sleep." Yes, he was aware he sounded bossy and gruff. But the more she just stood there, the greater his urge to take over became. To undress her himself. To take her to the bathroom and help her get ready for sleep. To tuck her into bed. Wrap her in his arms. And . . .

Fuck. He needed that cold shower. He hadn't reacted to

another woman like this since . . . since Jacqui died. Okay, that reminder worked better than any cold shower.

You can't let yourself feel anything for her.

"Yes, you're right. I'll do that."

Right. Fuck. Shit. He should leave. Let her get ready for bed. He walked out, turning back at the door. "Need anything?"

"N-no. I'm fine. Thank you."

She didn't sound fine. She sounded lost and alone. And he hated it. He wanted that smile back on her face. That carefree way she approached everything and everyone. As though she'd never met anyone she couldn't charm.

"Sleep in tomorrow. Don't want you up before nine." He walked out into the hallway before he could say anything he might regret.

Like . . . come sleep with me.

He strode into the master suite after checking that the house was secure. The master suite was much the same as the room he'd put her in. Utilitarian. Boring. He didn't care. He only used this room to sleep in. But the whole house was like this.

Maybe he should have let her go stay with Damon. His house was easily four times the size. Luxurious. And even more secure. He had several armed guards roaming the grounds and inside the house.

Spike ground his teeth together at the thought of her with Steele and Grady. He just hadn't been able to stomach it.

Stripping off his clothes, he chucked them in the dirty laundry and made his way into the attached bathroom. He turned the water on and climbed in while it was still cold.

Unfortunately, it did nothing for his raging hard-on. Leaning one hand against the shower wall, the water cascading down his back, he took hold of his dick, running his hand up and down the length.

He closed his eyes as he moved his hand harder. Faster.

Hazel eyes dancing with laughter. Looking up at him in concern. Soft hands touching him.

His balls tightened as his orgasm grew closer. He imagined those red lips wrapped around his shaft. Those breasts, loose and free, bouncing up and down as she rode him. Taking her from behind, slapping his hand down on her ass as he took her hard and fast.

Fuck. That was ridiculously fast. He groaned as he came, his heart racing, body taut.

Yeah, bringing her home with him was most likely going to turn out to be the dumbest thing he'd ever done.

13

All right.

No need to panic.

She'd faced down a man holding her at gunpoint. A room filled with rough, scary-looking bikers. A gang member intent on dragging his ex-girlfriend away with him.

She'd done all that without letting on how damn well terrified she was.

So she should be able to handle sleeping in Spike's house without freaking out. Right? Right. It was no different than staying in the motel. Well, except for the fact that this was . . .

Spike's house.

And he was just down the hallway. There was no lock on her door. She barely knew the man. And what she did know . . . well, he was bossy and abrupt and stubborn.

And protective. And caring, in his own weird way.

"You can do this. It's not like he's going to hurt you."

Maybe it would be a good idea to let someone know where she was, though.

She shook her head. Who would she tell? It wasn't like anyone was close enough to help her. She wouldn't have come here with him if she'd even had an inkling that he might harm her.

Nope, that wasn't the issue.

The issue was that she was attracted to him. And it was freaking her out.

Not to mention that everything that had happened tonight was piling up on her. Threatening to crack that box inside her, where it was all locked up tight. She tried to push all her fear into the box. But it felt like it was rocking, about to explode.

Calm. Down.

Reacting to what happened wouldn't help her. It wouldn't rewind the last few hours, hell the last few days.

The last few years.

She squeezed her eyes shut as a few tears dripped down her face. None of this would break her. She was strong. She could take on as much as she needed to.

Managing to calm herself down, she unzipped her suitcase. No one back home was going to understand why she'd agreed to come here. She didn't get it herself. There was no way that Devil's Sinners guy could find her at the motel.

This was a total overreaction on Spike's part. Although it seemed like Damon and Grady had goaded him into it. She paused as she pulled out her dinosaur night light, plugging it in. She needed to remember to put it and Chompers away in the morning in case Spike came in here and saw them.

Had they done it on purpose? To get Spike to take her home with him?

Nah. That was stupid. Why would they do that? And Damon had more reason to want her with him since she was the only one who could point out the traitor. Well, her and that asshole, Luther. But she didn't think he'd be spilling his guts anytime soon.

Anger flooded her as she remembered the way he'd talked about selling women for sex. He preyed on the young and vulnerable. Treating them like they were a commodity. She sat on the side of the bed and took a few deep breaths to stop herself from crying again.

Crying never helped a situation, Millie.

Grabbing out her onesie next, along with her toiletries, she cautiously opened her door. She looked up and down the hallway.

Yes, she knew she was acting like an idiot, but she just wasn't sure she could take any more of Spike tonight. Not without breaking down and begging him to hug her.

Or fuck her.

Millie wasn't ashamed of her sex drive, exactly. But she had been raised by her grandparents. They'd never really talked about sex or boys. Everything she'd learned had first come from school then books. Then her few relationships.

She slipped into the bathroom and turned the lock. The bathroom was surprisingly nice. White subway tiles on the walls and grey tiles on the floor. A big sunken bath that made her sigh longingly.

Could she?

Biting her lip, she put the plug in and turned the water on. Then she searched through the cupboards and found a fresh towel. She opened up her toiletries bag and drew out her bottle of shower gel that came in a dinosaur container.

Yes, there was a theme going on here.

She poured a generous amount into the bath and nearly squealed in delight as bubbles appeared. She loved a good bubble bath. It was soothing. Relaxing. She stripped off her clothes then reached back into her toiletries bag.

Sticking her tongue out in thought, she glanced over at the lock on the door.

He'd never know. He was all the way down the hall. This door had a lock, unlike her bedroom door. So if she was going to do it, surely this was the safest place? The water would likely muffle any noise, not that it made much. She'd bought this one because it was extra quiet.

Oh, and also because it was shaped like a dinosaur.

Purple and long, the top of the vibrator formed the dinosaur's head and could be used to stimulate the clit. Down the back of the vibrator were small scales and at the base was the power button.

If she didn't do something about the buzzing in her body, she was certain she'd struggle to sleep. Mind made up, she turned the water off and climbed in, setting the dino vibrator on the lip of the bath next to her. She washed herself first then she reached for her breast, plucking the nipple.

Felt so good.

She bit her lip to hold in a moan of pleasure. Even though she didn't think he'd hear her, she didn't want to do anything to embarrass herself.

Reaching for the vibrator, she set it on low to begin with and rubbed the head of it over each of her nipples. Throwing back her head, she slid it lower, between her spread legs. She imagined Spike's face between her legs, pleasuring her. His tongue against her clit. Then thrusting in deep.

A small moan escaped.

Careful. Careful.

She slid the vibrator into her pussy then turned up the vibrations, using her middle finger of her other hand to toy with her clit.

So good. So good.

Her orgasm grew closer and closer.

Her imagination turned to Spike pressing her legs apart, to his firm, thick cock thrusting deep inside her.

A scream escaped her as she came.

Oh. Oh.

She panted, trying frantically to turn off the damn vibrator even as her hands shook.

Her pussy still clenched, her clit tingling as aftereffects ran through her. Shoot.

"Millie! Millie! Are you all right?"

She winced as Spike banged on the door. Damn. This was so embarrassing.

"Millie! Answer me now." The door handle rattled as he tested it. Crap! The lock was one of those ones that you pressed in on the door handle. All he'd need to do was get a pin or needle to press in the hole on the other side and he'd be in here.

He'd see her. Naked. Flushed. With a purple dino vibrator in her hand.

Not good. Not good.

"I'm fine!" she managed to croak out.

There was silence on the other side of the door. Her heart pounded as she waited for him to reply.

"Fine?"

She could hear the skepticism in his voice and she closed her eyes in chagrin. What had she been thinking? She'd never been able to keep quiet when she came. Doug had been horribly embarrassed by it. He'd even asked her to wear a gag so he didn't risk his parents hearing her.

Yes, he'd still lived at home.

"Yes, I'm fine."

"I heard you scream."

Shoot. Crap. Drat.

Damn it!

"Sorry, I, uh, thought I saw a mouse." She rolled her eyes at herself. Like she'd scream if she saw a mouse. But he didn't know that.

"A mouse?"

"Yep. A mouse. But, it, uh, must have been my imagination playing tricks on me."

"Sure you're okay?"

"Me, I'm fine. Just taking a nice relaxing bath in this mouse-free bathroom. Nothing else going on, nope."

Stop rambling, Millie!

She wanted to sink under the water with embarrassment. Thank God he couldn't see her.

Wait! He wouldn't have cameras in the house, would he? No, that would be just wrong.

Why. Why her? Why did she have to scream?

"Millie? Millie? Damn it, answer me!"

"Oh, sorry, what?"

"Open the door."

"No!"

There was grumbling from the other side of the door. She bet he was regretting bringing her back here now. She should get out. Her relaxing bath had kind of turned into something else. Not that she was going to let him in. No way. What if he could tell what she'd been doing just from looking at her? She wasn't sure if that was possible. But some of the heroes in the romances she loved to read claimed to be able to.

So she wasn't taking any chances.

"Millie!"

She let out a screech of fright as his voice penetrated her musings, accidentally dropping the vibrator. It slipped under the bubbles.

Shoot! Where was that slippery sucker? She searched through the water, trying to find it, sending water sloshing over the sides. She moaned at the mess she was making.

Such a klutz. Why couldn't she be graceful? Svelte. Delicate.

"Why did you cry out? Did you see the mouse again?" he snapped.

"Oh no, I just slipped."

"You slipped? Trying to get out of the bath? That's it. I'm coming in."

"Nooo, I'm naked."

"Seen naked women before."

What kind of answer was that? He'd never seen her naked before. And she wasn't ready for him to see her naked now.

One day, maybe. . .

No, Millie. Focus. He's like this gorgeous, muscular specimen of a man who is way out of your league. Women probably threw themselves at him.

"Don't come in here," she cried out desperately.

"You got nothing I ain't seen before."

"That's just . . . that's just rude!" she sputtered out. What? It would be nice to feel special.

There was a thump on the other side of the door. Was he planning on breaking it down?

Or was he banging his head against it in frustration?

Both were possible, to be honest.

"I'm coming, all right? I'll get out and put my pajamas on then you'll see I'm fine."

"No, wait!" he barked.

She froze, halfway out of the bath already.

"You'll slip and hurt yourself."

"I won't slip and hurt myself," she scoffed. "I've been taking baths on my own since I was five."

"Fine. Go slow. Watch where you put your feet."

This was ridiculous. Why would she slip? Sure, she could be somewhat clumsy. But it was just getting out of the bath.

He was being over the top ridiculous.

And you're objecting because . . .

Also, you already told him you slipped. Idiot.

She climbed out but her foot stepped directly onto a pool of water, sending her sliding and she landed on the tiled floor with a thump and a cry.

Ow. Ouchy. That really hurt.

"What happened? Millie!"

She sat there for a moment, feeling thoroughly humiliated. Then she screeched as the door slammed open and Spike loomed in the doorway. Dressed in just a pair of black pajama pants that hung low on his hips, it took her a moment to drag her tongue back into her mouth with all that skin and muscles on display.

How was it possible for a man to be that ripped?

He had to be older than her, at least she thought he was, and he was in such good shape he could be one of those fitness models.

"Millie! What happened?" He strode forward, reaching over to snag the towel she'd left on the bathroom counter.

She remembered then that she was stark naked. With a cry, she brought her legs up to her chest and wrapped her arms around them.

Then she promptly burst into tears.

Sᴘɪᴋᴇ ꜰʀᴏᴢᴇ as Millie started to cry.

She'd had a lot thrown at her tonight and she hadn't once cried. He'd thought she might have broken down into tears after what happened with that Devil's Sinner fucker.

But she hadn't.

Then he'd figured she might after her break down at Pinkies when she'd vomited in the bathroom.

But she hadn't.

Then he'd thought she might have cried when they'd banged heads at the motel.

But again, she'd proven him wrong.

She was crying now, though. Tears dripping down her face. Ragged sobs filled the room. The whole nine yards.

Fuck.

What should he do? Was it something he'd done? Or had she truly hurt herself?

Well, you should do something other than stand here, holding a towel while she sobs her heart out, sitting naked, wet and cold on the floor, dipshit.

"Oh, baby girl. It's okay. Here." He crouched down and wrapped the towel around her. But she didn't release the tight hold she had on her legs and the towel wasn't big enough to wrap around her. He grabbed another one, pressing it to her front.

"It's okay. You're okay," he told her over and over as she continued to cry.

"It's not. It's not. It's all a mess. It's all a big m-mess."

Fuck it.

Bending down, he wrapped one arm around her back and the other under her legs and picked her up. He waited for an objection. But to his shock, she just buried her face into his chest and continued to cry.

He hated it. Wanted to do whatever he had to in order to stop those heart-shattering tears. He'd raze cities, destroy lives.

Just for her to stop crying like her heart was breaking. These weren't simple tears. They didn't stem from surface-level pain. He might not be a man who understood emotions well. But he knew pain. And hers was coming from deep inside her. Something bad had happened to this girl.

And it was tearing him in two.

Because he now realized the happy, easygoing, naïve persona was just that. A put-on, a front. No way could she skim through life, not letting things get to her and have this deep well of pain if it wasn't all pretend.

"Come on, baby doll, stop crying."

He settled on her bed with her on his lap. Even the dog looked up from his bed to give a small yip of sympathy.

Fuck. She felt too nice pressed to his body. The scent of

bubblegum clung to her skin from whatever she'd put in the bath. Had to be something she'd brought with her since he sure as shit didn't have anything in the house that smelled that good.

Her face was turned to his chest as he rocked her back and forth.

"Hush, little baby, don't say a word."

He didn't know where the words came from. She'd likely think him ridiculous for singing a child's lullaby to her.

And fuck knew, his voice was shit. Gravelly and broken. Definitely not suited to singing.

"Daddy's gonna buy you a mockingbird."

She didn't move. Didn't say a thing, but her sobs seemed to ease.

Well, shit.

"And if that mockingbird don't sing."

Sniffle. Sniffle. But she eased into him, turning her face from his chest.

"Daddy's gonna buy you a diamond ring."

Her small hand wrapped lightly around his bicep as she struggled to get her breathing under control.

"And if that diamond ring turns brass."

He gave in to temptation. Fuck. Where was his iron control now? He kissed the top of her head. She'd piled her hair up and secured it with a big clip. He reached up and undid it, letting those strands of silken hair fall around her shoulders.

"Daddy's going to buy you a looking glass."

She tilted her head back, looking up at him through swollen eyes. Her cheeks were wet, her face blotchy, her nose red.

She wasn't a pretty crier.

And he'd never wanted to kiss someone more.

He closed his eyes on a wince. That was wrong. So wrong.

He had to pull back from her. This wasn't what he wanted. He couldn't do this again. He couldn't allow himself to feel anything for her.

Fuck. He had to find some way of putting some distance between them.

"Spike?" she whispered. "Are you okay?"

He opened his eyes, gazing down at her in shock. "Am I okay?" Pretty sure it should be him asking that.

"You looked to be in pain. Oh." She glanced down as though just realizing that she was sitting on his lap. "I'm so sorry. I got you all wet."

I'd like to get you all wet.

Ahh. Shit. Did he really just think that? Was he that much of an ass? He wasn't eighteen anymore. He was pushing forty. He had more restraint than this.

And he really shouldn't be able to get it up again so quickly after he'd rubbed one off in the shower, right?

Fuck. She was killing him here.

She scrambled to get off his lap and he held her tight. He doubted she had any idea what she was doing to him with all the jiggling, especially as her towel was resting rather precariously on her breasts. It wouldn't take much for it to fall off.

"Sit still," he growled.

She froze and he cursed himself for being an asshole.

"About to lose your towel," he used as an excuse. Even though he wouldn't object at all if that towel were to slip.

That glimpse he'd gotten of her body before she'd realized she was naked and had curled into herself . . . well, there was a reason he was hard again.

Fuck. Him.

"Oh shoot. I'm so sorry. I just . . . oh goodness." She grabbed the towel, frantically wrapping it around herself before she slid off his lap onto the bed. This time he let her, hoping she didn't catch the raging hard-on he was sporting.

Although that was probably a fruitless dream considering her ass had been nestled against it.

Get yourself under control, man.

"Umm . . . I . . . I'm sorry for losing it like that . . . I . . ." She sniffled, looking around the room. "Can you hand me my handbag? I've got some tissues in there."

Of course she did. That thing was a Tardis, considering how much stuff she managed to get in it. He handed her bag to her.

"Be back." He stood and walked out into the bathroom, hoping that would give him some time to calm down.

When he returned, she'd blown her nose and wiped her face. He sat next to her and gently grabbing hold of her chin, he cleaned her face with a warm washcloth. She'd taken the opportunity to secure one of the towels more firmly around herself. But he'd also grabbed the clothing she'd left on the bathroom counter, figuring she'd want to get out of that wet towel.

He held it up, blinking in surprise as he realized it was a onesie. A dinosaur onesie.

"Oh that's . . . it's . . . I . . ."

"Cute."

"C-cute? Really?" She stared up at him.

He nodded. "Need help?"

She was still staring at him in shock.

"Millie? You okay?"

She seemed kind of spacey and out of it. And earlier when he'd been calling to her through the bathroom door there had been long moments when she wouldn't answer him. Just tiredness? Or something more? And he wasn't sure he bought the whole mouse excuse for why she'd screamed.

"Did you hurt yourself?"

"What? Oh, no." She shook her head.

He eyed her doubtfully.

She gave him a wry smile. "Believe it or not, but I fall over a lot."

"I believe it." He didn't like it though. Maybe the bubble wrap was the way to go. Perhaps knee pads, shin pads and a helmet?

She sighed sadly. "Yeah, I'm just one big klutz."

He frowned at her. "Not a klutz."

"No? What do you call it then? Seems like I can't go five minutes without tripping over my own feet."

Cute. He called it cute. But he couldn't tell her that.

"You need sleep."

She nodded tiredly and yawned. "Yeah."

"Get this on. I'll be back."

After giving him a surprised look, she reached for the onesie, her cheeks still blushing. Her fingers brushed against his, sending warmth through his body. He snatched his hand back, unprepared for the sensation.

Millie flinched at his reaction. Inwardly, he cursed himself.

"S-sorry," she whispered. "I'm a terrible house guest. I've already broken your bathroom door and made you carry me half-naked while sobbing on your chest. I promise I don't usually behave like this. I can't even remember the last time I cried. How embarrassing. I'll be much more normal tomorrow."

He frowned at that. Normal? Who said she had to be normal? Or who got to say what normal was? He didn't like the way she'd hunched her shoulders, as though trying to appear smaller. Invisible.

"I broke the door, not you."

"Only because you were worried about me," she whispered.

A small tinge of red hit her cheeks, making him wonder again why she had screamed that first time. But he decided not to push. She was fragile right now. She needed comfort, not for him to push and prod at her until she bled.

"You're fine," he said. As far as reassurances went, it was pretty crap. But she gave him a small smile.

"You're a good man, Spike . . ." She snorted. "I not only don't know your last name, but I don't know your actual first name either."

"Lochlin. Quillon Lochlin."

He didn't know why he told her that. So few people knew his real name. And he liked it that way.

"Quillon. I like it."

"I don't use it."

She nodded. "I understand. My lips are sealed."

Hmm. He'd rather they were wrapped around his cock.

Fuck. What was wrong with him?

"Get dressed. Back soon."

He strode out of the room and across to the bathroom, deciding that tidying it up might help him bring himself under control. He pulled the plug out of the bath and got a towel to mop up the excess water on the floor.

He spotted the dinosaur shaped bottle on the floor. Opening the lid, he took a sniff.

Bubblegum.

It was children's bubble bath and that just added to the overall picture he was building of her.

He wished he knew what was going on in her head. Why she'd acted so weird in the bathroom. Why she'd lost it, sobbing in his arms.

As the bath emptied, something caught his eye.

Was that?

Huh . . . well, that explained some of her behavior.

Amused, Spike reached in and grabbed the small vibrator that had a face and scales down the back. He cleaned it off and placed it in her toilet bag.

When he walked into the bedroom, he found her pulling

down the blankets, yawning loudly. She was dressed in a dinosaur onesie that went over her feet and, he noted as she bent over, also had a drop seat.

That made it so much easier to get to her bottom.

Especially good for naughty little girls who used toys to get themselves off in the bath then claimed to have seen a mouse.

Hmm... if she was his...

But she's not. Because if she was, she'd be in a hell of a lot of trouble for getting herself off without permission. She also wouldn't be having a bath by herself. Little girls didn't bathe themselves. That was far too dangerous. They could slip and fall. They could hurt themselves.

Much like she had.

"Hop in," he commanded.

She let out a cry, turning, her feet nearly slipping out from under her. He grabbed her, steadying her.

"Oh, you scared me. You need to learn to make some noise."

"Why? So you could get away with mischief without getting caught?"

"Well, yes, hey! I wasn't getting up to any mischief." She pouted but climbed into bed, he grabbed the covers, tucking them around her.

Her eyelids were already drooping. Poor baby. She'd had an eventful night. Sitting on the side of the bed, he resisted the urge to brush back her hair, to offer to braid it for her.

She yawned. There was something so real about her. Yet at the same time, there were secrets swirling in her eyes. There was a reason she acted so blasé about her own safety. He didn't like that. Not one bit.

What was he thinking, bringing her here?

Just how the fuck was he going to resist her?

14

She had to pee so badly.

She'd woken up with a dry mouth, her hair sticking to her cheek where she'd obviously been drooling in her sleep. Something she did when she was really tired.

Gross.

With eyes still half-open, she stumbled out of bed and shuffled her way towards the door. She hadn't even fully registered where she was when she opened the door and stepped into the hallway.

Yawning, she tried to orientate herself. Where was the bathroom?

Stretching, she walked towards the door opposite her.

"Good morning."

She squealed, pressing her legs together as she nearly wet herself in shock. Blinking, she stared down the hallway to where a huge, bald man stood staring at her.

Spike.

She was at Spike's house.

She was standing in front of Spike, in his house, wearing her dinosaur onesie.

With another squeal, she dove back into her bedroom, looking around frantically before pulling open the closest door and jumping inside.

Heart thundering, she pulled her legs up to her chest and tried to ignore her complaining bladder. What was she thinking? Why didn't she get dressed first? Or make sure the hallway was clear?

Idiot. Idiot.

"Millie?"

She groaned and buried her face in her knees.

"Millie? You okay?"

"Millie no longer exists," she called back.

"Then who am I talking to?"

That couldn't be a thread of amusement in his voice. No way. Because this was so not funny.

"Agnes," she said. Agnes? Really? That's the best she could come up with?

"Agnes, huh? Well, Aggie, why are you in the closet?"

"I like closets. They help me think. They're quiet and dark and cool."

"You like the dark?"

She hated the dark. She was starting to wonder why she'd hidden in here. It was getting a bit creepy and claustrophobic and . . . okay, she was starting to panic.

Stop being an idiot, Millie.

"Come out of the closet, baby doll." The voice he used was almost . . . tender. It did weird things to her insides. Made her shiver in pleasure.

Made her want things she knew she couldn't have.

"I'm okay."

"Your voice is shaking."

"It's always like this before I have a coffee." *Liar. Liar.*

There was a long beat of silence.

"You hiding from me?"

Well, duh.

She bit her lip on that reply. "No, like I said. I like closets. Closets are great. Not scary at all. Nope. Nuh-uh. They're really useful. Good for lots of things. Like hanging up your clothes . . . why is the ground not opening me up and swallowing me whole?"

"Millie—"

"I'm not Millie." Okay, at this point she just sounded ridiculous. "I've lost the plot."

"Come out now." His voice was firmer this time.

Shoot. It was hard not to obey him immediately.

"I can't."

"Why not?"

"I'm too embarrassed."

"Why?"

Wasn't it obvious?

"Is this because I found your vibrator?"

He found her vibrator? Oh no! She groaned. "This isn't happening. It's not happening. This is all some awful dream."

"Everyone masturbates. It's normal." His voice was gruff and tight. As though he wasn't nearly as relaxed as he was pretending to be.

Everyone masturbates? It's normal? Really? This is where he was going?

"Kill me. Kill me now."

"No need to be embarrassed."

Really? How did he expect her to react? Sure, it might be freaking normal. But it wasn't normal to do it in the bathtub of a stranger's house with a dinosaur vibrator! Or to have that stranger find her vibrator in the bottom of the bathtub after she'd fallen asleep.

In her dinosaur onesie.

"Millie, come out now."

"No. Never! I'm going to die in here. I'm gonna apologize now for the smell of my decaying flesh and for the flies and buzzards."

"Buzzards hardly gonna get you in the closet."

That's what he wanted to say? Really?

Suddenly the door opened, flooding the closet with light. Before she could protest, she was picked up and pulled out into his arms. He carried her to the bed and sat with her on his lap.

"Don't! Leave me!" She tried to fight her way free.

A slap landed on her ass as she froze, gaping up at him. He scowled down at her. Normally, that face might have intimidated the hell out of her. But she was beyond that right now.

He'd found her dinosaur vibrator.

"Settle down," he growled at her.

"Please, please let this be a dream."

He sighed. "Already told you. Don't be embarrassed."

"Just because you tell someone to do something or in this case, not do something, doesn't mean they're going to do it. Or, urgh, not to do it. Oh, you know what I mean!"

He gave her a look of disbelief then he just shook his head. "Be a lot easier if you just did as I said."

"For you, maybe," she muttered, keeping her gaze on her hands. "Can't believe you found my vibrator. That you know what I was doing in the bath." She hunched her shoulders. "And I was embarrassed over being caught in my onesie."

"Your onesie?"

"Yeah."

"That's why you hid in the closet?"

"Uh-huh. Turns out I should have just jumped out the window."

He sighed. "How can you face down a gang member without flinching and this makes you want to jump out a window?"

She shrugged. "Guess I didn't much care if he hurt me. I was just worried about Tawny. Getting hurt or dying doesn't scare me."

He tightened his arms around her, surprising her. "Don't like that."

It was what it was.

"Can't believe you spanked me."

"You think that was a spanking? That was a little tap to stop you getting hysterical."

"I wasn't hysterical."

"Uh-huh, you talked about jumping out a window just because I saw your vibrator."

She groaned. "Please can we stop talking about it? Can we just pretend it never happened? In fact, let's pretend we never met. I'll get dressed, pack up and leave. Okay?"

"Not okay."

He was intent on torturing her.

"Meanie-bo-beanie."

Crap. Did she really just say that? The verbal diarrhea was bad enough but now she was resorting to an insult a three-year-old would use.

"Look at me."

"Nuh-uh."

"Millie," he said in a low warning voice.

"I don't wanna." If she looked at him, then this definitely wasn't a dream. She'd definitely made a complete fool of herself.

And she wasn't sure she could handle that.

So she buried her face in his chest. He smelled nice. If she just hadn't thoroughly humiliated herself and still really needed to pee, like, she was starting to worry about having an accident, she might have enjoyed being held on his lap, surrounded by his thick arms.

But she really should move. She was likely squishing him by now.

She started to wriggle, hissing at the pain in her bladder.

"What's the matter?" He tightened his hold on her.

"Nothing. Let me up."

"Little girl, if you don't stop lying to me, you're gonna find out what that drop seat can be handy for."

She froze. He did not just say that. No way. That did not happen.

Did it?

"Listen. You are not running. You are not hiding. You're gonna look at me. Right. Now."

Darn it.

She raised her eyes, unable to keep her gaze from his any longer. His gaze was serious but not unkind as he took her in.

"Good girl."

She shivered. Those words. The only thing that would make them sound better? Hearing the word 'my' in front of them.

Oh, Millie. You're not falling for him, are you? He's rude and gruff and grouchy. And he threatened to spank you. All cons.

He was also protective and could be caring and kind. All pros.

He knows you got off in his bath tub. Huge con. Massive.

Shoot. She should really offer to scrub his bathtub. Not that she had any diseases or anything. But it just seemed like the thing to do.

"I'll clean it."

"What?"

She knew her cheeks were bright red. "The bathtub. I'm so sorry. I'll clean it. Or buy you a new one." Yeah, I'll buy you a new one."

"Baby, not worried about the damn bathtub." His hand cupped the side of her face.

She swore for a moment that he was about to kiss her. But that was crazy. He wasn't attracted to her. Irritated by her. Perplexed. Angered.

But not interested in her.

"Not worried about any of this. You shouldn't be either. Got me?"

She stared up into his eyes, saw how genuine he appeared to be. Even though she knew she wouldn't let go of her embarrassment so easily, she did feel a small burst of relief at how calm he was.

"You good?" he asked.

"No. But I think I'm about as good as I'll get."

He nodded.

"I'm really sorry you had to clean up after me last night." There went her cheeks again. Hot enough to fry eggs on.

"Hush," he said, not unkindly.

"Right. Hush. I can do that."

He raised an eyebrow. "Like to see that."

She wrinkled her nose at him. And tried to climb off his lap again.

"Stay still."

"Aren't I squashing you?"

"Nope. Could hold you all day."

Oh, wouldn't that be nice. Nope, not going there. Not right now anyway. "There's just one problem."

"Just one," he drawled.

"Jeez, who knew you could be such a smart-ass."

He scowled.

Okay, so probably the big, bad, biker dude didn't want to be called a smart ass.

"I really have to use the bathroom."

He nodded. Then helped her off his lap.

"Meet me downstairs after. We have to talk." He walked to the door then turned back. "No more hiding in closets."

Fine. She was sure she could find somewhere better to hide anyway.

15

Spike pulled out the ingredients for a smoothie, chopping up fruit and adding it to the blender. But his mind wasn't really on what he was doing.

It kept circling back to the woman upstairs.

In her dinosaur onesie. Her face bright red from embarrassment. The way she'd hidden in the closet.

Everything pointed to her being a Little. But what was he going to do with the information? Sit on it or address it?

And what about this attraction he had to her? He could tell from the way she looked at him, reacted to him, that she felt it too.

"Fuck it," he muttered to himself.

He hadn't asked her the thing he'd really wanted to. Whether she'd been thinking about him when she'd gotten herself off last night.

He blended the fruit with ice and poured the smoothie into two glasses before poaching some eggs and placing them on wheat bread with slices of avocado on the side.

"Mr. Fluffy? Mr. Fluffy?"

She raced into the kitchen, a towel wrapped around her, her

hair dripping. She'd obviously been in the shower and had jumped out to come find her dog?

"Have you seen Mr. Fluffy? I can't believe I forgot about him. He's not in my bedroom. I don't know where he could be..."

He placed a hand over her mouth. "Over there."

He nodded to the living room. Where Mr. Fluffy sat sleeping in front of the fireplace. The fire wasn't on, but Spike had found an old rug and set it down there for him.

"Oh, thank goodness."

"Heard him scratching at your door. Let him out. Fed him. Now he's sleeping. Again."

"I'm so sorry. I didn't hear him. Thank you for looking after him." She glanced around the kitchen. "Wow. You can cook?"

"Yep. Go get dressed. It's nearly ready."

"Okay. Thank you."

"Don't need to thank me."

He set everything out and she returned a few minutes later dressed in an ankle-length skirt that was black with red poppies on it and a fitted black shirt. Her hair was pulled back in a pony tail and still dripping down her back. He shook his head.

"Sit."

She sat on a stool and he left to grab a clean towel. When he returned, she wasn't at the counter but was crouching, talking to that ridiculous dog.

"Come here."

When she grew close, he lifted her back onto the stool.

"Oh. You need to stop doing that."

He grunted. Seemed to him that the only way he could get her to do what he told her was to pick her up and move her around himself.

Grabbing her ponytail between the ends of the towel, he squeezed, drying it off.

"I can do that." She tried to turn, to take the towel, but he held it out of her reach and gave her a look.

She sighed but turned around again, letting him dry her hair until it stopped dripping.

"Gonna catch a cold, going around with wet hair."

"Pretty sure that's just a myth. A cold is a virus. You don't catch a cold from being cold."

Another grunt.

"It was really nice of you to cook, but I don't really eat breakfast."

She would while she was here.

Without thinking, he leaned over her and started cutting up the toast and eggs into bite-sized pieces.

"Um, what are you doing?"

He froze. Shit. He placed the knife and fork down. With a sigh he sat next to her and reached over to grab his glass. He drank some smoothie down before replying.

"You're a Little, aren't you?"

Did he really just ask her that?

Her heart raced. Well, she guessed it might be obvious. At least to someone who knew about age play. She licked her dry lips, unsure about how to respond. Was he horrified? Upset? Happy?

Damn it! Why was he so hard to read? Why couldn't he give her some clue here?

"You . . . I . . . it . . ." She took in a deep breath. "Should have just stayed in bed this morning."

"I did tell you to sleep until at least nine." He nodded over at the clock on the oven which said it was just before eight.

She swallowed. "Yes."

He gave a nod and took a bite of food. "Thought so."

"Are you? I mean . . . you obviously know about . . ."

"I was a Daddy Dom. Once. My wife was my Little."

She gave him a surprised look but didn't say anything. She realized how little she knew about him. Especially considering she was staying in his house.

What was she even doing here? How long would it take for that asshole to forget about her?

Where was his wife now? Had they gotten divorced? The way he looked as he spoke of her though . . .

"She was?"

"Yep. She died. About ten years ago."

"I'm so sorry." She wished she could give him a hug, but she was too scared of being rejected.

"Haven't had a Little since. Haven't wanted to be anyone's Dominant or Daddy. Haven't been in any sort of relationship since."

That was so sad. She guessed he'd loved her so much that it hurt to imagine being with someone else like that. Tears welled in her eyes.

He watched her curiously then leaned over to brush away a tear. "You crying for me?"

She nodded.

"Don't," he whispered. "It was a long time ago."

"You must have loved her a lot, though." To not have been with anyone else for ten years.

He gave a nod. "Eat. Drink."

She reached for the smoothie, taking a sip and barely refraining from wrinkling her nose. That tasted very healthy.

"Do you mind if I grab a coffee?"

"After the smoothie."

He wasn't serious? But the look he gave her told her that he was. Well, she guessed it was his coffee. But what if she didn't want the smoothie?

He went to a lot of trouble to make breakfast, Millie. Don't be a brat.

She wasn't really a brat by nature. But she really did love coffee.

"Little girls shouldn't drink coffee."

Her mouth dropped open. "Just because I'm a Little doesn't mean I can live without coffee. Coffee is life. It's what gets me out of bed each morning. I can't function without coffee."

"Drink your smoothie and you'll get one."

She scowled. "Just because I'm a Little doesn't mean you get to boss me around."

"You're right."

Okay, that surprised her. She also sensed a but.

"I'd boss you around regardless."

She sighed. She just bet he would.

Bossy, arrogant biker.

"I'm really sorry about losing it like that last night. I don't usually cry."

"You don't?"

"Crying doesn't make anything better, right?"

He just eyed her.

"You had a Daddy before?" he asked.

She picked up her fork, moving her food around on her plate and hoping that he was fooled into thinking she was eating it.

"Yes, but only online."

"Online?"

"I had the same boyfriend since high school. After he broke up with me, I felt lost. Alone. I didn't have many ways of meeting people. Not many eligible bachelors came through the doors of the library. Anyway, my ex had always been embarrassed by my Little needs. So I decided I needed to find a Daddy. I met him online on a BDSM dating site. He seemed really nice. Kind but firm. Protective. Polite." And why was she telling him all this?

"What happened?"

"We talked for months online. But he lived in Texas. My

Grandma wasn't very well. She raised me and I was taking care of her. He wanted me to come visit him but I couldn't leave her. I guess he got annoyed and found someone who lived closer to him."

She glanced up to find him scowling. "Why the fuck didn't he come to you?"

She shrugged. "He said it was my job to come to him. That he was the dominant. He made the rules."

"Bunch of bullshit."

"But . . . the Dom does make the rules, right?"

"Yeah, but you agree to them. They aren't fucking forced on you. And you had a good reason for not visiting. He should have got on a fucking plane and come to you."

"He said he needed someone with a less complicated life. That if I'd really wanted to be with him, I'd have found a way. Once he made me kneel on rice for two hours because I missed a phone call from him and didn't call back for several hours. I'd had to call Grandma an ambulance. She'd collapsed. I was in such a panic; I left the house without my phone. I called him back as soon as I could. But he was so mad."

"Mother-fucking bastard."

"I should have remembered my phone. The rule was I had to call him back within an hour if he called me."

"Fucker can make an exception for emergencies. Your Grandma was being taken away in an ambulance."

"I was so sure she was going to die. I just wanted . . . I wanted him to tell me it was okay. That everything would be all right."

"Instead the asshole punished you."

"You wouldn't have punished your wife?"

"My wife wouldn't have been going through that alone. If by some chance, we were apart, you can bet your sweet ass I'd be getting myself on a plane back to her. And then I'd hug her tight. And tell her everything would be okay."

"I bet she'd have believed you too." How she wished she'd had someone like Spike to help her. Someone capable and caring.

"All this time, I've thought I was the problem. That it was my fault things didn't work out between us. That I should have made more of an effort."

"Sounds like that's what this asshole wanted you to think. Relationship goes two ways. Dom isn't always right. The sub doesn't have to do all the work. Doms make mistakes. Believe me."

She wanted to ask more, like how his wife had died. But it didn't feel like she had the right. It wasn't like she was volunteering everything about herself.

Reaching over, he grabbed her fork from her hand and used it to pick up a piece of egg, holding it to her mouth.

She sighed. "I can feed myself."

"Clearly not. Since you're not eating."

She took the mouthful, knowing he could out-stubborn her.

"I don't like breakfast."

"Don't talk with your mouth full," he chided in an almost absentminded voice.

She noticed he'd already eaten all his breakfast and drunk all of that way-too-healthy smoothie.

"I need something lighter for breakfast. Like cereal."

"Muesli?"

"I was thinking of Lucky Charms or Fruit Loops."

"That's just sugar."

She sighed. "I like sugar."

He shook his head, forking up some more food. Was she really going to sit here and let him feed her? Maybe she was.

"Four more bites and drink your smoothie then you get a cup of coffee."

Darn it. She might have been able to put her foot down if he'd gone all commando on her. But bribery worked all too well.

With a sigh, she took the next bite. For someone who claimed to no longer be a Daddy Dom he was definitely acting like one. She didn't know what to make of it. Or how to ask him. Because if she pointed it out, maybe he'd stop.

And her Little was lapping this up like parched ground in a rainstorm. It felt like she'd been starved for affection.

Would he give her a hug if she asked?

That was likely taking it too far.

He fed her in silence and she managed to down the smoothie with only a few grimaces. He rolled his eyes at her dramatics but he made her a coffee afterwards.

"I'll do the dishes," she offered as he started tidying up.

"Stay." He pointed at her.

She refrained from barking like a dog. Just.

"Starting to think you have some control issues."

The look he sent her clearly said, *well duh*.

"Spike?"

"Hmm?"

"How is this going to help? Me staying here? Are we just outwaiting that Devil's Sinners jerk, Corey? How long will that take? I have things to do. I can't just stay here and twiddle my thumbs all day."

He had made quick work of tidying the kitchen and now leaned back against the counter, facing her, his arms crossed over his thick chest. His T-shirt was tight around his biceps and she felt her heartbeat pick up.

"What things do you have to do?" he asked.

"Stuff."

"Not going to tell me exactly why you came here?"

"I told you, I'm looking for someone." It wasn't a lie. It just wasn't the full truth, either.

He simply stared at her. She had to fight hard not to fidget. The man should have been an interrogator. He had the whole intimidating act down pat.

"This isn't a long-term solution."

"It's not." He leaned forward, placing his hands on the island in front of him. "Best solution would be you going home. Steele doesn't want that until he knows who the rat is, but that's his issue. You wanna go, I'll get you home safe."

"I don't. Not yet. I can't."

"Then you stay here until I'm sure you're safe."

"Why? Why do you care?"

He stared at her for a long moment then turned away. "Gonna hit the gym then do some work. If you go outside, stay on the patio. Watch TV, there's books and magazines. Help yourself."

Her shoulders slumped as he walked off. He wasn't going to tell her.

Then he stopped in the doorway, his shoulders tensing before he turned back. "Couldn't save my wife."

Oh, so that was it. He was helping her because of his wife.

"Am I like her?" she asked.

"Not at all."

Ouch. For some reason that hurt. A lot.

He walked out.

"Wait!"

He turned again; his face shut down. She knew she wouldn't get anything else personal out of him.

"Can I use your Wi-Fi? I have my laptop."

He nodded and walked over to a drawer, drawing out a pen and paper. After writing something down, he left it on the counter. She looked over to read it as he left.

Jacqueline2010

Oh hell. Was that his wife's name? Was that the year she'd died?

16

Millie frowned at her laptop screen. She'd tried searching for any information on Luther Franklin. His father. Even Jared Bartolli.

Sure, a few things came up. Especially around the murder of Luther's father. But nothing that told her much that she didn't already know.

With a sigh, she closed her eyes, leaning her head back. She'd been on her laptop nearly all day with nothing to show for it except a sore neck and aching temples. It didn't feel like a migraine was developing but she knew she should probably take a rest for a while. Too much screen time could affect her and she wasn't doing that well at managing her stress levels.

Perhaps she should take up yoga. It was meant to help with migraines. And that had to count as exercising, right?

"Come on, Mr. Fluffy." She opened the sliding door and picked the puppy up, taking him outside so he could walk around and pee. When he'd done his business, she walked back into the house. She'd barely seen Spike today. He'd quickly popped in to grab a sandwich for lunch, making one for her as well. Then fled again.

Was he avoiding her? Worry sat like a brick in her stomach. She hated that she might be making him feel awkward in his own house. Deciding it might be better if she just went up and hid in her bedroom, she grabbed Mr. Fluffy and headed towards the stairs.

But instead, she found herself moving towards the other side of the house. The one he hadn't shown her.

Yes, she was nosey as hell. But what was the harm? So long as she didn't get caught.

There was a faint noise, like a bass. Did he have music playing?

"Just a small peek, Mr. Fluffy. Shh." She walked down the corridor and knocked on one door. "Spike?"

No answer. She opened it and peeked in to see what looked like an office. There was a huge wooden desk, a chesterfield sofa and bookshelves along the back wall. This room had the most lived-in look of the whole house.

She wondered what he did for a job?

"We probably shouldn't go in there, aye, Mr. Fluffy?"

"That would be a wise decision," a deep voice said from behind her.

With a scream, she turned and gaped up at him, her free hand on her racing heart.

Mr. Fluffy wriggled to get down. She set him on his feet and he trotted off down the corridor.

Traitor.

Was he really going to leave her here? To face Spike's wrath on her own?

"I . . . um . . . well, you could make some noise!"

He crossed his arms over his chest. "You're telling me off for being too quiet when I move because you got caught sneaking around?"

"Well, I, ahh . . ." Shoot. When he put it like that, it sounded bad.

"I wasn't sneaking around!"

"No? Then how come you look so guilty?"

"This isn't my guilty face. This is my surprised face. You nearly gave me a heart attack is all."

"Maybe if you weren't sneaking around you might have heard me."

"Don't think so, you move around like a ballerina. All light and graceful."

"Graceful?" he growled. "Ballerina?"

"What's wrong? Don't you like to dance?"

"No," he snarled. "I don't."

Hmm, might be time to leave. "Is that Mr. Fluffy I hear? I think he needs to go out. Gotta go. Bye!"

She knew she looked ridiculous as she fled. But she needed to get away from him before she said something else stupid.

Suck a dork.

∽

A KNOCK on her bedroom door later that evening surprised her.

"Hello? Who's there?" she called out then she whacked her palm against her forehead. Like there was more than one person who it could be.

Well, he could have a friend over.

A friend. Right.

Doofus.

"Spike," he said dryly. "Dinner's ready."

"Oh, I'm not hungry," she lied.

"Stop hiding and come eat."

Nope. Not happening. She'd just stay in here, thank you very much.

"Your butt isn't on a stool in five minutes time at the kitchen counter then I'm coming back up and carrying you down. Can tell you now, I won't be in a good mood if I have to do that."

Was he ever in a good mood?

But if this was him in a good mood, did she want to see his bad mood?

Hmm. No.

With a sigh, she forced herself to get up and walk downstairs. She grabbed Mr. Fluffy, carrying him. After giving him his dinner, she sat at the counter staring at the baked potato, with fixings to put on it sitting on the counter. There was also a green salad and a three-bean salad.

The back slider opened and Spike walked in carrying a plate with a steak on it.

"Don't mind if I eat meat, do you?"

She shook her head. It was his house, after all. He could eat what he liked. But no, it didn't worry her.

"Need to get you some food. You need some protein sources. Best I could do was the beans."

"This is ... more than enough. Thank you. It's better than what I feed myself."

Her tummy felt kind of queasy from the amount of sugar she'd binged on this afternoon.

He gave her a sideways look that told her he wasn't impressed. But she was starting to think he wasn't impressed by much, anyway.

They ate in silence but it wasn't awkward, surprisingly. Once again, he wouldn't let her help clean up. So she figured she'd head upstairs, find something to read on her eReader.

"Go sit down. Choose something to watch on TV."

"Umm, okay." Seemed kind of rude to say no, that she wanted to run up to her bedroom and hide. With a sigh, she let out Mr. Fluffy then once he was inside and settled on the rug in front of the fire, she turned on the TV. The news came on with coverage about a warehouse at the docks in Seattle catching fire.

"What the hell?" Spike muttered behind where she stood with the remote.

She jumped. Holy. Shit. He need not worry about that Devil's Sinner guy getting to her, because Spike would kill her himself with a heart attack.

"Sorry," he muttered. "Pass me the remote?"

She handed it over and he turned the volume up.

"Hope they can get it contained," she said as the story ended and he gave the remote back with a frown. He seemed worried about it.

"Hmm. Yeah. Find a movie or something. Be back soon."

That was strange. She flicked through the channels, wishing she could watch some cartoons. She wouldn't mind watching something upbeat and funny right then.

"Find something?" he asked.

"If I keel over from a heart attack, you know it's gonna be your fault, right?"

He gave her a pointed look. "You need to be more aware of your surroundings."

She handed the remote back and sat on the sofa as he spread out in the recliner.

"What do you do for a job?" she blurted out, trying to ignore his muscular forearms. Was it weird to notice a man's forearms? They were just so sexy. Same as his hands. They were large, like dinner plates.

What would it be like to feel his hand smack against her bare butt cheek?

Okay, don't go there, Millie.

"You daydreaming again?"

"What? No!"

"Uh-huh. You always ask people questions then zone out?"

Oh no. She had done that, hadn't she? "Sorry. What did you say?"

"I'm an investor."

"An investor?"

He shrugged. "Find start-up businesses or people with ideas and I think they'll make money; I might offer funding."

But to do that . . . wouldn't it mean he already had a lot of money? But that would be rude to ask, wouldn't it?

He sighed. "Ask. Can see you're dying to."

Well, she wasn't dying to . . . it wasn't like it was her business. But . . .

"Are you rich?" She smacked her forehead with her palm. "Shoot. Didn't mean to ask it quite like that."

He snorted. "I'm okay."

Uh-huh and did okay equate to hundreds of thousands or millions?

Yeah. That was definitely too rude to ask. He just stared at her as though waiting for her to ask something else.

"Suppose you don't need any of old Dan's counterfeit money then huh?" she said lamely.

"Guess not," he murmured. "I've placed that money in my safe in the study, by the way. Remind me to show you. Sounds like an interesting place, where you live."

"Oh, it's that all right."

"You like it there?"

"The people are really nice. It's where I grew up after I went to live with my grandma and grandad."

"How old were you?"

"Four. My granddad died a few years ago. My grandma died ten months ago. I miss them all."

She really needed to change the topic before she burst into tears.

"Should I go to the police about Luther?"

Spike switched off the TV and turned to look at her. "What?"

"Well, he was talking about hurting you and Steele. I mean, maybe I should speak to the cops."

"Cops aren't going to do anything based on something you overheard. He didn't out and out say he was gonna hurt us."

"What about his plans? We can't just let him take up where his father left off. From what you and Steele said, his father basically forced women to sell their bodies for sex. He bought women, took advantage of young girls. We can't let him do the same."

He tapped his finger against the remote and turned to look off into the distance. But he didn't say anything. He wasn't going to just let it go, surely.

"I can't let him do that," she told him. "I have to stop him."

"Luther Franklin is a slimeball. He's annoying. An idiot. A pissant. That doesn't mean he's not dangerous. You'll be going nowhere near him."

"But—"

"Steele said he will take care of him. He doesn't want him selling skin in his city. He also knows that Luther had something to do with the rat in his ranks. But he'll likely figure out who the rat is first. Maybe even feed him some bad intel to get back to Luther. Don't know."

"So I just have to sit around and wait? Like with this Devil's Sinner guy? Will Steele take care of him too?"

Spike grunted. "Yep."

That's all he was going to say?

"How?" she said with frustration.

"Sick of being here already?"

"No, it's not that." She had things she had to do.

"I'll talk to Steele. See what his plan is. But you need to know that you're having no part in any of it, understand?"

His protectiveness was kind of surprising and charming. But at the same time, annoying. Because as nice as it was to have someone care about her, sitting still and doing nothing wasn't something she was good at.

17

Today, she was making lunch.

She felt pretty useless. She'd basically been told she couldn't help with Luther or Corey. She didn't know how she was meant to point out this rat when she was hidden in Spike's house. And there was very little for her to do here.

Basically, she was sitting here twiddling her thumbs.

Well, she'd tried to do some more research. This time into the Devil's Sinners. But she knew what she'd found would just give her nightmares so she'd given up.

She hadn't seen Spike since breakfast. She couldn't say if she was relieved or disappointed.

Maybe a bit of both.

Would he mind if she made lunch? She felt like she should since he wouldn't let her lift a finger at breakfast.

With a groan, she searched through the cupboards and fridge, deciding to make grilled cheese sandwiches. She picked up a frying pan and started heating it up on the stovetop. She got the sandwiches put together then placed them on the hot pan.

Oh. Wait. She just thought of something to add to her notes.

Moving back to her laptop, she reminded herself not to forget about the grilled cheese.

∼

THE ALARM BLARED, and he jumped to his feet.

Shit!

Smoke alarm.

Racing out of his office, he ran down to the living area. Where was she? Why hadn't he been keeping a closer eye on her? Fuck it! He'd holed up in his office all morning to avoid her and the way she made him feel. The things he was tempted to do.

And now he had no idea where she was.

Doing a great job of watching over her.

Smoke drifted out from the kitchen as he raced in. He found her at the stove, picking up a smoking frying pan from the cooker.

"Millie!"

Mr. Fluffy started barking and she screamed, the pot slipping from her hand and landing on her foot. She cried out in pain, dropping to the floor and grabbing hold of her foot. Fuck! Racing over, he picked her up off the floor, setting her on the counter. He quickly checked the stove to make sure it was off. All the smoke must be from whatever she'd been cooking.

"What happened? Did the pan hit your foot?" he yelled.

She nodded, tears dripping slowly down her face as she sobbed.

"It's okay, baby. Hang on."

He grabbed a clean cloth and wet it, placing it on the red patch on the top of her foot.

"Hold that there." He raced over and opened the sliding door then hastened over to the pad on the wall by the backdoor, turning off the alarm.

He ran back into the kitchen. She still sat where he'd put her, holding the cloth to her foot. He turned the cold water tap on then gently turned her, placing her foot under the stream of water.

"Keep your foot there. I'll get the truck. Get you to the emergency room."

"I'm . . . I'm so sorry!" she wailed.

"Shh. You'll be okay."

"I j-just wanted to m-make lunch. I m-mess everything up."

"Hey," he warned, clasping hold of her chin and turning her face towards his. "You do not mess everything up. Now I'm gonna get my truck to drive you to the emergency room. Keep your foot under the cold water."

She swiped at her cheeks with her arm. "Don't need to go to the emergency room. It's all right. It's just a burn."

"It could be broken."

"It's not. Look I can wriggle my toes." She moved her toes back and forth. But the redness of her skin worried him. That could be a nasty burn. And the pan was a heavy one.

Nope. His mind was made up.

"If you don't want to go because you're worried about the cost then I'll pay for it."

"No, I have insurance," she grumbled.

"Then you're going to the emergency room."

She shook her head. "I don't want to. I can't believe I'm such a klutz. First, I forgot I left that pan on and then I dropped it. I'll get a new one for you."

"Don't give a fuck about the pan. I care about your damn foot. And you're going to the emergency room, so stop arguing."

18

Several hours later Millie was exhausted, embarrassed and she could feel the tingling warning of an impending migraine.

Which didn't surprise her. First there had been the stress of burning lunch and dropping that hot pan, then the blaring noise of the alarm, plus hours spent at the emergency room under fluorescent lights, talking to nurses and doctors, having them poke and prod her.

Yeah, no wonder she was done in.

Then there was the fact that she'd never gotten to eat lunch. Not that she could eat now with how nauseous she felt.

"Want something to eat?" Spike asked.

He hadn't said much since they'd left home, but he'd managed to intimidate the hell out of most of the nurses and doctors as he'd lurked beside her, glaring at them. She was certain they'd been rushed through because they were eager to get rid of them.

Nothing had been broken at least. Just a bad bruise and a burn. Her foot was wrapped up but she'd been told to give it some air tomorrow.

Thank goodness she could now afford health insurance. Spike had offered to pay

"No thanks," she said hoarsely. How had she managed to mess up grilled cheese? "I'll pay for whatever damages I caused."

Seems she was doing that a lot. First, she owed him a bathtub and now a new frying pan.

"You're not paying for anything," he grumbled at her as he turned up his driveway.

Mr. Fluffy stuck his head out of her handbag and gave her a look that loosely translated to, *you owe me lunch, bitch.*

Mr. Fluffy could be quite mean.

Spike pulled up inside the garage. He'd driven her to the emergency room in his enormous, manly, badass truck. It totally suited him.

He turned to her once he'd parked. "Wait there."

She undid her belt as he walked around to her side of the truck, opening the door and lifting her out. She held onto her handbag, containing Mr. Fluffy. Instead of setting her down, he carried her into the house. It still had the faint stink of smoke in the air and she groaned. "I'm so sorry."

"Hush," he said firmly and started for the stairs.

She squeaked. "What are you doing?"

"Carrying you upstairs. While I air the place out and make us some dinner you can have a bath and relax. Or do other things."

Oh no. He did not just go there. He did not.

She gaped up at him, but his face remained as impassive as always. She finally convinced herself that he didn't mean to imply that she could play with her dino vibrator.

"I can walk."

"No."

She bit her lip. "You shouldn't be carrying me around."

He made a grumbling noise.

"I'll come down and help you." She wasn't going to relax while he was working.

"No. You won't."

He walked into the bathroom and set her on the counter.

"But—"

"I don't want you inhaling any more smoke fumes."

There weren't any smoke fumes left in the house. Just the lingering stench. He was full of shit. Then again, maybe he didn't want her in his kitchen, because he was afraid she'd mess something up and actually set the house on fire.

She sighed as he started a bath. She closed her eyes. The side of her face felt numb and tingly. Shoot.

"You're pale. You in pain? Your foot?"

"My head," she whispered with a wince. "Migraine."

"Shit. You get migraines?"

"Yep."

"What can I do?"

She appreciated him not asking her a whole bunch of questions. "Quiet. Dark. Pills. Bag. Toilet."

"Okay, baby. Let me find them."

She heard a rustling noise. She didn't open her eyes.

"Gonna pick you up, put you to bed. Then I'll get some water for you to take these."

Even though he was gentle, she still whimpered as he moved her. It felt like a screwdriver going through the left side of her head and eye. The pain was excruciating. Dizziness assaulted her while nausea bubbled in her stomach.

Then he laid her down on the bed. She lay there, trying to convince herself that she didn't need to vomit. There was blessed quiet and she risked opening her eyes to find the room was empty, the curtains were pulled.

The door opened and he reappeared with a bottle of water.

"Fluffy?" she croaked. She could barely think and it was hard to get her words out. To figure out what she wanted to say.

"I'll take care of him. Don't worry. Is there anything else?"

"Cold cloth. Head."

"Okay. Gonna help you sit to take these."

He sat next to her on the bed and propped her up against his chest. Then he fed her the pills and held the bottle of water to her lips.

Maybe she should protest that she could do it. But truth was, she was tired. It was nice to have someone else look after her.

And he was so damn good at it.

"Gonna get you into something more comfortable. That okay with you?"

She grunted. She was beyond worrying about anything. It was so hard to think. She felt him moving her around. A wave of nausea rose over her.

She made a distressed noise and he quickly rolled her over. She vomited everywhere, sobbing in distress.

"Shh. Shh. Shh. I got you. You're safe."

She was picked up once again and carried.

"Chompers," she whispered as he laid her down. The scent of leather and cherry surrounded her. But thankfully, it didn't make her feel any worse.

"Get him for you."

More silence. Then she felt something being pressed into her arms. A cool cloth washed over her mouth and face and she sighed in pleasure.

"Rest."

"Thanks, Daddy," she whispered.

SPIKE STARED DOWN AT HER. She whimpered and curled up into a ball as though trying to protect herself.

Thanks, Daddy.

Fuck. He hated that she was in pain. His hands clenched into fists. This wasn't an enemy he could see or fight.

A wave of protectiveness washed through him. There was just something about Millie that urged him to take care of her. Maybe it was because she didn't seem to care enough to do it herself.

He hated that too.

Another whimper.

Daddy.

She'd called him Daddy.

He didn't want this, right? Jacqui had been the only love of his life.

You don't have to love her to be this for her. There are plenty of Daddy/Little relationships that have nothing to do with love.

Bringing her back here had been a major fuck-up. He should call Steele, get him to take her off his hands.

But would Steele look after her when she got a migraine? Would he watch over her to make sure she didn't burn down the house or hurt herself?

Like you've been doing a good job of that.

He'd been hiding from her. If he decided to do this, then he'd watch over her far more closely. It would make it easier to take care of her. He could set rules and boundaries.

Consequences.

His cock hardened at the thought of putting her over his knee. Lord knew, she needed a damn good spanking for all the worry she'd given him. And for all the lies. Not to mention the way she talked about herself.

This would take some thinking about. There wouldn't be an issue of commitment or feelings.

Should he be her Daddy when he wasn't able to be anything more?

For now, he needed to know how best to take care of her.

Striding out of his bedroom, where he'd carried her after she'd vomited in her room, he bundled up the dirty bedding, and took it downstairs, putting it in the wash. Then he grabbed his phone, calling someone he knew could help.

"Darling, you've got to stop calling me at home. My wife's getting suspicious."

Spike snorted. "If I was going to have an affair it would be with someone much prettier."

"Shot down! Damn. We'd make such ugly babies together too."

"Can you be serious?"

"What's going on?" Hack asked immediately. "You shot? Run over? Stabbed? Kidnapped?"

Spike sighed. "Why did I call you?"

"Can't answer that, my man."

Millie. He needed to remember Millie. "What can I do for someone with a migraine?"

"Migraine?" Hack's voice became more businesslike. "How bad is it?"

"Pretty bad. She vomited. Can't really talk. She's whimpering in pain."

"Has she taken some medication? Has she had migraine's before?"

"Yeah, she took these." He rattled off the name on the medication bottle. "It's half empty."

"Right. That's a prescription drug. She might get these often. She's lying down? In a dark, quiet place?"

"Yep."

"Best thing you can do is just keep an eye on her, but don't bother her too much. Try to keep her hydrated if you can. Although sometimes caffeine can also help. Some people react well to a cold compress or a heat pack. It all depends on the individual. Since we can't ask her, I would just try to keep her comfortable. She's staying with you?"

"Yep." He knew it would kill Hack not to know more. The guy was as nosey as they came.

"Huh. That really all you're gonna say?"

"Yep."

"Is she a Little?"

He wasn't sure that was Hack's business. So he didn't say anything.

"Say no more. I get it. If she's experienced lots of these, she likely knows her triggers. It can be certain smells or food or stress. I'll send you some articles. I mean, that's assuming she's going to be around for a while?"

Spike didn't answer that either.

Hack sighed. "You're no fun. I'll send the stuff anyway. Along with my bill. Let me know if you need my help, nothing I love more than making a house call."

Spike ended the call. Then he walked back to the bedroom to check on Millie, who appeared to be asleep.

Time to do some reading. And decide if taking care of her was something he could do ... without developing anything more.

19

Migraine hangovers sucked.

The excruciating pain in her head was gone. Drugs and sleep had taken care of that. But her body felt like she'd been run over by a truck. Drained and exhausted.

But at least she could open her eyes and move without feeling like her head was being drilled or wanting to vomit.

So, yay her.

Glancing around, she realized she wasn't in her bedroom. Was this Spike's room? Why was she in here? Memories rushed back at her and she groaned. Had she really vomited in her bed? Oh no. And he'd had to take care of her. She ran her hand down her side, realizing that she was now dressed in her onesie.

He'd undressed her.

He'd seen her rolls. Her stretch marks and cottage cheese thighs.

This was beyond embarrassing.

She groaned loudly. The door opened and then the man in question walked in, carrying Mr. Fluffy.

"Morning," he said to her.

"Morning," she croaked, knowing she was bright red.

He came over to the side of the bed where an armchair had been pulled close.

Mr. Fluffy basically jumped from his arms, landing on her chest. She let out a whoosh of breath.

"Easy, dog," Spike muttered as the puppy enthusiastically licked her face.

Urgh. Puppy breath. Lucky he was so darn cute.

"Morning, Mr. Fluffy," she crooned. "Did you miss me, baby?"

"He chewed his way through a pair of my socks and left one of his slobbery chew toys in my boot."

"Oh no. I'm so sorry." She had to bite back a grin.

"Didn't find it until I went to put my boots on this morning." Spike gave Mr. Fluffy a look.

He just settled on her chest with a yawn, looking unworried.

She bit her lip to hold in her giggle.

Spike turned that warning look on her. "Are you about to laugh?"

"I wouldn't do that," she told him.

He grunted and picked up the dog who let out a low grumbling noise that sounded suspiciously like the one Spike had just made.

He settled Mr. Fluffy in his dog bed, which he'd obviously gotten from her room and put in here. That was so thoughtful.

She tried to push herself up as he turned.

"Here." He came closer and arranged some pillows behind her back. His scent surrounded her and she felt her body heating at his closeness.

It wasn't until he drew back that she managed to take a full breath. He was potent.

"Thank you for taking care of me," she whispered. "I'm so sorry about everything yesterday. Is the smell of the smoke gone?"

"Yep." He sat on the armchair and studied her. "You're still pale."

Great. No doubt she looked like crap. Had she been drooling again? Please don't let her have been drooling.

She ran a shaking hand over her face. "Migraine hangover. I get them sometimes. Just means I feel kind of tired for a day or so. I'll be fine."

"You get migraines a lot?"

"Ah, it all depends. I've gotten them quite a bit these last few months."

"There a reason for that?"

She shrugged. She didn't really want to go into it.

"Let me check on your foot." He drew the blankets back.

"It's fine. I don't even feel it." Which was kind of a lie. And the look he gave her told her that he knew it was.

Gently, he peeled back the bandage. Be brave. Be brave.

Then he grunted. She wondered if that was a good grunt or a bad grunt. He stood and grabbed something off the bedside table. Burn cream. Slowly, gently, he ran it over the burn, leaving tingles in his wake. Then he replaced the bandage.

Yikes.

"Need to get you some breakfast."

"Oh, I can do that."

"Stay where you are," he commanded as she tried to get out of the bed.

She froze. "Oh, you don't want me in your kitchen? That's fair enough. Are you sure you got the smoke smell out? Maybe I should replace the curtains? They're hard to get smoke smell out of."

Millie felt terrible about yesterday. Not only had she set off his smoke alarms, stunk his house up with smoke and dropped a frying pan on her foot, but he'd had to spend all afternoon at the emergency room then take care of her.

She had this feeling that he hadn't just let her sleep it off alone, either. No, she had this vague recollection of opening her eyes at one point and seeing him sleeping in the armchair.

Not that she was going to ask him about that. It would be embarrassing if it was just a dream. And she didn't want to know if it was. Because the idea that this muscular, scary-looking biker might have slept in her room, watching over her ... well, that was a thought that would keep her warm at night for a long time to come.

So yeah, even if it was made up, she was going to keep that memory close to her heart.

"For the last time, don't give a fuck about the kitchen, the curtains, the flooring, any of it. But you also won't be trying to cook again. The stove is off-limits to you."

Chagrined, she bit her lip.

"Little girls don't cook."

Her eyes widened. Why did he say that? Did he mean that he wanted to ... no, that wasn't right?

"Read that stress can trigger migraines. So can skipping meals and not getting enough sleep."

He'd ... he'd read all that? Why?

So he can take care of you better? That was silly, though. He barely knew her.

"You read up on migraines?"

He frowned "Was worried about you. Didn't know how to take care of you. Called a doctor I know. He sent me some stuff on migraines. Told me best idea was to keep you in dark and quiet."

"Thank you. That really was the best thing. I'm so sorry I vomited everywhere. I should go clean that up."

He gave her an incredulous look. "Do you think I left it?"

"Oh no. Of course not. I'm sorry. I'm not thinking entirely clearly. You must think I'm an idiot. Bet you're regretting bringing me here now huh? I understand if you want to—"

He sighed and leaned forward, taking her nervous hands in his. "Stop."

She ceased her babbling. It was a relief to have him stop her before she said something truly idiotic.

"Do you remember what you called me last night?"

What she'd called him? No, she didn't. "No. It wasn't something rude, was it?"

He raised an eyebrow. "Something rude? You been calling me rude names in your head?"

"What? No!"

Amusement warmed his eyes. He was teasing her! She gaped at this more playful side of him. She hadn't realized it existed.

"Easy, baby doll," he soothed as she tried to pull her hands free. "You called me Daddy."

Oh God. Would the humiliation never end? Seriously, how much could one woman take?

"I'm so sor—"

He leaned over and covered her mouth with his hand. "Swear to God, every time I hear you say sorry, I'm gonna give you a spanking."

Her eyes grew wide. Spank her?

She tried to speak; the words muffled by his hand. Without thinking, she licked his palm. His gaze heated.

"Did you just lick me?"

She shook her head. He grew closer, moving his hand from her mouth to whisper in her ear. "You did. If you're not careful, I'll give you something else to lick."

A shiver washed through her body.

"Are you . . . are you saying that you'd . . ."

She couldn't seem to get the words out. He leaned back. "I want you, Millie. Tried to ignore it. Look where it got me. You in my house, my bed. Feel protective of you. Want you in my bed, under me, riding me, my mouth buried in your pussy, my cock in your mouth."

"Right. Well. You could have just said you wanted sex." She was pretty certain that was the most she'd ever heard him say.

"Could have."

She licked her dry lips.

"Well, I, ahh, want you too." *So eloquent, Millie.* But really, what could she add to what he'd already said?

"I know," he said arrogantly.

She rolled her eyes. "Oh yeah, and how do you know?"

"Because every time I get close to you, I see a shiver work its way across your skin. A small tinge of red fills your cheeks. Your breath grows faster. Bet your pussy gets wet."

"You're so arrogant."

"It's not arrogant if it's the truth."

Yep. Arrogant.

Darn it. She kind of liked it.

"Never had any intention of ever getting involved with someone again. Not after my wife's death."

He still loved her. That much was clear. It was so sweet. This huge, rough-looking biker was still deeply in love with his dead wife.

But what does that mean for you?

"While you're here, we could help you explore your Little side and this attraction."

"Explore my Little side?"

"Thought I'd never be interested in being someone's Daddy again, but you, little girl, desperately need one."

"I do not," she muttered.

He reached out and tilted up her chin. "You're a menace," he said bluntly. "You jump from one dangerous situation to another. You need rules. Consequences. Protection. A Daddy who will take care of you but also be firm with you. Who won't let you wrap him around your little finger."

She pouted. "I do not need rules and consequences."

"That pretender-Daddy give you any rules or consequences?"

"He wasn't pretending. He just didn't like being in a long-distance relationship."

"Guy was a selfish jerk. He didn't care about your needs or emotions, just what he wanted."

"Yeah, I had rules. Obviously calling him back within an hour was one."

"I get that. I'd even use that. If you were out without me and I called you, I'd want a call back quickly. But if there was an emergency, if you couldn't call back for some reason, I wouldn't punish you. Certainly not by making you kneel on rice for hours. Fucker. Was that even an agreed punishment between you?"

"Umm, agreed punishment?"

He swore under his breath. "You have control in this. You need to tell me your limits. And even if those limits change while we're in the middle of something you can speak up and say something. Say your safeword."

"What would you do if I didn't call you back and didn't have a good excuse?"

"Well, without knowing your limits, I'd likely make you write lines. Or ground you from going out without me for a week."

She let out a spluttering gasp. "Ground me?"

"Yep. Consequences depend on the rules broken. Put your health or safety at risk and you'll likely find yourself over my knee or the sofa or table, getting your behind reddened with my hand or your hairbrush or my belt."

His belt?

She wanted to be horrified. But she was kind of intrigued.

Seriously. What was wrong with her?

"So you're saying that while I'm here that you want to be my . . .

to be my Daddy? And my, um, lover?" she squeaked out the last word.

"Lover?" Amusement filled his face.

You're a super dork, Millie. Like, there are dorks and then there is you. Their Queen.

Queen Dork.

That was kind of catchy. Queen of the Dorks. Hmm.

"Millie. Millie! You okay?" He gave her a concerned look. "You need some food. And drink. Shouldn't have brought this up until you were feeling better."

"No, wait, I—"

"Don't feel pressured. Think about it. Doesn't matter what answer you give; I'll still protect you. But I don't think I can be your Daddy without wanting to fuck you. And vice versa. Gonna make you breakfast. Stay in bed. You're not getting out of bed today. You need to rest."

Still bossy as hell.

When he was gone, she slumped back against the pillows. Hell. What was she going to do? It wasn't that she didn't want him.

No, that wasn't the issue at all

Problem was, she wanted him too much. So much so that saying goodbye to him when she left just might break her heart.

But then, when was she likely to get an offer like this again? If she survived her mission, she'd go back to her hometown without even a hint of a romantic prospect in sight.

This might be her only chance to experience what having a Daddy would be like. To have sex with a man who made her whole body tingle when all he did was lean over her and whisper in her ear.

Was she really going to say no?

20

"Yes!"

The word flew out of her like a stone from a slingshot. Spike froze, a tray of food in his hands. He walked forward and set it down on the bedside table. She glanced over and saw a bowl of fruit salad.

Urgh.

Didn't the man believe in things like French toast and croissants and donuts?

Fruit salad was not a meal. It was garnish.

You know garnish on the side of a big slice of chocolate pie.

"There a reason you're scowling at the fruit salad?" Spike asked as he sat in the armchair and reached for the bowl and a fork.

"Umm, no."

"That 'yes' mean what I think it means?"

She blushed and nodded, feeling like an even bigger idiot than normal.

"Kind of meant for you to think about it longer than fifteen minutes."

"Oh. Well. When you know, you know," she said lamely. "I

mean, I haven't had a D-daddy in real life. So maybe I won't... I'm not sure I'll know what I like exactly... I don't want to disappoint you."

He didn't brush off her fears, instead he watched her closely. "You're scared."

"Yes."

"Don't be. I'll take care of you so you don't need to be afraid."

There was that arrogance. How could she trust him to take care of her? They barely knew each other.

And yet she did. She felt it deep inside her.

"You couldn't disappoint me even if you tried."

The statement was so sweet. So unlike Spike, that she just gaped at him.

Looking slightly awkward, as though he hadn't meant to say that, he held up a piece of pineapple to her mouth.

She stared at it with offense. The only pineapple she liked to eat came on a pizza.

Yes, she liked pineapple on her pizza.

"Open," he commanded.

"I'm not real hungry."

"You're going to eat something. You hardly ate anything yesterday." He frowned. "Unless you feel nauseous?"

"A bit," she admitted.

"I can make you a smoothie."

Oh, awesome.

"And coffee?" she asked.

"Eat some food first."

Damn, was he the coffee police or what?

Her bottom lip popped out in a pout.

"And put that away, it doesn't work on me."

With a long, dramatic sigh, she opened her mouth and he slid the pineapple in. She quickly chewed and swallowed.

"Good girl."

Oh no. There went that shiver again. He eyed her as though he knew the effect those words had on her.

"What happens next?" she asked.

"Eat this up and I'll get you some coffee."

"Oh, thank you, God."

"You're gonna stay in bed all day. Only acceptable reason for getting up is the toilet." He eyed her. "You need to go?"

"No, I, um, went before."

"Did you? When I told you to stay in bed?" he asked calmly.

"Well, yes, but I didn't think you meant that I couldn't go to the bathroom. I was busting."

"And what if you'd gotten dizzy and fallen, hmm? You could have hit your head. Lucky you hadn't already agreed to be my Little girl," he told her in that low, gravelly voice. "Or you'd find yourself in trouble."

"You wouldn't spank me while I'm sick." He was far too protective to do that.

"Don't have to spank you to punish you."

Crap.

"You ever been spanked?"

"No," she whispered.

"You want to be, though, don't you?"

She wasn't sure she wanted to talk about this. "Nobody *wants* to be spanked, right?"

He speared a piece of apple and fed it to her. She figured it was better to eat it than risk saying something stupid.

"Think you know better than that. How'd you learn about BDSM, about age play?"

She licked her lips. "Romance books."

He nodded. "Any of those subs enjoy being spanked?"

"Well, yes." She cleared her throat. "Doesn't mean I want it."

"You've never thought about being put over someone's knee,

having your panties lowered and a hand slapped against your bottom? Before you answer, lying would earn you spanking."

Well crap.

He fed her a piece of strawberry. Yum. Okay, the fruit salad wasn't that bad. Not that she'd tell him so.

"Need to talk about your hard limits."

Oh. She'd never done limits before.

"You didn't have a set of limits with that wannabe-Daddy, did you?"

"Not really," she whispered. "He said because we were long distance that I didn't need a safeword or to set limits."

"That fucking asshole. Listen to me. Long distance or not, whenever you have a relationship with a Top, you have a safeword and you go through limits. This is an agreement. Got it? You have choices. Always."

She nodded, shocked by his vehemence. "Yes, Sir."

"Sir is acceptable. Daddy is better. When you're ready."

She bit her lip. She wanted to say it. Could feel the word hovering on her tongue.

What's holding you back then?

"So, if I didn't want to be spanked?"

"We'd explore other discipline. But remember, no lying."

"Okay," she whispered. "Maybe I'm a bit curious. But since I've never had one, I'm not sure how I'll react..."

"We try it and see." He nodded easily, feeding her some more fruit.

Funny how she hadn't pegged him as the type to take care of someone else like this.

Shows how you shouldn't stereotype, Millie.

"Any ideas of what your hard limits might be?"

"I don't want to do anything that draws blood," she said quickly. "Nothing in public."

"Sure? If you broke a health or safety rule, I'd usually want to deal with it immediately. No one has to see. Could take you into the family bathroom, have you bend over and raise your skirt. Could take you out to the truck and place you over my lap in the back seat."

Oh hell. Why was the thought of that turning her on? She'd never imagined she'd be into any sort of voyeurism.

Maybe it was just the thought of it. The reality probably wouldn't be as enticing. Perhaps.

"I . . . I . . ."

"Too much too soon," he summed up. "Thought turns you on though, huh?"

"Oh man." She covered up her red cheeks as he winked at her.

He fed her a few more pieces of fruit and she drank some juice. Then he sat back and studied her, hands on his flat abs, elbows on the arms of the chair.

"Other limits?"

"Umm, well, I wouldn't like to be humiliated. To be called names or told that I wasn't desirable or anything." She kept her gaze on the covers as she told him that.

He leaned forward and grasped hold of her chin, raising her face. When she stared up at him, she gasped at the fury in his face. "He did that to you?"

She bit her lip. "Not just him. My previous boyfriend, Doug, he often made remarks about what I wore or the way I acted. My online Daddy said I was too excitable. A lot of the time I was only to speak to him when he asked me a question."

He gaped at her. Yeah, now that she said it out loud, she realized how messed up things had been with that jerk.

"Those bastards. You're fucking beautiful. Sexy as fuck. Their fault they didn't recognize when they had something special in their grasp. That they didn't take care of you the way they should."

"You know, for a man who doesn't say a lot, you sure have a way with words."

He shrugged. "Fuck them. You're fucking perfect."

"Really?" she whispered, his words were like a balm on the ragged edges of her very soul. When had she become so tattered and torn? When had her self-confidence eroded away? She didn't used to be like this.

"Wanted to fuck you the moment I saw you."

"You were so mean to me! You ignored me. You practically ran away from me."

"Still wanted to fuck you."

She grumbled at him, but her mouth twitched with a smile. "You really like the way I look?"

"You don't know how often I've fucking rubbed one off thinking about you these past few days."

Her cheeks blazed red even as happiness made her giddy. "Oh."

"Oh? That all you got to say?"

"Umm." What did he want from her? *Perhaps for you to tell him that you think he's handsome?* "You're gorgeous too."

A knowing look entered his eyes. "Were you thinking about me when you used that dinosaur vibrator in the bath? Did you imagine it was my tongue against your clit? My cock slipping inside your slick passage?"

She placed her hands on her hot cheeks. "I thought we agreed not to talk about that!"

"Well?"

"This is so embarrassing. Yes, all right? I was thinking about you while I used the vibrator on myself."

This smug look entered his face. "Gonna watch you next time."

Gonna watch her what? Use her vibrator? "I don't think so!"

He tilted his head to the side. "Why not?"

"B-because you c-can't watch!"

"Minute you agreed to be my Little, you just gave me all your orgasms."

"What does that mean?" It was like she'd gone to sleep in one world and woken up in a completely different one.

"Means you don't get an orgasm unless I give my permission. So no using that vibrator without me watching you."

He didn't mean it. He couldn't mean it. But as she stared into his firm face, she saw he did.

"Well, shit."

"Need to talk about your other rules."

She wasn't sure she wanted to know.

"No putting yourself down. No lying. Communication is important. There's something you don't want, that scares you, if you're hurt, then you need to tell me or say your safeword. What do you want your safeword to be?"

"Um, how about sausage?"

His eyes widened. "Sausage?"

"Yeah, is that a bad safeword?"

"It's just, uh, why sausage?"

For the first time since meeting him, which admittedly, wasn't that long ago, he seemed almost flummoxed.

"Well, Mr. Fluffy is currently chewing on one of his sausage toys so I thought . . . " she trailed off as something occurred to her. "Oh no, I didn't mean your sausage, I wasn't thinking of that when I said it. I mean, I don't think of your . . . your . . . you know, anytime you want to stop me from talking right now that would be awesome – eek!" she cried out as he reached over and plucked her from the bed, placing her on his lap. "Guess that works. Maybe I need a new safeword, I'm not sure that one will …umm."

This time he stopped her by placing his mouth against hers. She froze. It felt so nice. His lips were warm. Firm but gentle.

Thank goodness she'd brushed her teeth when she'd gotten up to pee earlier. Wouldn't pay . . . to . . . umm . . .okay bye-bye thoughts.

His tongue slid into her mouth, dancing against hers. She

wrapped her hands around his biceps as he ravaged her mouth. Something firm and definitely not at all sausage-like pressed against her hip. At least, it wasn't like any sausage she'd ever eaten.

Oh hell. Now she was thinking about eating him.

He grasped hold of her chin, pulling it down so her mouth opened further. Then there was nothing but him. His taste. His touch. His smell.

More. She wanted more. She wiggled on his lap, trying to get closer, letting out a pained cry when he drew back from her.

"Easy, baby."

"Noo," she cried, reaching up to place her hand around the back of his neck.

"Got to slow down."

"Why?" she wailed.

"Because if we go any further then I'm going to end up fucking you right now."

"And that would be bad because . . ."

"You're still recovering from a migraine. You're pale. You need food, drink and rest. Also want to know that you're really sure. Once you're in my bed, you're not leaving for a long while."

Until this supposed threat to her was gone and he kicked her out, he meant.

Shoot. No point in thinking about that now.

"I know what I want," she told him.

"Good. So do I. That doesn't mean you're not resting today."

She pouted as he placed her back on the bed. He tapped her lower lip. "What have I told you about that?"

She huffed out a breath. "If you kissed me, I wouldn't pout."

"Ultimatums don't work on me either," he warned. "Maybe I need to make no pouting a rule."

"I don't think so," she said hastily.

He eyed her for a moment. "What triggers the migraines?"

"What?"

"If I'm to look after you properly, I need to know what triggers them."

Spike studied her closely. Her hair needed a good brush and her lips were slightly swollen. She was wearing that dinosaur onesie.

She looked fucking adorable.

Shit. He was in trouble here.

"What sets them off?"

"Oh, I think yesterday it might have been a combination of things, some scents do it. The smoke and the stress probably set me off yesterday."

"What else? Diet? Sleep?"

"Hmm. If I don't get enough sleep that can be an issue."

"Diet?" he prompted again.

She sighed. "Meat is an issue which is part of the reason I went vegetarian, but mostly it was because I love animals so much."

"Skipping meals an issue?"

She winced. "Um, yep. You know, I've managed these migraines for a long time. I don't think we need to go into any great detail about them."

"How many you had in the last two months?"

"Around five or six."

That many? Hell. Poor baby.

"Seems like a lot to me."

"I've had a lot of stress on me lately. And when I'm stressed, I find it hard to sleep. It's a bad pattern."

"Other triggers?"

"Strong smells and alcohol. Caffeine is good for them, though." She gave him an innocent look.

Uh-huh, like he was buying that.

"If you drink enough water to remain hydrated."

"I hate water. Yuck."

Okay, it seemed like her Little side was close to the surface today. Probably because she was tired. And out of sorts.

"It usual for you to be tired and grumpy after one?"

"Yes. I'm sorry. I don't mean to act like a grouchy two-year-old."

"Anything else?"

She blushed and her gaze went to her hands. A sure sign there was something else she just didn't want to say what it was.

"Millie," he warned.

"My cycle, I guess. It can be hormonal."

"Got it," he said briskly. He wanted to tell her that she could talk to him about anything, including her periods. But he could tell this wasn't a subject she wanted to delve into. Once she was more comfortable with him, he could discuss them with her.

Oh yeah? And how long do you think she's going to be around for?

"When you get a migraine, what helps?"

"I usually try to lie down in the dark and quiet."

"Nothing else? Cold packs? Hot packs? Massage?"

"I'm not sure, I'm usually too ill to get any of that and I can't massage myself."

What the fuck? Was she fucking kidding him right now? He could tell by the lost, lonely look on her face that she wasn't.

"Hasn't anyone taken care of you during one of these?"

"Uh, no. My grandma used to help me lie down and stuff. But she just thought they were a bad headache. And Doug would just stay away until I felt better."

"Mother-fucking bastard," he muttered to himself. "Mind if we try a few things next time?" He thought about the ideas he'd read about.

"No, not at all."

"Got some more rules."

"Oh, awesome," she said quietly.

"What was that?"

"Nothing." She smiled brightly.

Brat.

"You feel a migraine coming on, tell me immediately."

"Okay."

"You start getting stressed, you tell me."

She nodded, chewing at her lip worriedly.

"Words," he prompted.

"Yes, Sir."

"Gonna need a bedtime too."

"A bedtime?" she squeaked. "I don't think that's really necessary."

"Nine for your Little. Ten the rest of the time."

"You . . . you what? I never go to sleep before one in the morning." She stared at him with big, pleading eyes. "That's so early."

"You need a better routine. And more sleep."

"Darn it."

"Any idea how old your Little is?"

She chewed at her lip. "Well, not that young. Maybe around four."

"Four-year-olds still nap sometimes. And you're going to start taking naps when you're in Little space."

She gaped at him. "Naps?"

"Uh-huh. Naps."

"I don't need to take naps."

"You said you haven't been sleeping well. That could be a trigger for your migraines."

"But I must have slept around fourteen hours last night. I'm all caught up."

Yeah, right.

"I really don't think this is necessary. If I nap in the day, how will I get to sleep at night?"

"Go for a week without a migraine and you can skip the naps."

"Well, hell."

"Wanna change your mind?"

She shook her head but she looked a bit uncertain.

"So far all we've talked about are rules and consequences. Let's talk about the fun stuff."

Ooh. Fun stuff? "Fun stuff? Like sex?"

"While that is definitely fun, I was talking about what you like to do when you're Little."

"Oh." Dork. "Do?"

"Play with."

"Play with?" she asked.

"You gonna just repeat all of my questions?"

Shoot.

"What toys do you like playing with?" he asked.

"Toys?"

He sent her a look.

"Sorry," she whispered. "I guess I've never played much. I don't have toys for my Little. Well, other than Chompers."

"What did you do while in Little space with that wannabe-Daddy? Didn't you play? Maybe color him a picture?"

"He didn't want me to do any of that. Mostly he would call and talk about his day. Then he'd like me to tell him what I did wrong that day, and he'd lecture me on how I could improve. Sometimes give me a punishment. And then he'd, uh, get himself off while I was on the phone."

She was so embarrassed right now. She wished she could tell what he was thinking but he was so hard to read.

"That so? And you? Did you get to come?"

"No."

"You'd wait until later and use your vibrator?"

She shrugged. "Yeah."

"Selfish prick. Baby girl, sounds to me like you found a fucking idiot for a Daddy. Selfish and a dickshit."

"I'm beginning to realize that. Do you mean that I . . . that you'd be okay with me playing while in Little space?"

He stood and walked towards the door. She stared at him. Was it something she'd said?

"Stay."

He disappeared and she sat there.

When he walked back into the bedroom, he was carrying a tablet in his hand.

"Scoot over," he told her. Then sat next to her so she could see the tablet screen.

Which was showing a website . . . selling toys.

"Choose what you want. Add it to the cart and we'll get it."

He really wanted to buy her some toys?

"I can't."

"Don't know what to choose? What do you think you'd like? Legos? Coloring pens and shit? Soft toys? You like dinosaurs, huh?"

Oh hell. She was going to cry. She could feel herself welling up. And she hated crying. The other night had been the first time she'd cried in months.

"I, uh, yeah. But I can't let you get me things. Not when we ..." Are just a temporary thing.

She didn't want to say that. She didn't want to make the words real.

"You need shit to play with. Got nothing here. You like music?"

"Yes," she said immediately.

He glanced over at her and she blushed. "I like to sing. And dance. I'm no good at it, though."

"Hmm." She noticed him adding a keyboard and a kid's karaoke machine to the cart.

"Really, I don't need all this."

"I say you do. And last time I checked; I was in charge."

She sighed. "So it's your way or the highway?"

"No, it's my way or the corner."

"What?"

"Keep arguing with me and you'll find yourself in time-out."

"I don't think that's at all fair."

"Noted."

Jeez. She sulked for a moment then she realized how much stuff he was adding to the cart. She reached for the tablet with a squeal. "I'll do it."

He gave her a look. "All right. But I want to see several things in that cart or you're in trouble, understand?"

"Yes, Daddy."

Okay, that just slipped out. But a pleased look entered his face.

"Gonna clean up the kitchen. Then I'll be up to pay for it."

No, he wouldn't. Because she knew her credit card number off by heart.

"What's the address here?"

"I'll put it in when I get back up," he told her.

Shoot. There went her plan.

"And don't think I don't know what you were planning on doing, brat," he said in a low rumbly voice that did things to her. "Just so you know, if you'd succeeded, you'd be lying on your tummy for the rest of the day."

Her mouth dropped open in shock as he walked out of the room.

21

She was so bored. After ordering some coloring pens and a coloring book, the karaoke machine and a microphone, along with a board game, he'd taken the tablet from her and then he'd gone through some limits with her. That had been kind of embarrassing, nothing like talking to the man you thought was hot about how you felt about anal play.

Which, by the way, she was totally hot for, but tried to downplay in case he wasn't. Which she then got told off about and was informed that if she held back again, she'd be made to keep a ginger plug in her bottom for ten minutes.

She'd been totally truthful after that.

Although now she couldn't stop thinking about ginger plugs.

After that conversation, she'd been given orders to rest, then he'd left. But resting was boring. Especially when she wasn't tired. So she'd snuck into her bedroom and grabbed her eReader and laptop.

After Skyping back home and talking to everyone, she'd

settled under the covers of the bed with Chompers and one of her favorite books to reread.

This was one written by CJ Bennett. About a Little on a ranch in Texas who had three daddies. Three! She couldn't believe it. She couldn't even find one.

Well... that's not quite true now, is it?

She couldn't find one who wanted to keep her, that was.

Push the hurt deep inside, Millie.

She'd just gotten to a scene where the naughty heroine was about to be spanked for putting herself in danger by going out riding alone when the door opened. She gasped. She'd gotten so caught up in the story that she hadn't realized it was close to lunchtime. She was also so turned on that she could feel the slickness on her thighs when she rubbed them together.

Uh oh.

"What are you doing?" Spike rumbled.

"Umm, oh, reading a story." She fumbled with her eReader, quickly turning it off.

"You shouldn't be on a screen," he scolded.

"I got bored. I can't just lie here all day. Can I get up and rest in the living room?"

He set the tray down on the bedside table. "So long as you promise to lie on the sofa and not move."

"Pinky promise." She held up her pinky.

As he stood there, staring at her finger, she realized what she was doing. Idiot. She started to drop her hand, when he reached out and wrapped his little finger around hers. "Pinky promises are sacred."

Warmth flooded her. He wasn't rejecting her.

"Oh, I know. They're the most sacred of all the promises."

"After lunch I'll carry you downstairs."

"You don't have to carry me, I'm..." she broke off as he scowled at her. Right, no putting herself down. She didn't want a spanking.

Well, maybe she did.

She really wasn't sure.

"I'm not an invalid," she added hastily.

"Nice save, but I'll carry you. Eat."

"Yum, cheese sandwiches are my favorite," she sang, grabbed a sandwich and bit into it enthusiastically.

Then she realized he was watching her.

"Oh, sorry." She placed the sandwich down and tried to eat like a normal person.

Such a doofus.

"Why?"

"Umm, I've been told I get a bit too enthusiastic about things."

"Seems to me that you just enjoy life. And you like to show that. Nothing wrong with being enthusiastic." There was something almost sexy in the way he said that. Was he talking about enthusiasm in the bedroom?

Holy. Hell.

"My ex used to gag me while we were having sex because I was too loud."

He blinked.

Oh shit. Oh shit. Oh shit.

"I cannot believe I just blurted that out." She groaned and whacked her face with her palm.

Queen. Of. The. Dorks.

"Stop that," he gently chastised. "Look at me."

"I don't want to."

"Why not?"

"Because maybe then I can pretend I never said that?" Where was that hole when she needed it?

"Baby, look at me."

Shit. Maybe if he'd gotten all growly, she could have resisted. But that was his gentle voice. That croon that just did it for her.

Of course his rough, growly voice did it for her too.

So, you know, she was screwed either way.

"That guy was an asshole. Sometimes I might gag you, but mostly I want to hear every cry, every shout, every sigh that comes from your mouth when I'm fucking you."

"He didn't want his parents to hear us."

He leaned over her, his hands on the mattress on either side of her. "I don't give a fuck who hears us." He kissed her. And it was every bit as amazing as earlier.

More. She wanted more.

Reaching up, she wrapped her arms around his neck, drawing him into her. "Please. More."

"Easy, baby."

She groaned as he drew back. "Finish your sandwich."

Millie was starting to think he was just a huge tease.

"I'm not hungry."

Not for food anyway. Holy crap. CJ's book was obviously turning her mind dirty. She rubbed her thighs together. She needed to clean up before going downstairs.

"I don't want to stop," she confessed.

"Fuck. Neither do I. But we're not rushing this."

Why not? She wouldn't be here forever. They didn't have a lot of time. And she was on fire here. So much so she wondered if she could sneak a session with her vibrator in the shower. But then he'd told her she wasn't allowed to do that anymore, hadn't he?

She stuck her lower lip out. "It's not fair."

"What's not fair, baby doll?" He tapped her lower lip.

"Oh. Um. Nothing. Didn't mean to say that out loud."

He gave her a knowing look. "You turned on?"

Her breathing quickened as he ran a finger down her cheek.

"Just what were you reading before, huh?"

"Nothing." Her voice was high-pitched and sounded guilty as hell.

"Nothing, huh? You're looking a bit flushed. Too hot?"

"No. I just need to go clean up a bit."

"Clean up?" he asked.

Oh, she really didn't want to explain that.

"I'll help you clean up."

"That's not necessary," she said frantically.

"It's Daddy's job to make sure his girl is clean. And settled. And happy."

Shoot. Kill her now.

"Let's see where you need cleaning up."

Holy. Crap.

He started pulling down the zipper of her onesie. She suddenly remembered that all she wore underneath were a pair of damp panties. While he'd already seen her naked, she wasn't ready to repeat that in broad daylight while she was conscious.

She grabbed his hand, stilling it. "I'm not wearing anything underneath."

"I know."

"You just said we weren't rushing into things."

"We're not having sex. I'm just making you more comfortable."

"How is this making me more comfortable?" All it was doing was pushing her arousal higher. And if he wasn't planning on doing anything about it, then they should probably stop now. He undid the zipper some more but didn't pull the onesie apart to reveal her breasts.

She watched him, her heart racing.

"What were you reading, Millie? Be a good girl and tell Daddy the truth and he'll reward you. Be naughty and Daddy will have to punish his girl."

His girl.

Shit.

Where was he getting this stuff from? What happened to taciturn, grouchy Spike? Him, she could handle. This side of him . . .

She wasn't sure she could ever let him go.

"Millie, last chance."

"It was a Daddy Dom romance."

He kissed down her neck. "Tell me about it."

"There are these three men, brothers, who live on a ranch in Texas and they hired a housekeeper who is a Little. They're all Daddies. They end up sharing her."

He leaned back, glaring down at her. "Share? I don't share."

She blinked at him. "I didn't think . . . I mean, it's fiction. That sort of thing doesn't happen in real life."

"You have no idea of what goes on in real life."

Did he mean that really did happen? Wow.

"I can barely handle one Daddy let alone three," she muttered.

"You won't be handling me at all. I'm in charge in this relationship."

But they didn't have a relationship, right?

Semantics, Millie. He didn't mean it like that.

He'd reached her collarbone by now. She wished she was dressed in something sexy. Not a darn dinosaur onesie.

"It turned you on, reading about that, didn't it?" He cupped her breast.

"Umm."

He stopped moving his hand, drawing his head back to look down at her. "Remember, honesty."

"Yes," she squeaked.

"What scene were you reading when I came in?" He grabbed her by the hips and drew her further down the bed so she was flat on her back while he sat, looming over her.

Oh no. She really didn't want to tell him that. But he'd stopped again. And she decided that was worse

"She was about to get spanked," she blurted out.

"Is that so? What had she done to get spanked?"

"She disobeyed her Daddies and went riding on her own when she wasn't familiar with the ranch. She got lost and was away for hours and they were worried. So when she got back, she got bent over a hay bale and that's where I was when you came in," she told him. As she finished, she took in a gasping breath.

"Very naughty, worrying her Daddies. You wouldn't do that, would you? Because you're my good girl."

"I don't know how to ride."

"That wasn't the issue and you know it. She disobeyed a rule. She put herself at risk. She worried her Daddies. They need to whip her ass with a belt. Then ground her."

He ran his hand up between her legs.

"Hmm, still haven't found where you need cleaning up."

Her heart raced. "I . . . I . . can do it."

"Oh no, it's definitely Daddy's job. Pull your legs up to your chest and hold them there."

"W-what?"

"You heard me."

Holy crap. She raised her legs up, holding them behind the knees. He undid her drop seat, pulling it open and running a hand over her bottom.

"Damn, this ass. Fucking edible."

She gasped as he leaned in and bit her bottom cheek lightly. Oh God, she was already so wet. She really wished she'd had the chance to change her panties before he had his face down there.

"Somebody is very wet." He ran a finger along her slit. "This all because of that scene?"

"N-no."

"No? Why else are you wet?"

"How come you're so talkative now?" she moaned. "I've never had someone talk to me during. . . during whatever this is."

"Want me to shut up?"

"Yes . . . no. Shoot. I think I like it."

He actually chuckled. "This wet pussy is anything to go by, you definitely like it."

A groan escaped her. "I need to go to the bathroom. Two minutes is all I need."

"You're not going anywhere. I'm going to clean my girl up." He pushed her panties to one side then leaning in, he ran his tongue along her lips. "Such a pretty tasting pussy."

She gasped as he circled her clit.

Shoot. Shoot.

Whimpers escaped her mouth as he lapped at her, feeding from her. He ran his tongue over her outer lips. "Got to get all of you clean."

Sliding his tongue down, he thrust it deep into her passage. She cried out, her back arching.

Hell! Nobody had ever done this to her. Doug went down on her a few times, but it had always felt awkward and she'd finally told him that she didn't like it.

He'd seemed relieved.

But this. . . far out, he was eating her like he couldn't get enough of her. Like her taste was something he desired.

"Fuck, yes, baby. Cream for me."

Sweet heaven above.

"Please. Oh, please."

Two fingers slid deep inside her, curling and rubbing against that spot that drove her insane.

He sucked on her clit. "Fuck, could eat you out for hours and never get tired. Hmm, not a bad idea. How many times have you come in one session?"

"Uh, um, once?"

"Remedy that."

"You mean that multiple orgasms are really a thing? I don't think I can do that. I get too sensitive."

"We'll see," was all he said before he reached up with one hand to free her breast. He toyed with the nipple, pinching it slightly as he tapped at her clit with his tongue.

And that was all that was needed to send her up and over the edge. She spun. Her entire world contracted to just this moment, to the joy flooding her. He gentled his touch, prolonging the orgasm, making her shake, her pussy clenching.

Slowly, he lapped at her, moving his tongue over her lips then he drew his fingers free from her pussy and sat up.

"Open." She parted her lips and he pushed his fingers inside. "Good girl. Suck."

She sucked. She couldn't believe she was doing this. She wasn't this sort of girl. Under the sheets, in the dark, missionary style. That was her.

But didn't you always wonder if there was more?

She used her tongue to clean his fingers, watching as heat filled his face.

When he withdrew his fingers she whimpered in protest.

"Someone likes sucking on things, huh?"

There was definitely some innuendo in there.

"Just Daddy's big girl? Or his Little girl too?"

What did he mean?

He slid his wet fingers down to her nipple. "Does my baby ever suck her thumb? Or use a pacifier? A bottle?"

"I've never . . . no."

But that didn't mean she hadn't thought about it. She'd always imagined her Little was too old for that.

Except when she was tired or feeling a bit down, she liked to snuggle with Chompers. And sometimes she'd wondered what it would be like to suck on her thumb, to use a bottle.

"We can explore that." Leaning in, he suckled on her nipple.

She gasped. Oh hell. She felt that all the way down in her clit.

Then he drew back with a sigh. "Got to stop before I'm tempted to go too far."

"But, umm, would you like me to, umm . . ." She stared down at his crotch. She'd given blow jobs before but she wasn't sure she was all that good at them.

"Look at me." She raised her gaze to his.

"Much as the thought of your mouth around my dick is a fucking good one, this ain't tit-for-tat. Another time, you can suck me off. But right now, you're going to go relax on the couch, eat some food, rehydrate and rest. When you're at a hundred percent, then we can explore further."

Wow. She'd never met a man who just gave without expecting anything in return.

"Are you sure you're real?"

The skin around his eyes crinkled, as though he was fighting a smile. "Pretty damn sure. Stay here, I'm gonna get you some more clothes."

She lay back as he left the room. Her skin still felt all tingly, her nipples sensitive, the taste of her pleasure was on her tongue.

When he walked back in, she was still lying there in a post-orgasm daze. He placed another onesie on the bed, along with a clean pair of panties. In his hand, he held a washcloth.

"These are cute," he said, holding up her blue onesie. It had a hood with white ears on it. "We should've ordered more of them."

She was blushing as she realized he'd gone through her panties.

He'd touched her panties.

Yikes.

"Oh, um, I made them. I make all my clothes. Well, not my panties and bras. Could probably make panties, but I need bras with wire in them for my huge boobs."

His gaze went to her breasts and she realized one was still bare. Holy shit! How had she not noticed that? She squeaked and sitting, zipped up the onesie.

"Fucking sexy breasts."

Well, he would think that. Most men loved boobs, right? They didn't realize what a pain in the ass they could be.

"Thanks for getting me my clothes, but I need to shower first."

He frowned. "Don't want you showering alone. What if you feel faint and fall?"

"I'll be fine. Honest. I'm just tired now."

"No, Daddy will give you a bath tonight. Besides, you shouldn't shower with your foot. I'll just clean you up a bit. Lie back again."

"I don't ... I'm not sure I'm comfortable with you seeing me ... naked," the last word was whispered and she nearly rolled her eyes at herself.

"Seen you naked already," he pointed out.

"Yes, but I wasn't awake."

"That makes me sound like a pervert," he said dryly.

"What we just did ... I've never before ... I ..."

"No one's ever gone down on you before?"

Christ. He was so blunt!

"Yes, they have. Well, not like you did. That was ... spectacular."

A smug look filled his face.

"But only in the dark, under the sheets," she explained. "I didn't feel comfortable being exposed."

"We need to work on that, don't we? Because when I look at you, I see someone beautiful and sexy. Someone who has made cold showers a constant thing in my life. That body of yours is fucking sin. And there isn't an inch of it I don't want to taste or touch."

"Really?"

"Really. And I'll say it as many times as you need to hear it. I don't lie, Millie. Trust me."

She let out a deep breath. He didn't seem the type to say something he didn't mean. He really thought she was sexy?

"Gonna make you see yourself the way I do." He sat next to her and leaned in to kiss her. "Daddy is gonna get you cleaned up and changed, okay?"

She let out a breath, trying to rid herself of her nervousness. "Okay, Daddy." She lay back on the bed.

He unzipped her onesie. It took a lot to let him expose her. But with every inch that was revealed, his face grew more heated. She could see the hunger there.

"You really do think I'm sexy," she whispered in wonder.

"My cock is so hard it's fucking painful." He stripped off the onesie and threw it onto the floor.

"We totally defiled my poor, innocent onesie."

"Oh, we can do a better job than that."

She blushed bright red. Although she wasn't sure if that was due to his words or because he was pulling her soaked panties down off her legs.

"Part your legs," he growled.

Oh hell. She drew her legs apart, knowing she had to be as red as a tomato. He ran the cloth over her folds, cleaning her. This was so intimate. It wasn't precisely sexual, even though she was turned on.

It was him taking care of her.

In a way no one ever had. And she wasn't just talking about him cleaning her pussy. It was the way he undressed then dressed her. How he'd brought her food. How he wanted her to rest. How he gave her an orgasm without expecting anything in return.

He slid some clean panties over her feet. She raised her hips to help as he drew them up her hips.

"We need to get my girl some pretty panties," he murmured. "What would you like? Some dinosaur ones?"

"Ooh, yes. Dinosaur panties."

He helped her into her clean onesie. When she was dressed, he stood and held out his hands to her. She took them, letting him pull her up. But she was barely standing before she found herself swung up into his arms.

"You shouldn't carry me down the stairs," she protested.

"Baby doll, you are dancing dangerously close to a punishment," he warned. "I'll carry you where and when I like. Got it? Anything else out of that mouth that even strikes me as slightly self-derogatory and you're spending time in the corner. And before you say anything more, if you weren't recovering from a migraine it would be a spanking and lines."

Okay, time to zip it. Not something she was good at. Blurting things without thinking? She was all over that shit. Staying quiet, not so much.

He carried her bridal style and wowed her by not even breathing heavily by the time they got downstairs.

Seriously, he was fit. He settled her on the couch. "Going to get you some water and make you a new sandwich. What do you want to watch?" He picked up the remote and switched it over to cartoons. "Good?"

"Um, I don't like this one."

He clicked onto another channel.

"Ooh, yes, this one."

He gave it a skeptical look. "I don't think so. Too violent."

"Hey! No fair." She crossed her arms over her chest.

Spike just raised his eyebrows and gave her a look that she was beginning to realize meant she was about to get herself into trouble.

"How about this?" He chose another channel and she nodded reluctantly.

"Fine. I'll watch that."

"Watch that tone. I'm sure I can find something far less pleasant for my girl to do."

"Like what?" she asked suspiciously.

"Like lying on her tummy with a piece of ginger lodged in her bottom."

"This is fine," she squeaked.

"Thought so." He leaned in to kiss her forehead.

He returned quickly with a new sandwich and a big bottle of water. "I want that eaten and all the water gone by the time I come back to check on you."

"Urgh, water. Yuck."

"You need to rehydrate."

She sighed. "I just don't like the way it tastes."

He looked thoughtful. Then he picked up the bottle of water. "Back soon."

She gave him a curious look as he moved away. He was gone for around ten minutes or so but when he returned, the water was a faint pink color and it had cut up pieces of strawberries floating in it.

"Ooh, pretty."

"This is special. It's fairy juice."

"Fairy juice?" She sat up, staring at the water. "Fairies aren't real, Daddy."

"You so sure about that? Because if fairies aren't real how come they live in my garden?"

"Do not!" She gaped at him. This was a side of him she never thought existed. Sure, he'd told her he was a Daddy Dom, but she hadn't expected him to be, well, playful. Stern, yes. Demanding, yes. Caring, sure. But playful and fun? Not really.

"They do. And if you're good, one day I'll take you on a fairy picnic. But that won't happen if you don't drink your fairy juice."

"Why not?"

"Because you won't see them. You've got to drink the juice every day to build up the magic. See?"

That was genius. She stared at the juice. "Okay, Daddy. I can do that."

You're such a sucker.

But she grabbed the bottle and started to drink. Okay, it didn't taste so bad with the faint hint of strawberry in it.

"Drink. Eat. Do not move off the couch. Hear me?"

"Yes, Daddy. I hear you."

"How is your foot? Do you need some more cream?"

"It's fine."

He shot her a skeptical look.

"Promise."

He grunted.

"Have you heard anything from Steele about that Corey guy?" she asked anxiously.

He shook his head. "Will call him. I've got some friends looking for him too. We'll find him."

"And Luther? What about the threat to you?"

Surprise filled his face before he cupped her chin, kissing her lightly. "You're too fucking sweet. I will be fine. Rest."

22

Spike sat in his office and turned the camera feed on for the living room. He had cameras in every room of the house that fed through to here. He didn't usually monitor them. They recorded then erased after forty-eight hours.

But they served a purpose now since he didn't want to make these calls with her listening in. He opened his phone and saw a text from Hack.

How is our Little patient?

Spike rolled his eyes at his nosiness.

Better. Thanks.

Maybe I should come check her.

Spike didn't answer. He didn't think so.

Does she like glitter?

Nope. He knew how that went. He did not want a house filled with glitter.

She hates glitter.

She does or you do? Never mind. Will ask her myself when I meet her.

Spike growled. Oh no, he wouldn't. Hack was a flirt. He was charming. He was fun.

He was almost the exact opposite of Spike. Crap. Was he really worried Millie would like Hack more?

He wasn't. This wasn't serious. They were just having fun while she was here. He hadn't realized how much he missed having someone to take care of . . .

Shit.

Spike couldn't get attached to her.

He'd missed having a Little around. And while it wasn't what he'd had with Jacqui, it was still filling a hole inside him he hadn't realized was there.

Ignoring Hack, he called Ink.

"Tell me you've found this asshole," he growled down the phone.

"Hello to you too, Spike. How are you today?" Ink replied.

Spike groaned. Ink was cheerful. Fucker had been that way ever since meeting Betsy. Oh, he could still be a shit. He still liked to stir the pot with Reyes, only now he did it with a grin on his face.

It was sickening.

"Ink," he warned.

"Got nothing. Sent guys out to where we know the Devil's Sinners hang out. No one matching the description of this asshole."

"Fuck."

He wanted this guy found. The threat to Millie taken care of.

Only then, you'll have no excuse to keep her here, will you?

He pushed that thought aside.

"Thanks, man."

"We'll keep on it. You heard anything about the fire at Senior's warehouse on the docks?"

"Nah."

"Hmm. You don't think Reyes..."

What? Would organize that? He didn't think so. But then he wasn't sure.

"He'd tell us."

Would he, though? Reyes could be secretive as shit.

He ended the call. He needed to get out there and talk to people. He had contacts in the underground that Ink didn't. When it came to finding out information, Spike was good. Maybe only Grady was better.

But he couldn't leave Millie here alone. His place was secure, but nothing was completely foolproof. Well, maybe that bunker Reyes talked of. But he couldn't see him leaving her there.

Steele's place is pretty secure.

Yeah, but he wasn't taking her near that fucker without being present himself. He'd seen the light of interest in Steele and Grady's eyes. No way he'd hand her over on a platter to them.

Ink's place? It was secure too.

But that didn't feel right. No, he'd wait a bit longer, see if Ink or Steele found this asshole.

He called Steele next.

The other man answered quickly. "Spike."

"Steele."

"How is the lovely Millie?"

"She's fine," he said shortly.

"Good. Hope you're taking care of her."

"Stop the bullshit. You found him yet?" Spike snapped.

"I have not," Steele said darkly. Spike knew that had to be pissing him off. That this asshole had gotten into the club, then escaped under his watch. Steele didn't let stuff like that slide. "But I will."

"Millie's been asking what we're going to do about Luther." She was sweet to worry about the threat to him, but he could take care of himself. However, he didn't like the idea of Luther starting up where his father had left off.

"I'm setting something up to see if we can figure out the traitor. Someday soon, I'm going to need Millie at Pinkies to point out this guy."

"Don't want her leaving the house."

And not just because of the risk to her.

"Nobody will get to her in here," Steele promised. "If I find the traitor I can go after Luther."

Fuck it.

"I'll talk to her."

"Talk to her, huh? Hmm, you do that."

Spike rolled his eyes. Steele wasn't the type to ask. He demanded. But he'd never been with a woman for longer than a weekend. He didn't get that there was a time to make commands and a time to be flexible. While he'd never allow Millie to be in danger or put her health at risk, Spike knew he couldn't make all the decisions for her.

And if he could, then Steele would be disappointed because he'd order her ass to stay at home.

Being a Daddy gave him more control. But she wasn't his Little 24/7. At the end of the day, she always had the ultimate control. He thought that Steele hadn't ever entered into anything more with a woman because he'd never found one he'd be willing to compromise for.

Or maybe Steele hadn't found someone who would be willing to give him all of her. To allow him as much control as he needed to function.

Fuck it. It wasn't his life.

"I'll set it up." Steele ended the call. Spike had been watching the camera feed the whole time, satisfied to see she was drinking her fairy juice.

That reminded him. He quickly went online and ordered the

toys she'd put in the cart. He added some more things as well. Stuff he thought she might like. Then he moved over to an online age play and apparel shop that he'd heard about from Ink.

Hmm. He ordered a bottle. Just in case. He spotted a pacifier with a dinosaur on it. That went in the cart. There were also some damn cute panties that he thought would be perfect for her. Satin with bows. Others with ruffles. An adorable romper set went in too. And a form-fitting onesie in pale yellow with pictures of puppies on it and a snap crotch.

There was a ballerina outfit as well. He remembered what she'd said about liking to dance and sing.

She'd also told him that she made her own clothes. If it took them awhile to find this Devil's Sinners jerk, then maybe he should get something for her to do when she wasn't in Little space. But was ordering a sewing machine taking things too far? She wouldn't be here for long.

He didn't want to send the wrong message.

Fuck it. He did a bit of research to find the one with the best reviews then he ordered it. He forced himself to do some work even though all he wanted was to return to her. He should stay away from her for a while. Give them both some space.

But she'd been ill and she was injured, so he shouldn't leave her too long. Having justified his need to be around her, he returned to the living room. Mr. Fluffy was asleep on her lap. He saw with surprise that she'd drunk all the water.

"I drunk it all!"

"You sure did, baby doll." He leaned down and kissed the top of her head. "That deserves a reward."

There was a flash of heat in her gaze, which filled him with satisfaction. However, that wasn't what he'd meant.

"Not that, baby doll." He tapped her nose. "How about a movie date? Popcorn. Your choice of movie. Might even find some chocolate."

"That sounds great." She clapped her hands. Mr. Fluffy didn't even flinch.

"Never known a dog to sleep that much."

"Do you think I should take him to the vet?" she worried.

"Maybe. He should go anyway. There's shots he likely needs."

Her face dropped. "I'm a bad puppy mama."

"You've had a lot going on. And you found him in an alley, you're taking care of him, not everyone would do that."

She sighed. "I guess. I've always loved animals. My grandma wasn't a fan, but grandad always helped with all the strays that I brought home."

She had a big heart. That much was clear. He knew he should bring up Steele's plan. Tell her that ink hadn't found anything, but he wanted her to be worry free for a while.

That stuff could all wait until tomorrow.

23

Millie sat on the bathroom counter, watching as Spike filled up the bath.

When was the last time someone ran her a bath? Hmm. She guessed when she was young, but she couldn't remember. Spike had sat through *The Secret Life of Pets* one and two without complaining. She'd even gotten some popcorn and some chocolate. Although she'd had to drink another bottle of fairy juice.

It surprised her how easily she had slipped into Little space with him. She was holding back a bit though, waiting to see exactly how much he wanted. She knew that all of her was probably too much. No matter what he said, she knew he wouldn't want someone who was too needy. Or too emotional. Or too loud.

So she just had to gauge how much he was comfortable with and give him that.

Last thing she wanted was to scare him away. And since they were only going to be together for a short time, she knew she could easily hide those parts of herself.

Much as she might wish this didn't have an expiration date, she knew it was a good thing. She was batting way out of her league. No way was a country bumpkin who sewed her own clothes, was clumsy as hell and had a terrible habit of blurting out her thoughts, be good enough for him.

He'd used her bubble bath to make it nice and sudsy, at least. So that would cover her up.

"Don't think I'm gonna like those thoughts, am I, girl?"

No, she didn't think so either. She bit her lip in consternation. He strode over to her, placing his hands on the counter on either side of her. He leaned in to whisper into her ear. Christ, he'd picked up awfully quickly how much that turned her on.

"Know what I'm tempted to do?"

She shook her head. Nope. But she was certain he would soon tell her.

"I'm tempted to make you go naked for a day. I'd take you into my office. Have you lie on my desk with your legs spread wide and when I needed to play, you'd be right there for me to feast on."

He wouldn't.

Would he?

Her breath sped up at that thought.

Drawing back, he stared into her eyes. His eyes were wicked. And filled with heat and promise.

"Oh, you like that idea."

The being naked part would suck ass. But the being feasted on part?

Yeah, she could probably get behind that.

"Christ, woman. What are you doing to me? I'm like a fucking horny teenager when it comes to you."

"Sorry?" She bit her lip to hold back a smile.

His look told her that he thought she was full of shit.

"Daddy might just have to spank you for teasing him." He

started unzipping her onesie. She held herself still and forced herself not to stop him.

"That's not fair. I didn't do anything wrong!"

"Teasing him is naughty. But I didn't say this would be a punishment spanking."

Oh? Ohh.

She swallowed heavily as he drew her arms free, then pulled the onesie down to reveal her full breasts. The nipples were hard and she fully expected him to lean in and lick them or touch them. But he grabbed her around the waist, slipping her off the counter so he could crouch in front of her and draw down the onesie.

"Hold onto my shoulders while you step out," he commanded.

Probably a wise idea. She'd been known to trip and fall while getting dressed. Then she found herself standing in front of him, only wearing a pair of panties.

He reached for the top of her panties, slowly pulling them down. She swore she heard him groan, but he didn't say anything and his touch didn't linger.

When she was completely naked, he sat back on his heels and ran his gaze over her. She covered up her tummy and pussy, feeling exposed.

"Hands to your side," he commanded.

"Can I get in the bath?"

"No. Not yet. Daddy's not finished looking. Turn around and grasp hold of the counter and bend over. Legs spread."

Crap. Crap. Crap.

She knew he could see everything. Could likely see her pussy lips glistening in arousal.

"Fucking beautiful. Never seen an ass more beautiful than this. Makes me wonder what it's gonna be like to see my handprint on it."

She squealed as he smacked his hand on her right cheek. Then he did the same to her left.

"Daddy!"

"Yep. Fucking beautiful. Christ, woman, the things you do to me."

He stood up behind her, grabbing her hips and her imagination went straight to what it would be like to have him enter her. To thrust deep inside her while she watched in the mirror.

Holy. Hell.

"And these breasts. Fucking amazing." He reached around and cupped each breast. "Straighten. Watch yourself."

She couldn't do anything but stand there, transfixed as his large hands cupped her breasts. He lightly twisted her nipples and her heart raced. She leaned back against him.

"Look how pretty you are. Face flushed. Eyes sparkling with arousal. Too. Fucking. Much."

He pressed her hair to one side and kissed his way down her neck. "Creamy skin. Smell so good. Eat you up." The words were mumbled between the kisses he laid on her skin. But she heard him. A shiver ran through her.

"Spike," she groaned.

"I know, woman. Feel it too." He leaned back and slapped her ass again.

"Hey!" She reached back to rub the offending spot. "Why?"

"Like I said, teasing me. Supposed to be getting you clean and you're distracting me."

She was distracting him? Was he insane? If anyone was doing the distracting it was him.

"You got any hair ties? Or you want me to wash your hair?"

"It takes too long to dry. I've got some in my toilet bag." She reached for the bag on the counter and drew some out, raising her hands to tie back her hair. But he held out his hand and she gave him a curious look.

"Give them to me. Please."

She raised her eyebrows at the 'please.' That sounded almost foreign coming from his lips. But she passed him the hair ties.

He drew her hair back and braided it. He must have done this for his wife. She felt sad at the thought of how much he must have loved her. How much he must miss her. She wondered how she'd died.

He twisted the braid into a bun and then secured it with the second hair tie. Then he took hold of her hand and led her to the bathtub.

"You need to keep your injured foot out of the water." He helped her sit while laying her foot on the outer edge of the tub. She sighed as the warm water soothed her muscles.

Spike grabbed a clean washcloth from the cupboard and then walked over to crouch beside her. She foolishly reached for the cloth.

He drew his hand away, giving her hand a light tap. She flushed even as her insides danced. He really was going to wash her, wasn't he?

Sliding the cloth around in slow circles, he had her sit forward to do her back and arms first, then he moved around to her front. To her surprise, he didn't linger on her breasts.

"Lie back, baby doll."

She lay back so her neck rested on the edge of the tub. Then he tapped her shoulders. She opened her eyes to find he'd rolled up a towel. She sat up slightly and he put it behind her head before guiding her back.

Wow.

She hadn't realized men this thoughtful existed. Who were protective and caring, who would also find her attractive. Sexy.

Seriously, he was ruining her for all other daddies.

The washcloth went lower down her stomach and she stiffened slightly. Having someone touch her stomach wasn't her favorite. But he must have sensed what she was thinking, because he rubbed the cloth back and forth until she relaxed.

Then he moved to her feet, cleaning them more thoroughly than she ever would have, avoiding her burn of course, before moving up her legs. He slid the cloth over her pussy lips. She let out a small groan. Opening her eyes, she saw the way he was bent over the tub, concentrating on his task.

Oh, she knew she shouldn't.

But she just couldn't resist.

He was so serious all the time. He needed a bit of messing with, right? She put her hand under the water, cupping it then quickly pushed it forward, splashing a whole lot of water up into his face.

Far more than she'd meant to, actually.

And she'd been aiming for his shoulder.

Whoops.

He froze. Almost as though he couldn't believe she'd just done that.

Truth was, she couldn't believe she'd just done that either. She sat there, staring at him, her heart racing. Either she'd made a huge mistake and she was in a world of trouble . . . or he'd find the funny side.

Somehow, she thought it might be the first.

When he turned to face her, water dripping off his face and down onto his T-shirt, she squealed and slid under the water.

Oh Lord save her.

Strong hands slid under her arms and he drew her up with a stern look.

"Don't do that. You could drown."

"In a bathtub? I don't think so. I know how to swim, or you know, sit up."

"You want to watch your sass right now, Millicent Margaret."

Uh-oh. Two names. Definitely in trouble.

"How do you know my full name?"

"Looked at your license."

He'd looked at her license?

"When?"

"When you went to the bathroom at Pinkies the other night. Needed to check you were who you said you were."

Leaning back, he whipped off his T-shirt, putting all those muscles and abs on display.

Had she ever seen a man so ripped before? If she had, she'd certainly never been close enough to touch. Leaning up, she ran a finger down his abs.

"Wow."

"Like?"

She pulled her hand away, blushing. Doofus. *Way to make an idiot of yourself.* She attempted to submerge again, but he grabbed her, drawing her back up.

Then he pointed at her. "Stay there."

Drat. She really thought it would be better if she could just hide at this point.

"Want to explain yourself?"

"Umm. I thought you looked hot, Daddy."

He gave her a skeptical look. Yeah, he wasn't buying what she was selling.

"Hot?"

"Uh-huh. Like you needed cooling down."

Although she hadn't factored in him removing his shirt. She couldn't decide if that was a good thing or a bad thing. She wiped at her chin, making sure she wasn't drooling.

"Little girl, splashing is naughty."

"Sorry, Daddy. I won'ts do it again." She could feel herself regressing further and tried to pull herself back.

"Wish I believed that."

"I'm good girl, Daddy. Perfect little princess."

He snorted at her silliness but she thought she saw a hint of a smile. Maybe.

He helped her out and dried her off as she stood on the fluffy bath mat. That feeling of being taken care of flooded her again. Then he helped her get dressed in a clean pair of panties and these soft, flannel pajamas she'd made for herself with dinosaurs on them.

Finally, he cleaned up while she brushed her teeth then he checked her bandage. Her burn looked really good so he left it off. He grabbed her hair brush and led her back to the bedroom. His bedroom. She eyed the hair brush worriedly.

He wasn't really mad over her splashing him, was he?

"You look worried," he murmured as he drew her over to the bed. "Concerned about going across my knee and getting a well-deserved paddling?"

"It is not well-deserved. I is a good girl."

"Uh-huh. Splashing Daddy should come with consequences." He stood in front of her and smacked the smooth side of the hair brush against his thigh. "Wonder what that should be."

Her eyes widened. He wasn't being serious, was he?

"I'm sorry, Daddy. I won't do it again. Promise."

"Don't make promises you can't keep."

He sat on the bed and leaned back against the headboard, then he pointed to the mattress between his open legs. "Sit."

But then he undid her braid and dried it with the hairdryer before brushing it. By the time he was finished, she was so relaxed and sleepy that she was barely able to hold herself up. Spike helped her into bed and then kissed the top of her head.

"Sleep, baby."

See? She was a good girl because she obeyed him straight away.

∽

HELP ME.

Help me, Millie.

Please. I need you.

SHE CRIED OUT, sitting up with a gasp. Her breath came in sharp pants, the panic from the nightmare still clinging to her.

"Hey, what is it? Did you have a nightmare?"

She let out a scream, turning to find a huge man sitting beside her, almost looming over her. A dog let out a small bark as she shrank back.

"Millie. Millie, it's me. Spike. Daddy."

Spike. Daddy.

Oh shit. She suddenly realized where she was. She ran a shaking hand over her face then lay back on the bed with a sigh.

"Sorry. Sorry. Confused. Sorry."

"It's okay. Shh. Calm down. Can I touch you?"

She liked that he asked. "Please."

Lying on his back, he gently pulled her over so she was on top of him, her cheek against his chest. She tensed slightly.

"Shh," he told her, running his hand up and down her back. Gradually, she started relaxing. She'd move before she went to sleep so as not to get too heavy for him. But damn, this was nice. Especially when he started rubbing her bottom.

"Nightmare?"

"Yeah. And then I got confused about where I was."

"Poor baby," he crooned. He ran his fingers through her hair, massaging her scalp gently.

Ohh. So good.

"Want to talk about it?" he asked, his voice still low and calm.

"Not now." There was nothing that talking could do. She started to tense up again as she thought of the nightmare.

"Shh. Close your eyes. You're safe. Daddy has you. You're safe in my arms."

If only she could stay there.

Before she could remind herself to shift, she found herself slipping off to sleep.

24

She stared down at the omelet the next morning. Were those vegetables in there? Eww. Seriously what did the man have against carbs?

Another bottle of fairy juice was placed in front of her. This time it was a light green color and had slices of cucumber in it. She gave it a doubtful look.

"Try it. Don't like it, I'll make you the strawberry one."

Well. Okay. She took a small sip. That wasn't too bad.

Spike had already left the bed when she'd woken. She still couldn't believe she'd fallen asleep on his chest. Shockingly, the man was a damn good cuddler. Like sleeping with a giant teddy bear, except harder. After brushing her teeth and getting dressed, she'd walked downstairs to find him. When he wasn't in any of the obvious places, she'd given Mr. Fluffy a sausage link from the fridge to keep him occupied while she'd searched the rest of the house.

And she'd found him in the gym.

Holy. Hell.

She was still hot and bothered from watching him work out.

That man could make sweat look good. She'd never thought that was possible.

A buzzer interrupted her musings. She gave Spike a startled look, but he didn't seem concerned as he checked his phone. He'd already showered and eaten most of his breakfast. He tapped her plate. "Want to see most of that gone by the time I return."

She sighed, but nodded as he got up.

"Where are you going?"

"Some packages have arrived. Will be the stuff we ordered for you. Gonna go down to the gate and grab them. Stay here. Eat. Drink."

She waited until she heard the front door open and close then she stood.

"Mr. Fluffy, want some omelet?"

Spike had already cut it up into bite-sized pieces. She pushed them into Mr. Fluffy's bowl. He waddled over and stuffed his face into the bowl while she ran upstairs to where her stash of sugar was. She ate a Twizzler and some M&Ms.

Racing downstairs, she was nearly at the bottom before he opened the door.

"What are you doing running down the stairs!" he barked.

She cried out and tripped. Tensing, she brought her arms up to her face to try to prevent it from being smashed against the wooden stairs.

To her shock, she didn't hit hard stairs, instead she smashed into a firm chest. A pair of arms surrounded her as he grunted at the impact, slamming into the railing.

She shuddered, her breath coming in pants at her near-miss.

Shit. Spike was quick.

"Little girl," he growled at her.

"Yes?" She risked a glance up at him.

Oh, he was really not happy.

"What do you have to say for yourself?"

"Umm, good catch, Daddy?"

"What were you doing, running down the stairs like that? Damn foolish thing to do."

She'd come to understand that his grumbling was because he was concerned.

It was all just part of his charm.

He carried her into the kitchen and set her down on the counter. Then he ran his hands over her, checking for any injuries.

"I'm fine, Daddy."

"Could have hit your head. Broke your neck. Smashed your nose. Twisted your foot. Banged your toe."

Banged her toe? She'd done that twice this morning already.

Although perhaps she wouldn't tell him that. He seemed stressed enough as it was.

He leaned his hands on the counter on either side of her. "You took ten years off my life, baby doll."

"Bet you're glad you don't have hair to pull out huh, Daddy?"

"No more running up or down stairs. No more running at all."

That she could happily agree to. She nodded.

"Swear, I should've bought damn shin pads and a helmet for you," he muttered.

She shrugged and went to slide off the bench. He turned and pointed his finger at her. "Stay."

She waited until his back was turned to poke her tongue out at him.

"Saw that."

Oh, he so did not.

"Ate it all?" He moved to where her empty plate was and gathered it up, placing it in the dishwasher. Shoot, she should have done that. She was becoming lazy.

"Sorry, Daddy."

"For what?"

"Not tidying up."

Way to be a terrible houseguest, Millie.

"Hey. Are you allowed to touch things in the kitchen?" he asked, placing his finger under her chin to raise her face up.

"No."

"Then don't apologize for following Daddy's rules."

She didn't exactly follow them, though, did she? She hadn't eaten the omelet and now her tummy was empty except for some licorice and chocolate.

Please don't let it growl.

Maybe she should ask for something else to eat. But then it would make it obvious she hadn't had breakfast.

See the mess you've gotten yourself into, Millie?

"Can I get down now?" she asked as he tidied up the kitchen.

"No."

"But—"

"If you stay there, you're out of trouble. Don't move." He gave her a firm look then disappeared out of the kitchen. With a sigh, she sat there. What was he doing? Where were the packages?

She'd just slipped off the counter when he walked back in. Drat. "Where are you going?"

"Nowhere, Daddy." She gave him her best innocent look.

"What did I tell you to do?" He gave her a stern look.

"Stay put."

He took hold of her hand. "Need to start tying you down to get you to stay put."

"Daddy!" she said with a mock gasp of horror. "That's illegal."

He gave her a sharp slap on her ass that made her squeal and glare at him.

He led her down to the study. As he opened the door, his phone rang.

"Go in. No touching."

She walked in to find some boxes in the middle of the room.

Movement caught her eye and she saw Mr. Fluffy jump off

Spike's desk to one of the boxes. He must have used them to climb up there. Cheeky monkey.

"Mr. Fluffy, you shouldn't be in here."

He waddled over to her and she picked him up, scratching his belly. His very full belly.

Guilt flooded her. She shouldn't have fed him that whole omelet.

Bad puppy mama.

Bad Little girl.

Her shoulders hunched. How awful was Spike going to feel when he heard what she'd done? And after he'd bought her all this stuff? She didn't deserve it. Not any of it.

Setting Mr. Fluffy down, she crawled behind the sofa and sat there, her legs pressed to her chest, her arms wrapped around them.

Bad Millie.

"Millie? Where are you?" Spike's confused voice called out. "Playing hide and seek?"

No. Although that sounded like a lot of fun. She could have been doing that, if she hadn't been so naughty. Spike was so good to her.

And she was awful.

His face popped over the edge of the sofa. "Found you."

She buried her face in her knees.

"Come out?"

She shook her head. Nope. She wasn't ready to face him yet.

"What happened?"

She shrugged. Speaking was beyond her right now. She wished she had Chompers. She needed the comfort.

She sensed him moving away. That was good. He should just leave her be. Suddenly the sofa was shifted. A gasp escaped her and she glanced up at him.

"What are you doing?" she asked

"You wouldn't come to me, so I'm coming to you. What's wrong?"

"I don't deserve any of that stuff," she whispered.

He sat facing her then reaching over, pulled her into his lap, wrapping his big arms around her. She wished she could just give in to the comfort he was offering.

"Why not?"

"I lied! I'm a terrible person and you should just send all this stuff back 'cause I don't deserve to be your temporary little girl."

SHE'D LIED? About what? Obviously, it was about something bad given her reaction.

He tensed, ready to push her away. He detested liars.

"I didn't eat the omelet. I fed it to Mr. Fluffy instead. I'm sorry!" she wailed.

Wait. What?

That was the big lie? Not eating the omelet?

"Now you know I don't deserve all these toys you bought me. I'm so sorry! You should send it all back as punishment. Or give it to a good Little girl."

Dramatic little thing, wasn't she? He thought it through for a moment. It wasn't that big of a deal. But she did lie. And she had been sneaky. However, it wasn't the end of the world either. There had to be a balance here.

He could scold her. But that didn't seem like enough, not when she felt this guilty. He definitely wasn't sending all of this back.

"Well?" she cried, drawing away to look up at him.

"What?"

"Are you going to send all this back? Or are you . . . are you going to send me away?"

Send her away? Was she insane?

Gently, he grasped her chin, tilting her face up. "I would never send you away. You did something naughty. But you didn't betray me. You didn't hurt anyone. This stuff stays. And you're definitely staying. Understand?"

"Yes, Daddy."

"Have you eaten anything?"

She sniffled. "A Twizzler and some M&Ms I had in my bag."

He frowned. "That isn't breakfast food. Skipping meals isn't allowed."

"I know. You really won't give my toys to some better-behaved Little girl who deserves them?"

"I have a good Little girl who deserves them right here."

She heaved a sigh. "I'm really not, Daddy."

"You made a mistake. You're still good."

"So I gets to keep them all?"

"Yes."

A bright smile flooded her face. Christ, he loved seeing her smile. "I'm not getting punished?"

"I didn't say that."

"Oh." She chewed her lip. "How am I getting punished then?"

"They're three things you did wrong. Not communicating that you didn't want the omelet. Lying about eating it. And skipping a meal to have candy instead. Five spanks for each transgression, so fifteen in total. Followed by fifteen minutes of corner time."

Her mouth dropped open and then she gave him a pitiful look. "Isn't the spanking enough, Daddy?"

"No. It is not." And he was glad he'd added on the corner time. He thought that might be more of a punishment for her than the spanking since she'd have to stay still and silent. Not things she was good at.

"And you'll give Daddy your candy stash."

Her mouth dropped open. "Daddy, no!"

"I'll make sure you don't eat too much at one time." He set her on the floor. Standing, he leaned down and helped her up. Then he gave her a sharp swat on the ass.

"Ouch! Are we starting my spanking now?"

"Nope. That's an extra for saying you don't deserve the things I bought you."

"I don't though. I'm only going to be here a short time. You shouldn't have spent the money on me. Although I suppose you could keep them if you ever have another Little girl."

The sadness in her face did strange things to his insides. He tried to harden himself against the feeling.

"There won't be another girl after you. Never intended to have another one after Jacqui died." He inwardly winced, knowing he could have worded that better.

But all she did was nod understandingly. "You sure you still want to do this with me? I get it if you don't."

"I don't say or do things I don't want to do."

"If you want to stop, you'll tell me?"

So he gave a sharp nod. "And if you want to stop, you'll tell me."

She smiled and nodded.

"What's your safe word?"

"Sausage."

"Good." He took hold of her hand and led her over to one of the chairs in front of the desk. "Stay here. Gonna put the dog out. Don't want him getting upset."

Grabbing the dog, who was dressed in a top that had, *I love my Mommy*, written on it, he set him down out in the hallway. The puppy gave him a reproachful look as he shut the door.

He resisted the urge to apologize to him. Turning, he moved to the chair. Millie was right where he'd left her. Sitting on the seat, he patted his lap.

"Over you go."

25

Oh hell.

Swallowing heavily, she looked at him nervously. He gave her a calm glance back.

"Do you think you don't deserve this, baby doll?" he asked gently.

Okay, that wasn't what she expected him to say. She'd almost thought he might grab for her, force her over his lap.

Instead, he was asking what she thought. What did she think?

That you most definitely deserve a spanking. That you need it to let go of the guilt.

"I deserve it," she whispered and lay herself over his lap. She fleetingly worried about the sight she must make with her ample ass on display. Then he didn't give her a chance to think anymore. He just grabbed the bottom of her skirt and raised it up over her ass.

"Eek!" she cried out.

"Spankings are on the bare unless we're in public," he told her as he drew down her panties.

Oh hell.

His hand touched her ass and she jumped, startled even though it was just a light touch. He rubbed then pulled his hand back, giving her a sharp smack.

She let out a small cry. More in surprise than pain. Another spank to her next cheek.

Two more. Smack! Smack!

Slap! Slap!

Her breath came faster, her pulse racing as her bottom grew hot. The spanks became heavier and she let out another cry. Two more and she started kicking her feet as the pain increased.

"Daddy!"

He paused. "Are you using your safeword?"

Was she? No. While the spanking was painful, it wasn't anything she couldn't take. And she had been naughty.

"No, Daddy."

"Seven more."

Smack! Smack!

She cried out again, unable to stop herself from wriggling around.

Slap! Slap!

Oh the last few really did hurt. Her bottom was throbbing by now. And she knew she wasn't going to be comfortable sitting for a long while. But as he turned her over, and held her against his chest, careful to keep her weight off her hot bottom, she felt lighter.

The guilt was gone.

"Okay, baby doll?"

"Yeah, yeah, I am."

He rubbed his big hand up and down her back. "Why'd you get a spanking?"

She snuggled into him. Ooh, this was nice. If she got held like this every time she got a spanking she might have to earn more of them.

Bad Millie. You can't act up just to get a spanking.

"For not eating my omelet and pretending I did. And for eating candy for breakfast."

"Are you going to lie again?" His big hand squeezed one red bottom cheek.

"No, Daddy," she squeaked, raising her hips up to try to get away from his grip.

"Good. Because do it again and the punishment will be harder. Went easy on you because it was your first spanking."

Yikes. That was easy? Maybe she wouldn't act up to get another spanking then.

"Gonna go make you something else to eat while you stand in the corner." He grabbed hold of her chin, raising his face. "Take it you don't like omelets?"

She wrinkled her nose. "It was more the spinach and mushrooms in it."

"Right. My fault for not asking you what you liked in it first."

"I still should have eaten it. I was rude. I'm sorry, Daddy."

"Forgiven. How about scrambled eggs on toast? You like that?"

"No veggies?" she asked suspiciously.

"No veggies."

"Thanks, Daddy."

He kissed her gently. "You're a good girl, baby doll. And you deserve the world. Don't ever forget that."

∽

MILLIE SPENT a painful fifteen minutes in the corner. Painful because she'd had to stand still, with her skirt up over her red ass and her panties down around her ankles.

And because she couldn't talk. Oh, the horror. That was far harder than getting spanked. In fact, she'd rather have two spankings than experience corner time again.

That was for sure.

Now, though, she'd done her time, eaten the second breakfast he made her and they were back in his office with all those tempting boxes.

"I think we need to talk about the bag of counterfeit in my safe." He shifted one of the end tables by the sofa then pulled up a section of the floor to reveal a safe.

"That is so cool! What do you keep in there?"

"Some cash. Not much else." He opened it and pulled out the bag. It took up most of the room in the safe. Opening it, he examined it. "Shouldn't keep this here. Should burn it."

"Daddy, no! Dan will be so upset."

He muttered something and set it back. "Figure something out."

"Can I start opening things now? Please?"

"Go ahead, baby doll."

With an excited squeal, she started opening packages.

"Wow! Oh Daddy, look at this! It's so cool!" she yelled, ripping the packaging on the microphone. Then she moved to the karaoke machine. She oohed and aahed over the coloring pens and book. "And look at this! So cute!" She grabbed hold of a huge stuffed dinosaur. It was almost as big as she was. And she didn't remember ordering it. "So, so cute!" She dived on top of it.

Suddenly, she realized Spike wasn't saying much. Turning, she found him just watching her.

Darn it, Millie. What are you doing? You're acting like a crazy lunatic over a big, stuffed toy.

"What you gonna call that huge beast?" He nodded over at the dinosaur.

"Daddy, there's only one thing to call him."

He raised an eyebrow.

"Tiny!" She raised her arms into the air and giggled like a loon. Her giggles turned to cries of mercy as he tickled her to the ground. Mr. Fluffy got in on the act, barking and trying to pounce on her as he licked her face.

Gradually, she called for mercy, fearing she was going to pee herself.

But the huge smile didn't leave her face for a long time afterward.

26

Spike knew he was going to have to tell her about Steele's idea to find the traitor.

But right now, he liked that she was carefree. Every night, she slept in his bed, after he'd given her a bath. Then an orgasm to help her sleep. He hadn't let her return the favor yet, and he knew she was starting to wonder why.

He wasn't quite sure himself. There was something holding him back from going further.

Maybe it was because he felt like he would be betraying Jacqui.

He strolled into the living room with a bowl of popcorn in his hand. Millie was sitting at the coffee table, coloring. Well, she was kneeling not sitting because earlier today, she'd earned herself a punishment for saying something derogatory about herself. He'd given her ten with his hand, followed by five with the back of her hairbrush since this was something she continued to do.

Then she'd had to spend fifteen minutes in the corner, which he knew was pure torture for her.

The woman sure did like to chat. And she was very rarely still. He'd often catch her dancing around the house, singing loudly.

The first time he'd heard her voice . . . well, he'd been shocked. She had this big, deep voice that seemed to fill the whole house. He'd stood there frozen as she'd used the microphone he'd bought for her and belted out a song that he thought came from some cartoon movie.

Then she'd danced around the room. When she'd seen him standing there, watching her, she'd frozen, her eyes wide.

Silly girl seemed to think he'd be embarrassed by her. Everything she did was so genuine. She was an open book. Well, almost. She didn't talk much about her reason for being here. He'd heard stories about the people in her hometown. They all seemed crazy as hell. She filled the house with her chatter, normally talking to the dog since Spike spent most of his days in his office.

He'd come out to make her meals. To bathe her and put her to bed or down for a nap but otherwise, he kept some distance. Tried to convince himself that he didn't feel anything other than affection for her.

"How is the picture going?" he asked, setting the popcorn down. Tonight they were watching a movie called *Sing*. He glanced at her picture, wincing slightly. What was that?

"It's going great! What do you think of it, Daddy?"

"Hmm. Looks great."

"What color should I do this?" She pointed at some sort of scribbly mess that went along the bottom of the picture.

"Uh, black?" he suggested. He had no freaking idea since he couldn't tell what on Earth it was.

"Black? Daddy those are the flowers in the garden! You can't get black flowers!"

"You can't?" he asked.

"I don't think you can. Maybe there's black tulips. I like tulips. Okay, Daddy. I'll do some black for you."

"Movie's on soon." He sat in the chair and felt something sharp pushing into his back. Standing up, he pushed aside the cushion. "What the fuck..."

He drew out a chop bone. "Baby doll, you want to explain this?"

Millie looked up at him in surprise. Then she glanced over at that fluff ball dog of hers. Today he was dressed up like a dinosaur. "Mr. Fluffy, did you put your chop bone on Daddy's seat?"

The puppy yawned, looking completely unconcerned.

"Did you give him a chop to eat?"

"He was hungry." She gave him big, innocent eyes.

He shook his head. Damn dog was always leaving chewed up things around. But only where he sat or slept. Or in his boots. The day her toys arrived, he'd found a chewed-up sausage on his office chair.

"It's only because he loves you that he leaves you these presents."

Uh-huh.

"Come sit with me."

Leaning down, he picked her up and carried her to his large recliner.

"My Daddy, what big muscles you have." She slammed her hand over her mouth after blurting that out.

He rolled his eyes at her. She really was crazy.

And you like it.

She was so different from Jacqui... he put that thought out of his mind. Jacqui had been the love of his life. The only woman he would ever love. Maybe that's why he was okay with getting involved with Millie. She was so different that he wasn't likely to want anything more.

Jacqui had been quiet and reserved. Graceful. He usually had to prod and push her until she would tell him what was going on inside her head.

Not so with Millie. Generally, if she thought it, she said it.

He settled them both into the recliner.

"Big muscles, huh?"

"Can't believe I said that. Of course, they look even bigger when you're working out in the gym. And who knew that sweat could be so sexy."

"You've been watching me in the gym?" he asked casually. He knew she had. There were mirrors on one whole wall of the gym. He'd caught her that very first day, but he hadn't said anything.

Truth was, he kind of liked the way she watched him. Drooled over him.

"Oh crap." She smacked the palm of her hand against her forehead. He grabbed hold of her hand, pulling it back. "Umm. Maybe. Sorry?"

"You should join me next time."

"Me? Workout? With equipment? I don't think so. Last time I tried exercise; I accidentally kicked my gym instructor in the balls. I got banned from that gym for life."

He gave her an incredulous look and she just grinned. But he thought he saw a hint of something in her gaze. Hurt? Vulnerability? Whatever it was, she was trying her best to hide it.

"Let's watch *Sing*, Daddy. Trust me, you'll love this one. It's got a singing pig. Who doesn't like a singing pig?"

He had no reply to that.

But he did spend the next hour and a half watching her as she sang and laughed her way through the movie.

~

SHE YAWNED as Spike finished drying her off after her bath. He insisted on bathing her every night and she never said no. She actually liked this time the best.

Well, and the orgasm that usually came after.

But instead of helping her climb into one of her onesies, he wrapped a towel around her and picked her up. He was constantly carrying her around, usually telling her to stay put in that rough, gravelly voice of his. She knew better than to protest, though. Her bottom was still a bit tender after her introduction to the hair brush earlier today.

When they entered the guest bedroom, she stiffened. She'd slept every night since her migraine in his bed. Was he trying to tell her he didn't want her in there anymore? Did he not want her next to him? Did she snore? Talk in her sleep?

"Can hear you thinking. Whatever it is, stop," he commanded, setting her down on her feet.

"Why are we in here? Did I snore? You should just roll me onto my side if I do that. Or is it the nightmares?"

They'd become more frequent since she'd come to the city. She was wondering if it was guilt causing them.

Because she was here on a mission. And that didn't include playing out a fantasy with Spike. She hadn't asked him at all today about that Devil's Sinners.

Because you don't want to leave here. Leave him.

"Brought you in here because some more things arrived for you today." He pointed over at the bed where a number of items had been laid out. There were several rompers, one with a dinosaur and another with puppies and a third one with ruffles on the bottom.

"That is sooo cute," she exclaimed, immediately picking up the one with the ruffles. She glanced over at the panties, blushing at the thought of him buying them for her.

There was also a pale lavender dress with a layered bottom that would barely cover her ass.

Although maybe that was the point. Combined with the panties with ruffles and it would be freaking adorable.

"This one?" He pointed to the one in her hand.

She nodded and he helped her get into the romper. Apparently getting dressed on her own was a thing of the past. The romper was tighter than she would usually wear and she worried for a moment that she looked ridiculous in it.

She twisted to try and look at her ass in the short pants. "My bottom isn't sticking out is it?"

"Oh yeah. Fucking hot." His gaze was riveted on her ass and she found herself blushing.

Well, okay, maybe if he thought she looked good she should stop worrying so much. It wasn't always easy and she knew she would still feel self-conscious at times, but it helped to see the hunger in his gaze when he stared at her.

To know this sexy, gorgeous guy wanted her.

Even if he would never be hers. She had to make sure to remind herself of that so she didn't get caught up in the idea of having him for good. That would just lead to heartache.

And she couldn't afford any more of that in her life.

"Can I wear this tomorrow?" She held up the lavender dress and he gave her a nod, although she saw the way the skin at the corners of his eyes crinkled. That was about as close to a smile as he got.

She spotted another outfit. It was a pale pink leotard with a tutu attached.

"For my dancing girl," he told her.

Tears actually filled her eyes. He'd bought her an outfit to dance in? It was seriously cute. Even though she didn't think there was any way she could wear it.

"I love it, Daddy. Thank you."

"Dance for me in it."

She knew he didn't mean right now. But truth was, she wasn't sure she could be comfortable wearing it in front of him, let alone dancing in it. So instead of saying anything, she set it down and skipped over to him and kissed him on the cheek. "Daddy, you're spoiling me."

"You deserve it."

She wasn't so sure about that.

"Something else to show you." He took hold of her hand and led her to the last bedroom. She'd never been in this one.

Opening the door, he led her inside. She froze just in the doorway, looking on in shock.

"What is this?"

"This is for you." He cleared his throat. "Don't know how long you'll be stuck here."

Stuck? She didn't like the sound of that, but she pushed that thought aside as he kept going.

"Remembered how you said you liked to sew, so I got you this?"

He got her this? He'd just bought it for her? She walked closer, looking at the sewing machine reverently. It wasn't just any sewing machine; it was the best on the market. And she knew that wouldn't be a coincidence. Spike was methodical. He would have done his research and bought this one because it was the best.

And also the most expensive.

"I'll pay you for it," she blurted out.

Immediately she wished the words back as his face grew dark. "What?"

"Um, it's just I know this is really expensive. I might not be here much longer. I mean, I shouldn't stay much longer. I can't. I have things I'm supposed to do. And it cost too much money for me to use for only a few days. And I suppose you could sell it when I'm gone. But if you're gonna do that then I might as well buy it from you." She paused to take in a gasping breath. She kept her gaze from his. She wasn't feeling quite brave enough to look at him.

Then he grasped her under the chin and lifted her head, forcing her to look at him. "No."

She blinked, waiting for more.

Really, she should have known better.

"No? That's just it. No?"

"No. You are not paying for it." The words were pushed out through gritted teeth.

"But I have the money."

"No."

"But—"

He placed his hand over her mouth. "For God's sake, woman. Stop arguing. One more word about paying for it and that's thirty minutes in time-out."

Well, that didn't seem very fair. She wasn't breaking any of the rules. And she didn't think it was fair for him to pay for this on top of everything else.

She stomped her foot in frustration. Then she slid her tongue out and licked him.

"What'd I say to you about that tongue?" he drawled, removing his hand and giving her a hard, hot look.

Uh-oh.

She licked her lips. "You wouldn't let me talk."

"Talking gets you into trouble."

Darn it. She certainly couldn't argue with that. She watched him warily.

Spike suddenly took a step towards her and with a squeak, she turned and raced off, heading down the hallway. Where she thought she was going to go, she had no idea, since she'd turned in the direction of his bedroom.

27

Running from him was a bad, bad idea. Didn't she know never to run from a predator? He didn't give a shit whether she had money or not. She wasn't paying him back for a gift.

Spike strode down the hallway, making his footsteps deliberately heavy to warn her he was coming. Normally, she'd accuse him of walking like a ballerina.

Tonight, she got the hulk.

He opened the door and stood in the doorway, looking around the room for his naughty girl.

She wasn't anywhere obvious, but he knew her preferred hiding places. Walking inside the room, he shut the door behind him and stalked over to the closet. Pulling the door open, he soon discovered she wasn't in there. Climbing down so he could peer under the bed, he caught sight of a little foot. Grabbing the ankle, he gently tugged her out.

"No! No, Daddy!"

"Come out here, Millicent Margaret," he said sternly. She froze, no longer fighting him. Nothing like the power of two names to tell a Little when Daddy was being serious.

When she was out from under the bed, he picked her up and plonked her on the mattress, crouching over her. He grabbed her wrists in his hands and pulled her hands above her head.

Her breath came in sharp pants, her breasts pushing against the buttons of the romper.

"You're in big trouble, little girl."

"I didn't do nothin'."

He arched a brow. "Offering to pay for a gift? Stomping your foot in a tantrum? Running from Daddy?"

"Well, when you put it like that it doesn't sound so good. But Daddy, I was just—"

This time he didn't quiet her with his hand but with his mouth, pressing his lips to hers, he kept kissing her until she was soft and relaxed beneath him. Then he slid his lips along her jaw to her ear. He knew how much she loved that.

"You will not mention paying me again." He kissed that spot beneath her ear. "Or there's gonna be trouble. Hear me?"

"Okay, Daddy. Thank you for my gifts."

"You're welcome. I like your onesies." He kissed his way down her neck. "Especially the drop seats." He moved his mouth along her collarbone. "But these have something I like too. Can you guess what?"

SHE KNEW she was blushing as he ran his finger over her nipple. The romper still covered her but her nipple grew instantly hard. Leaning in, he licked his tongue across it and she groaned.

"Well?" he murmured. He toyed with her other nipple until her breath was coming in sharp pants, arousal flooding her.

Christ. He always got so talkative during sex. Well, not sex since they hadn't done that yet. He hadn't even had an orgasm.

Although he had promised to show her another use for that tongue if she ever licked him again.

"The snap crotch?" she guessed.

"Clever girl. Since you were naughty, you have to put your hands behind your head. No touching."

She pouted at that.

"No sulking." He tapped her lower lip.

She sighed. "Daddy, that's rather mean."

He gave her a look. "Could order you not to talk."

"No, no, let's not be too hasty. No pouting. I get it."

"Something else arrived for you today." He reached over and opened the drawer, pulling a damn anal plug.

"Got you some training plugs. This is the small one."

That was the small one? Yikes.

Next, he drew out a bottle of lube. Followed by a pair of handcuffs that had pink fluff on the inside but were made of solid steel. They could be fun.

"Time for your punishment. Put those hands behind your head."

She slowly obeyed him. "Good girl."

Would she ever become used to hearing those words from his lips? Somehow, she thought not.

"Gonna play with you but you cannot come. Understand? Come without permission and you'll spend an hour in the corner tomorrow with a butterfly vibrator on your clit and a plug up your ass."

Oh hell. Was he serious?

She studied his face. She should have known better. When did Spike ever joke around?

Leaning down, he sucked on her nipple through the cloth of her romper. She groaned, wanting to feel him without the material between them. He slid lower on the bed, lying between her legs, pressing them apart.

Then he slowly undid the snap crotch. Her breath caught; her pulse raced. She was already wet. Hell, sometimes it felt like she was always wet around him.

She couldn't help it.

He pushed the material away from her slick lips.

"Is my baby already wet for me? Hmm?"

She didn't reply. Wasn't like he couldn't see the evidence himself. He kissed along the top of her thigh then smacked his hand lightly down on her pussy, making her cry out. "Answer me."

"Yes. Yes, I'm wet."

"Good girl. Fuck, you smell so damn good." He spread her lips apart. She lay there with her hands behind her head. She wondered why he didn't use the cuffs. It was so hard to keep her hands where they were, to stop herself from reaching for him.

Maybe that was the point.

He took a long slow lick that had her groaning, his tongue flicked at her clit. Once. Twice.

God, yes.

Felt so good. So darn good.

Jeez, this was going to be even harder than she thought. How was she supposed to stop herself from coming when with every little touch nearly set her on fire?

Her breath came faster as he ran his tongue slowly around her clit then he flicked it again. Once. Twice. Circled it.

More. More.

Suddenly, he sat up and flipped her over. He pulled her romper up over her butt. What was he doing? Was he going to spank her? But he ran his tongue along one ass cheek and over the other. Then he nipped her bottom gently.

She whimpered.

"Bend your legs, on your knees," he commanded. "Keep your arms out in front of you, face pressed to the bed. No moving."

She curled her legs up, raising her ass. He ran a finger down the seam of her bottom then pulled it away. She half-expected a smack, instead she heard a squirting noise and then his finger was at her puckered entrance, slick with what had to be lube.

"Deep breath in. Now out. Good girl. That's it. Let me inside you." He slid his finger inside her. "Fuck. So tight. So hot. Do you want Daddy's cock inside your ass, baby girl?"

He was killing her. Seriously. She had never had anyone talk to her like this. Not during sex. Not even that other Daddy Dom. Or wannabe-Daddy, as Spike liked to refer to him as.

"Gonna answer me?"

"Yes," she groaned, knowing she wouldn't get away with not saying anything. She also wouldn't get away with lying.

"That's a good girl." He drove his finger in and out of her ass. Holy. Hell. Felt so good. How could that feel so hot?

He slid in a second finger, stretching her. There was a slight burn that soon morphed into something else. Something hotter.

"Please. Please."

"What is it, baby girl?"

"More. I need more."

"You want the plug?"

What she wanted was to come. But she was also curious as to what being plugged would feel like.

"Yes, please."

"Fuck, that's sexy, seeing my fingers disappear into your ass. Do you need to come, baby?"

"Yesss."

He slid his finger free from her ass then he nipped the back of her neck, her shoulder. "Too bad you were naughty and don't get to, huh?"

She groaned. He was so mean.

He moved off the bed. She concentrated on trying to bring her breathing under control, to soothe the arousal surging through her blood. But before she could calm herself much, her ass cheeks were being parted and something slick and solid was pressed against her asshole.

"Breathe in. Relax as you breathe out." As she let the breath out, the plug was pushed deep inside her. Okay, it wasn't much bigger than his fingers. But it felt so strange inside her ass. Solid. Thick.

And damn, she was turned on. She heaved in a breath, feeling like she'd run a marathon. Every nerve ending had flared to life. More, she wanted more. She whimpered, wiggling her bottom, trying to get him to touch her.

"Uh-uh-uh." He smacked his hand down on her ass cheek. "No moving."

She let out a whine. "Pretty please."

"Nope." Another smack on the other cheek.

"With sprinkles on top?"

"Definitely no." Two more smacks. She cried out.

"How about cherries and whipped cream?"

"Dreaming, baby. Get on your back, baby doll. I'm gonna go wash my hands."

She turned carefully, the plug in her ass moving around.

"All right, how about pretty please with a protein smoothie, sliced avocado and a shrimp on top?" she asked when he returned from the bathroom.

He gave her a strange look. "That's the most disgusting combination ever."

She shrugged. "Did it work? Please touch me."

"Touch you where?" There was a wicked glint in his eyes. Oh no.

"Everywhere. My pussy. My clit. My breasts. Please."

"I'll touch you."

Oh, thank goodness.

"But you still don't get to come." Grabbing her legs, he drew her down to the edge of the bed. He knelt on the floor and spread the lips of her pussy. "Now stay very still. And no coming."

Torture. It was pure torture. The things he did with his tongue . . . well, if she knew something to confess, she would have given it up in the first thirty seconds. He drove her up to the edge of orgasm again and again before pulling back.

By the time he moved away from her pussy, she was certain hours must have passed. Sweat coated her skin, her nipples were hard, her breath coming in sharp, ragged pants.

He stood and leaned over her, kissing her. The taste of her was on his tongue, but she didn't care. She needed his kiss. Craved it.

When he drew back, she whimpered and tried to reach for him.

"Uh-uh, stay where you are," he reminded her.

She put her hands back down. He stripped off his shirt. Holy shit. The man was gorgeous. He didn't have as many tattoos as she'd thought a biker might have. She studied the one down his right arm. It was an image of a woman praying and a rose. She wondered if that was for his wife.

Then he reached for his belt, undoing it and pulling off his jeans. She leaned up on one elbow so she could continue watching him. With his back turned to her, he slid down his boxers.

Holy. Crap. Was she finally going to see him naked?

He turned to her. His cock was thick and long.

Delicious.

Her heart felt like it was going to beat right out of her chest. Did he think that his cock was ever going to fit in her ass? Because she didn't think it likely.

"You look terrified."

He crossed his arms over his thick chest as he stared down at her. She licked her lips.

"No, nope, not at all. Me? Scared? Why would I be scared?"

Jesus, you doofus. Way to be sexy and worldly. You're acting like a complete dork.

He raised his eyebrows, taking her in.

"Sit at the end of the bed."

She slid down to the end of the bed then sat up. He knelt in front of her. His bed was high so they were now at about the same height. Leaning in, he took her lips in a far gentler kiss than she'd expected.

"I would never do anything to hurt you, trust me?"

She did. She really did. She didn't care that she hadn't known him that long. She wouldn't have shown him her Little if she didn't trust him.

So maybe you should tell him everything.

She wasn't sure why she was holding back. In the beginning, she hadn't wanted to talk about it with anyone. Now, she thought maybe it was because he didn't offer anything personal about himself. He kept this wall up between them. It was probably for the best. He was so protective he might insist that she forget her mission and go home.

And she couldn't do that.

"I trust you," she whispered.

The look he sent her was filled with satisfaction. An alpha male who'd gotten exactly what he wanted. And expected. Because nothing less would be acceptable.

Moving between her legs, he kissed along her inner thigh. He slid his lips closer to her pussy. Maybe she should have felt in a position of dominance. Of power. But there was no mistaking who was in charge.

It was him. Always him.

The boss.

He spread her pussy lips and buried his tongue deep inside her.

"Please, oh please. More. I need to come."

Flicking at her clit, he slid a finger deep into her pussy. She groaned. The plug in her ass just drove her arousal higher and higher. She wasn't going to be able to hold back much longer. She needed to come so badly. Just as she thought she was going to come, he drew away.

"Noo," she groaned. Why was he torturing her?

"Think you won't offer to pay me for a gift again, yes?" he said in that evil voice.

She glared up at him, her whole-body quivering with need. "Damn it."

"That your answer?" He cocked an arrogant eyebrow.

"Nooo. I won't, Daddy. Promise."

"Good." Suddenly, he stood. What was he doing? Wasn't he supposed to be giving her an orgasm? "Time to show you what happens when you stick that tongue out."

Oh crap. Her gaze went to his cock.

She licked her lips, nerves and excitement dancing inside her. "I might not be very good."

"Doll, just get your mouth around my cock."

She leaned in, wrapping her hand around the base. He was smooth but hard. She ran her tongue over the tip, jerking back slightly as he groaned.

"Wrong?"

"Fuck no. Only wrong thing is if you use too much teeth. Or stop. Got me?"

Okay then. She swirled her tongue around the head again, then took him slowly into her mouth. She ran her hand up and down the base.

"Squeeze harder, fuck yes. That's it."

Sucking on him harder, she squeezed him tighter.

"Fuck, doll. So fucking good."

Her confidence grew as she drew back and swirled her tongue around the head once more. Then she sucked him in quick, taking as much of him as she could into her mouth. She choked slightly; he was big but the groan he emitted made it worth a bit of discomfort.

She slid her hand down her stomach towards her clit. Maybe she could multi-task. Her clit was throbbing, his need was driving her own higher and higher.

"No touching yourself," he commanded.

She froze, gaping up at him. He stared down at her through half-lidded eyes.

She slid her mouth off his dick. "But that's not fair."

"Punishment, remember?"

This punishment sucked. "Can't I just have a spanking?"

"Keep sulking and you'll end up in the corner with the butterfly vibrator on your clit."

Oh, hell no. "Not sulking. See?" She gave him a wide, big smile.

He gave her a knowing look. "Get on the bed on your knees, arms out in front of you, face pressed to the mattress."

Was he taking out the plug? She got into position as he walked around the side of the bed. She turned her head to watch him sliding on a condom.

Holy. Hell. It was happening. He was finally having sex with her.

He crouched down so they were at eye-level. "Okay?"

"Yes," she squeaked then cleared her throat. Rising, he moved behind her, spreading her legs. He ran his hands down her ass then slapped one cheek. Then the other. She groaned. They weren't hard smacks. Just enough to warm her cheeks. To make her heart race.

Tugging at the plug, he slowly drew it out.

Oh hell. Oh hell.

When it was completely out, she almost begged him to put it back. She must have made some noise because he ran his hand over her bottom.

"Easy, doll. There will be lots of chances to plug you."

That sounded rather ominous. But she wasn't worried. Unless he was talking about a ginger plug. Then maybe she should be slightly worried.

She didn't see where he put the plug. Frankly, at this point, she didn't care either.

Moving in behind her, he ran a hand down her back. Almost soothingly. Then his cock nudged at her entrance.

Their groans mixed together as he entered her. "Fuck me. Wet. Hot. Fuck."

She was shocked at the feel of him. He was huge, stretching her but there was no pain. She was wet and ready for him. He slid in deep then paused.

"Doll. Feels so good."

She was incapable of speech, of anything except for the small cries that escaped her as he started to move. In and out. Slow at first. Then he built up speed until he was slamming into her.

The urge to touch herself was so strong. She knew it wouldn't take much. Just a few flicks of her finger and she'd fall over the edge. It was only his threat of making her wear a butterfly vibrator that kept her from moving.

"So fucking close."

She needed to come so bad.

He slid over her, his chest against her back, surrounding her in his warmth, his strength. His teeth grazed the outer shell of her ear. "I shouldn't let you come. Should teach you a lesson. You've made me soft."

She doubted it.

Please, please, please.

She was uncertain whether she said those words out loud or not. She clenched down around him. Needing him.

Finally, he flicked at her clit.

"You can come, doll."

Just a few short flicks of his finger and she was screaming as she squeezed his dick, coming, her entire body shaking. She barely heard his own release. Barely even felt him drawing out of her as she collapsed on the bed.

She was so relaxed. She couldn't even bring herself to roll over as he climbed off the bed. There was the sound of running water then Spike turned her onto her back. She kept her eyes shut. He could do what he wanted. She was just going to lie here.

"Legs apart," he commanded.

She spread her legs, then tensed as a warm cloth was placed over her pussy. She reached down to grab the cloth and he gave her hand a light slap.

"Leave it. I'm big. You're small. It will soothe you." He peered down at her thoughtfully. "Do you need a bath?"

She yawned. Maybe she should be embarrassed at lying there naked with a warm cloth between her legs. But for some reason, she wasn't. Perhaps because he was so matter-of-fact about it all.

"No. Tired. Sleep."

Spike gave her a searching look then nodded. "All right. If you're sore tomorrow you can have a bath."

Heat filled her cheeks at the thought. But she nodded. He removed the cloth once it had cooled then climbed into bed.

He pulled her onto his chest so she was lying on top of him, his favorite position for sleeping. And frankly, it had become her favorite too. To the point that she wondered how she was ever meant to sleep again without him surrounding her.

28

"Hi everyone!" She smiled into the laptop. Or she tried to. For some reason, she'd woken up feeling a bit melancholy. Last night had been amazing. And Spike had woken her up this morning with his tongue on her clit. But then he'd pulled back. Instead of holding her afterwards, he'd immediately gotten up to shower. Which is where he was now.

You're expecting too much. This isn't a proper relationship.

It's just that he ran so hot and cold sometimes that she couldn't keep up. He was protective to the point of being ridiculous. She wasn't to touch anything in the kitchen on her own. She couldn't run up and down the stairs. She couldn't bathe by herself. Or go far from the house.

He'd even done some research on good nutrition for vegetarians and had groceries delivered with plenty of protein alternatives for her. She'd never eaten so well in her life.

But at the same time, it felt like he kept this distance between them. He spent most of his days in the office. Sure, he came out for movies or to feed her meals and snacks. He always got up early and let out Mr. Fluffy then would bring her coffee in bed. He would ask her if she was feeling okay, and get on her case if she didn't eat right or drink enough fairy juice.

However, spending most of her days alone was wearing on her. So was the fact that she had things to do and couldn't even leave the house. She was kind of lonely. And she didn't feel like she had the right to ask him for more. Maybe he didn't want to play with her Little. Maybe all her singing and dancing around the house just annoyed him.

It's all for the best. You can't go getting attached. Or falling in love with him.

That would be a disaster.

"What's wrong?" Mr. Spain barked through the computer screen. "Why is she grimacing? Is she in pain? Did she hurt herself?"

"I'm fine, Mr. Spain," she told him patiently. "I was smiling."

"What? She was what?"

"She was smiling, you old fart," Mrs. Spain said.

"What? Why do I care if she's going to Walmart?"

Millie shook her head with a real smile this time.

"How are you, dear?" Mrs. Larsen asked. "Are you still staying with that boy?"

Mrs. Larsen considered anyone under the age of sixty to be a boy.

"Yes. I'm still here."

"What's wrong? Are you unhappy there?" Reverend Pat asked. "Has he done something to you?"

"Who did something to our eagle?" Andrey asked in his big booming accented voice.

"Eagle?" He'd never called her that before.

"Ya. Others say dove, but why would you wish to be a dove when you could be an eagle?"

Okay, she wasn't in the mood to explain that one.

"I'm fine. No one has done anything to me. I'm just impatient and cranky from sitting around and doing nothing."

Which wasn't a lie. She'd never been good at waiting around. And it felt like nothing was happening, even though Spike had explained that he had people working on finding Corey, the Devil's Sinners' jerk.

"What's going on with all of you?"

She heard the shower turn off as Mrs. Spain started talking about her garden and how the rabbits had gotten into her carrots.

Suddenly, her voice dried up and her mouth dropped open. "Mrs. Spain? Are you all right?" Was she having a seizure? Drool actually appeared in the corner of her mouth. Was she having a stroke?

"Mrs. Spain?"

"Is that your man, Millie?" Mrs. Larsen said loudly.

She turned to look over her shoulder, finding Spike there. His back was to them, his towel hanging precariously around his hips as he grabbed a T-shirt from his drawers.

"Umm. That's Spike." He wasn't her man. But she didn't want to get into that with her friends.

"Well, hello there, handsome," Mrs. Spain practically purred.

"Mrs. Spain," she managed to splutter out.

Spike turned and gave her a curious look.

"Um, these are some of my friends from back home. This is Spike, who I'm staying with." *And fucking. And who is my temporary Daddy. But there's no real emotion between us. Well, that's not true there is from me to him just not vice versa. Because he still loves his dead wife and how can I compete with that?*

News flash. I can't.

Spike gave everyone a wave. "You okay?" he asked her.

She nodded woodenly and he walked into the bathroom again, presumably to get dressed where he wouldn't be ogled.

"Who was that?" Mr. Spain demanded.

"Millie's man," Mrs. Spain replied.

"The milkman? Why is the milkman in Millie's bedroom?"

Millie started giggling as everyone tried to correct the deaf older man. Even Mr. Fluffy started barking as though to add his two cents worth.

Okay, so maybe Spike would never love her. Or want anything more from her than what they now had. But she did have people who loved her.

And she should be grateful for that.

~

"PLEASE, pretty please with kale and chia seeds on top."

"Kale and chia seeds?"

Standing on the other side of his desk with her hands in the prayer position, she batted her eyelashes at him.

He should send her away. After all, begging didn't work with him. He was immune to it.

Right. Sure you are, idiot.

When he'd first insisted on bringing her home, he'd known he was making an idiotic move. He'd told himself that he could keep her safe without caring about her.

Yeah. That had worked.

All too soon, she'd started working her way under his skin. He had to keep reminding himself that this wasn't a forever thing. He'd been keeping as much distance as he could from her physically. But he knew that hurt her. He'd seen the flashes of pain in her eyes when he'd brushed off her attempts to pull him into one of her games.

The house was filled with laughter and sunshine again. He should hate it. After all, she was bringing out feelings in him. Things he didn't want. He liked his lonely, dark existence.

It was his punishment for his failings.

So yeah, he should tell her no. Send her away so he could hide in his study and pretend that he didn't long to play with her. To watch her as she danced and sang. To wince as she attempted to play the damn keyboard he'd bought her. The woman sang like a dream. But she couldn't play the keyboard for shit.

"Too dangerous," he told her shortly. "Order it online."

He knew his words were too harsh when she winced. "Okay." Her shoulders slumped and she turned away.

Stay strong. Stay strong.

Fuck. Even that damn dog gave him a reproachful look. Great, he was likely to end up with something disgusting in his shoes later or under his pillow or between the sheets on his side of the bed.

Stay strong.

Fuck it.

"Wait," he said on a sigh. "We'll go."

She half-turned. She shook her head. "No, it's fine. I'm sorry. I should never have asked. I'm gonna take Mr. Fluffy to play outside for a while, okay?"

"Doll, come here."

She shook her head.

Oh, being stubborn was she?

"Gonna count to five, and if your cute butt isn't over here in that time then it's gonna be a cute red butt."

Her eyes narrowed and he could tell she was thinking about defying him.

"One."

She didn't move.

"Two."

Nothing.

"Did I mention you'll be standing in the corner with your butt on display for ten minutes after? Th—"

Before he even got the number out, she was flying across the room and flinging herself into his lap. She placed her hand over his mouth.

"I'm here. I'm here."

He carefully removed her hand. "Here's what's happening. No arguments. I'll take you to the store but you'll follow the rules."

"What rules?" she asked suspiciously.

"You do exactly as I say when I say."

"Well, that sure covers a lot of ground," she muttered.

He gave her a stern look.

"Okay, but are you sure? Because I don't want you to think you have to take me. I'll order the material online and just wait."

He placed a finger against her lips. "Hush."

She pretended to zip her mouth and throw away the key. Right. If only he believed that.

"You won't be out of my sight. At all."

"What if I have to pee?"

"Pee before we leave."

"But what if I still have to go? I have a rebellious bladder."

A rebellious bladder?

"It always needs to go whenever I tell it that it can't."

Dear. Lord.

"Then we'll be going in the family bathroom."

Her eyes widened. "I'll tell it to behave."

He nodded. "We go to one store. No more than an hour. No complaints."

"Sir, yes, sir."

He set her on her feet with a sharp smack to her bottom for her smart mouth.

"Go upstairs. Walk," he warned knowing her penchant for rushing everywhere and getting hurt. "Change your clothes into something less noticeable."

She stiffened.

Fuck. He realized too late that he'd likely insulted her. Today, she was wearing a pretty blue dress with white polka dots that he knew she had made herself. She looked cute as fuck.

And you just told her to get out of it.

"I didn't—"

"Okay," she said quietly. "What would you like me to wear?"

He sighed. "Listen to me. I didn't mean to insult you, doll. Think you look cute in that dress. I love all your outfits. But if we're going out, I don't want to draw attention."

"I highly doubt that any of the Devil's Sinners are going to be shopping at the fabric store," she pointed out.

He just gave her a look. She sent him a salute.

Brat.

29

It kind of hurt. She wouldn't lie.

How often had she been told to be less? To be less exuberant? To make herself smaller by dressing down, by being quieter, by keeping her mouth shut?

She hadn't expected it from him.

Stop being silly, Millie. He didn't mean it like that. This is because of safety. She gave herself a pep talk as she climbed into the only dark, boring clothes she owned. Which was a pair of black yoga pants and a long T-shirt. She grabbed one of Spike's hoodies, which she swam in but she didn't have anything suitable.

Taking a deep breath, she let it out slowly, trying to push away the pain. She knew he hadn't meant to hurt her. Had seen the regret in his face. Still, she should try to keep things low-key while she was out.

She didn't want to embarrass him.

Forcing a big smile on her face, she walked out of the bedroom and down the stairs.

"I'm ready, Daddy!" she said.

Oh. He probably didn't want her calling him that in public. Spike. Spike. Spike.

She grabbed her shoes and huge handbag from the closet.

"Mr. Fluffy, come on! We're going for a ride."

She set her handbag down to put on her shoes. She hopped around on one foot as she drew the left one on. Then she tried to do the same with the other foot, only she jumped on top of her loose laces and nearly went flying forward headfirst.

"Little girl, what are you doing?" Spike growled at her, grabbing her by the shoulders and steadying her.

"Putting on my shoes."

He grumbled something under his breath as he crouched down in front of her and took hold of her shoe. "Shoulders."

She held onto his shoulders as he put the shoe on and did up both of the laces. Then he stood and turned her toward the internal garage door. A slap on her ass got her moving.

"Hey!" she protested, rubbing at the sore spot.

"Next time, ask for help."

She strode into the garage, glancing at his big, black truck before her eyes spied a gorgeous looking motorcycle.

"Ooh, can we take that?"

Spike looked over to the bike then shook his head. "Nope."

"Why not? Oh, because there's nowhere to put the shopping? Do you have a backpack? I could wear it?"

He shook his head. "Got no gear for you."

That was sad. "It's so pretty."

"Doll, my bike is not pretty." He gave her an offended look. Whoops.

Note to self, don't insult the big, bad biker's bike by calling it pretty.

"But it's so shiny. Can I touch?" She walked closer to run her finger lightly along it.

Shiny.

Spike just grunted and she looked over to see him holding

open the passenger door. She supposed it was too wasteful to buy some motorcycle gear just to go for a ride. And he didn't seem too thrilled at the idea of taking her anyway.

She walked over to his badass truck. This thing seemed even bigger than it had the other day. Big hands grasped hold of her waist, lifting her into the air.

Seriously. Those daily gym workouts? Really working out.

She put Mr. Fluffy into the back seat. Spike set her into the seat then grabbed the seat belt and pulled it over her. She could barely resist bouncing around in excitement.

"This is so fun! I wonder what sort of material I should get. Is there anything you need? I wonder if Mr. Fluffy would like a new outfit?"

Today the puppy was dressed in a glittery red shirt. She didn't take offense when Spike didn't answer. She took over the radio, turning it to a station where she knew most of the songs and started singing along as he drove. Soon they reached an outdoor mall with a large fabric store. She was so eager that she had her belt off as soon as they entered the parking lot.

"Belt!" he barked.

"But we're in the parking lot."

"Belt."

With a sigh, she did as ordered. He parked out front and she undid her belt. Then she turned to grab Mr. Fluffy, putting him in her handbag. Gosh, when had he gotten so heavy? She was going to need a bigger bag soon.

Spike came around and opened her door. He lifted her down and took her hand, closing the door and beeping the locks.

He gave her ass a sharp slap. "Don't ever take your belt off unless we're stopped, understand?"

"Sorry," she said quietly.

Smiling, she led the way into the shop. Spike kept his gaze moving, never lingering on one thing.

"Oh, look at this one! So pretty!" She gathered up different pieces of material. "Hmm how much to get? What do you think of this one?"

Spike didn't answer. She shrugged and kept chattering to herself as she strolled around the shop. Gradually, she had too much to hold. Stuff kept slipping out of her arms.

"I think I should have gotten a cart."

He took most of it off her. "Do you need anything else?"

She glanced over at him. He was tense, his eyes continuing to search for any threats. Was he really that worried about safety?

Likely he's just bored. This isn't exactly exciting stuff for most people. And she'd been bouncing around the shop like a kid in a candy store. She was probably annoying him.

"No. I'm good. Let's go."

Fuck it.

What had he said? But before he could work out how to retract his statement, to make things better, she was turning towards the counter.

She'd seemed so happy, dancing around from place to place and now she'd shut down. He knew he should be happy they were leaving but he couldn't help but feel like he'd stomped on something precious.

And broken it.

Unsure what to say to fix things, to put that light of happiness back in her eyes, he was quiet as he drove them home. When they arrived, he carried everything up to her room where the sewing machine was. They'd stopped at a drive through to eat and she'd chosen a salad.

That concerned him too. Since when did she like salads?

You've done something. Fix it.

"Want to watch a movie?" She loved watching movies and

eating popcorn. And he had to admit, he looked forward to their daily movie together.

"No, thanks. Think I'll organize all of this."

"Want something to eat?"

She gave him a quizzical look. "We just ate."

Yeah. But she hadn't eaten much of it.

"Dessert? Make you a sundae."

"Are you okay, Spike?"

He grunted. He wasn't used to hearing her call him Spike. It was always Daddy. She'd called him Spike a few times while they were out today and he'd almost not answered her. He'd figured it was because they were in public. But they were home now.

And he did not like it.

"Daddy," he growled.

Her eyes widened. *Okay, calm down, man.*

"Are you okay, Daddy?"

He let out a satisfied grunt. "I'm fine. Gonna be in my study."

∾

MILLIE HUMMED HAPPILY as she sewed a skirt for her Little. It was layered and would end about mid-thigh, so not something she'd wear in public. Ever since Spike took her to the store yesterday, she'd been sewing up a storm.

A knock on the door startled her and she glanced over as Spike came in. He sat on the bed, watching her at the table. "That looks good."

"Thanks." She smiled happily.

"You really enjoy this."

"I do. I'd love to do this as a job. I mean, I enjoyed my work at the library before I got laid off, but this really makes me happy."

"You should do it."

She shrugged shyly. "Not sure anyone would want to buy my stuff."

"Don't know until you try. I could give you the capital to start up a business."

She stared at him, shocked. He looked a bit surprised himself.

"Oh, thank you. But that's okay. It's really just a hobby. And I have some money set aside anyway, if I need it."

He looked like he wanted to ask her something then he seemed to think better of it. "Just got off the phone with Steele. He wants to know if you'd come to Pinkies tonight, see if you could spot the traitor."

"Oh, is he going to have some of his men there?"

"Apparently a few of them are drinking there tonight."

It could be a good opportunity. Plus, she really wanted to have a chat with Damon about what was happening with Luther. And Corey.

Spike scowled. "Don't like you leaving the house."

"I'll be fine. I need to do this. I need to find this guy for Damon. Then he can find out who he's working for. And maybe then he can focus on Luther. And nobody can find the Devil's Sinners asshole. He's likely left the city. I'll stay with you the whole night, I promise. I'll do everything you say. But please, Spike. I need to get back to my life. And this is a step towards that. I can't hide here forever."

He studied her for a long moment then he grunted. "Fine, we'll do this. But you will do exactly as I say when I say it."

"Pinky promise."

30

Irritation filled him as he turned his truck down the street leading to Pinkies. He had a bad feeling about tonight.

But how long could he keep her with him? Nobody had found asswipe, Corey. It looked like he'd left the city. Not to mention that the longer Millie stayed with him, the harder he was finding it to keep some distance between them. And he badly needed that distance.

So they were here. Against his better judgment.

This was better for her too, because he couldn't give her anything more than he was. Not when his heart still belonged to his dead wife.

Right?

As he pulled into the parking lot at Pinkies, she undid her belt. He hadn't even come to a stop before her door was open and she was jumping out, her dog in one hand, bag over her shoulder.

His heart nearly leaped into his throat. Quickly, he turned off the truck and grabbing the keys, climbed out. He beeped the locks as he strode over to where she was nearly at the door. Reaching out, he took hold of her hand, halting her.

"What was that?"

"What?" She gave him a surprised look.

"You just jumped out of a moving truck."

"It wasn't moving."

"It damn well was. And you're in trouble."

Mr. Fluffy growled up at him.

"Trouble?"

"Yes. Trouble. You're getting a spanking."

He kept hold of her hand as he led her through the front door, barely acknowledging the bouncer. He kept his gaze roaming the room, ever watchful for danger as they walked towards the door to Steele's private rooms.

The guy guarding it merely opened the door and stepped to one side. He wondered what happened to Jerry, the guy who'd been knocked out while he was supposed to be watching Corey. Steele didn't tolerate mistakes.

Upstairs, Steele was standing at the window looking out while Grady was working on a laptop at the table.

"Spike, Miss Millie," Steele greeted them.

"Um, hi," Millie said as they walked past.

"Need your bedroom," Spike told him, taking the dog from her and handing him over to Grady, who looked shocked to find himself with an arm full of dog.

"Really?" Steele grinned like a lunatic.

"Spike!" she protested as drew her into the bedroom.

He stopped and turned to her, his hands on his hips. Maybe he was overreacting. She hadn't gotten hurt. Which was surprising, considering how often the damn woman stubbed her toe. But he also wanted her to know that taking risks, even small risks, wasn't acceptable.

"What are you doing? You can't spank me!" she protested, her cheeks red.

"Am I your Dom?"

"Temporarily."

That word bit deeper than he'd expected.

"Am I your Dom?" he repeated.

"Yes."

"Yes, Sir or Yes, Daddy."

"Yes, Daddy."

Okay, that soothed some of the rough edges.

"Did we agree that I'm in charge of your safety?"

She bit her lip, looking worried. "Yes, Daddy. But I wasn't in danger—"

"I could have sped up. You could have tripped and fallen under the tires." Okay, it was unlikely he'd speed up while parking or that she would fall beneath the tires, but you never knew.

"I've done it heaps of times before."

He grimaced at the thought, feeling ill. "Don't care. You don't put yourself at risk under my watch and expect to get away with it."

Chagrin filled her face. "Do you really have to spank me here? Couldn't we wait until we go home?"

"You risked your safety, so no it can't wait. Stand at the end of the bed, bend over and place your forearms on the mattress.

"But Damon and Grady will hear!"

"This room is soundproofed. They'll just think we're having sex."

"Oh God, that's almost worse!"

He raised an eyebrow at that. She was blushing bright red. He twirled his finger in the air.

Trepidation filled her face as she turned and bent over in position. He raised her skirt then took a moment to take her in. She was wearing the same red dress she'd worn when she'd first approached him in the parking lot at Reaper's. Her panties, though, were a pair that he'd bought her. They were pink with ruffles.

He turned the lock on the door, not that he thought anyone would come in, but to make her feel better. Then he slid her panties down over her ass.

Standing to the side, he rubbed her bottom. Then he laid a smack on one cheek. "From now on, you are not allowed to undo your own seat belt without permission.

Smack! Smack!

She let out a small groan.

Smack! Smack!

"Tomorrow you are also going to write a hundred times, *I will not jump from a moving car*."

Smack! Smack!

He rubbed her ass then decided to move lower, to her thighs. He wished he had a paddle or her hairbrush.

Slap! Slap!

He gave her thighs two hard smacks then he sat on the bed and pulled her onto his lap. She was sniffling but not crying. Rubbing her back, he kissed the top of her head.

Tilting up her chin, he kissed her. "Don't do that again. Understand? I don't want anything bad happening to you."

"Why?"

"What?"

"I mean, I guess I don't understand why you care so much. We're not . . I'll be leaving soon."

Fuck. He didn't like the idea of that. "But while you're here, you're mine to care for. To look after. And I take that seriously. You're far too precious to put yourself at risk like that, understand me?"

"Yes, Daddy."

"Good girl. Let's get this done and then we can go home."

"I can't go out there." She looked appalled as she gaped up at him. "Isn't there like a back door we can sneak out of and go home?"

"Don't you want to find Steele's rat?"

"They think we had sex." Her face was as bright as a tomato.

"Well, I can tell them that I spanked you if you want."

"No," she shouted. "No, I don't want you to do that."

"Don't worry. You're not the first woman to have sex in here or get spanked, for that matter."

She groaned and hid her face against his chest. "I have to go out there."

"Yep."

"I'm gonna be bright red with embarrassment."

"Yep." She already was.

"I really would appreciate that hole to open and swallow me right now."

"Afraid that's not happening, doll." He stood and set her on her feet. "Come on. Won't be so bad."

∽

HE WAS RIGHT.

It wasn't so bad.

It was worse.

Damon had run his gaze over her, studying her then he'd turned to Spike. "See you went easy on her."

Spike had just raised an eyebrow while she'd hidden behind him. She'd spotted Mr. Fluffy sleeping in a corner of the sofa.

"Josh told me she jumped out of your truck while it was still moving. Said you had a face like thunder and he figured your woman wouldn't be sitting for a week."

Holy crap.

Who was Josh? The bouncer? This was so embarrassing.

Spike grunted.

Grady walked over and took hold of her chin, inspecting her face. "She didn't even cry. You're losing your touch."

Spike slapped his hand away. "Don't touch. Mine."

Her heart raced at the possessiveness in his voice even as she cautioned herself to keep her heart safe.

Oh, who was she kidding?

Her heart was already involved. She was going to be a mess when this was all over and she had to leave him. There was no way around it.

Grady gave Spike a strange look that she couldn't interrupt. "Water, dear? Or a daiquiri?"

"A daiquiri please."

"Virgin?"

"Yes."

Spike led her over to where Damon was standing by the windows. "My men are starting to trickle in. I wanted you here first. Most of them are here tonight celebrating. See if you can spot the traitor."

She nodded, still feeling embarrassed but, grateful to have something to focus on.

"Spike, talk to you a moment?" Damon asked.

Spike squeezed her hand then walked away. Grady stepped up next to her with her drink in hand. She took a big gulp.

"Don't be embarrassed, love. I bet you look gorgeous with a red bottom."

"Grady!" she spluttered.

"Millie?" Spike asked sharply from across the room.

She turned and waved him off then she gave Grady a quelling look. He just smiled, looking pleased with himself.

"So protective, isn't he? I'm glad he's taken an interest in another sub. Never thought I'd see him this way again after Jacqui's death."

"This is just a temporary arrangement between us. While I'm

having to stay with him. Then we'll go our separate ways." She didn't want him to think this was anything more.

Grady studied her. "And is that what you want?"

"Doesn't matter what I want. It is what it is."

Sympathy filled his face. The last thing she wanted was his pity.

"We live in two different states. And we're very different people. It would never work."

"Anything can work if you want it badly enough," he told her.

But Spike didn't want it.

"Don't lose hope, my dear. I think he'll pull his head out of his ass eventually. Now, do you see our traitor?"

She let out a breath of frustration. "Not yet."

※

SPIKE KEPT his gaze on Millie as Steele spoke to him.

". . . and then I murdered him in cold blood and beheaded him, putting his head on a spike."

"What?" Spike frowned and turned to him.

"Oh, so you were listening? I thought you had tuned me out completely."

"What do you want?" Spike asked, irritably.

"She's beautiful. I don't blame you for not being able to take your eyes off her. She reminds me of Jacqui in some ways."

"She's nothing like Jacqui."

"Not in looks or temperament perhaps. But there's something about her . . . maybe that's why I didn't try harder to get her to come home with me. Because there's something that reminds me of Jacqui."

Jacqui had been slight, but feisty. Strong, but somewhat broken inside. She'd been everything to him.

"She's not a replacement of Jacqui. What's between Millie and me is temporary."

"Does she know that?"

"She does."

"Hmm, because the way she looks at you . . ."

"What do you want to talk about?" he asked abruptly.

Damon studied him closely. "You're not betraying Jacqui's memory by falling in love with someone else. She wouldn't want you to be alone, you know."

Spike scoffed. "Jesus, if that's what you drew me over here to talk about then let me put your mind at ease. I don't love her. I never will. I still love my wife."

Suddenly, he realized that his words were too loud. He glanced over to see Grady glaring at him with anger and reproach in his eyes. He forced himself to look at Millie. A flash of pain flooded her face before it was gone, hidden behind a cool mask he'd never seen her wear before.

And one he really didn't like.

"Millie . . ." he started with no idea what to say.

A knock on the door interrupted them.

Grady walked over to open the door, still scowling at Spike.

He got it. He'd fucked up. He tried to catch her gaze but she wouldn't even look at him. Shit.

Mitchell, who managed Pinkies, stood on the other side. He was an older man. Slim-built and dressed in a suit. But he ran Pinkies like a well-oiled machine. Normally. Spike was surprised that asshole from the Devil's Sinners had gotten past Mitchell's bouncers.

"Mitchell, come in," Grady invited.

"Sorry to interrupt," he said. "Damon, wonder if I could borrow you for a moment."

"Sure. Mitchell, this is Millie. She's the one who stepped in to help Tawny the other night when that asshole tried to take her."

Mitchell held out a hand to Millie who shook it with a small smile. "So nice to meet you. I apologize for all that unpleasantness. I still feel guilty that Devil's Sinners bastard somehow snuck his way in here. He used the back entrance. Unfortunately, the door hadn't been shut properly. I'd love to have a few minutes with him."

"We'll find him," Steele said. "But you'll have to wait until Spike's had his turn. There might not be much left."

Damn right there wouldn't be.

Mitchell's gaze turned to Mr. Fluffy. "Is that a puppy?"

"Oh yes, that's Mr. Fluffy. I'm sorry if he's not allowed in here. He gets separation anxiety if left alone."

Mitchell blinked at her. "Of course. That's fine. What kind of puppy is he?"

"I'm not sure, I found him in an alleyway. We have to take him to a vet."

Mitchell walked over and sat next to Mr. Fluffy, who ignored him. He ran a finger over his head, patting him. "Very cute. Are you going to keep him? I'd gladly take him off your hands. He reminds me of the dog I had as a child."

"Oh, I'm sorry. Yes, I am going to keep him. I'm far too attached to him now."

Spike could tell she felt bad for Mitchell.

"Maybe you could go to the pound and find another one?"

"Maybe," he replied, standing.

"Let's go," Damon said.

Damon left with Mitchell and Spike watched as Millie turned to look out the window, her shoulders tense.

Fucking hell. How did he fix this?

Millie stared out the window, trying to keep her composure. She was all too aware that Spike was only a few feet away.

I don't love her. I never will.

God. That hurt. So much.

"Millie, we need to talk," Spike said.

She tensed. Talk about what?

Pull yourself together.

I don't love her and I never will.

She'd known going into this that it wasn't going to turn into a great love story. He'd made that clear. So why was she so hurt?

His words had clawed their way deep. Tearing holes in her heart.

Because you already fell in love with him, that's why. Idiot.

She watched as one guy stood up from the table, his phone in his hand, texting. She frowned. There was something familiar about him.

"Millie? Are you all right?" Grady asked.

No. Of course she wasn't.

"I'll take care of her," Spike snapped, coming up to stand on her other side.

Right. Breaking her heart was taking care of her really well.

Not fair, Millie.

She took a deep breath in, studying the guy. "That guy there, the one standing . . . he kind of looks familiar."

Both men tensed.

"You think he could be the guy from the alleyway the other night?" Grady asked, bringing out his phone.

"Maybe. I need to see his face, can we go down there?"

"No," Spike said abruptly.

She let out a sigh. "He never saw me."

"She'll be perfectly safe," Grady added. "This place is filled with Steele's guys. No way he could get to her, even if he did know who she was. You can wait up here."

"No fucking way." Spike took hold of her hand. He grabbed Mr. Fluffy, holding him in his other arm. She didn't pull away, despite knowing she probably should. She should put some distance between them, like he'd been doing all this time.

Foolish her, letting her heart get involved.

But she let him lead her out of the room and down the stairs. Grady followed. They walked into the room and towards the bar. She was sandwiched between the two men.

As they stood at the bar, watching. The man turned and headed towards them.

"It's him," she said hoarsely. She didn't know why but her heart started racing. Hard. He didn't know who she was. There was no reason to be afraid.

His gaze slid over her, no hint of recognition on his face. He gave a nod to Grady, who nodded back.

"Damon is going to be pissed," Grady said as the man settled in at the other end of the bar. They slowly strolled away to a quieter area. "His name is Regan Jones. He's been with us for two years." Grady drew out his phone and tapped off a message.

"That could mean Fergus planted him if he's working for the Bartolli's," Spike said, his gaze roaming the room.

Grady made a sound of agreement. "I've got to go speak to Steele."

"I'm taking Millie home."

Grady narrowed his gaze at him. "Steele will want to speak to her."

"I still need to talk to Damon about Luther," she whispered. She wanted to make sure that Steele didn't forget his promise to take care of him.

"Another night," Spike said. "I have a bad feeling. Let's go."

She gave Spike an exasperated look. To her shock, Grady drew her close.

"He didn't mean what he said," he whispered to her. "He's scared."

Spike, scared? Yeah, right.

Spike pulled her away from Grady, glaring at the other man as he slid his arm around her waist. Then without a word to Grady, he led her away.

"That was rude," she told him.

He just grunted.

"We should have said goodbye to Damon."

He was silent as he led them outside. They were nearly at his truck, when someone called out his name from the club. Turning, they both saw Damon standing there.

"Spike! Talk to you a minute?"

Sighing, he turned to her. She shivered slightly. "If you give me the keys, I'll hop in."

He just gave her a look and beeped the truck open. He walked over to open the door, but she paused, turning to give Damon a wave good night.

As she turned, the sound of tires squealing caught her attention.

She looked over as a car screeched down the street. Mr. Fluffy started barking.

"Spike!" Damon roared.

"Millie!" Spike yelled.

It felt like everything was in slow motion. Steele raced towards her, a look of horror and fear on his face.

There was a rat-a-tat noise then something lodged in her shoulder. Pain screamed through her as something heavy slammed into her, pushing her to the ground.

She screamed. Or she thought she did. She wasn't sure. There was a lot of noise. The sound of her heartbeat drowned everything else out. Her arm was burning, like her skin was being flayed straight from her.

Struggling for breath, she lay on the ground, wondering what was lying on top of her. *Too heavy. Get off.*

Did she say the words or just imagine them?

She tried to wiggle free but whatever it was held her tighter.

Black circles appeared in her vision.

Oh shit. Was she getting a migraine?

Then all other thoughts fled from her mind as darkness overtook her.

31

What was that beeping noise?

It was so annoying.

"Sorry, princess," a male voice said to her. "But the beeping is a good thing. It tells us you're alive."

She tried to open her eyes, but it was all blurry. The only thing she could see was a giant rabbit standing over her.

"Go away, rabbit. Shoo."

There was silence.

"Rabbit, huh?" he asked, sounding amused. "First time I've been called a rabbit."

"Shh. I'm sleeping."

"Sorry, princess, please, go back to sleep."

"I would if you'd stop with all your jibber-jabber."

"I don't think rabbits jibber-jabber," the rabbit replied.

She drifted off.

~

MILLIE FORCED her way through the fog.

Help me, Millie. Help me.

"I'm so sorry."

"What do you have to be sorry for, princess? Calling me a rabbit? I will accept bribes of beer and pot roast as an apology."

She glared up at the giant rabbit. So annoying. "Are you still here? Shoo rabbit. Before Mr. Spain shoots you."

"And why would he shoot me?"

"For getting into Mrs. Spain's garden." How did he not know this? "Silly rabbit."

"Why is she talking like this?" a gravelly voice asked, one that sent a shiver along her skin.

"It's the drugs. They affect people differently," the rabbit said soothingly.

"Silly rabbit, thinks he's a doctor." She turned to the gravelly voice. "Shoot him."

"So bloodthirsty," the rabbit said. "I thought you said she likes animals."

~

MILLIE WOKE up with a dry mouth and a need to move. Her entire body ached. She tried to sit up. She cried out in pain as she put weight on her arm. What the hell?

"What are you doing?" a deep voice barked. Then gentle hands eased her back onto the bed. "Easy, baby. Lie still."

"W-what's going on?" She blinked to clear her vision and stared up into Spike's concerned face. "You look terrible."

He had dark marks under his eyes. There was a few days growth on his cheeks and his clothes were rumpled. Glancing around the strange room, worry flooded her.

"This isn't your bedroom. Where are we?"

"Hospital."

"Hospital? Why are we in the hospital? Did I have a bad migraine?"

"Your migraines often get that bad?"

"It's happened a few times," she prevaricated. "What happened? Why can't I move my arm? The last thing I remember . . ." she trailed off. "Leaving Pinkies and someone came screaming up in a black car . . ."

Her heart started to race and she whimpered.

"Easy, baby. You're getting too stressed."

He placed his hand on hers. Why was she here? All she remembered was pain in her arm, then she was slammed to the ground . . . had she hurt herself?

The door to her room opened and an older woman wearing scrubs stepped in. A nurse.

"Hi, what's going on in here?" She gave Spike a look of disapproval as she walked over to Millie's other side. "It's past visiting hours, Mr. Lochlin."

"And like every other night, I'm not leaving," Spike replied.

Every other night? How long had she been here?

The nurse huffed as she grabbed a compression cuff and put it on Millie's arm to take her blood pressure.

"Being friends with Doctor Anderson might get you special privileges," the nurse stated coldly. "But if your presence is upsetting my patient, then you will have to leave."

She had no clue who Doctor Anderson was. But she did know she didn't want Spike to go.

"I want Spike to stay," she blurted out.

The nurse gave her a look filled with sympathy. "Are you sure, dear? Your blood pressure is high. You were shot. You lost quite a lot of blood and your body went into shock. You need peace and quiet to heal. Not to be upset." The nurse sent Spike a withering look.

She'd been shot? Holy shit.

"Shot?"

"In the shoulder. You had surgery to repair it and the doctor will go through everything tomorrow. Drive-by shooting apparently."

"The people in the black car?" she asked Spike who just gave a nod. She guessed he didn't want to say anything with the nurse here.

"I want him to stay. Please."

"Fine. He can stay tonight. But after that he'll have to stick to visiting hours."

Spike made a low, grumbling noise and she thought it might be best to get the nurse out of his sight.

"Can I have a drink?"

"Certainly." The nurse grabbed a clear jug from the table by the bed and poured some water into a glass with a straw.

She wrinkled her nose as the nurse held the straw up to her mouth. Water. Yuck.

"She hates that water. I have some for her here." Spike grabbed a bottle from the bedside drawers. The nurse gave him a disgusted look. The water was pale pink.

Spike just glared back at the nurse then gently pushed away the straw before holding the bottle up to Millie's mouth. She took a few grateful gulps.

The nurse huffed. "I'll leave you to sleep. Here is the button for more medication if you need it. Don't worry, it won't give you more than you're allowed. This here is the buzzer to call me. I'll be on until morning."

"How long do I have to stay here?" she asked.

"You'll need to discuss that with the doctor. You were very lucky that the bullet only entered your shoulder, too much lower and it could have gotten your heart. Get some rest."

Once they were alone, Millie turned to look at Spike.

"Who the hell shot me?"

. . .

Fuck.

Spike ran his hand over his face. He'd barely slept in days. Just nodded off now and then. He'd only slipped into the bathroom attached to her private room for a quick shower when Hack was able to sit with her. Ink had arranged round-the-clock security for her, but he didn't trust anyone but those in his close circle. Spike was just grateful Hack did some work in the hospital and was able to get himself assigned as her doctor.

Christ, how was he ever going to let her out of his sight again?

He couldn't.

Over and over, it kept playing in his mind. The car screeching around the corner. Something sticking out the window.

Steele's horrified shout.

The realization that they were being shot at.

Diving for Millie and tackling her to the ground.

Too. Fucking. Late.

He'd nearly lost her. Like Jacqui. He couldn't do this. Could he? Fuck. This is why he was supposed to stop himself from feeling anything.

But he'd never expected her to nearly die.

"Spike? Are you all right? Spike?"

His breath came in sharp, shallow pants. The world spun around him.

Fuck. Get it under control, man.

"Spike! I'll call the nurse."

"No!" he said sharply. "No. I'm fine." He forced his gaze back to hers. Tears were dripping down her cheeks and he quickly moved closer to her, wiping them away. "What's wrong? Are you hurting? Where is it sore? Press the button."

He picked up the pain relief button, giving it to her.

"It's not that. It's you. Are you sure you're okay? You look so upset."

Shit. Fuck. He was supposed to be keeping her calm and here he was scaring the shit out of her. He cupped her face between his hands. "I'm fine, baby doll. I'm all right. Just worried as fuck about you."

"What happened? Who shot me? Was it a random drive-by?"

He sighed. "It was the Devil's Sinners."

"What?"

"After you were shot, I stayed with you. Waiting for the ambulance." And trying hard not to lose it. Even though he'd wanted to roar in pain, thinking she was going to die. "Some of Steele's guys gave chase, but it was too late. They couldn't catch up to them."

"What makes you think it was the Devil's Sinners then?"

"Steele caught a look at the shooter. It was that asshole, Corey."

"Oh God. He tried to kill me? Really?"

"I should never have let you go to Pinkies that night. I should have kept you home."

Where she would've been fucking safe. As soon as she was well enough to leave the hospital, he was taking her home and keeping her there.

Forever.

Shit. Fuck.

"It's not your fault. You couldn't have known." She frowned. "How did he know that I was there or was it all just a coincidence?"

"Good question," Spike said. "Dunno. But not sure I believe in coincidences."

She swallowed heavily.

"Nobody else got hurt?"

"Just you, baby doll. Because I wasn't fucking close enough or fast enough."

"It's not your fault, Spike. You were only a few feet away from me. I'm so glad you didn't get shot."

He scowled. "Better me than you. Fuck, I thought I was gonna lose you."

And what would you have done then?

He tried to tell himself that he was just feeling guilty that she got hurt while under his protection. But it wasn't as simple as that.

"There was so much blood. The ambulance seemed to take forever. You passed out. I was worried I'd hurt you even more by tackling you."

"Spike, I'm okay." She reached out for his hand with her good one. "I'm alive. It's just my shoulder."

"Just your shoulder? Baby, they had to operate to reconstruct it. You don't know how much damage a bullet can do."

"I'm alive. You're alive. Nobody else is hurt. Things are okay."

He stared at her for a long moment. Then he shook his head. She amazed him. Here she was, injured, in the hospital, trying to comfort him.

Her eyes started to drift closed. Poor baby. She was exhausted.

"Sleep, baby."

"Mr. Fluffy?"

"He's with Ink and Betsy."

"He'll be missing me," she murmured. "Did they take his favorite toy?"

"I told them to grab it."

"And his clothes?"

"Yes," he growled, even though he knew Ink was going to give him shit for that. Fuck his life.

"Good," she sighed.

Spike watched her drift off to sleep.

Fuck.

He was so messed up. He needed sleep, but he knew he

wouldn't be able to. He needed to guard her. Watch over her. Make sure nothing bad ever happened to her again.

And what about when she leaves?

Panic flooded him again. He couldn't let her go. Couldn't let her leave him.

Shit. Closing his eyes, he saw Jacqui's face. Heard her pleas. Then her face morphed into Millie's.

It was Millie begging him to save her.

He couldn't keep her fucking safe. Just look what had happened to her on his watch.

She'd been fucking shot!

And yet what was the alternative? Letting her go?

Not happening. Mine.

The door to the hospital room opened and he shot up, on the defensive.

Hack raised his hands. "Easy, man. Just here to check on our little patient. Rachel said she woke up."

"That rude nurse?"

Hack raised his eyebrows. "I see you've met her."

"She's sleeping again."

"That's good. She needs lots of sleep to help heal." Hack turned to him. "You look like you could use some sleep yourself."

"I'm fine."

"Uh-huh."

"I said I'm fucking fine."

"And in a better mood than usual, I see," Hack said cheerfully.

Spike just grunted. So he didn't smile all the time like Hack did. So what?

"She's going to require quite a bit of care when she leaves," Hack told him. "Do you know if she has any family who can care for her?"

Anger filled Spike. "I'm going to look after her."

"You are? I'm talking about around the clock care."

"I can take care of her."

"She must mean a lot to you then."

"Stop fucking poking your nose into my business," Spike snarled.

"Why don't you go home, get some real sleep. I'll call Ink, he can drive you. You'll be no good to anyone if you collapse."

Fuck. He was so annoying. There was no way he was leaving her.

But maybe that's why you should. Distance. You need some sleep to get some perspective.

"I'll stay the night," Hack promised. "One of Ink's guys is just outside. Nothing will happen to her. And I think the nurses are about one encounter away from calling security on you."

"No. I need to stay."

"Spike, unless you get some sleep, I'm not releasing her to you."

"What?" he growled. He couldn't fucking do that!

Hack stared back at him calmly. "Go home. Ink should be here any minute."

"You already called him."

"Yep. I did. Because you need to rest. If you don't go, I'll call security and have you hauled out of here."

"You fucking bastard."

"I'll watch over her. And you're no good to her if you get sick."

"You won't leave her."

"I promise."

He ground his teeth together. He didn't want to leave. But maybe he had to. In order to get his head on straight.

"Fine. Fuck. I'll go. But if anything happens to her, I'll rip out your insides and spread them from one end of the city to the other."

"You always say the nicest things."

As soon as he stepped into the house, he knew he'd made the wrong decision.

He stomped up the stairs to his bedroom. Their bedroom. It smelled like her. Bubblegum.

Fuck. He stripped and showered. Before getting into bed, he opened the window to let some air in. He was so fucking tired the room spun.

Yet he knew he wouldn't sleep.

The house was so fucking quiet. So fucking cold.

How had he not noticed that she'd filled the house with warmth? With laughter. With her singing. Dancing. Talking to that damn dog.

He'd nearly lost her.

What was he doing? How had he ever thought he could say goodbye to her?

He couldn't.

Fuck. He couldn't.

Because he fucking loved her.

Christ. She'd wormed her way into his heart with her unfailing generosity. Her spirit. Her never say die attitude. No matter what was thrown at her, she bounced up and came back swinging.

"Jacqui, baby, I'm sorry."

A warm breeze suddenly drifted through the open window. Tears rose in his eyes as he stared out the window at the stars. Could have been coincidence. Or his lack of sleep.

But he swore he almost felt Jacqui touch him. Smile. Give her blessing.

He knew that Millie had been holding back some things. So had he. The time for playing things safe was gone. He ran his hand over his face.

The only question was, how did he hold onto her? How did he

keep her safe? How could he balance his need to protect her with still letting her breathe?

He couldn't lie to himself. He knew he'd want to lock her up, keep her away from everyone who threatened her. Especially after what just happened.

But Millie wasn't the type to be locked away for her own good.

She actually liked people.

He grimaced.

He'd have to find some sort of compromise. All he knew was that he wasn't letting her go. And with that decision made, he finally gave in to exhaustion.

32

Millie help me.
Help me.
Why won't you help me?

"Millie? Millie, wake up."

She opened her eyes on a gasp, looking up into a pair of strangely familiar eyes. They were a deep emerald color. Unusual. Long sooty lashes surrounded them.

"So pretty. Jealous."

"Millie? You all right?" the owner of those pretty eyes asked her. She shied back, groaning as pain lanced her, engulfing her arm and shoulder.

"Easy, princess. Easy. Don't hurt yourself," pretty eyes said. He held his hands up in a placating gesture. He was dressed in a pair of jeans and a button-up flannel shirt.

"Who are you?"

"I'm Doctor Anderson."

This was Doctor Anderson?

"No way," she scoffed. He didn't look like a doctor with that beard and his casual clothes.

"I assure you I am. You can call me Hack, though. Or rabbit."

"Why would I call you rabbit?"

"Why indeed."

"Rabbit is kind of a strange nickname." Then again so was Hack. Especially for a doctor. How had he gotten that nickname? And did she really want to know?

"Tell me, how many rabbits does Mr. Spain actually hit?"

"Oh, none. He's a terrible shot."

Wait.

"How did you know about Mr. Spain?" she asked suspiciously. Who was this guy? How did he know about her neighbor shooting rabbits? Or trying to.

Like she'd said, he wasn't very good. Just as well since she loved bunnies.

"You talk in your sleep."

"I do not," she said, outraged. And horrified. What had she said? "Wait, where's Spike?" The drugs must be messing her up not to have noticed that he wasn't here. Panic flooded her. Where was he?

"Millie? Millie, it's okay. He'll be here soon."

She shook her head. "No. Where is he?"

"Shit. Calm down, sweetie. It's okay. He'll be here soon."

Tears dripped down her face. She needed her Daddy. She was alone in a strange place. She was in pain. And sure, maybe the drugs were messing her up a bit, but she was scared.

"I want him."

"Easy, aww sweetie, don't cry. Hush. Hush. It's all going to be all right." Hack awkwardly patted her hand. "Fuck, he's gonna kill me for letting you get upset."

She shook her head. "He doesn't want me."

"Doesn't want you? Of course he wants you."

A sob broke free. "Not like that. Not forever. J-just temporary."

"Oh, baby girl, I don't know what that idiot has been telling you, but he hasn't left your side the whole time you've been here. He wouldn't have left last night if I hadn't threatened to have him forcibly removed and told him that I wouldn't release you to his care unless he got some sleep."

"W-what?"

Hack brushed her hair off her face. "Let me get you a tissue." He grabbed a tissue then sat on the bed facing her as he carefully wiped her face. Maybe it should have been weird to have a stranger do that for her. But the honest truth was, she just didn't care at this point.

"He's kidding himself if he thinks he doesn't love you, princess."

Before she could say anything, the door opened.

"What the fuck is going on?" Spike snapped, walking in. "What are you doing? Why is she crying?"

Hack scrambled off the bed quickly, holding up his hands. "She was upset and I was reassuring her."

Spike couldn't believe it.

What the fuck was Hack doing sitting on her bed, brushing her hair off her face?

And she'd been crying?

"Why the hell is she crying?"

"Because she missed you for some Godforsaken reason. Maybe the poor girl enjoys having her eardrums blown." Hack pulled at his ear while Spike sent him a look.

He walked closer and took Hack's spot on the bed. "Mine."

"I know. Wasn't trying to steal your girl."

He narrowed his gaze at the other man. "Go away."

"Well, I do have to get going. See you later for rounds, princess. Good luck with the beast."

Spike growled and Hack hastily left. He turned back to Millie, who had her mouth open, gaping at him. "Spike! That was rude. He's my doctor."

"He was hitting on you."

"He was not hitting on me."

"Sitting too close to you. Touching you."

"Again, he's my doctor. He kind of has to touch me."

"Don't like it."

"Are you okay?" she asked.

"Shouldn't that be my question?"

"You look better but you seem kind of on edge. Short-tempered. Angry, I guess."

Closing his eyes, he took a deep breath. "Not angry at you." When he opened them, his gaze held something she'd never seen before.

He almost looked tender. He brushed her hair off her forehead. Then took her good hand in his, holding it gently.

Okay . . . what was going on? Who was this man? What had happened to her Spike? The gruff, blunt, take-no-prisoners man?

"What's the matter?" she asked.

"I lied."

She stiffened. "About what?"

"Do you remember the night you were shot? We were in Pinkies and I said I didn't love you and never would. That I'd never love anyone the way I did my wife?"

"I remember," she said hoarsely.

"That's when I lied."

She stared at him in confusion. "I think you're going to have to tell me more than that because I'm not getting it."

The look Spike gave her told her that he didn't understand how she was missing his point.

She was all drugged up. She'd been shot! So sue her for her confusion.

"I lied about not loving you. Only I didn't know I was lying at the time. But having you nearly die. Fuck. I can't lose you, Millie. I can't."

His voice cracked and she stared at him in shock. Spike didn't crack. He was solid as a rock. Granite. Stone. And he was looking at her like he was going to lose control at any moment.

Then his words penetrated.

"You love me?"

"I love you."

"But how?"

He snorted. "How? What do you mean, how? You're beautiful. Smart. Kind. Sweet. Bit naïve. But that doesn't matter, because you'll have me to protect you from now on. And nothing will happen to you. I won't fucking have it."

His voice became a low, savage whisper and she could tell he meant every word.

Holy. Hell.

"You love me?" She had to repeat it just to be sure.

"I love you, baby doll. More than fucking anything. You're my whole fucking life. Think I fell for you the minute I saw you pull that arsenal out of your bag at Pinkies."

"No way. You hated me."

"Never hated you."

"All right. Was annoyed by me. You think I'm nosy and annoying and crazy."

"Well, yeah. But I can think that and still fucking love you."

She gaped at him. Then a freaking miracle happened. His lips twitched.

They. Actually. Twitched.

"Did you make a joke? Was that a joke? What is happening

here? First you tell me you love me. Then you make a joke. Then you nearly smile! Am I dying? I'm dying, aren't I?"

"You're not fucking dying," he growled. "Don't even joke about it."

"Then what's happening here?"

He ran a hand over his face. "Truth is, I didn't want to love again after Jacqui died."

"Because you loved her so much."

"Yeah. And because it was my fucking fault she died. And I can't ever forgive myself for that."

33

Her heart skipped a beat.

His fault? No way. She didn't believe that. It was clear to see how much he loved his wife. He wouldn't have caused her death.

"There's no way it was your fault," she whispered. "I don't believe that for a second."

He ran his finger over the scar on his neck. It was the first time he'd ever done that. Ever touched his scar. She'd never worked up the courage to ask him how he got it.

Now she was guessing he'd got it the night Jacqui died.

"What happened?"

He sighed. "We lived in Chicago. It was late at night and we'd just flown in after visiting Steele."

"Visiting Steele? You guys were all friends then?"

Surprise filled his face. "Can't believe I haven't told you. Jacqui was Steele's sister."

Okay, that explained some things. Sadness filled her. So Spike lost his wife and Steele lost his sister.

"He basically raised her. Even though he's only a few years

older. They had shitty parents and he did pretty much everything for her. She hated living in a different city from him. I had a deal go south and I wasn't in a great mood. We were stopped at a light when these guys with guns approached. They had Jacqui's door opened before I could do anything. If I hadn't been so preoccupied, I would have noticed them. Could have done something."

"Spike, no one could have anticipated that."

He shook his head. "They demanded we get out of the car. I fought back. Stupid move. There were four of them against me. Don't know why I did it. One of them had a knife, he stabbed me several times, got close to slashing my throat. They left me beaten on the ground, obviously they thought I would bleed out before help arrived. All I could remember as I lay there, unable to move, was Jacqui crying my name."

"Oh, Spike." How awful. Her heart broke for him.

"I must have lost consciousness, I don't remember them leaving. I guess they thought I was dead or close to it. Instead, I woke up in the hospital. Alive. Steele and Grady sitting on chairs on either side of me. I looked into Steele's eyes and I just knew. Without him telling me, I just knew she was gone. They left her about half a mile up the road. Bullet in her brain. She never stood a chance."

"Oh, Spike. I'm so sorry." She tried to shuffle over, tried to reach for him, needing to comfort him. She winced as she moved.

Jumping to his feet, he crowded over her, lightly putting pressure on her good shoulder. "What are you doing? Stay in place. You shouldn't move."

Tears dripped down her cheeks. "I'm so sorry."

"Ahh, baby. Don't cry. Don't cry for me. I don't deserve it."

"It wasn't your fault!" How could he think that?

He gave her an incredulous look. "If I'd been paying attention, if I hadn't fought back—"

"Then you might have ended up with a bullet in your brain as well! They likely had no intention of letting either of you live. They're the ones who took her. Who murdered her. It's *their* fault not yours."

She couldn't believe he'd lived with this guilt for so long.

"Did they find them?"

"Yeah, fucking bastards didn't get rid of the car quick enough. They're doing life in prison. It's still not enough."

God, her heart was breaking for him.

She reached for him with her good hand. "Spike, it wasn't your fault."

"I failed to protect her. I failed to protect you. I nearly lost you."

"You couldn't have predicted that I would get shot. No one could have." She got it now. Why he was so overprotective. Why he'd brought her into his home when he barely knew her.

"Should never have let you leave the house. It won't happen again."

"What? Me leaving the house?" she joked. But she noticed that his face didn't change expression. Holy. Shit. He meant that.

Okay, one issue at a time.

"Spike, it wasn't your fault. Do you really think that Jacqui would want you to blame yourself? To live your life alone and in guilt? I didn't know her, but she must have been pretty special for you to love her this much."

"She was special." He brushed some hair back from her face. "I need to warn you."

"Warn me?" She felt like her head was spinning. She couldn't keep up with him. Maybe this wasn't the best time for this conversation. The drugs were obviously still messing with her head.

"I couldn't let you stay with Steele, yet I couldn't let myself feel anything for you. But I failed at that. Every day I think I fell in love with you more. You're crazy and caring. Klutzy and cute. Loving."

"Not sure all of those were compliments," she muttered.

"They were. It's just you. I love you, baby doll. I want you. But that might not be what's best for you. I'm going to give you this one chance to tell me no. Because if you tell me you love me then there is no going back. You will be mine. In all ways. Your life will change. There will be no holding back. For either of us. I will know all of you. You'll know all of me. It won't be one of those relationships where we lead different lives. Unless I'm doing something dangerous, you'll be with me. By my side. As my woman. And my baby doll. I will love you. Take care of you. Keep you safe. Sometimes my protection will feel like I'm smothering you. And I probably will be. But once you're in, you're all in. So this is it. Do you love me or do you want me to leave?"

She sucked in a breath. Say no to him? Was he kidding her? And whoa, who knew he could say so much at one time?

Before she could reply, the door to her room opened and Hack peeked in.

"Is it safe to come in?" Hack asked. "Or do I need to come back in combat wear? Should I bring Green in with me as protection?"

She giggled then hissed as it jolted her shoulder. The drugs seemed to be wearing off a bit.

"Don't make her laugh," Spike snapped with a scowl.

"Right. Don't sit next to her. Don't touch her hair. Don't make her laugh. Now, am I allowed to touch her shoulder or is that off the table as well?"

She rolled her eyes at Hack's questions. Spike wasn't that bad.

"Only for medical purposes."

Umm. Okay.

"Make her cry again and you're gonna lose a limb."

Right. She was beginning to see what he meant when he said things would go to another level.

Her being shot had triggered something inside him. Understandable given what happened to his wife. But the beast was out of the cage and he wasn't going back in. She had a feeling she was barely going to be allowed to pee on her own.

Hack gave her a sympathetic look as though sensing her thoughts. "Right, business time." Hack's humor drained away. "Millie, you were a very lucky girl."

"I was lucky to get shot?" That was an odd thing to say.

"Sounds like if Spike hadn't tackled you, then that shot could well have hit something vital."

"I owe him my life." She looked over at Spike who appeared unconvinced.

"You should never have been in that parking lot to begin with," he grumbled.

She sighed.

Hack rolled his eyes at her. "I see he's going to take the blame for everything. Hey, Spike, I stubbed my toe earlier, you gonna feel guilty for that?"

Spike just crossed his arms over his chest, looking menacing.

"Right," Hack said cheerfully, looking unperturbed by Spike's surly attitude.

"Even though the bullet didn't hit anything vital, it did do quite a bit of damage to your shoulder. We were able to save your arm when we operated but you're looking at a lot of recovery time. So long as there are no signs of infection, you'll probably be able to leave the hospital in about a week's time. You're going to need someone to take care of you at home since you won't be able to use that arm. I know you don't live here. I'm not sure what your plans are?"

"She's coming home with me," Spike told him.

"So you're still prepared to care for her?" Hack asked.

Still? Had they discussed this already?

Spike grunted.

"One grunt for yes? Two for no?" Hack asked.

"Are you ever professional?" Spike asked.

"Very rarely. It gives me a rash." Hack turned to her. "After you're discharged, you're going to need more time to recover, then physical therapy to help that arm. It might never be the same again."

"Oh." She hadn't really thought that far ahead. What did that mean exactly?

"She likes to sew and make clothing," Spike told him. "Will she be able to do that?"

Hack gave her a look filled with sympathy. "Hopefully."

Pain flooded her. To not be able to make her creations . . . yeah, it hurt. But she had to be realistic here. She pushed the pain deep. Into that box.

"Okay."

"Okay?" Hack drawled the word, looking over at Spike for some sort of explanation.

Spike just frowned at her.

"Yeah, okay."

"You don't seem too upset by that. You're probably in shock. It might hit you later," Hack warned.

"No, I get it," she reassured him, attempting a small smile. "I'm lucky to be alive. Anything else I can deal with, right? That's what life is, just dealing with the punches and getting back up."

Hack studied her. "How many punches have you had?"

"Enough."

"And does anyone ever help you get back up?" Hack asked.

"I have friends back home," she said defensively.

"Okay, that's good. But this could hit you harder later and if you ever need to talk, I have the name of some good therapists."

"I'll be fine. Thank you." She gave him a big smile.

Hack appeared puzzled. He turned to Spike, but Spike continued to stare at her. She swallowed. She had the feeling that Spike saw more than he was letting on.

"If you need them you can ask for them at any time. There are people here in the hospital who can come see you."

"I'll be fine," she said more firmly. "Thank you."

"Spike, you got anything to say?" Hack asked.

Spike glanced over at him. She braced herself, knowing he would side with Hack.

"She'll be fine," Spike told him.

Okay. That surprised her. It surprised Hack too, if his expression was anything to go by.

"All right. I've got to get going. Rest when you can. Drink plenty of fluids. You might not feel like eating yet, and that's okay. Just keep up the fluids. Spike, try not to terrorize the nurses too much. I don't want to come back to save you from them. If you need me, call."

He left and silence filled the room.

"You're not going to pressure me to talk to someone?" she asked.

"You will be fine. I won't allow you to be anything else. But you will talk to me. You're gonna tell me why you react the way you do."

"React the way I do?"

"Hmm. Other people, they hear they might not be able to do something they love because they were shot by some asshole, they'd likely get angry. Upset. They might cry or shout or go into shock. You just moved on. And not the first time you've done it. We'll talk about that. And everything else. If I get the answer I want. So gotta know, what's your answer, Millie?"

She licked her dry lips. "My answer."

"You should know I'll take care of you no matter what."

"You don't have to."

"I do."

"Because you feel guilty?"

"Because I love you."

"I love you too," she whispered back. "I'm in this."

"All the way?"

"All the way."

A look of such stark possessiveness filled his face that her breath was stolen for a moment. Then he leaned in to kiss her lightly.

"Thank fuck." He leaned his forehead against hers. "Gonna look after you, baby doll."

"I know you will."

"I'm not easy. Not simple. At times you'll want to kill me. But now one will ever love you like I do."

She knew that. She felt it in her soul.

34

"Right, Millie, it's time for a sponge bath." The nurse who walked in spoke cheerfully. As though this was something she should be happy about.

Having a stranger bathe her. Umm, no thanks. Definitely not on her list to do today.

Even though she'd tried to send him home last night, Spike had insisted on staying. Much to the night nurse's irritation. She knew he can't have gotten much sleep sitting in that chair.

She couldn't wait to get home. She missed Mr. Fluffy. Spike had brought her Chompers, which helped. And he'd actually Facetimed Betsy earlier so that Millie could check on Mr. Fluffy.

But it wasn't the same. She wanted to be home in Spike's bed. In his house. Not in the hospital surrounded by strangers. The police had been by earlier to interview her, but they hadn't had many answers for her either. Spike wouldn't answer any questions about what was happening with the Devil's Sinners. If she wasn't feeling so sleepy and dopey, she might have been irritated at being kept out of the loop.

"No thanks," she replied as the woman started to fill up a bowl with warm water and soap at the sink. Urgh, hospital soap? She so didn't think so.

"It will make you feel so much better."

Right. So she said.

"Sir, you'll have to leave to give my patient some privacy," the nurse said to Spike.

"No," Spike said. He stood and reached for the bowl and cloth.

"Sir—"

"I'll be bathing her myself. You can go."

"Look, I can't just l-let you . . . " the nurse spluttered.

"She's mine to care for. I will do it."

"You can't get her bandages wet."

He gave her a look that clearly told her that he wasn't stupid.

The nurse sighed. "Millie, is this all right with you?"

"Yes," she said immediately. She'd much rather have Spike bathe her than some stranger.

A buzzer sounded and the nurse gave them both a harried look. "All right. I'll be back later to take your vitals."

She left and Spike moved to the door, having a quiet word with the man outside. Then he tipped the water down the sink.

She sighed in relief. But he started to fill it again, moving into the bathroom and coming back with her own shower gel.

"Couldn't I have a shower instead?" she whined. She wasn't usually a whiner but this was all getting to be too much. She hated how helpless she was.

"Baby doll, you're hooked up to a drip. Not to mention you're weak as a babe. No way I would let you shower like this."

"Maybe I can wash myself."

He gently cupped one side of her face with his big hand. "Millie."

That was all he said, but she knew what he wanted. She raised her face so she was looking at him. She braced herself for his commands, knowing she'd likely give in.

"Let me do this. Please."

He couldn't have shocked her more if he'd told her he had a lifetime goal to become a clown in the circus.

"P-please? You just said please... am I hallucinating?"

He shook his head at her, but the skin around his eyes crinkled.

"You don't know how hard it is to feel helpless," he told her. "When you're hurt, in pain, I just want to do something. Let me take care of you."

"You are doing something by just being here. You're keeping me sane."

"Keep me sane and let me help you."

"Are you sure you were ever sane?" she asked suspiciously.

"It's debatable," he admitted.

She snorted with laughter then groaned.

"No laughing. And you need more pain killers."

Damn it. He'd caught on far too quickly that she didn't like pushing the button to release more medication She huffed out a sigh.

"Millie," he said warningly.

Only thing was he couldn't back that up with a threat, right? Because he couldn't punish her while she was injured.

He leaned over her, careful not to bump her. "Oh, I know that look. That's the look of a Little girl who thinks she can get away with things because Daddy is wrapped around her finger and won't do anything while his baby is hurt. But you will get better. And Daddy has a long memory."

"Well, shoot. There should be an expiration date. Like if a week passes, I can no longer be punished for something."

"You wish, baby doll."

"That's just mean, Daddy."

Something like relief filled his face. Had he been waiting for her to call him that again? Maybe he had.

"It's hard for me to slip into Little space here. I feel on edge. Watched."

"I get it, baby doll."

And she knew he did.

He moved over and grabbed the bowl and cloth, just waiting. She gave him a nod. He drew the curtain around the bed, although she was certain he'd told her guard at the door not to allow anyone entrance.

Then he carefully pulled back the blankets. She was half-wearing one of the awful hospital gowns. Her injured arm couldn't fit in the arm hole.

He gently pulled the top half down, leaving her breasts naked.

Picking up the cloth, he squeezed the water out.

"I'm gonna resemble sasquatch by the time I can shave again," she groaned.

"I'll get you a razor and take care of it."

She blushed. She wasn't sure what was worse. Being a hairy beast or having him shave her. Gently, carefully, he washed her body. And she started to relax. His touch was almost reverent.

As if he cherished her.

Tears filled her eyes.

"What's wrong, baby doll? Did I hurt you?" There was an urgent note in his voice.

"No. It's just . . . the way you're touching me. You're so careful. You really do love me, don't you?"

"There was doubt?"

"No one has ever loved me. I mean, my family and friends. But not like this."

"No," he agreed. "Not like this."

∼

"Millie!"

"Are you okay?"

"Does she look okay?"

"Millie, what happened? We've been worried about you."

She smiled into the laptop screen as everyone tried to speak over each other. "Hi, everyone."

Spike had moved out of screenshot after setting the laptop up for her.

"What's going on?" Mrs. Spain asked. "Why haven't you answered our calls?"

"And where are you?" Mrs. Larsen asked.

They all started talking at once and she frowned, trying to work out who to answer first.

"Quiet," Spike demanded without raising his voice.

To her shock, they all acquiesced. Well, except for Mr. Spain. But that was to be expected when he couldn't hear anything.

"What's going on? What?"

Spike turned the laptop so he was looking at them all.

"It's that young man. What was his name?" Mrs. Spain said as though Spike wasn't sitting right there. "Pike?"

"No, it's Mike," Mrs. Lancaster said.

"Spike!" yelled Mr. Spain, surprisingly getting it right for once.

"Quiet, you old coot," Mrs. Spain scolded. "Young man, where has our Millie gone? What have you done to her? If you've hurt her, we'll make sure you pay."

"Millie is fine. She's in the hospital but she is well. I am caring for her."

She let out a sigh when he didn't tell them the full truth. The last thing she wanted was to cause them stress.

"You're taking care of her?" Reverend Pat demanded.

"I am."

"You better be," Andrey threatened. "Or I come cut off your dick."

"I'm good," she called out. She wasn't sure, but she thought

Andrey might have ties to the Russian mafia.

Spike turned the laptop back around and she smiled at everyone. "I'm fine. Spike is taking very good care of me. Promise. Sorry I worried you. Tell me how everyone is back home."

That distracted them and she settled in to listen to the gossip she'd already heard last time they spoke. Gradually, her eyes started to grow heavy-lidded.

"Millie needs a nap now," Spike said abruptly. "Say goodbye, Millie."

She forced her eyes open. "Oh, no. I'm fine."

"Say goodbye," he said more sternly.

She sighed but knew he wasn't going to budge. "Bye all."

Everyone waved off and she frowned at Spike. "I was still talking.

"No, you were about to fall asleep. It's your naptime."

She sighed. "Don't wanna nap."

"Too bad. My baby doll is getting grouchy. That means she needs a nap." He grabbed Chompers and settled him in beside her.

"You must need the world's biggest nap then since you're the king of the grouches," she muttered sleepily.

Lips brushed her forehead before she drifted off to sleep.

~

"Right, I bet you're ready to see the back of this place," a nurse said cheerfully as she pushed a wheelchair into the room.

It was the first genuine smile she'd seen on one of the nurses' faces since she'd arrived. Not that she could blame them. Over the past week, Spike had done his best to alienate every one of them. Not that he was trying on purpose.

He was just being Spike. Blunt. Gruff. Protective. Possessive.

He didn't like them touching her. And Lord help them if any of them accidentally hurt her. Changing the dressing was bad. At first, they'd tried to make him leave but he'd refused. She'd worried they were going to call security and have him forcibly removed. But there must have been something about her situation that made them hesitate. Maybe it was the guard at her door 24/7 or perhaps it was Hack's interference, she wasn't sure.

But any time she cried out in pain, he'd snarl at them. He'd reminded her of a dragon. Her very own, protective, sometimes vicious dragon.

But never with her.

Oh no, with her he was as sweet as maple syrup. He had the gentlest touch, the softest voice.

They'd removed the catheter a couple of days ago and he'd insisted on carrying her to the bathroom. That had been a bit embarrassing since he'd also refused to leave while she'd peed. Finally, he'd ran the water and turned his back.

He hadn't been joking when he said he wouldn't leave her side. Even when he showered, he did it in the attached bathroom and only when Hack was here to watch over her.

Thankfully, the only migraine she'd had while here had been a pretty mild one. Spike had quickly gotten on top of it, turning off all the lights and making sure no one was allowed entrance to her room.

She was certain that endeared him to the nurses too.

"I see you're all dressed." The nurse shot Spike a look of reproach.

He simply stared back at her, his expression not changing. He wasn't going to apologize for taking care of her.

And she wouldn't want him to.

Her arm was in a sling and would likely remain in one for several weeks. She felt weak as hell. All she'd done was let Spike dress her and she was ready for a nap. Spike had bought her some new clothes online. Soft tracksuit pants, camisoles and cardigans.

Things that were easy for her to wear. As well as cute pajama bottoms with matching sleeveless tops.

He'd thought of everything.

"Let's just get you into this wheelchair then I can push you out," the nurse said.

"I'll do that," Spike told her.

The nurse opened her mouth, frowned then sighed. "Fine. Fine."

She stomped out of the room.

"Don't think you've made any friends there," she half-joked.

"Not here to make friends."

He carefully picked her up and settled her into the wheelchair. She had to hold back a wince. The painkillers she was on now just weren't as good as the morphine. As he pushed her down the corridor, Hack walked up to them, whistling.

"Spike! There's a party going on in the nurses' lounge. You'll never guess what they're celebrating."

She had to bite back a smile as Spike growled at the doctor. She'd gotten used to Hack's ways. He came across as carefree and irreverent. But he cared deeply about his patients. He crouched down in front of her.

"Right, Miss Millie," he said, giving her a firm look. "You're going to follow all of my rules, yeah?"

"She will," Spike replied.

"Don't push too far too fast. Rest. Let the big guy do all the hard work, yeah?"

"Yes. Thank you, Hack. For everything."

"Hey, you're talking like we won't see each other again. I'll be over for Sunday lunch, yeah?"

"No," Spike told him.

He pressed his hand to his chest. "Cuts deep, that does."

She giggled and he quickly kissed her cheek and jumped up, moving away with a whistle before Spike could say anything.

With a grumble, Spike started pushing her wheelchair down the corridor again. While she might miss seeing Hack, she wasn't going to miss being in the hospital.

∼

Forty-five minutes later, they pulled up to his gate. She was exhausted. Her body covered in a fine sheen of sweat. She wanted a bath. She wanted sleep. She wanted drugs.

Not necessarily in that order.

"Bastards," Spike muttered as he drove up the driveway. She looked at him, startled. Then she spotted a black sports car sitting outside the front of the house.

"Who's here?"

"Steele and Grady. Knew I'd regret giving them the alarm code. They got me in a weak moment. Said they wanted to do something for you." He sighed. "I'll get rid of them quickly."

He pulled into the garage then came around and undid her seatbelt, carefully lifting her out. "I'll take you upstairs then get rid of them."

"I'd like to say hello. And I have some questions for them."

He grumbled something under his breath. "I don't want them upsetting you."

"They won't upset me." Then she got it. "You think talking about being shot will upset me."

"It should. But this is you. I don't know what you do with all of your fear and anger, but I plan on figuring it out."

"Maybe I'm just weird and don't feel things like normal people."

He gave her a look like he knew she was full of shit.

Spike walked into the house with her in his arms. Instead of going up the stairs, he turned towards the kitchen. "You can be up for twenty minutes, no longer. Then you're going to bed."

"Yes, Daddy."

When he carried her into the kitchen and living area, Damon was standing at the stove, stirring something.

Grady was seated at the counter, sipping from a glass of red wine and watching Damon. He turned with a smile.

"My dear, you're here. Finally, we can see you. Spike has been very selfish, keeping you all to himself."

"Hello, Grady," she said.

Damon flicked off the stove and turned, wiping his hands on a towel. "Sweetheart, how are you?" He came over and brushed his hand over her forehead.

Spike grumbled at him and walked away, carrying her into the living room, where a giant giraffe lay on the sofa. Her mouth dropped open as she stared at it.

"What the fuck is that?" Spike snapped.

"That's a giraffe," Damon said, picking it up so Spike could lay her carefully on the sofa.

"I'll go get you a pillow and blanket. Need anything else?"

She shook her head, grimacing slightly.

"Stay put."

She wasn't planning on going anywhere. He quickly disappeared upstairs. Grady sat on one of the recliners while Damon grabbed a chair from the table and sat close to her.

"How are you, my dear?" Grady asked.

"I'm fine. Really," she insisted as they gave her doubtful looks. "You brought me a giraffe?" A giant giraffe.

Grady sighed. "I told him it was gauche. He insisted that bigger is better. I tried to point out that isn't always true."

Damon sent him a cheeky grin. "And sometimes it is."

Not for the first time, she wondered if there was something between them. Not that it was any of her business.

"What are you doing here?" Spike demanded as he re-entered

the room. He set a pillow behind her then carefully laid the blanket over her.

"Spike," she chided

"It's all right, my dear. We're well used to Spike's idiosyncrasies."

"It's not an idiosyncrasy," Spike grumbled.

Damon grinned. "He likes to pretend that he doesn't like us, but really he would be lost without us."

Spike just shook his head.

Damon lost his grin. "How are you, Millie? Spike is terrible at keeping us updated."

"I'm fine."

Both men's faces grew stony hard. Spike grunted. "She's doing okay. Surgery went well. No sign of infection. We're not sure how much use of that arm she'll get back, though."

"See, fine," she said cheerfully.

"I can't believe this happened on my watch." Damon shook his head. "And then they fucking got away."

She sighed. "I'm surrounded by people who seem to want to feel guilty for things that are beyond their control. It's not your fault I got shot."

"Any idea how they knew she was there?" Spike asked

"Someone had to have told them," Grady said.

"Who?" Spike asked.

"That's the question," Damon said darkly.

"It could have been a coincidence," she said weakly.

All three men gave her looks that said they didn't believe that. Neither did she.

"Could it have been the rat?" she asked, trying to think of who might have warned Corey that she was there. "Except that doesn't make sense unless..."

"He's been working for the Devil's Sinners all along," Damon said grimly.

"That would mean Luther was too," Spike said.

"I know," Damon replied. "Which is why we need to find out for sure. We're going to set a trap using the rat."

"What kind of trap?" she asked.

"Less you know the better, my dear," Grady said.

"But you will deal with Luther, right?" she asked. "You won't let him take over from his father. Because if you're not going to take care of him, I will."

"And how would you do that, my dear?" Grady asked in a deceptively casual voice.

"I don't know. Pay someone, I guess. Maybe we should do that. Do you know someone who could kill him? I can pay for it."

Damon shot a look at Spike. But he sat there, watching her with that too-knowing gaze of his.

"Is there some reason you're so adamant about Luther being taken down?" Damon asked.

"Other than all those poor women that he abuses?" she asked.

"Yes," Damon said. "Because while most people would feel horror over that, they wouldn't be willing to part with their cash to take him out. By the way, that would take a significant amount of capital to achieve."

"I have money."

"And just how does an out-of-work librarian from Nowhere, Nebraska have that sort of money?" Grady asked.

"I won it."

"You . . . won it," Grady said slowly. "In the lottery?"

"How much money are we speaking of?" Damon asked.

"I think it's a little over a million now. I used a bit of it already."

Damon crossed his arms over his chest. "If you didn't win the lottery, how did you win it?"

"Well, I'm not really sure." This was the bizarre part. "I must have entered a competition. This man came to my house with a check for two million dollars."

They'd all grown tense. "What? It's not that strange, is it?" *Of course it's strange, Millie.*

"Actually, it's very strange. Do you remember the name of this man? Or the name of the competition? Where the money came from?" Grady questioned.

"He had some sort of normal name. Like Ken Jones. But I do remember the name that was printed on the check of the company who ran the competition because it was so unusual."

"What was it?" Spike spoke up for the first time in ages.

"For Fox Sake."

Spike sat there for a long moment.

That couldn't be right.

He had to have heard wrong. Right?

"What did you say?" he asked slowly.

"For Fox Sake. I remember it because it sounds like for fuck's sake. And there was this image of a fox's head. I guess I entered a competition that was maybe at a pet store or something. Although I hadn't been to a pet store. Maybe it was one of those ones where you're entered into the draw just by purchasing something."

Spike got to his feet, no longer able to stay still.

"What's going on?" Damon demanded. "What's wrong?"

Spike shook his head. "Nothing. I just . . . I need you guys to go."

Damon scowled. "Spike, if you're in trouble . . ."

"There's no trouble. And if there were, I can take care of myself."

"We'll go. I'm sure Millie could use some rest. She looks rather fragile right now," Grady cautioned.

Millie frowned at his words, but Spike knew the other man was right. She was fragile. Injured.

Was she who she portrayed herself to be, though?

How could someone be that innocent? And what about the strange way she reacted to things? Was there something more to it than having a warped processing system? Fucked if he knew, but he had to find out.

"I made you lasagna and put it in the fridge. You just need to heat it up. On the stove is some caramel sauce to go with the ice cream for dessert," Damon told him.

"Thank you."

He waited for them both to say goodbye to Millie then he walked them out.

"You sure there's nothing we can do?" Damon asked.

"When's the trap being set?"

"Don't know. Soon. You want to be there for it?"

"Yeah. I'll find someone to stay with Millie."

Damon whacked him on the back and Grady nodded to him before they left.

He took a moment to gather himself. Had it all been a lie? No, it couldn't have been.

Then what was going on?

Well, there was only one way to find out. He walked back into the living room and sat on the coffee table in front of Millie. She was staring at the giraffe. "What am I going to do with him?"

"Don't worry about the giraffe. Millie, be honest with me."

"No good conversations usually start that way, but okay. Honest about what?"

"Just how do you know the Fox?"

Umm.

Had he lost his mind?

Was he tricking her or something? Was fox a code word for something?

"How do I know the fox?"

He stood and paced back and forth in front of her, which was bizarre in itself. Spike wasn't a pacer. He sat back. He observed. He looked for weaknesses.

Then he pounced.

The fact he was pacing, well, she wasn't quite sure what to do with that.

"Just tell me. Whatever it is, we'll deal with it," he told her.

"Whatever what is?"

"Your connection to the Fox." He stopped and stared down at her. She hadn't seen such a cold look on his face since the first night she met him. And it stole her breath.

"Spike, I don't know what you're talking about."

Whatever it was, it was something he felt deeply about. He was masking his feelings. She attempted to do the same. To push her hurt deep. But it wouldn't go. It danced just below the surface, punching at her with a staccato beat.

"I don't know any foxes. I told you it must have been one of those competitions that—"

"I know what you said." He waved his hand dismissively. "But it has to be him. That's not a coincidence. But if you know him you wouldn't give me the name of the company so that means..."

"Who is it I'm meant to know? Obviously, you know something about this company that I don't. Maybe you'd like to fill me in."

He sat on the coffee table, slumped on it as though all his energy had left him in a rush.

What was going on here?

"You don't know the Fox?"

"Spike, are you okay? I mean, I'm not sure if by Fox you're meaning a person... is it a character on a show? Oh, on one of those marvel shows. Like Spiderman? Is it a superhero I'm not aware of? Except why are you so mad that I don't know him? No, you're upset because you think I do know him and didn't tell you, is that it?"

She was getting horribly confused.

"Okay, baby doll. I want you to listen to me carefully. Have you ever encountered a man who calls himself the Fox?"

"I can safely say that has never happened."

He nodded. "The man who brought you the check, what did he look like?"

"Umm, he was tall. Probably your height but he had a big belly. And he was older."

"Okay, doesn't really mean anything, he can disguise himself. The way he looks, his voice, fuck. Why would he do that? Give you money?"

"You're kind of starting to scare me."

That was a lie. He was fully scaring her.

And instead of reassuring her, the way he normally would have, he just stared at her.

"Spike?"

He shook his head, closing his eyes. "Shit, baby doll. Sorry. I just . . . he's got me messed up."

"Who has?" She turned her legs around, trying to shuffle so she was fully facing him.

He must have sensed her moving because his eyes shot open and he leaned forward, grasping hold of her thighs. "Easy. What are you doing?"

"What's going on? Tell me. I can help. I promise."

He leaned forward and brushed her hair off her face. There was her Spike. "I need you to do something for me."

"Of course, anything."

"Tell me more about you. I need to know why you're here. Why did you come to the city?"

Even though she thought it odd he was asking now, she knew the time had come to tell him.

"I came here to find the person who murdered my sister."

35

He knew he was staring.

"You came here to find who murdered your sister?"

"Yes. I told you that my grandma and granddad raised me?"

"Yes, but you didn't mention a sister."

"Technically, she was my half-sister. Apparently, my mom isn't big on raising her own kids. Having kids, yes. Taking care of them, no. She kept me until I was four before dropping me off with my grandparents. My sister, she only kept until she was three. I was thirteen when she came to live with us. I've always watched out for her. My grandparents did their best but they didn't have the energy by the time she came along. They were living off their pension. My granddad took a job driving a taxi when she came to live with them to help. Unfortunately, Nowhere is pretty small and most of the people that live there are older."

That explained why all her friends looked to be in their eighties.

"Deedee hated living in Nowhere. I don't blame her. There were no young people around. We had to take a bus for an hour just to get to school. I did my best to take her places, the park, to sports things, but she just seemed to grow up resenting all of us. My granddad died several years ago. My grandma got sick with breast cancer a few years ago. I was working a lot to pay her mounting medical bills as well as taking her to appointments. I neglected Deedee. She needed me and I wasn't there."

"Baby, what happened to her wasn't your fault."

"Wasn't it? I was working late at the library. Deedee was supposed to be with Grandma. When I got home, Grandma was passed out on the floor. I called an ambulance. I wondered where Deedee was but I didn't have time to go find her. When I finally got home from the hospital it was after midnight and she wasn't in her bed. I started to panic. I called her. I drove the streets looking for her. All my neighbors were elderly so I couldn't wake them to help. She was gone. It wasn't until I got home, I found the note from her. She said she'd had enough of living in some tiny town filled with old people. She'd only just turned seventeen."

"I'm sorry, baby."

"I reported her missing, of course. But the cops didn't have much to go on. And I couldn't just leave Grandma. I was torn between my runaway sister and my sick grandmother. If I'd had the money, I would have hired someone to find her."

"So this was before you won the money?"

"Oh yes. After Grandma died, I was in a lot of debt from her medical bills. I'd lost my job. I was going to have to sell the house. I didn't have anyone who could help. Then I got a knock on the door. It was the police. They told me that DeeDee's body had been recovered. That she'd been murdered."

She took in a long breath. "They couldn't tell me who did it, but they did say that she'd been working as a prostitute and they figured she'd been killed by a customer." Her breath hitched. "My baby sister. She'd left because she was searching for a better life and then she ended up in hell."

"Oh, baby doll." He came and sat beside her, lifting her onto his lap.

"I was in shock. I think I just sat there and nodded like a lunatic. I don't even remember them leaving. Three days later, there was another knock on my door to tell me I'd won two million dollars. I didn't even ask questions. It was like a Godsend. I paid off all her medical debts."

"That's where the rest of the money went?"

"Oh, I also helped out a few of Grandma's friends."

He bet she did. She was always taking care of everyone else and forgetting about looking after herself.

Now she didn't have to. Because she had him.

"And then I decided I was going to come here. That I was going to find out who killed her. I know it was stupid. I mean, how was I possibly going to find the killer? I'm such an idiot."

"Stop that," he growled at her, placing a finger over her lips. "No calling yourself names."

"But I'm just some country bumpkin from Nowhere, Nebraska. I have no idea what I'm doing. I worked in a library. I grew up surrounded by people who think a late night is if they're not in bed by eight. My sister ran away from me because my life was so boring. I was stupid to think I could ever do any of this. I just kept moving forward because stopping or looking back would be failing. I failed her once. I couldn't do it again. I just couldn't."

"Hush, baby. Hush." He gently rocked her. "You didn't fail her. You had far too much on your plate. And no one to help you."

"I've got to keep myself together. Because there's no one else to do it all. I don't have the option of falling apart."

"You can fall apart. Because I'm here. And I will always put you back together."

She slumped against him. "That's so sweet."

"I don't ever want to hear you call yourself stupid again, understand me?"

She huffed out a sigh. "There's the grump again."

"Why were you staying in such a crappy motel if you had money?"

"I chose a motel close to where she was found. I thought it was a good idea to pay a week upfront, it was definitely cheaper. It wasn't until I got here that I saw why it was so cheap. But I couldn't get my money back so I figured I'd stay for the week. It really wasn't so bad."

He grunted in disagreement. His mind turned everything over. Sister murdered. Staying close to where she was found. The Fox.

"Baby doll, what's her real name? Your sister?"

"Daria. Daria Marshall."

He tensed. Daria Marshall. The girl from the photos that they'd been forced to use to blackmail that sick fuck, Senator Jonathan Robins. "Shit. Fuck. Christ. So that's the connection. But why would he do that?"

"What is it? What's going on?" she asked.

"I think I might know who gave you the money. I just don't know why he did it."

"Who? What? How would you know?"

He shook his head. "It's so far-fetched. But it fits."

"Spike," she said. "Are you going to tell me what's going on?"

He blew out a breath. She rubbed at her forehead.

"You're getting a migraine. This is stressing you out."

"What? Getting shot? Learning that you know something about the money I suddenly won? Or you acting all strange and cold when you told me you loved me and always would."

Fuck. He'd fucked this up hugely.

"Baby doll," he started to say. He didn't know what to say to her. He didn't want to hurt her and he knew what he had to say would do that.

"I'm fine, Spike. Just tell me."

"You'd tell me you were fine if you were bleeding out on the sidewalk."

Christ. That imagery was a bit too close to what had happened to be comfortable.

"I just . . . there's no use dwelling on problems, right? I mean, growing up as I did, I was just always so grateful that Grandma and Granddad took me in. That I didn't go to a foster home. That I had so many friends to help me when Grandma got ill. There's no point in thinking too hard about the bad things."

He studied her, piecing together what she was telling him. "Is that what you do? When bad things happen you push them aside and think only about the good?"

"Sort of. If something is really painful then I just push it deep. I imagine this box and it holds all the bad thoughts and memories and things that have happened to me and then I lock the box. Sometimes it feels like it's going to explode from being overloaded. But yeah . . . that's how I deal with it."

"Baby doll, that's really not healthy."

"Says the man who has blamed himself for his wife's death for the last ten years," she replied dryly.

"I don't know if it's a good idea to tell you this."

"If it's about my sister then I deserve to know."

"You do. But you just got home from the hospital. You're exhausted. You need time to heal. You shouldn't have to think about this right now."

"Spike, I need answers. If you have the answers I came here to find, then you have to tell me."

She was right. She needed to know. And he had to be the one to tell her. Much as he hated to do that.

"She's already dead. How much more can this hurt?" she asked.

Oh, baby girl. If only she knew.

"Spike."

"I'll tell you. Just let me talk to the guys first."

She rubbed her temples again. He'd noticed how pale she'd grown. "The Iron Shadows guys?"

He nodded.

"Why? What do they have to do with anything?"

"This is their story to tell as well. You getting a migraine?"

"Yes," she said in a soft whisper. "I need to lie down."

Fuck it. He wished he hadn't said anything now. As though it wasn't enough that she'd been shot. On his watch. Now learning he knew something about her sister's death had caused her enough stress to get a migraine.

He stood with her in his arms, hating her whimper of pain.

"After all this, you're never going to stress again."

"Pretty sure that's impossible," she rasped as he reached the bottom of the stairs. He was careful not to jostle her too much as he slowly walked up them.

Not if she stayed in Little space the whole time it wouldn't be.

Fuck. Okay, maybe it was impossible. But he was going to do what he needed to in order to mitigate the stress in her life. He would ensure that she knew she didn't have to do everything on her own.

Laying her down on his bed, he quickly pulled all the drapes. Her bag was still downstairs with Chompers in it. Striding into the bathroom, he wet a cloth. When he walked back to her, she was curled up on her side, holding herself stiffly.

Gently, he drew her hair off her neck and placed the cloth down. Then he ran downstairs, made her a fresh bottle of fairy juice and grabbed her bag, carrying everything back up. Setting the bag down, he pulled out Chompers and placed him beside her.

Then he pulled her pills out.

"Baby doll, you need your pills."

"No," she groaned. "Can't."

Poor baby.

"Come on, it will help make you feel better."

She opened one eye to glare at him. "No."

"I know you're hurting. Let Daddy help you. Please. I don't like you in pain." He hated it. He wanted to do whatever was necessary to fix it. And knowing he couldn't, it killed him.

"Okay," she muttered.

She opened her mouth and he gave her the pills then held the bottle to her mouth. Some fairy juice dripped out of the side of her mouth.

This would be easier with a proper bottle. It was something he'd usually discuss with her first, but she had shown some interest. And if it helped him get her hydrated it could only be a good thing.

Fuck, he hated leaving her but he needed to get some of the things he'd ordered for her. Including a baby monitor with a camera.

Walking out, he made a few calls while he was grabbing stuff. After setting up the camera and making sure it worked, he mixed some more fairy juice up into the baby bottle he'd bought for her then set it by her lips.

He didn't want to wake her if she was sleeping. But to his surprise, her mouth opened and he slid the nipple in. She started sucking on it.

When it was half gone, her mouth went slack and he guessed she was in a deeper sleep. After brushing a light kiss on her forehead, he stood.

"You're not alone anymore, baby doll. I'm gonna take care of you."

∼

RAZOR WHISTLED as he entered the foyer. "Some nice digs you got here, bro. So how come we never come out here for Sunday barbeques, huh?"

"Because I don't want you all in my house," Spike said dryly. "Wouldn't have you here now if I could leave."

But there was no way he was leaving her.

"What's this about?" Reyes snapped as he followed Razor. "What was so urgent we had to come all the way out here?"

"You have something better to do?" Ink asked Reyes. "You gonna get laid or something? Spike, you should let the man get laid, maybe he'd be in a better mood."

"Certainly worked for you," Duke shot at Ink.

Ink handed over Mr. Fluffy to Spike, placing his bag of stuff in the foyer. "Thanks to you, Betsy and the boys now want a puppy. Only they can't decide on a breed. I'm gonna end up with three damn puppies."

The last one inside was Jason who just nodded his head.

"Keep your voices down," Spike told them. "Millie's asleep. Don't need you all waking her."

"Even more reason we shouldn't be here," Reyes said. "Couldn't you come in?"

"Not leaving her." He led the way down to his office. He set Mr. Fluffy down on the floor and the dog promptly jumped on the sofa and settled in.

So well trained.

Spike set the monitor down so he could see her sleeping.

Spike hated that she was in pain. They needed a routine. Something that would help with her stress levels and teach her to lean on him.

He had a feeling he was going to need a notebook to keep track of all her transgressions while she was injured. He was going to find it hard to get stern with her at the best of times.

Fuck, this girl. She had him wrapped around her little finger.

"Couldn't we have had this chat over the phone?" Reyes asked.

"Not private enough."

Ink rolled his eyes at him. "Who do you think is gonna listen in?"

"I dunno. Maybe the Fox."

"What?" Duke snapped.

"I've gone over this house with a bug detector. It's clean."

"Explain yourself," Reyes demanded.

They'd all moved throughout his office. Jason was leaning against a wall, as usual. Both Razor and Reyes were sitting in the chairs across from him, while Duke and Ink had taken seats on the sofa. He looked over them all.

"Millie came here to try and find who murdered her sister."

"Fuck," Ink said. "She's only just told you that now?"

He winced and ran his hand over his face. "My fault. I haven't exactly been forthcoming with my own shit. Was trying to keep some distance between us."

"Yeah?" Ink asked with amusement. "Seems to have gone well for you."

Spike shot him a look. Asshole.

"Anyway, she's always been adamant that we couldn't let Luther pick up where his father left off. I figured it was just because she didn't like the idea of Luther selling pussy. But it's more than that. Her sister was Daria Marshall."

Silence fell through the room.

"What the fuck?" Reyes spat out. "How?"

"They're half-sisters. Different last names from different dads. Millie is ten years older than Daria. Millie's mom couldn't be bothered looking after her kids. She dropped Millie off at her grandparents when she was four. Years later, she dropped off Daria. But by then, the grandparents were quite old. Millie had to help out a lot. The granddad died then the grandma got ill and Millie was taking care of her and working and trying to watch over Daria. When she was seventeen, Daria ran off and Millie couldn't find her. She didn't know where she was until two cops knocked on her door and told her that Daria had been found murdered. Oh, and that she'd been working as a prostitute."

"Fuck," Razor said. "That poor girl."

"She blames herself," Spike said. "Feels guilty for her death when it wasn't her fault."

"I know someone else like that," Duke said dryly.

Spike shot him a look. He got it. It was the same thing he'd been doing all this time. But he wasn't going to let Millie make the same mistakes he had.

"Wait. How did she know about Luther's connection to Daria?" Reyes asked. "Was she following him that night and that's how she overheard that conversation between him and that rat who was inside Steele's ranks?"

"No. That was total coincidence. She doesn't know that Luther's old man was the one who recruited Daria. Who fucking sold her to the senator. Or that the senator killed her."

"You haven't told her yet?" Duke asked incredulously.

"She's got a migraine. I can't tell her right now. And I asked her to let me talk to you guys first. Because there's more."

"Fuck me," Ink groaned. "Why can't things ever be simple?"

That just wasn't their lives, it seemed.

"Few days after the cops told her about Daria, she lost her job. Thought she was going to lose her home. Her friends are all elderly, they couldn't help. She gets a knock on the door. Seems she'd won a contest she can't remember ever entering."

"Let me guess, she won enough money to pay all her bills," Razor said dryly.

"And to help her grandma's elderly friends with theirs. With enough left over to want to hire someone to take out Luther. Something she's quite keen on doing."

Jason whistled.

"So what was this contest?" Reyes asked.

"Well, she didn't remember much about the guy who brought her the check. He was tall, with a belly. But the contest was run by a company called For Fox Sake and there was a picture of a fox's head on the emblem."

"Fuck. Me," Ink breathed.

They all looked to Duke, waiting for him to explode. Duke was normally a very calm guy. But the Fox knew how to push his buttons. Mainly because the Fox adored Sunny and he wasn't afraid to send her expensive gifts or threaten Duke if he thought Sunny was at risk in any way.

"Why would the Fox send money to Millie?" Duke asked.

Spike shrugged. "Who knows why he does anything? Why did he save Betsy from being buried alive? Why did he save Sunny from Horse and Rory? Why give us alibis?"

"The guy is a loose unit," Reyes muttered. "His behavior is erratic. He almost seems to do things on a whim. Like a child. He takes interest in something shiny then moves on to something else when it dulls."

"He still finds Sunny shiny," Duke muttered.

"Do we call him? Ask?" Jason said. "Sunny has his number, right?"

"I don't want Sunny calling him. I don't want Sunny having anything to do with him," Duke stated.

"You have to get past this hatred of him," Ink told Duke. "At the end of the day, he's saved all our asses. We owe the guy. And the fact that he saved Betsy means I'm forever indebted to him. Cut him some slack."

"All right for you to say, he didn't send Betsy a motorcycle for her birthday," Duke muttered. "Who knows what he'll send her for Christmas? A damn plane?"

"He enjoys getting a rise out of you," Razor said.

"Let's get back on track," Reyes demanded. "So Millie is Daria's half-sister. She gets a huge amount of money from the Fox. Only she doesn't know who he is?"

Spike nodded. "She has no clue or she likely would be trying to hire him to kill Luther."

"So she decides to come here to find her sister's killer," Reyes continued. "Which is a damn stupid idea. She overhears a conversation. Which leads her to us. Well, to you."

"Yep."

"And it's all one fucking big coincidence," Reyes muttered. "Except for the Fox sending her money. He obviously did that deliberately."

"Remember when he stole that money from Sunny's ex and donated it to a charity for foxes?" Jason asked.

"What? You think he used that money to send to Millie?" Ink asked. "But Sunny's ex didn't have that sort of money."

"Nah, I'm saying that what if he took money from someone else and gave it to her. Someone he considered had wronged her."

Spike straightened. "The senator. Who knows what sort of dirty funds he had? If he'd taken that money, he might have thought it was a weird sort of justice to give it to Daria's sister."

"Fuck," Ink stated. He then looked over at Spike. "What are you going to tell her?"

Spike ran his hand over his face. "The truth, I guess."

"Don't envy you that, man," Duke told him.

No. He was dreading it. "I think she'll react one of two ways. She'll either try to ignore the pain." Push it into her box. "Or she'll completely lose it."

"Anything else we can do?" Duke asked.

"Umm, yeah, there is one more thing I need help with."

36

Millie reached the top of the stairs just as Spike appeared at the bottom.

He scowled up at her. "Just what the hell do you think you're doing, baby doll?"

"Coming downstairs to see you?" She'd woken up feeling out of sorts. Part of it was aftereffects from the migraine and the fact that she'd slept so long. But mostly it was because she'd remembered that Spike knew something about her sister's death.

It cut her to the quick. She wanted to know.

And yet she didn't.

He strode up the stairs. "Stay right there."

When he reached the top of the stairs, he placed his hands on her hips and studied her closely. "How are you feeling?"

"Like I got shot, had a migraine then slept for fifteen hours straight."

He grunted. "If you'd wanted up, you should have called for me."

"I didn't feel like screaming. How did you know I was up anyway?"

He wrapped his hand around the back of his neck. "Ah, I might have put a camera in the bedroom."

She raised her eyebrows. "That's kind of kinky."

"Not a camera that records. More like a baby camera."

"Oh." She blushed. "You've been watching me sleep?"

He shrugged. "I don't like leaving you when you're injured or ill. This lets me keep watch over you while I'm somewhere else in the house. And you obviously need watching since you got out of bed without permission."

"I need permission to get out of bed?" He had to be kidding, right?

"You do," he replied, completely serious.

"Spike, I can get out of bed on my own."

He shook his head. "Nope. No can do. You could get light-headed and fall, hit your head, knock yourself unconscious and end up back in the hospital. Do you want to be in the hospital again?"

"Not sure they'd let us back in after last time," she muttered.

"From now on, you want out of bed, you call for me. And there is no going up and down the stairs on your own."

She sighed. "More rules."

"More rules."

"I'm not made of glass."

"To me you are. To me you're more precious than anything."

Tears entered her eyes and she leaned her forehead against his chest.

"Hey, what is it? Did you hurt yourself? Fuck it, from now on, I'm just carrying you everywhere. Come on, back to bed."

"I didn't hurt myself. I'm not in pain."

He ran his hand up and down her back and just waited for her to continue. She drew away to look up at him, aware of a tear escaping. "Don't know what I did to deserve you."

He snorted. "Think that's my line. From what I know of you,

baby doll, you deserve everything." He gently ran his fingers through her hair. "Sounds to me like you've spent most of your life taking care of everyone else. Time to let me take care of you."

She gave him a tremulous smile. "I'd like that. Just, try not to go too far overboard, huh?"

"I did warn you."

He was right. He had.

"I want to have a shower and get changed. Then I need you to tell me about my sister."

"Sure you're ready for it?"

"I'm ready." Not really. But then she never would be. There was a ball of dread in her tummy telling her that she didn't want to know.

"No shower. I'll give you a quick sponge bath and get you dressed."

She sighed but let him fuss. And by the time she was dressed in clean trackpants, a camisole and a cardigan that hung off her injured shoulder, she was exhausted.

Spike held her shoulders, studying her intently. "How are your pain levels? Is your migraine completely gone? Feeling dizzy? Hungry? Thirsty?"

She placed her good hand over his mouth. "Spike." Enough procrastinating.

He nodded. "Right. But before I tell you though, you're going to eat and take some painkillers." He carried her downstairs and had her lie on the sofa with a pillow at her back and a blanket over her legs as he heated up some soup. Mr. Fluffy managed to rouse himself enough to toddle over to her for a cuddle before settling in at her feet. A fresh bottle of fairy juice was placed on the floor by the sofa. Then Spike pulled the coffee table closer and sat on it. He spooned up some soup, blowing on it and held it out for her.

"I can feed myself."

"Nope. Daddy will feed you. I need to. Please."

There was a flash of pain in his eyes and she knew that her being shot was going to haunt him for a long time.

Maybe forever.

This connection between them was something special, maybe something that some people never experienced in a lifetime.

"Okay, Daddy."

"Good girl." He proceeded to feed her, checking every mouthful to ensure it wasn't too hot. His caring almost brought tears to her eyes again and she had to take a deep breath after he finished and left to grab her pain pills. What was wrong with her? Her emotions were bubbling just beneath the surface.

Where had her control gone?

After taking the pills he handed her, she settled back into the sofa while he sat by her legs, facing her. "Good? Too hot? Too cold?"

"Spike just tell me. It can't be . . . it can't be worse than not knowing, surely?"

He glanced away from her and she braced herself.

"I'm going to start a bit further back so you understand how I know this. See, before Reyes was the President of the Iron Shadows, we had this asshole called Smiley. He started laundering money through the bar, got us mixed up with some bad characters. Reyes came along and got rid of Smiley. But by then it was too late, the bar was in the red and we were in deep with the Bartolli family."

"Bartolli? I've heard that name."

"Yeah, Luther is connected to them. He married Fergus Bartolli's niece. Fergus was the head of the family. Asshole man. Involved in human trafficking, drugs, guns. Anyway, Reyes was trying to put the bar in the black and made some deals with the wrong people. Bartolli had us over a barrel. He got us to blackmail US Senator Jonathan Robins."

"Whoa," she stated. "What was the blackmail over? Wait,

wasn't the senator murdered? Didn't he have some young girl in his cabin?"

He scowled. "Yep. Robins was scum. He bought young women from Luther's old man, raped and murdered them. Bartolli gave us photo evidence to use. We handled retrieving the cash and dropping it to Bartolli. You gotta know, none of us wanted to do it. We started watching the senator, trying to work out where he was hiding the girl in the photos so we could rescue her."

"Did you find her?"

He sighed. "No. Not in time." He grimaced. "Baby doll, the girl in the photos, it was Daria."

"No," she whispered. "It . . . it what? How can that be? The police . . ."

"They never knew about her connection to the senator. Although if they did their job better, they might have worked it out. We think the senator's father probably has connections with the cops and got things pushed under the rug."

"Oh God. Oh God."

"I'm so sorry." He reached for her hand and she drew it back. She just couldn't be touched right then.

A flash of hurt crossed his face but she was too deeply in shock to say anything to soothe him. It wasn't him. It was just . . . Daria. Oh God, Daria.

A sob broke free.

"Baby," he said, his voice broken. "I'm so fucking sorry. We tried and failed. Failed her. Failed you."

"I . . . you said he bought her from Luther's father? The pimp?"

"Yeah. Don't know how she ended up with Frankie. She could have been picked up as soon as she arrived in the city. Frankie had a woman that he'd send to hang around the bus terminal to lure runaways in."

She could barely process it. Couldn't handle that this had happened to her sister.

"Why didn't she call me? I would have come for her. I would have done anything for her."

"I don't know, baby. I'm so sorry."

Oh Daria.

"Robins killed her then?"

"Yeah. Or one of his men."

"How many women do you think he did that to?"

"I don't know, baby."

"The one found at his cabin? Is she all right?"

"I don't know. I can find out."

She nodded. "Maybe she needs help. I have money . . . I can help her."

"Fuck, baby. You have the biggest heart of anyone I've ever met. Why don't you just concentrate on you right now. I know this has to be a fucking shock."

"You didn't know she was my sister when you met me?" she asked. She didn't know what she would do if he'd kept it from her all this time.

"No. You have two different last names. We didn't look into her background once she was . . ."

He trailed off but she knew what he was going to say.

Oh Daria.

Keep it together, Millie. No point in falling apart. But she could feel the strain of locking everything down.

"But when I told you about the money, you acted strange, why?"

He sighed. "Like I said, we were keeping watch on Robins, trying to find out where he was keeping, umm, Daria."

"Right," she whispered.

"Turns out, he was being watched by someone else. Someone called the Fox."

"A person who calls themselves the Fox." Her mind could barely put the pieces together.

Oh Daria.

"The Fox is an assassin for hire. He was there to take out the senator."

"An assassin for hire murdered the senator?"

Spike was watching her carefully. "Yes, but you can't ever say anything. The Fox is, he's different. He could well be a psychopath. We're not sure. But he helped us."

"Helped you?"

"He took a shine to Sunny, rescued her from two men who had kidnapped her and then he hid her away. He had us trying to find her while he was taking out the senator. But he's not a normal man. He might not like that I told you this. You must keep it to yourself. Promise me."

She nodded. "I won't tell. He did the world a favor. I only wish I could make Jonathan Robins pay. That sick asshole. And Frankie too. Wait, do you think Luther had anything to do with it?"

Spike sighed. "Don't know. Don't think he was in the city at the time."

"If he did, I want him to pay."

"I'll find out. I promise you."

"Wait. Fox. For Fox Sake. The company name? You think this assassin had something to do with the money I was sent?"

"I don't know, baby doll. But frankly, it wouldn't surprise me. That's something he might do."

"I don't get it." The more she learned the more confused she grew.

Oh Daria.

"He might have seen it as justice to take money from the senator and give it to you."

She blanched. "You mean it's dirty money." It was becoming harder to breathe. "I have to get rid of it."

"We'll do whatever you want," he reassured her. "Give it away to a charity, whatever you need to do."

"Yes. Yes. We'll get rid of it. Get rid of it."

"Baby?"

She was aware of his worried stare. Knew that he was waiting for her to lose it. She should be losing it, shouldn't she?

Instead, all she felt was this weird emptiness. It was like her emotions had drained out of her. Was she in shock? She wasn't sure. She felt weird. Out of it. Numb.

She was numb.

This wasn't right. She should be screaming. Crying. Mourning Daria. Mourning the loss of her baby sister, who she'd helped raise.

Who she'd failed. She'd failed to keep her safe.

"Millie, talk to me."

"Think that's the first time anyone has urged me to talk. Most people want me to shut up."

"What?" Spike scowled.

"It's okay. I know I can be a lot. I get excited about stupid things. I dance around the house, I love to sing and be silly. I can be too much."

"Fuck that shit. You're fucking perfect. I don't want you to be anything but yourself. Do you hear me? If I find out you're trying to change yourself to be what you think I want, I'm going to be fucking mad, understand?"

"You wanted me to change my outfit to fit in more."

"What? When?" he demanded.

"At the fabric store."

"Fuck. Baby, that wasn't because I didn't like the way you looked. Liked it too fucking much. You're gorgeous. I'm going to spend all my time fucking keeping men from staring at you."

"I doubt it."

"I don't," he growled. "And I was wrong to tell you to do that. Safety be damned. Should never have demanded you change.

Fucking kills me that I hurt you. Understand? I was wrong. And you, are perfect."

She blinked at him.

"Christ, baby doll. I think you're in shock."

"I think so too."

"I'm going to call Hack," he said urgently.

No. No, she didn't want to deal with anyone else.

"No. I just. I think I need to just sleep. I feel tired. I need to sleep."

∼

Spike paced back and forth in the kitchen. What the fuck should he do?

For over an hour, she'd just sat there, staring into space. He'd called Hack. The asshole had told him just to give her some time to process everything. How much time did she fucking need? He just wanted to hold her. He wanted to make her feel better. To take away her pain.

Fuck, he wished he knew how to do that. To put that spark back into her eyes.

He couldn't believe that she thought he wanted her to be less. To hide who she was. Fuck, how many people had done that to her? Told her that she was too much as she is? No wonder she'd started locking down any emotions that she thought people might react negatively to.

No more.

A cry came from the living room, he raced in there. Her eyes were shut, a fine sheen of sweat covered her brow. Fuck! Was she too hot? He placed his hand over her forehead, sighing in relief when her temperature felt normal.

"No, Daria, no!"

Fuck. She was having a nightmare.

"Millie! Millie, wake up!"

He didn't want to jostle her. She started to thrash around, crying out as she obviously hurt herself. Fuck!

Carefully, he picked her up. He sat on the sofa with her nestled on his lap.

"Millie, wake up! Wake up, baby doll. Daddy needs you to wake up."

Her eyes shot open and she took in a gasping breath. "Daria... oh God, Daria!" She attempted to suck in a breath, panic filling her face. Suddenly, he realized she was having a panic attack.

"Shit! You're panicking. Breathe in. Slow. Out slow. In. Out." He reached for her hand, placing it on his chest. "In. Out. That's it, baby doll. In. Out."

Her breathing started to slow and panic gradually gave way to despair.

"Spike," she sobbed.

"It's okay. It's okay." He held her as tightly as he dared. "Let it out."

"I can't!"

"Baby doll, you have to. You can't keep it inside you. Let it free, baby doll. There's just me and you. Give me your pain. I'll take it all. Give it to me."

He didn't think she was going to. Then she turned her face into his chest as a sob broke free. And he held her tight as she lost it.

∼

SHE'D NEVER CRIED SO MUCH in her life.

When her grandma died, she'd struggled with her emotions. Everything had been a mess. She'd tried to shed tears when she heard about Daria, but they just hadn't come.

But now she was paying for keeping her tears on the inside.

The pain burst out of her in huge sobs. Everything she'd shut down tight came out. Fear. Anger. Hurt. Pain.

The terror she'd felt when that asshole held a gun on her.

The fear as she'd crouched in the alleyway and listened to Luther and the rat talking.

Her worry when Spike wouldn't listen to her that night at Reaper's bar.

The terror when Corey tried to take Tawny.

Anger when Daria left. Anger at everyone dying on her.

"Why did they all have to die? I'm all alone. They all died."

She knew she should be feeling some pain in her shoulder. But she didn't. At least she couldn't separate that pain from the rest of the agony coursing through her body.

"You're not alone. You'll never be alone again."

"You can't promise that. What if something happens to you? What do I do if something happens to you?" she cried.

"Listen to me," he said in a hard voice. "Millie, listen."

She stared up at him, aware she must be a mess. Her eyes were almost swollen with tears, her face was likely blotchy and she really needed to blow her nose.

He carefully shifted her, then to her surprise whipped off his T-shirt. Was he trying to distract her with his muscles?

Then he held his T-shirt to her face, wiping her tears before holding it to her nose. "Blow."

"I . . . I can't."

"Blow. I don't want to leave you to get tissues. Blow."

She blew into his T-shirt. Yes, it was gross. But she'd make sure to wash it later.

"Millie, I've been where you are. For years I didn't want to love anyone because I was scared to lose them like I did my wife. Now, I realize I was just waiting for someone that was worth the risk of loving again. I was waiting for you."

"What if you decide I'm not what you want? You could do that. Other people have."

"Other people were idiots. Millie, listen. You have a huge heart. You're bubbly and sweet and fun. Somehow, we fit. You and me. You've always taken care of everyone else. You're worn down. You need someone to take care of you. You deserve it. Maybe I don't deserve you. But I'm not letting you go."

She sniffled. "Are you sure?"

"Never been more sure of anything in my life."

"I feel broken."

"I know. And I know it feels like you'll never be whole. But you will be. And I will help. I promise."

37

She looked down at the French toast in disinterest. She hadn't had an appetite since Spike told her about her sister two days ago.

Afterwards, he'd held her while she'd cried. Spoken softly to her. Reassured her. Kept her safe. She'd spent all day crying off and on. He hadn't pushed her to do anything. To talk. The only time that he'd grown bossy was when she'd refused to take her pain pills.

Every night, he held her as tight as he could without hurting her. And each time she'd had a nightmare, he'd been there. He'd wiped her tears. Spoken to her quietly until she slipped back to sleep.

Yesterday it had been much the same. She'd felt like a zombie. Numb. Only for it to hit her once more and she'd start crying all over again.

"Baby doll, you need to eat."

She shook her head.

He sighed, forking up a piece and holding it against her lips.

Reluctantly she ate it. For him. The relief on his face was worth it. But it sat like concrete in her belly. Heavy and hard.

She rubbed her stomach.

"Sore tummy?" Spike guessed.

Nodding, she frowned. Sadness was a veil around her. It was drowning her. Making it hard for her to breathe. To see the light at the end of the tunnel.

Spike sighed, then cupped her face with his big palm. "I'm gonna ring Hack. Get him to come out and check you."

"I'm not ill."

"Baby doll, you were shot. You've been through a huge shock. And you get debilitating migraines that are often triggered by stress and not taking care of yourself. Or in this case, me not taking care of you."

There was a bitterness to his words she didn't like.

She reached over and took his hand in hers. He looked down at it like he'd never seen it before.

"Spike?"

"I know you blame me. I blame me as well." He stood suddenly, slamming his fist against the countertop of the kitchen island. The display of emotion, of barely controlled anger, shocked her.

This wasn't Spike.

You're doing this to him.

"I don't blame you." How could he think that? None of this was his fault.

But it was as though he didn't hear her. He started pacing. "I should have done more."

"Spike."

"I should have saved her."

"Spike."

"Too late. We were too late."

"Spike!" She slid off the stool and suddenly he was there, his hands wrapping around her waist.

"What are you doing?" he questioned. "You need to be careful."

He was treating her as though she was fragile. And she got it. Because that's how she felt right now. However, the old Spike wouldn't let her get away with half the stuff she had. She'd have already found her way across his knee. He hadn't threatened once to keep track of her transgressions.

"Spike, listen to me."

He stared down at her, his eyes tormented. She cupped the side of his face, the way he often did for her.

"You're right."

Agony etched into his face and he flinched, closing his eyes briefly. When he opened them again, he was calm. Poised.

As though waiting for a blow.

"You were right that it wasn't healthy for me to bottle everything up. To go through life pretending it would all be okay if I just smiled more. I . . . this isn't just about Daria's death. That was the trigger. But this is about more than that. Daria's death was in no way your fault."

"If we could have found her in time . . ."

"And if I had noticed she was so unhappy. If I'd tried harder to find her. There are so many what ifs."

"None of that is your fault," he told her. "You couldn't have known she was going to run."

"No. And it's not your fault either," she said gently.

He gave a short nod.

"Sometimes I think things happen for a reason, you know? And I have to realize that even though everything that has happened is terrible, that there is still a lot of good in my life. What's good in my life is you. If all of this hadn't happened, I would never have met you."

His shoulders sagged. "Christ, I thought you were going to tell me you wanted to leave."

"Never," she whispered fiercely. "Not as long as you want me. Maybe not even then."

"Thank fuck." He drew her closer. "I can't lose you, baby doll. I can't."

God, how selfish she'd been, wallowing in her guilt and pity without realizing he was going through the same.

"I'll be okay, Spike. I just need some time."

"And I want to give you that time," he said gruffly. "But not at the expense of your health."

"I know. I'll try to eat and sleep. It's just every bite makes me feel ill and when I close my eyes . . . having you hold me helps."

"Then that's what I'll do. I won't let you go."

"I know." She smiled up at him.

"Do you need to talk to someone? A professional? I know you said no before to Hack's offer. But maybe you should reconsider."

"Maybe I should." Even though the thought of talking to a stranger was scary, she couldn't go on like this.

"I'll talk to him. Gonna ask him about the food issues too. Is there anything else I can do?"

"You don't need to treat me like I'm made of glass. I won't shatter if you get all bossy with me."

Arrogance filled his face. "You like it when I'm bossy."

"Well, no, I didn't say that! You're just not you when you're not grumbling over something ridiculous and threatening to spank me."

"Aww, do you miss being spanked, baby doll?" he drawled.

"I didn't say that." For the first time in days, she felt a spark of something. Of heat. Of amusement. "Think I just need a bit of normalcy. Well, as much as I can get with my injured arm."

And the sadness in her heart.

"Come into the study with me. You can lie on the couch and

read or color while I make a few calls. I'll bring you some snacks and if you're a good girl and eat for Daddy, he has a surprise for you."

Ooh. A surprise.

∽

SPIKE WATCHED her as she lay on the couch in his office. He'd placed a blanket over her and gotten Chompers for her. Mr. Fluffy was sleeping at her feet. She had a coloring book on her lap, but mostly she spent her time looking off into the distance.

She had some earphones in, listening to an audiobook at the same time. It was hard for her to concentrate enough to read at the moment. But listening to books seemed to relax her.

He put through a call to Hack first.

"How's our girl?" Hack answered.

He ground his teeth together. "Not our girl. Mine."

Hack just laughed. Asshole.

"She's not doing that great," Spike admitted.

All sounds of amusement stopped. "What's going on?"

"She's not eating. Barely sleeping. Nightmares. I'm worried she'll have another migraine soon on top of the one she just had a few days ago. She's too stressed. Sad."

Hack blew out a breath. "She's dealt with a lot lately."

"That's just it. Millie doesn't deal with things, she suppresses them."

"And now that's biting her in the ass," Hack surmised.

"That your official diagnosis?" Spike snapped.

"Asshole." Hack was silent for a moment. "Is she willing to talk to someone now? I know a guy in the lifestyle. He's a Daddy Dom. Has his own Little. He actually shares her with his brother." Spike had told Hack about Millie coming here to find out what happened to her sister. But he hadn't gone into any detail. Hack knew nothing about the Fox and they wanted to keep it that way. The less people who knew, the better.

"Yes. If you can recommend someone."

"Yeah, I have an idea. I'll set it up, but probably won't be able to get her in for a few days. You said eating has become difficult?"

"She said she feels nauseous each time she eats."

"Protein drinks could help. I can get some sent to you by the end of the day. It will be from all the stress. Anything you can do to ease that will help. Distract her. Treat her like you normally would. Has she been in Little space since?"

"No. But I have an idea about that."

∼

MILLIE FOLLOWED Spike down the hallway, wondering where he was leading her to. They reached a door she hadn't opened before.

She knew he was upset that she'd barely eaten any lunch on top of her miserable attempt at breakfast. She had to do better or she was going to find herself getting more and more migraines.

Suddenly, he stopped and looked back at her. She was surprised to see he was nervous. Whatever was beyond this door meant something to him.

"If you don't like it, we can change it. Or you don't have to have any of it if you don't want. I just thought it could be somewhere special for you." He was rambling which was so unlike Spike. Her heart melted.

"Show me."

He opened the door and stepped inside. She followed him, coming to a stop, her heart racing. She slowly turned in a circle, trying to take it all in.

"You did this for me?" she finally managed to ask.

"The guys helped."

"How . . . I never even imagined . . . this is all for me?" Tears welled in her eyes. Shoot. She'd have thought she was all out of tears.

His face grew panicked. "It wasn't supposed to make you cry! I can take it all back."

"Spike—"

"It's too much—"

"Spike—"

"Too soon, isn't it?"

"Daddy!"

He stopped, stared at her. His face flushed slightly. "That's the first time you've called me Daddy since the day we got home from the hospital."

She hadn't let her Little out in a while. But maybe that was a mistake. She'd kept herself from slipping into that Little space out of guilt. To punish herself. But she was punishing him too. And maybe they both needed this in order to heal.

"Daddy, this is perfect. I wouldn't change a thing." Because he'd done this for her.

Well, maybe the time-out chair she'd spotted in one corner. That could go.

The walls were painted cream, but along all four walls, decals had been stuck on. There was a large tree in the corner, spanning almost two full walls and hanging from the branches were small, colorful houses. Fairies danced in the air, some of them close to the tree, but others appeared on the other walls.

A magical fairy tree.

But then in amongst all the fairies, dinosaurs roamed. Big ones, small ones, some flying ones. It was insane. It shouldn't have made any sense.

It was perfect.

The corner where the tree resided had a small book shelf along with lots of big, colorful cushions on the floor. A reading corner.

Across from her there was a platform with a microphone on a stand along with her karaoke machine. A gold metallic curtain had been hung from the wall behind the stage.

There was even a dog bed for Mr. Fluffy. It was white with his name written along the side of it. He padded over there, flopped down and promptly fell asleep.

Along one wall was storage. Big tubs that he now led her to. Even the giant giraffe that Damon bought her, who she'd named Jamie, was here.

"These are full of toys. Wasn't sure exactly what you liked." He pulled out one tub. It held a doll along with piles of clothes for her. Another tub was filled with Legos.

"Oh, this is amazing."

The baby corner had a rocking chair. A big, wooden one with comfy looking cushions. Next to it was a small set of drawers like you might use for a nightstand. On top of the drawers was a lamp in the shape of a dinosaur.

He drew her over there next, opening the drawers. Inside, she saw there was a baby's bottle with an oversized nipple, a gorgeous looking pacifier that had a dinosaur face on the front of it, and a dinosaur-shaped bib.

"You don't have to use any of those." He shrugged. "Although I used the bottle when you had a migraine to get some fairy juice into you."

"You did?" She could vaguely remember that. "I'm not sure I can…"

"It's okay. It's just in case. Would you like to play with something?"

She glanced over at the reading corner. "Want me to read you a story, Daddy?"

"Nothing would make me happier, baby doll."

∼

For the first time in a long, long time Spike actually felt at ease. He watched as Millie sat on the floor and built something with the Legos. It was slow going with one arm, but she didn't get grumpy. She'd already read him three stories before declaring that she wanted to play for a while.

He'd brought his laptop in to work while keeping an eye on her.

She liked the playroom.

Thank fuck.

Yeah, he'd been a bit nervous. But he was glad now that he'd done it. He was heartened to see the sadness lighten in her eyes. This was helping both of them, he realized. Hopefully, easing both of their stress levels.

When he saw her yawn for the third time in a matter of minutes, he knew that he was going to have to interrupt her play.

"Hey, baby doll. Time for a nap." He set his laptop down and walked over to crouch in front of her.

"Don't need a nap, Daddy."

"You've yawned several times and it's past the time that you usually nap."

"No, Daddy. I'm playing."

"Little girl, last warning," he said sternly.

She frowned up at him. "Daddy, I'm in the middle of building a princess castle. I can't be stopping. Where will she sleep tonight if I don't make it?"

"I'm sure she'll be just fine sleeping in the box."

"In a box." She gasped. "Daddy, a princess does not sleep in a box."

He tapped her nose. "If this princess doesn't do as she's told she might well find herself sleeping with a hot bottom."

"Daddy! You can't spank me! Chompers, get him!" she commanded her dinosaur.

He shook his head at her antics, then to his shock, he found himself whacked in the face with a dinosaur.

Spike sat there for a moment. There was a deafening silence.

He looked at Chompers then over to Millie's horrified face. "Did you just throw your toy at me, little girl?"

"Nuh-uh, Daddy."

"Nuh-uh? So you didn't do that?"

"Nope, Daddy. That would be naughty."

"It would be naughty. So how do you think Chompers ended up hitting me in the face?" he asked her.

"Well, he is a dinosaur. They aren't exactly well trained."

"Uh-huh, so Chompers did that all on his own?"

"I guess he didn't want to take a nap. Naughty Chompers," she scolded the dinosaur.

"Well, I guess Chompers is going to have to go into time-out then, isn't he?" He stood and walked to the corner of the room that held the time-out chair. He set Chompers into it.

"No, Daddy, you can't do that to Chompers," she cried.

Mr. Fluffy opened an eye and let out a disgruntled woof. Whether that was over Millie's distress or the fact that she woke him up, Spike wasn't sure.

"If Chompers is naughty he has to be punished. Come on, nap time."

"Not without Chompers."

"Chompers decided to hit Daddy rather than doing as he was told, so he's getting time-out while you take a nap."

"Urgh, Daddy! You know it wasn't Chompers. It was me." She frowned at him.

"So you hit Daddy in the face with Chompers and you lied to me?"

Her shoulders slumped.

He shook his head then came back and helped her up. He

walked her over to the time-out chair. "Ten minutes. For you and Chompers both."

He grabbed the toy and helped her sit, before handing Chompers to her.

"Daddy is being a big meanie today, isn't he, Chompers?" she muttered.

"No talking or that's extra minutes."

She let out a huge disgruntled sigh. He gave Mr. Fluffy a pat as he passed by to grab something from behind the bookshelf. He really needed to look into training the puppy. As well as getting him to a vet.

He drew out the whiteboard he'd hidden behind the bookshelf and grabbed some pens from a drawer. Then he sat down to write everything while she was in time-out.

"Come here, baby doll," he said after ten minutes. Standing, he held out his arms.

She moved quickly into his embrace and he held her gently, rubbing his hand up and down her back. "Do you know why you were in time-out?"

"Because I threw Chompers at you then lied and said Chompers did it himself."

"That's right. You also weren't listening, were you?"

"I's sorry, Daddy."

"I know, baby doll. But I think we need some help to manage your behavior. So I have made this chart."

He turned her towards the whiteboard that was leaning against the wall. "Here we have Daddy's rules listed." He pointed to the rules. "Over here, we can keep track of any naughty or good behavior. At the end of the week if there are more good ticks than naughty ones, my girl gets a reward."

"And if there is more naughty than good?" she asked suspiciously.

"She gets a punishment. Of course, if she breaks a health and safety rule she gets punished immediately regardless. But she also gets two ticks on the naughty side."

"But you won't spank me while I'm injured."

"No, but Daddy is keeping track. Once you're well enough to be punished, Daddy will be reddening that bottom. I have a feeling you won't sit properly for weeks."

"Daddy!" she cried. Then she eyed him. "What are my rewards?"

"Hmm, could be a new stuffy or toy. Or it could be getting to stay up later for a night or extra playtime. Or it could be Daddy's face between your legs for several hours while he licks your pretty pussy."

"Yeah, that sounds good," she squeaked.

Yeah, sounded damn good to him too.

38

Millie, help me.
 Help me. Where are you? I need you!

"Millie, wake up. Wake up, baby doll."

She came awake with a gasp, her body shaking. A strong arm rested over her belly as she lay on her back, fighting off the dream.

"It's okay, just a nightmare, baby doll. Just a nightmare. You're here with me. You're safe."

Her heart raced. She felt ill. Her breath sawed in and out of her lungs.

"I'm here. Daddy's here." He kissed her cheek before reaching over to the bedside table to grab her bottle of fairy juice, helping her sip from it. She took several sips.

"Want to talk about it?" he murmured, taking the bottle and putting it aside before leaning up on one elbow to stare down at her.

She shook her head. "It's always the same. Always Daria asking for my help."

"I'm so sorry, baby doll." He pushed some strands of hair away from her face.

"I know. Me too."

He lay back beside her, holding her gently. "Think you can go back to sleep?"

She felt restless, out of sorts.

"No," she replied, feeling guilty at keeping him awake. "I could go into the other room, let you get a peaceful night's sleep for once."

He let out a disgruntled growl. "You'll stay right where you are. You won't ever sleep apart from me. Never again."

"Well, there might be some instances where I have to sleep apart from you."

"Not happening."

"What if one of us needs to go away?"

"The other one goes with them."

"Spike—"

"No. I didn't find you to spend even one night apart from you. I'm a possessive bastard. You. Are. Mine."

Was it wrong to like his possessiveness so much? She really wasn't sure. And she didn't know that she cared.

"Got an idea how to help you sleep."

He slid under the blankets. She was lying on her back, a pillow under her arm to support it. All she wore was a camisole and panties. She didn't bother putting the strap over the shoulder of her injured arm. So when he reached up and tugged her top down, her breast popped free easily.

He pushed her legs apart, settling between her thighs, his fingers plucking at her nipple.

"Spike!"

He stilled and she knew what he wanted. Knew he liked to be called Daddy all the time.

"Daddy, please."

His tongue ran along the seam of her lips before dipping in to toy with her clit. Lapping at it, sucking, teasing.

Pleasure stole over her, her heart racing for an entirely different reason. She parted her legs further, allowing him greater access. His tongue left her clit and she let out a cry of protest. But then he thrust it deep into her pussy. Her hips arched up. His fingers left her nipple, his thumb circling her clit as he tongue-fucked her.

In and out. Slow then fast. Her breath came in sharp pants as his thumb now flicked at the swollen bud. She needed to come.

"Please, Daddy. Please!"

Her thighs were shaking. She was so close. So close.

Her pleasure crested and she cried out as she came. Her pussy continued to give pulses of ecstasy. He lapped at her, bringing her down slowly before shifting away. Lying on his side, he moved the camisole back up over her breast then wrapped his big arm over her waist.

"Can I do something for you?" she asked shyly.

He kissed her shoulder. "Not now, baby doll. Now is the time for sleep. You need that more than I need my cock sucked."

She surprised herself by huffing out a laugh. She felt his lips curling against her arm.

"Daddy?" she asked after a few moments.

"Hmm?"

"Do you think I could possibly . . . if you don't mind getting it . . . could I try that pacifier?"

He stiffened and she thought he might say no.

She should have known better. She had a feeling that unless he deemed it dangerous or bad for her health then he would rarely tell her no.

She just might become the most spoiled Little there was.

"Of course, baby doll."

He shifted from the bed, leaving her feeling at a loss and she had to stop herself from calling him back. It was crazy, how much he'd come to mean to her in such a short time. As though he really was a part of her.

Soon, he was back, nestled in close to her. The pacifier was slipped between her lips. It felt strange and she thought she might have made a mistake. But as she sucked, a soothing feeling came over her. Okay, she could kind of like this.

The longer she lay there, the more relaxed she grew until she drifted off to sleep.

39

"What are we doing, Daddy?" she asked as he walked into the living room.

He'd been outside for about an hour, telling her he was setting up a surprise for her. It had been hard to wait around inside without sneaking out to peek. But she also didn't want to ruin his surprise. He'd seemed so excited.

"We're going on a picnic."

"A picnic! Yay!" Then she bit her lip worriedly. She hadn't been having much luck with eating. She knew that Hack had sent over some protein powder, but Spike hadn't given her any yet to try.

What if she couldn't stomach that either?

Hack told Spike it was likely the stress made it difficult for her to eat and she guessed he was right. He'd also set up an appointment for her early next week with a therapist.

Spike walked into the kitchen and came out with a picnic basket. Where had that been hidden? He took some things out of the fridge and put them in.

"Daddy, you've been sneaky."

He winked at her then came over and offered her his arm. She slipped her good hand into the crook of his elbow.

"Mr. Fluffy, you want to come on a picnic?" she called out.

He heaved himself out of his dog bed and padded after them.

"Some of your other friends are already waiting," Spike told her.

"Really, Daddy?"

"And this is a special picnic. It's a fairy picnic."

"Ooh," she said excitedly.

"You know all that fairy juice you've drunk? Well, hopefully this means you can see the fairies living in my garden."

"Daddy, this is so much fun."

"Just walk slowly," he warned her. "I don't want you falling over."

If she did, she had no doubts that he'd catch her. He led her into the trees growing around his property to a small clearing where he'd set down a picnic blanket. Sitting around the blanket were Chompers, Tiny, Jamie and her doll, Aggie.

"Ooh, everyone is here."

"Picnic first? Or fairy hunting?" Spike asked, setting down the basket at the edge of the blanket.

"Silly Daddy. Fairy hunting of course."

He smiled at her.

"Come on, Mr. Fluffy!" she called.

Mr. Fluffy gave her a baleful look and plopped down on his belly. Okay, so it seemed Mr. Fluffy was not into fairies.

"Now, the rules."

"Daddy, there are no rules when fairy hunting!"

He gave her a stern look and she sighed. "Fine, what're the rules?"

"You have to hold onto Daddy at all times. No running. No sharp movements and when Daddy says it's time to stop and rest, no arguing."

"Oh, fine, Daddy. Let's go, though!" He worried way too much in her opinion.

They headed off through the trees and she was careful where she stepped, although most of the ground was pretty flat. She bet he'd scouted this area to make sure she could navigate it safely.

"Daddy, there! There's one!" There was a gorgeous yellow fairy house attached to the big tree trunk in front of her.

"Let's go have a look then."

She squealed as they moved closer. Reaching out carefully, she opened the tiny door and inside there was a small fairy sitting at a tiny table drinking tea.

"Oh my gosh, she's so beautiful!"

For the next fifteen minutes, they explored. She found fairy houses set between roots of the trees, some hanging from branches and there were even a couple of fairies flying around. After house number eight, she could feel her energy levels starting to plummet.

"All right, baby doll, that's enough. Back to the picnic. It's time for a rest."

"No, Daddy, I want to find more," she complained.

"What was my last rule?" he said sternly.

She pouted. "But I don't want to stop. I want to find all the fairy houses."

"We can come back after you've rested and gotten something in your belly."

"Daddy, please," she wheedled.

"No. Do I need to carry you back?"

"Daddy, you're being so mean." She slid her hand free of his arm and stomped her foot on the ground.

"Did you just stomp your foot?"

"Daddy!"

"You definitely need a rest."

"Do not."

"All that sulking is getting you is ten minutes in time-out for you and a tick on the naughty side of your chart."

Well, that just sucked.

She pouted the whole way back to the picnic. Once they were there, he had her sit at the corner of the picnic blanket, facing away from everyone. She fumed for the first few minutes. Then she started to realize that he was right. She was tired. And being tired meant she was more likely to trip and hurt herself.

He'd gone to all this trouble and she'd acted like a bit of a brat.

"Ten minutes is up, baby doll."

She turned to find he'd set out a feast. Big sandwiches filled with ham and cheese that were obviously for him. But there were smaller sandwiches cut into the form of a brontosaurus that just had cheese in them. Ooh, those were cute. There was also cut out fruit and chocolate dip to go with them.

"Daddy, this looks so good. I'm sorry I was naughty."

He leaned over and lightly kissed her forehead. "That's all right, baby doll. I know you're frustrated because you can't do everything you want to with your arm. Want to try a dinosaur sandwich?"

"Yes," she squealed. "I didn't know you could make dinosaur sandwiches, Daddy."

"Daddy has lots of hidden talents," he told her, handing her a sandwich. She nibbled on it. It still didn't sit right in her tummy, but no way she wasn't eating it.

"Chompers, want some of my sandwich? Hmm, no?" The sandwich had cheese and mayonnaise in it.

She managed one but shook her head when Daddy offered another one. He ate two huge sandwiches while she played with her toys.

"Aggie thinks this is the best picnic ever, Daddy!"

"I'm glad Aggie thinks that, what does Millie think?"

"I say it is too!"

"Would you like to try a strawberry dipped in chocolate?"

She nodded enthusiastically. He used a fork to spear a piece of strawberry then dipped it in the chocolate sauce. He held it out to her, with one hand underneath to catch the drips.

She bit down. "Yum! That's so good, Daddy!"

"Another one?"

"Yes, please. I think fruit should always be eaten with chocolate."

"I bet you do. But this is just a special treat."

She pouted a bit at that. But she managed to eat three pieces of strawberry before her stomach claimed it was enough.

"Good. How about you lie down for a while and rest, huh?" He drew one of the cushions he'd brought out with him over and put it against his thigh. Then he helped support her as she lay on her back, looking up at him, her head resting on the cushion.

She yawned. Oh. She was more tired than she'd thought.

Spike leaned over to grab something from the basket and she saw him shake a bottle. She recognized the baby's bottle he'd bought for her. It was filled with a pink colored liquid. But it wasn't her fairy juice.

"This is the protein shake Hack sent over," he explained to her before setting the nipple at her mouth. "Daddy wants you to give it a try, okay?"

"Okay, Daddy." She felt a bit self-conscious for a start. But soon the heat of the sun and the excitement of the picnic and fairy hunt caught up to her. She continued to suckle as she closed her eyes and drifted. Gradually, the nipple of the bottle was pulled away and replaced with her pacifier.

Hmm. Daddy. A picnic. Fairies. Her friends.

Yeah, this was a pretty good day.

NERVES FILLED her as Spike left the living room to let Sunny and Duke through the gate. Sunny had offered to call the Fox for her. To maybe get some answers.

Was this the right thing to do? What did she even know about the Fox? That he was an assassin? That he'd killed the man who murdered Daria? And likely sent her a whole lot of money? Was it a good idea to ask him why?

Or was she best just to leave it alone?

Feeling like she might throw up, she glanced up as Spike walked back in followed by Sunny, who was wearing a pair of black jeans paired with a pink shirt. She had her dark-blonde hair tied back in a braid but there were fly-away pieces everywhere.

"Millie!" she called out with a big smile.

Millie smiled back. It was hard to resist Sunny's infectious grin. She attempted to stand, pushing herself up with one hand, but Sunny waved her back down. "Don't get up for us."

Sunny leaned down and gave her a half-hug. "How are you doing? How is your arm? Are you in a lot of pain? I can't believe you got shot!"

"Take a breath, little rebel. Give Millie a chance to answer you." The dark-haired man from Reaper's the other night walked into the room, giving Millie a wink. He was carrying a hot pink backpack in his hand that was covered in rhinestones.

"Sorry," Sunny told her. "Did you meet Duke the other night?"

"Ahh, no. Nice to meet you."

"Nice to meet you too, sweetheart."

Spike glanced over at Duke. "Nice backpack, man."

Duke just shook his head as Sunny giggled. "I think pink is a good look on him."

"I don't think so, little rebel," he replied as he sat on an armchair. Sunny perched on the arm and he lifted her to sit on his lap, setting the backpack on the floor. "Millie, how are you feeling?"

Spike came over and sat on the sofa next to her. "I'm feeling really good."

"This guy taking care of you?" Duke nodded at Spike.

She smiled at Spike. "He is. He takes very good care of me. Although, I think if he had his way, he'd just carry me everywhere."

"Damn straight," Spike grumbled.

She rolled her eyes at Sunny, who grinned back at her. "These men of ours do tend to be overprotective."

"Well, if you wouldn't get yourselves into trouble, we wouldn't have gray hairs from worrying over you," Duke complained.

"Tell me about it." Spike ran his hand over his bald head, winking down at Millie as Sunny giggled. "Want a beer?" he asked Duke who nodded.

Both men stood and made their way into the kitchen.

"I brought you a get-well card," Sunny told her.

"You did? Thank you!"

Sunny pulled a card out of her backpack, showing it to Millie. It was handmade with a mess of glitter in the front and when she opened it, more glitter drifted out onto the floor.

"Whoops," Sunny said with a giggle. "I might have gone overboard with the glitter."

"I love it. Thank you."

"You're welcome," Sunny said shyly. "I'm so glad that Spike found you. Or that you found Spike. And that you're a Little too. Like me and Betsy. Duke said he and the guys helped Spike with your playroom. Oh, I hope you don't mind that he told me that?"

"Of course I don't. Would you like to see it?"

Sunny's eyes widened. "Yes. I wasn't sure if you'd want to show me or not. Some people aren't comfortable showing their Little side to other people."

She wouldn't be comfortable with just showing it to anyone,

but Sunny was so warm and genuine it would be difficult not to relax around her. "Do you have a playroom?"

"Uh-huh. It's awesome. It's got this scene from Alice in Wonderland on the walls because that's my favorite story. When you come over for one of our barbeques, I'll show it to you."

She scooted forward and went to push herself off the sofa with her good hand.

"What are you doing?" Spike appeared at her side, grabbing hold of her good arm to support her.

"I'm going to show Sunny my playroom."

"If you wanted to get off the sofa, what should you have done?" he asked sternly.

She bit her lip. "Asked you for help?"

"That's right." He slid her good hand through his arm and lead them all towards the playroom.

Sunny clapped her hands as she entered in behind them. "This is so cool! Ooh, look at your stage." Sunny skipped over to the stage, checking out the microphone. "Can you sing, Millie?"

"I'm okay."

"You're better than okay, baby doll," Spike told her.

She smiled up at him.

"Daddy, can I have a stage in my playroom?" Sunny asked Duke.

"Course you can, little one," he replied warmly.

"Millie, you know what you need for this stage?"

"No, what?"

"Dress-ups!"

"Ooh, yes." Millie looked up at Spike, taken by Sunny's enthusiasm. "Could we get some, Daddy? I could make some but . . ." She looked at her arm with a sigh. She couldn't even get down on the floor to play like Sunny was currently doing, let alone sew anything.

"You can sew?" Sunny asked.

Millie nodded.

"Millie makes a lot of her own clothing," Spike said proudly. "Including her onesies."

"Ooh." Sunny clapped her hands. "Can I see? Will you make me some?"

"Of course."

"Come on, little rebel. We can arrange a play date for when Millie's arm is better, okay?" Duke said to Sunny, holding out a hand to her.

"That would be so much fun. Betsy could come too. You can all come to my house. I have so much crafting stuff. I've got heaps of rhinestones and glitter and a glue gun. Although I'm only allowed to use that under supervision." Sunny sighed.

"You could burn yourself. And I can't have that," Duke said sweetly, kissing the top of her head as he led her out of the playroom.

"Head into my office," Spike told him. "We'll make the call in there."

She tensed as they made their way into his office. He led her to the sofa, helping her sit. Then he crouched in front of her, taking hold of her good hand. "You sure about this, baby doll? We don't have to do it."

She bit her lip. "I don't know. I'm nervous for some reason."

Sunny took a seat in one of the chairs that Duke pulled over. "I'll go get your phone," Duke said to Sunny who nodded with a smile.

"Millie, there's no pressure. If you decide not to call the Fox, that's fine."

What if the money had come from the senator? What would she do with it? She already knew she didn't want to keep it.

"In all likelihood, the Fox will turn up for Christmas dinner and you'll be able to ask him yourself," Sunny joked as Duke walked back in.

"Jesus. Why would you say that, little rebel?"

"Don't worry." Sunny waved a hand dismissively. "It will never happen."

"Okay, let's do it," she said, letting out a breath. "I want to know for sure whether the money came from him. And if it did, why he sent it to me."

Sunny nodded and tapped on her phone, setting it down on her lap on speaker.

"Hello, you've reached the Fox. If you are anyone other than my sweet girl, you need to hang up now before I hunt you down, skin you alive and roast your entrail on my firepit. If you are my sweet girl, then leave a message and I'll get back to you."

Millie felt her eyes widen as she looked over at Spike. He grabbed her good hand, giving it a slight squeeze. Sunny just shook her head. When there was a beep, Sunny spoke.

"Fox, it's me. Can you call me back? Thanks."

Duke reached over and ended the call.

"I didn't want to say too much," Sunny told her.

"He, umm, is definitely different," Millie said, squeezing hold of Spike. "You know what? I think I've changed my mind."

"Don't be afraid," Sunny reassured her. "Fox is really a big softie."

Duke made a snorting noise. "Maybe for you. For everyone else, he's a dangerous assassin."

"I've definitely changed my mind," Millie said in a high-pitched voice.

"I would never let him hurt you," Spike growled.

The phone rang and she sucked in a breath. Now or never, she guessed.

"It's him," Sunny said, answering the phone. "Fox."

"Sunny, my sweet girl. I don't have a lot of time. I'm playing with fire and I don't want to get burned. Are you all right? Duke better be keeping you safe."

Sunny patted Duke's leg as he scowled. "He is taking care of me just fine, Fox."

"Good. What's going on? Don't tell me someone else has been kidnapped?"

"No. Nobody has been kidnapped. You're on speaker. Duke and Spike are here. So is Millie."

"Millie?"

"Yeah, her sister, Daria was murdered by the senator."

"Ahh, yes. Hate to rush you, sweet girl. But I really do have a fire to attend to."

"Fox did you send money to Millie?"

"Now why would I do that?"

"I'm not sure. But she won some money that came from a company called For Fox Sake. Seems a bit of a coincidence."

"Does it?" the Fox said slyly. "Sorry, sweet girl. Can't stay and chat. Things to do, people to kill."

"Fox!"

"Bye, sweet girl. See you soon. Likely, very soon."

With that the call ended.

"Wait. So he didn't send me that money?"

Sunny looked at Duke then Spike. "My gut tells me he did. He didn't out and out say he didn't. But he likely wants to keep his reasons to himself."

"What I want to know is what the hell did he mean by I'll see you soon," Duke demanded.

Sunny shrugged. "It's the Fox. Who knows?"

40

Spike tapped out a message to Hack before walking back into the living room. Millie looked up from the sofa, giving him a worried look. He tried to smile for her, not wanting her to stress too much.

Just minutes ago he'd had his baby on his lap as they watched some movie about trolls who sang. Then Steele had rang. And now he had to head out to help deal with the trap Steele had set using the rat in his ranks.

"It's happening now?" Millie asked Spike.

"Yep, apparently, Ink's surveillance caught sight of a group of Devil's Sinners breaking into the warehouse that Steele leaked to the rat. They're gonna detain them until Steele arrives."

Already his mind was going through what he needed to do.

"And you're going as well?" she asked fearfully.

A response came from Hack quickly. He was on his way. He lived closest to Spike so he was the obvious choice to come sit with Millie while Spike was gone.

He leaned over her where she sat on the couch. They'd been watching *Sing* again. He had to admit the movie was growing on him. It was dark outside now and she'd been allowed to stay up later due to good behavior this week. Although it had been close. There had only been one tick in it.

Gently, he kissed her lips. "I promise I'll be careful. Steele will also have men with him. Hack is on his way."

Millie licked her lips, looking nervous. "Okay, you better go. You don't want to miss anything."

He frowned, not wanting to leave her alone. "Hack will be about another five or ten minutes."

"And I'll be fine until he gets here. Promise. No gymnastics, acrobatics or stairs until he gets here."

He grasped hold of her chin. "Promise."

"Pinky promise." She held out her little finger and he wrapped his around hers. "Love you."

"Love you too."

He grabbed his gun and made sure the alarms were all set before racing out of there. This was it. They finally had the Devil's Sinners where they wanted them. He just hoped that fucker who shot her was there.

∽

FIFTEEN MINUTES LATER, he pulled his truck up a block away from the warehouse. Steele had waited until the rat was in hearing distance to let the location of his supply warehouse slip out. Its location was a closely guarded secret.

Of course this wasn't the location of the actual warehouse. Brody, Ink's tech guy, had set up cameras around the perimeter. Alarms had been triggered by the Devil's Sinners when they'd snuck in and Ink's men, who had been waiting close by, had been alerted, swarming in to surround the intruders.

It was an expensive exercise, but Steele wanted nothing leaking to the Devil's Sinners.

Steele was already there. He climbed out of his car, followed by Grady. Mitchell, and a handful of other guys who were close to Steel were there too. Steele nodded at Spike as he adjusted his suit jacket. Spike knew the other man would be armed, along with all of his guys.

"Let's go have a chat, shall we?" Steele murmured.

Spike and Grady flanked him as he walked confidently towards the door. The other men fanned out behind them, watching their backs.

The warehouse was filled with containers. All smoke and mirrors since they were all empty. In the middle of the warehouse, four of Ink's men stood over a group of around seven members of the Devil's Sinners who were kneeling with their arms up behind their heads. And yep . . . there was Corey. Excellent. Spike cracked his knuckles then pressed his neck from side to side.

Asshole was in for a world of pain.

Regan, the rat in Steele's rank, was there too, looking ill. He should feel sick. Steele wasn't taking his betrayal well.

Spike stepped forward but Steele motioned him back. Damn it. Fine. He'd let Steele run the show.

But Corey was his. The bastard had shot his woman. And now he was going to pay.

"Who is in charge here?" Steele demanded.

A thin, bald guy with tattoos covering his neck and face stood up with a grin. Another guy with a similar build stood too.

"Name's Falcon. This is my brother, Jackal. We're in charge."

"Your mother didn't like you very much, did she?" Grady mocked.

Jackal snarled at him. "My mother was a cheating, lying slut. Just like all bitches are." He turned a sly look on Spike. "How's that cunt of yours doing after my bro, Corey shot her?"

Spike growled. Fucker was going to die. Murderous rage flooded him. He stepped forward, his hands clenching into fists.

"Spike, wait," Steele told him.

"Yes, Spike, wait," Falcon mocked.

"You chose the wrong town to come to," Steele told him. "This is my town. You're not bringing your business here. You should have just kept the fuck away. Would've been safer for you."

"Oh, I beg to differ." Falcon grinned.

There was the sound of a gun chamber filling. Spike half-turned to see Mitchell standing with his gun pressed against the back of Steele's head.

"Aww, you didn't think there was only one rat in your ranks, did you?" Falcon asked.

Corey laughed. Rage flooded Spike again. All that was holding him back was the gun being at Steele's head. All of the Devil's Sinners guys rose to their feet, cocky looks filling their faces.

"Thought you were so shit hot, huh? My town. Guess you got that wrong," Falcon gloated

"Mitchell, I'm disappointed in you," Grady drawled, as cool under fire as ever. "Were the benefits not good enough for you? We treated you like family."

"That was your fucking mistake, wasn't it?" Mitchell sneered. "Too fucking trusting. All of you put your fucking guns down."

They all set their guns on the ground. Regan started collecting them up.

"I take it you were the one who let that asswipe into Pinkies?" Steele asked, pointing over at Corey, who snarled furiously. Steele just gave him a calm look back. "I'm also guessing you're the one who freed him?"

"Took you long enough to work it out," Mitchell replied calmly.

"You all thought you were so smart setting this up," Jackal snarled. "But we always knew this was a set-up. We were one step ahead of you all along. Want to know how?"

"I'm sure you'll tell us," Steele said.

"It was the fucking puppy," Mitchell grumbled.

What?

"A puppy?" Grady said slowly. "Do tell."

"The fucking puppy that cunt of his found." Mitchell nodded to Spike.

"Shut your fucking mouth," Spike spat back. What did this have to do with Millie? And Mr. Fluffy?

"Luther was transporting a bunch of puppies for us and he lost one. All the idiot had to do was pick the up from the breeder and bring them to headquarters. They all look alike. When I saw that damn puppy with your bitch the other night at Pinkies, I knew it was the missing one," Mitchell snapped. "Needed to figure out how she got hold of it. I sent off a text to Corey to tell him the bitch was there. Then after work, I went to talk to Luther. Found out that he'd pulled Regan out of his cover to talk with him."

Fuck. Shit.

"Was suspicious as fuck, but I didn't know if she'd overheard them. Until the location of your secret warehouse was leaked in front of Regan," Mitchell added. "That's how I knew that you'd all figured out he was the fucking rat. It was too much of a coincidence. That location was always locked down tight."

"And now you've been caught in our trap," Falcon informed them.

"Actually, I'll have to disagree with you," Steele said before letting out a piercing whistle.

They came from everywhere. They'd slipped into the warehouse unnoticed and hidden behind crates. Reyes, Ink, Duke and Razor as well as the rest of Ink's guys. All of them armed, their guns pointed at the Devil's Sinners guys.

Falcon had a nice red dot on his forehead. Courtesy of Jason with his sniper rifle. Spike saw Falcon swallow heavily.

"Fucking hell," Jackal swore. "You fucking cunts are dead! You're all dead!"

"I don't think so," Steele replied. "Put the gun down, Mitchell."

"Fuck you," Mitchell spat at him.

"Be a shame if Falcon got his head blown off," Steele said calmly. "Or you."

The beam of light landed on Mitchell's forehead. "Fuck! Fuck!"

Mitchell stepped back and Grady reached over and grabbed the gun then he shoved Mitchell towards the other Devil's Sinners. Mitchell turned back with a snarl. "Fucking assholes. You'll pay for this."

"I doubt it," Steele replied. "See, you're not as smart as you think you are. All those shipments that were intercepted, the information that was leaked, it couldn't have come from Regan. He wasn't close enough to us. But you were."

Mitchell just glared at him.

"So you see, we did know there was another rat," Grady drawled. "We were just waiting for him to show his true colors. Your downfall was pairing up with an idiot like Luther Franklin."

"Where is Luther?" Spike asked.

"Running," Falcon replied. "Fucking bastard messed everything up for us. He knows we're coming for him."

"You five are staying here." Steele pointed to Falcon, Jackal, Corey, Mitchell and Regan. "Raul, call in some more guys and take the rest of them with you. All of you head over to their headquarters. Let them know they're no longer welcome in my city. Not that any of you ever were."

∽

A BUZZER SOUNDED and she walked to the front door to unlock it, checking the camera first the way Spike had taught her. Seeing Hack standing there, she opened the door with a smile.

He smiled at her. "Hello, princess." He held up one hand. "I bring with me treasures from the fairy kingdom. Magical candy."

He shook a huge bag of M&Ms. "And magic wands." The other hand held a bag of Twizzlers.

How did he know they were her favorites?

What did it matter? The man needed to get in here with his treasure.

She opened the door further. "Come in."

"Just hold this bag while I text Spike." He handed over the Twizzlers as he grabbed out his phone and sent off a text. "There, that will keep him off our backs. Now, my princess, shall we go eat our weight in junk food?"

"Are you sure you're a doctor?"

"That's what it says on my diploma back home."

Something black moved up behind him and before she even had time to warn him there was a sickening crunching noise. Then Hack slowly fell to the ground, his phone smashing to the floor. She screamed and tried to reach for him. Panic flooded her. She wasn't thinking properly or she might have run. Maybe. But she didn't run, and someone grabbed her, shoving her back. She landed on the ground and agony engulfed her side.

Her head slammed against the floor, dazing her. She heard a grunting noise. Someone muttering something.

"God damn bitch. Fucking stupid cunt. All your fucking fault."

Someone kicked her side and she screamed. Hands landed around her neck, constricting her air. She tried to fight with her good hand, she used her nails to scratch at her attacker, beat at him with her fist. He screeched but it just made him angrier. Finally, the lack of air started to slow her movements. Darkness encroached.

Then nothing.

41

Spike's knuckles were broken and bruised. His body had taken a few hits. But the enemy was in a far worse state. Falcon, Jackal, Regan, Mitchell and Corey likely thought they'd have the advantage against him, Steele and Grady.

They were mistaken.

The five of them lay on the ground, broken and bleeding. But not dead.

It wasn't enough.

"You need to go now," Steele told him as he slipped on his jacket. The big man looked invigorated. As though he'd just gone for a run. He and Grady hadn't taken many hits. Steele was an ex-cage fighter. He wasn't someone to underestimate. And despite his genteel appearance, Grady wasn't either.

"I'll stay." Corey shot his woman.

"You don't need to be here for this part," Steele told him, his pale blue eyes intense.

"It's my fight too."

"Yeah. And you fought your part," Steele countered. "You don't need to do this part. Leave it to us. Our souls are already fully black."

He shook his head.

"Listen to him, Quillon," Grady said, using his real name. "You should go home to that gorgeous girl of yours and leave this to us."

"The puppies," he muttered.

"What?" Steele and Grady exchanged a look.

"The other puppies like Mr. Fluffy. Luther was transporting puppies and lost one. But where are the other ones? I need to get those puppies. Millie will never forgive me if I don't take care of them."

"I've got guys circling in on their headquarters just out of the city. I can get someone to grab the puppies and bring them to you," Steele told him.

"I'll go myself and get them before I go home. You don't know how much Millie loves animals."

"Go," Steele said. "We'll take care of the trash here."

"It will be our pleasure." Grady smiled. It wasn't a pretty smile.

Spike walked out of the warehouse, rolling his shoulders. He grabbed out his phone to call Hack and saw he'd already received a text from him over an hour ago.

I'm here. We're fine. Have fun!

Idiot.

He sent a text back.

Be home in two hours. Keep my girl safe.

"Spike!"

He looked up and saw his brothers waiting on him. He slipped the phone into his pocket. He'd call home soon.

"Waiting for me?" he asked.

Razor grinned. "Figured we'd better make certain you were okay. Gotten used to seeing your ugly mug."

Spike just shook his head as Duke came up and whacked his back. "All done?"

"Steele and Grady are tidying up."

Reyes nodded. They all knew what that meant.

"Back to Reaper's for a drink?" Razor asked.

"I best get home to Sunny," Duke said.

"I better get home too," Ink added. "The boys wanted to come. They'll have driven Betsy nuts all night."

"I have to go retrieve some puppies," Spike told them.

"Puppies?" Razor asked.

"Yeah. But thanks guys, appreciate your help," he said awkwardly.

Ink grinned. "What else is family for, man, but to come armed to a beat down with a gang? I'm shocked I don't get asked to do that more often."

∼

SPIKE COULD BARELY HEAR himself think from all the barking.

While Mr. Fluffy might be narcoleptic, it seemed his brothers and sister were the opposite. They were boisterous. Energetic. And one of them was chewing on his damn seatbelt.

He needed to call home. He'd tried to check in on his way to the Devil's Sinner headquarters, but Steele had called him. Then he'd decided that maybe it was best to wait until after he had safely rescued the puppies. No use worrying Millie more than necessary. But now he really needed to hear her voice. Using the truck's Bluetooth, he was about to call home when his phone rang. "Yeah?"

"Ah, Spike, we got a situation here," Razor told him.

"Got a bit of a situation here myself," he yelled over the puppies barking.

"Well, think you best come deal with this one. Five, um, older folks just walked into the bar demanding to see you. One says he's Russian mafia, he's already threatened to skin several of the guys.

Another is deaf as fuck and is yelling everything. And then there's the one they're calling Reverend Pat. Spike, they've cleared out half the fucking bar."

"Fuck. They're Millie's family. Just get them out to Reyes' office and I'll be there soon."

"Well, put your foot down, man. Before everyone clears out."

42

Her head was pounding. Nausea bubbled in her stomach. Was she having a migraine? But why did her neck hurt so much? Why was she lying on something hard? And who was yelling?

Her shoulder was in agony. Where was Spike? What was going on? She took shallow breaths to try and manage the pain and nausea.

"It's all this bitch's fault!" someone roared.

Her heart raced. She knew that voice.

Who was it?

She wished she could think. But it was like all her thoughts were coming through sludge.

"Now I have nothing! Your fucking cousin is after me! Steele is gunning for me and the fucking Devil's Sinners want my guts."

There was another voice. Feminine. Her voice was low and quiet so Millie couldn't make out the words. Then there was the sound of skin slapping against skin.

Then a cry.

Had he hit her?

"All because I fucking lost one goddamn puppy and this bitch picked him up! How was I supposed to know she was listening in? That she would tell Steele what she heard? What were the fucking odds of that?"

Another slapping sound. Another cry.

Millie wanted to protest. Wanted to help the woman. As she forced her eyes open, she realized who that voice belonged to.

Luther.

"Wake up, you stupid bitch!" A kick landed against her thigh and she screamed in pain.

"Stop it, Luther!" the woman cried.

Millie groaned, trying to curl up to protect herself.

"Get out of the way, you ugly bitch."

More hits. More cries.

Millie forced her eyes open, her vision was blurred but she could see they were still at the house. What had happened? How had Luther gotten in here?

Hack!

He'd been hurt. Obviously by Luther. Had he killed him? Oh God, where was he?

She couldn't think over all the yelling Luther was doing.

She blinked a few times, trying to clear her vision. It was then that she saw the other woman. She was sitting on the floor, her arms over her head as Luther screamed down at her.

Oh no.

He reached down and started slapping at her. She had to stop him. She had to do something.

"Stop!" she croaked out. "Stop hurting her."

She didn't know who the other woman was, but she was obviously a victim to this asshole.

Luther turned, his chest heaving, his eyes wild.

"You fucking bitch! This is all your fault! I was gonna run this fucking town! Her fucking cousin was too much of a pussy to take over, so I was going to do it. I fucking had it all worked out until you ruined it all."

He reached down and grabbed her, dragging her up. She screamed as fire engulfed her shoulder and side. He shook her, not caring about her pain. Mr. Fluffy started barking and attacking Luther's ankles. He shook him off then kicked the dog, sending him flying. He let out a pained whimper.

"No!" she screamed.

"I ought to put a fucking bullet in your brain right now." He shoved her down against the sofa. Sweat coated her skin as she lay there, trying to manage the pain. Everything hurt, but nothing more than her shoulder and head.

"Luther, no! You can't shoot her. Please! Stop!"

She forced herself to look up, her vision was still blurry but not enough that she could mistake the gun aimed at her.

Fuck.

∽

SPIKE EXPECTED to walk into chaos.

So he was shocked when he found the bar was almost quiet. It had mostly cleared out of patrons which wasn't good for tonight's takings, but there were still about twenty people all gathered around one of the larger tables.

"Woot! Will you look at that? I've won again," a female voice said.

There were a series of groans as he walked forward to find a woman with frizzy, gray hair sitting at the table along with a couple of Iron Shadows guys. Behind her stood a slightly stooped man with thick glasses. Over at the bar, someone hooted with laughter.

A big, gray-haired man dressed in a flannel shirt whacked Razor on the back. "That is good joke, man. I remember that when we go back to Nowhere." The man spoke with a Russian accent.

Razor gave him a puzzled look. "That wasn't a joke."

Behind the bar, another woman was showing Jewel how to mix a cocktail. She wore a green floral dress and a huge, wide-brimmed white hat.

What the fuck?

Shock flooded him as he stared around, taking it in.

Someone poked him in the back and he turned to find a short, round man glaring up at him.

"It's about time you got here, young man," he said.

The bar went silent, watching on. Reyes stood behind the man, glaring at Spike.

"Reverend Pat, good to meet you. None of you mentioned you were visiting."

"We're here to check up on Millie," the woman who'd been playing poker said, coming around to stand by the reverend. The man who'd been behind her came and stood with her.

"Mr. and Mrs. Spain, Millie is fine. You didn't have to come all this way."

Especially without giving him a heads-up.

"We thought it would be a good surprise, yes?" the Russian man boomed. "Give you no time to try and hide anything."

"What would I hide?"

"I don't know. Dead bodies in the closet."

"Skeletons in the closet, dear," the woman from behind the bar said.

"Skeletons? Who would let them decay in the closet?" Andrey boomed. "The stink would be terrible."

"Take us to Millie," Reverend Pat said. "Now."

~

Millie licked her dry lips.

Her heart pounded. She had to do something. Fast. Not just for her but for the poor, broken woman lying across from her. And for Hack.

Oh God, Hack. Where was he?

"What do you want?" she rasped.

"I want you fucking dead," Luther snarled at her.

"That's not what you really want. Right? You want power. Money." An idea came to her. "What if I had enough money that you could get away from here? Start over. You could just take it and go."

"Banks can track fucking wire transfers, bitch. I won't even be able to access it without some fancy fucking off-shore account."

"I have cash. Lots of cash. All you have to do is leave us here. Alive."

"Or you can just give me the cash and I can still fucking shoot you."

Okay. So her negotiation skills needed work.

"Where's the fucking money?" Luther screamed, spittle flying from his mouth.

Gross. So gross.

Where was Spike? What about Hack?

"Tell me where the money is or I'll fucking shoot you! This better not be a fucking trick!"

"It's not! I'll get it for you!" She tried to pull herself up. Maybe if she stalled long enough Spike would get here.

She was shaking too hard and in too much pain to get her legs under her so she could stand.

"Get up, you fat bitch."

"She can't," the other woman said. "You hurt her."

Millie looked over at the other woman, urging her to stay silent. She didn't want him turning his rage back on the poor, small woman. Millie winced as she took in her face. One eye was swollen shut and there was dried blood under her nose. What other injuries did she have?

"Shut the fuck up! Or I'm gonna put a bullet in your brain!" Luther screamed at her.

The other woman whimpered and Millie gathered her strength, managing to push herself up using the sofa behind her. She swayed, black dots dancing through her vision.

Don't faint. Don't faint.

"Fucking hell! This is all such a mess! I should be in a position of power. I'm meant to be someone. Instead, here I am with two sniveling bitches, on the run. Where's the money, bitch?"

Spike, please hurry.

"Bitch, you better answer me!"

Didn't he know any other insults?

"In the office." She stumbled through the room, trying to stay upright.

"Stay here," he barked at the other woman. He followed so close behind her that she could smell the stench of his body odor. She was nearly gagging by the time she reached the office.

Spike, please, I need you.

"It's in the floor. Over here."

"This better not be a fucking trick, bitch, or you're dead."

She figured she was dead either way.

Please, Spike. Please. I love you.

She managed to slide down to her knees, holding onto the arm of the couch with her good hand. Everything hurt. God, it hurt. She had to take shallow breathes as she shook with agony.

"Hurry up!" Luther yelled, waving the gun around. "I don't know when that bastard will be back."

Hopefully soon. Please be soon.

She pushed aside the end table then tugged at the floor. "It's in here."

Oh no.

How had she forgotten that she'd need to get into the safe? What was the code? She had no idea. A whimper escaped.

"What is it? Open the fucking safe!" Luther screeched.

She winced. His yelling wasn't helping her think. With a shaking hand, hoping she was right she input six numbers into the office safe.

The date of Jacqui's death.

To her shock, a green light flashed and she grabbed the handle, pulling the door open. Then she reached in and heaved at the bag of cash. It was so heavy that by the time she managed to get it out, her breath was sawing in and out of her lungs and those black dots had returned. She sat back, shaking and pointed to the bag.

"In there."

"Open it," Luther told her, watching her suspiciously.

It took her a few attempts to pull down the zipper, but she finally managed it. Luther went to his knees, greed lighting up his face as he took in the cash.

Counterfeit cash.

But hopefully, he didn't look too closely.

As he was distracted, staring at the money, she spotted the woman creeping into the room. She had a metal poker that usually sat on a stand beside the log fireplace in her hand.

Millie tried not to watch her, not to tense up as she tip-toed into the room and raised the poker.

Luther was reaching into the bag when the woman got close enough to swing. Then he must have sensed something because he turned. "What the fuck!"

But as he swung around a ball of fluff attacked with a growl, distracting him from shooting and the woman swung the poker at his head. It landed with a sickening crunch. Millie stared on in shock as Luther stilled. For a moment, she thought the woman hadn't hit him hard enough. Then he rolled to the side, his eyes drifting closed.

Millie watched for a moment, hardly believing her eyes. Mr. Fluffy stood there, his hackles raised, snarling at the man on the floor. She forced herself to scramble over to grab the gun. She got it in her good hand as the other woman just stared down at Luther, a blank look on her face.

"Mr. Fluffy!" she cried out as the puppy came over to her, trying to lick her face, his tail wagging. "You did so good. Good boy. My good boy."

"I got him," the woman said.

"You got him. You got him. Everything's going to be okay, now. I'm going to call my Daddy. He'll come. Everything's okay," Millie rambled.

"I got him. He can't hurt me anymore."

"No, he can't."

Millie tried to stand, crying out in frustration as her legs wouldn't work.

"Hack! Oh God, where's Hack?"

"The other man? I think he's still outside. I think he's dead."

"No, no, no, I need to check on him. I need to call Daddy. Oh no." She tried to stand and slipped onto her bottom once more with a pained cry.

A small hand reached out to her and she looked up at the woman who smiled down at her. "Hi, I'm Tabby."

"Hi, Tabby, I'm Millie."

∼

HIS PHONE RANG as he gathered everyone up in Reyes' office. All five of Millie's friends as well as Reyes, Razor and Jason.

Pulling his phone out, he frowned as he saw it was his home line. Would Millie still be up this late? Fuck. He never did get around to calling her earlier. He should have known she wouldn't sleep until she heard from him.

"Millie?" he answered.

"Spike? Oh God, Spike. You're okay." Her voice sounded odd. Filled with tears and raspy as though she had a sore throat.

"Course I am. Baby doll, what's wrong?"

She'd started sobbing. Huge sobs that reached inside him and twisted up his gut until he could barely breathe. "Millie! What's wrong?"

He was aware of everyone staring at him, hyper alert.

"I w-was so s-scared," she managed to get out.

"Because I didn't call? I'm sorry," he crooned. "I'm fine."

Where the fuck was Hack? Why had he let her get into this state? She cried into the phone, breaking his fucking heart.

He was going to kill Hack.

"Baby doll, listen." He gave Reyes a look that told him to keep everyone here. Reyes nodded back, not looking at all pleased. Not that Spike blamed him. Reverend Pat was pissed that he wasn't being taken to Millie immediately, Mrs. Larsen was chatting to Jason about tattoos. Mr. Spain was snoring on the couch and Mrs. Spain seemed to be sharing recipes with Razor. That left Reyes to face off with Reverend Pat and the big Russian guy.

He slid out into the corridor. Millie was still sobbing. Fuck. He needed to get home to her. But first he needed to calm her down before she made herself ill.

"Baby doll, Daddy wants you to calm down. Nice, deep breaths. Can you do that for me? Stop crying please. Deep breaths. You can do it."

"D-daddy..."

"I'm here. I'm not going anywhere."

"N-need you."

"I'm going to be heading home soon. I've just got a small situation here."

"M-me t-too."

He frowned. What was she talking about? What situation?

"Millie, where is Hack?"

"H-he's still a-alive!" she wailed.

What the fuck? What the fuck did that mean?

"What do you mean he's still alive? What happened? Where is he?"

"S-still u-unconscious. Luther h-hit him so h-hard I t-though he was d-dead. But T-tabby has p-pressure on his w-wound. But Luther c-could wake up. We tried to t-tie him up. Tabby d-did while I h-held gun. But Daddy, I need you!"

43

He'd never driven so fast in his fucking life. He'd raced out of the bar, shouting at Reyes that there was something going on at his place. Reyes and Razor had jumped into his truck with him, leaving Jason to deal with their visitors.

Poor bastard.

He sped into his driveway and had barely put the truck in drive before he was out the door. Thankfully, Razor had managed to hold onto all the puppies. Although he left them in the truck as they raced up towards the house.

"Millie!" Spike roared as he ran. "Millie!"

He stormed towards the door, nearly tripping over Hack's prone body lying in the foyer.

"Fuck!"

A woman who'd been holding something to the back of Hack's head scrambled back with a terrified cry.

"Spike, rein it in," Reyes snapped.

Spike briefly took in the woman, noting her battered appearance. Shit. Fuck. What had gone on here?

"Daddy? Daddy!"

His attention turned from Hack and the woman as he leapt towards Millie. She was leaning against the hallway outside his office. Her face was deathly pale, her hair a mess, clothes rumpled. She'd obviously been through hell.

And he hadn't been here.

He gathered her close, holding her gently and still he heard her indrawn breath of pain.

There was a groan from behind him.

"Hack's coming around," Razor called out.

"We c-couldn't get him any f-further," she said to Spike. "He was t-too heavy."

She was shaking so hard she could barely speak. Poor baby.

Leaning down, he carefully took hold of her chin, lifting her face. That's when he noticed the mottled bruising around her neck.

"Who the fuck strangled you!" he roared.

∾

MILLIE SAT on Spike's lap, surrounded by his strong arms and for the first time since he'd left that night she felt safe. Mr. Fluffy was snuggled up on her lap and even though he was getting rather heavy she wasn't going to move him.

He was a hero, after all.

"All of you need to go to the emergency room," Reyes said.

Millie's gaze went to the woman sitting in the corner, her legs up against her chest. Razor was attempting to talk to her quietly. They were all in Spike's office. Hack had been helped in there by Reyes and was now sitting on the sofa as Reyes secured a bandage around his head.

"I'm fine."

Spike rumbled in disagreement. He hadn't spoken since she'd

started her recounting of what happened. She was starting to get worried about him. He was sitting on the chair with her on his lap, glaring down at Luther like he'd enjoy tearing him apart limb from limb.

Reyes had secured the man's hands behind his back with a pair of handcuffs with pink fluff around the inside of the cuffs. She might remember to be embarrassed about that later.

"You're not fine. You can barely speak. Both of you are covered in bruises and Hack has a huge bump on the back of his head," Razor pointed out in a soft tone, obviously trying not to scare Tabby any more than she was.

Spike snarled down at Luther who was still unconscious.

"What are we going to do with Luther?" she asked. "What happened at the warehouse? Is everyone fine?"

"Everyone is fine. But there was another rat," Razor explained. "Mitchell."

"Oh God."

"Don't worry." Reyes told her. "Steele was prepared."

"Your knuckles . . ." she whispered to Spike, no longer capable of speaking any louder. Her throat was so sore.

"He's fine, you should see the other guy," Razor said lamely.

She sucked in a breath then groaned in pain. Spike turned his gaze from Luther to glare at Razor who held his hands up in the air. "Sorry, man."

"I'm fine," she repeated.

"You need to go get checked out. Tabby too," Hack said.

"So do you," she insisted. "If I'm going to the emergency room, so are you."

"Right," Reyes said, standing. "All three of you need to see a doctor." He glared at Hack who went to speak. "But what are we doing with this asshole?" He kicked Luther and Millie whimpered.

Reyes whirled around, swearing quietly. "Sorry, sweetheart."

She blinked. She didn't know him, but he didn't seem the type to be gentle. His eyes narrowed on her then he turned to Spike. "She's in shock. And she's squinting? Another migraine?"

How did he know that?

"Millie?" Reyes prodded gently. "Answer me."

"I think it's just from where I hit my head. I'm okay."

Spike made a low, grumbling noise. She knew he didn't agree with her assessment.

She reached up and cupped the side of his face with her hand. "I'm fine. I promise. And this isn't your fault so don't even start thinking that."

She knew he would be blaming himself.

"No, it's Luther's," Reyes snarled. "Want me to take care of him?"

"No," a quiet voice protested.

They all turned to look at Tabby. She'd put her legs down, no longer looking so scared or defensive. Razor was crouched protectively next to her, a concerned look on his face.

"Don't tell me you want us to let him go?" Reyes asked incredulously.

She cringed then squared her shoulders. "No. Not at all."

"What happened?" Hack asked. "How did you come to be here?"

Millie heard the suspicious note in Hack's voice. She glared at him. Tabby had helped her. And she'd obviously been through hell with Luther. She didn't need them snapping at her.

Tabby rubbed at her temple gently. "I don't know. I really don't. I think he must have drugged me. He came home so angry, ranting about how everyone was after him. He started beating on me. Unfortunately, that wasn't an unusual occurrence. He's been hitting me almost from the day my uncle gave me to him."

"Gave you to him?" she whispered.

"My uncle thought women were a commodity. All of his wives were either given to him or he bought them. I was just a tool to be used. I knew there was no point in going to him when Luther started beating me. Then I basically became his prisoner, locked up in his house without any way of communicating with the outside world. I thought maybe my cousin would try to get in touch with me . . . we were close once."

"I'm so sorry," Millie told her.

"After Luther beat me, he gave me some pills to swallow. I wasn't in a state to refuse. I've learned that refusing just makes things worse. Of course, maybe if I'd said no, he'd finally have killed me."

She laughed bitterly then groaned in obvious pain.

"Tabby, no," Millie said. "If he'd killed you then you wouldn't have been here to help me. I'm sorry for everything you've gone through but I'm very glad you're not dead."

"I don't have much to live for."

She tried to shuffle off Spike's lap, but he tightened his hold on her. "Spike, let me go for a minute?"

"No. Not letting you go. Nearly lost you."

The words were the first he'd spoken in close to an hour and she knew she couldn't push him. He was on the edge.

"Then we need to find you reasons to live for, don't we?" Razor said quietly.

"Like me," Millie told her. "You saved my life, so we're family now."

Tabby blinked at her. "Not the way it works."

"It can be. We're connected now, you and I. And I need a friend so I'm gonna nominate you."

"Nominate me?" Tabby looked at Razor in confusion. "Can she do that?"

Razor shrugged, looking amused. "Guess she can."

Reyes kicked Luther. "Want me to take care of him?"

Spike snarled. "That should be my honor."

"Call my cousin," Tabby said suddenly. "He'll take care of him."

"Thought you weren't close to him, sugar?" Razor asked her.

"Not anymore. But we once were. Luther said Jared was after him. He'll make him disappear. My family is good at that."

"Do it," Spike said suddenly, surprising her. She thought he'd want to take care of Luther himself. "Don't want to leave Millie. Can't. Let Bartolli do it. Just don't want him coming here, near Millie."

Reyes nodded. "Tabby can call him and I'll meet him somewhere. Razor, you go with Spike and get these three to the hospital."

"No," Tabby said and she rose slowly. "I'll go with you. I need to see Jared. I need to know why he left me with him."

"Then I'm going with you," Razor said, standing too. He loomed over the petite girl with the pale skin and dark hair.

Reyes sighed. "Fine. Fuck. Spike, can you take care of these two?"

"Have been wiping my own ass for years, you know," Hack grumbled as Reyes helped him up.

Razor came over and picked up Luther, carrying the bound man over his shoulder.

"Spike, let me up for a minute. I'll come right back," she reassured him. "I won't leave your sight." He finally let her go with a grunt and she walked over to Tabby, giving the other woman a smile. "I meant what I said, Tabby. We're friends now. Anytime you need me, you call me." She grabbed a piece of paper from Spike's desk and wrote her number down.

Tabby looked at the piece of paper and Millie worried that she wasn't going to take it. Then with a hand that trembled, she reached for it, tucking it in her pocket. "Okay."

It was the best she was gonna get, but she'd take it. She just hoped the other woman would call.

~

Hours later, Spike carried her into the house. He'd taken her and Hack to the emergency room. They'd decided to keep Hack in for twenty-four hours due to his concussion. He wasn't happy about it, and she had a feeling he was going to make a terrible patient.

She'd been given the all-clear provided that she got plenty of rest and that Spike kept a close eye on her. She also needed to see her surgeon about her arm soon to make sure no further damage had occurred.

A giggle escaped her as Spike moved down the hallway towards their bedroom.

Oh, did she mention they gave her some really good drugs?

"Quillon. Quillon. Quillon."

"Any reason you got an obsession with my name, baby doll?" Spike asked. He'd been snarlier than usual while they'd been in the hospital and she could see he wasn't doing much better now, even though he knew she was unharmed.

"Unharmed? I would not call being choked until you passed out as unharmed."

Whoops. She must have said that out loud.

He laid her down on the bed and carefully undressed her. "You did."

"Relatively unharmed."

"You shouldn't have been fucking harmed at all," he snarled. "I should never have left you."

"You couldn't have known, Quillon."

"Stop calling me that. You call me Daddy." He loomed over her, his gaze intense.

She sighed. "You so pretty, Daddy."

He snorted. "They really gave you the good stuff, huh?"

"Daddy." She pouted, sniffling pathetically.

"What? What is it? Are you hurt?" he asked frantically.

"I never got to eat the magic wands and candy that Hack brought for me."

He sagged. "Christ, baby doll. Don't do that. You scared me."

She continued to sniff.

"Don't be upset," he told her. "Be a good girl and Daddy will get you some tomorrow, okay?"

"Okay. Promise, Daddy?"

"I promise. Now, let's get you to the bathroom so you can pee then you're going to bed. And you're staying in bed until I say you can get up."

"I don't gots to pee."

"Yes, you do."

"Nuh-uh. It's my body, Daddy. I'd know if I had to pee. Not you."

"Well, you're gonna try."

"Nuh-uh."

"Try for Daddy?" he cajoled.

"Oh, okay, Daddy. For you. But be prepared to eat your words 'cause this girl don't gots to pee."

He carried her into the bathroom. She could probably walk. Maybe. But why walk when he liked to carry her everywhere? Maybe she'd never walk again. Ooh or maybe she could float everywhere like a fairy? Or perhaps Tiny could come to life and she could ride him everywhere? Wouldn't that be something?

"It would definitely be something all right," Spike muttered.

Whoops. Talking out loud again.

Then he set her on her feet by the toilet and gently helped her sit. Moving away, he put some toothpaste on her toothbrush.

"See, Daddy? I didn't have to go. Bet you feel silly now," she sang.

"Baby doll, you're peeing," he replied dryly.

"What? No way." She tried to lean forward to see and nearly toppled off the toilet. Spike carefully grabbed hold of her.

"Careful! You'll hurt yourself."

"Sorry, Daddy. You sure I'm peeing?"

"Yep."

Weird. She couldn't feel a thing.

"They definitely gave you the good drugs, huh?" he said dryly.

"They sure did. I don't know why you got so growly at the poor doctor, he was just trying to help."

"He hurt you."

"Nuh-uh, that was that big meanie, Luther. Where is he? Did someone take care of him? What does that mean? Take care of him? What will happen to him?"

"Don't you worry about what that means," he told her firmly. He crouched in front of her and reached for some toilet paper to clean her up. Maybe later, she'd be embarrassed about that. Right now, she didn't care.

She loved these drugs.

"But—"

"Nope. I won't have you worrying about this. He is not your concern. Reyes took care of it."

"He handed him over to Tabby's cousin?"

"Yep."

"What about Tabby?"

By now he had her up and standing at the counter.

"Open up," he told her.

She opened wide and he started brushing her teeth.

"Tabby is fine. Spit."

She spat. "But where is she?"

"She went home with her cousin."

"What? Noooo." Tears dripped down her cheeks.

He cupped her face in his hands. "She wanted to go with him.

Razor tried to convince her to go with them, but she wouldn't. They couldn't make her."

"But what if he hurts her? Or marries her off to someone? Someone like Luther?

"We'll try to keep an eye on her, all right? I promise." He wiped her tears then drew her close. "I'm more concerned with you right now. You are my number one priority. From now on, nothing will hurt you. I won't let it."

She slumped against him. "And nothing will hurt you because I won't allow it."

Picking her up again, he carried her to the bed and tucked her under the covers.

"Daddy, I can't go to sleep right now," she told him.

"Why not? Oh, you need Chompers. I'll get him. Is he downstairs?"

"No, I mean, yes. But also, I'm naked," she whispered.

"So you are. That a problem?"

"Ooh, does this mean we're going to have some fun between the sheets?" She winked at him.

"Why are you blinking like that?" he asked. "Are you feeling all right?"

"I was trying to wink." She huffed. "Obviously."

"Sorry, baby doll. I can see that now."

Somewhat mollified, she reached out for him. "How 'bout you get naked too?"

"As much as I would like to, you're not up to anything more than a cuddle right now."

She pouted. "That's no fun." She sighed. "Hey, where's Mr. Fluffy? He must be so upset at being left here alone."

"If only that was the case," he muttered.

"What?"

"Nothing, baby doll. I'll go get him and Chompers. You stay in bed, understand me? Move from the bed and as soon as you're better that will be three ticks on the naughty side of your reward chart as well as thirty minutes in time-out."

"Daddy, that's just mean."

"Stay put."

She sighed. Honestly, it was like he didn't trust her or something.

She was singing to herself and staring up at the ceiling when she swore she heard something. That sounded like a dog barking. Mr. Fluffy? And there went another dog. Huh. That was weird. And was that... nah, that made no sense.

The door to the bedroom opened and Spike walked in with Chompers and a bottle of fairy juice in one hand and Mr. Fluffy in the other.

"Daddy! Chompers! Mr. Fluffy! You're all back! I waited such a long time. And I was a good girl. See?"

"Very good girl."

He placed the bottle on the bedside table then set Chompers down beside her. He gave her a moment to cuddle Mr. Fluffy before placing him on his dog bed.

Then he stripped and turned off the main light before he grabbed the bottle and joined her in bed. He lay on his side, his head resting on his hand as he placed the nipple of the bottle to her lips. She suckled on it, drinking the slightly flavored water until she was sated. After putting the bottle on the nightstand, he lay down next to her, resting his arm over her waist.

"Daddy?"

"Yeah, baby doll?"

"I think I was hallucinating."

He stiffened. "Why is that?"

"I heard puppies barking, like more than just Mr. Fluffy. Silly, huh?"

"Hmm," he replied.

"Daddy?"

"Yeah, baby doll?" he said with a note of amused exasperation.

"And I thought I heard another voice. It sounded like Reverend Pat. That's funny, huh?"

"It's funny all right. That's a story for in the morning."

"Can I have the story now?" she asked. She liked stories.

"No. You can sleep now," he told her sternly.

"Daddy?"

"Baby doll, are you going to ask me questions all night?"

"Just one more, I promise."

"Okay, ask."

"Were you scared tonight? Cause I was."

He tightened his hold on her. "I was fucking terrified."

"Daddy?"

"Baby doll," he said sternly. "It's time for sleep. Let me get your pacifier."

Not only did the pacifier help her relax into sleep, but they'd discovered one day by accident that it could help during her migraines. It seemed to loosen her jaw.

"Oh yeah, that might help. You know what else might help?"

"What's that?" he asked as he climbed out of bed and moved around to her side of the bed. She wondered why he didn't just reach over her. But she guessed maybe he didn't want to bump her.

"A kiss."

"All right, you can have a kiss." He climbed back into bed and leaned in to kiss her lightly.

"Daddy?"

He groaned. "Yes, baby doll?"

"Love you."

"Love you too. Now sleep."

She slept. Held in Daddy's arms. Because she was always a good girl.

"No, no, that's in the wrong place. They should go more to the left," Mrs. Spain called out.

"Go right," Andrey countered.

"I really think they're perfect where they are," Mrs. Larsen added.

"What?" Mr. Spain barked.

Millie giggled as she sat on the porch watching as poor Spike tried to hang some fairy lights in the trees around the house. She bet he hadn't anticipated having so many helpers.

Turning on the ladder, he gave her a look that promised retribution. She didn't know why he was blaming her. All she'd done was made the suggestion that some fairy lights in the trees might look pretty.

She hadn't expected Mrs. Spain and Mrs. Larsen to demand that Spike drive them to the store to buy them. Or that they'd all expect him to hang them then and there.

She just smiled widely back at him.

One of the puppies barked and another one ran across the porch and onto the lawn, a shoe held tightly in his mouth.

Uh-oh. That looked suspiciously like Spike's shoe. Seemed all the puppies had caught onto Mr. Fluffy's games with Spike.

It was only because they liked him so much.

Or that's what she tried to tell him, anyway.

All the other puppies raced out of the house, chasing him. Well, all of them except Mr. Fluffy who was sleeping on the porch in one of his dog baskets. Mrs. Spain and Mrs. Larsen had also done some shopping for all the puppies.

"You're happy."

She glanced over as Reverend Pat walked towards her, carrying two cups of coffee. He set them down on the small table that sat between the two rocking chairs. Then, leaning over he adjusted her blanket on her lap, making sure it covered her legs even though it wasn't that cold out here.

Everyone was fussing over her. She'd barely been allowed to lift a finger in two weeks. But she knew she'd given them all a fright. It was their way of showing they cared. Although she'd never have thought Reverend Pat would worry so much.

She guessed, deep down, he really did love her.

"I am. I really am."

He handed her a coffee then sat and took one for himself. She took a sip. Ahh, made perfectly.

"He's a good man. Wasn't so sure for a start. The tattoos. The motorcycles. His gruff manner. But he loves you."

"He does. And I love him. Gruffness and all. Although he still hasn't taken me for a ride on his motorcycle." She pouted. She'd have to wait until her arm was fully healed.

"Probably a good thing," Reverend Pat muttered. "Not sure I want you on the back of one of those things."

She rolled her eyes at him good-naturedly.

His face grew serious. "I've been worrying about you since the moment you left Nowhere."

"Really? Because you seemed awfully happy to see the back of me at my good luck party," she teased.

He sighed. "I admit, there have been times over the years when I thought you were sent to test my patience. But I've missed you, Millicent Margaret. Your smile. Your joy. Even your clumsiness."

"Aww, Reverend Pat, you love me, don't you?"

"Wouldn't go that far," he said gruffly. But she noticed his cheeks growing red. "You're a good girl. Your grandparents would be very proud of you. Daria would be proud of you."

Sadness filled her. She was still coming to terms with her sister's death. "I still feel like I failed her."

He reached over and patted her knee gently. That was about as affectionate as he got.

"You aren't responsible for everyone, Millie. And you couldn't fail anyone if you tried."

She sniffled at his words. "Thanks, Reverend Pat. Wish you could all stay longer." They were headed home the day after tomorrow. And the puppies were all going to their new homes. She was a little sad that Spike wouldn't let her keep Mr. Fluffy's littermates. But she guessed having five puppies might be a bit much.

"It's time to get home. I fear we might be outstaying our welcome." He grinned as Spike let out a frustrated groan.

"Well, don't worry, we have to come pack up the house and get my stuff. Spike just doesn't want me travelling that far at the moment."

Overprotective as always.

Reverend Pat nodded. "I look forward to it."

"That's it. That's where they're staying." Spike stomped his way down the ladder and she had to bite her lip to stop from laughing. He took down the ladder, lying it on its side as he walked towards her.

"Time for your nap, Millie."

Which was code for *I need a time-out from all these people invading my house.* He walked up the steps and she put her coffee down as he gently picked her up in his arms. Mr. Fluffy rose with a yawn and stood to follow them. Seemed he felt the same way about his brothers and sister.

Spike kissed her forehead as he turned. Her insides melted at the gesture. Then he froze.

"What the hell is that dog doing with my shoe?"

She tried. She really tried to hold it in.

But she couldn't stop the giggles from escaping.

EPILOGUE

Spike slid down her body, wrapping his lips around her plump nipple he tugged at it softly.

"Daddy," she groaned.

Fuck. Yeah.

Finally, the house was empty. It was just him, his baby doll and that damn dog.

Two weeks.

Two weeks he'd put up with her crazy friends, with barking puppies who weren't nearly as well behaved as Mr. Fluffy. Honestly, he appreciated the narcoleptic ball of fluff much more now. Even if he had barfed in his shoe yesterday.

Well over two weeks since he'd made love to his girl. Because she'd been in hospital and recovering before their visitors arrived and she hadn't felt like she could relax enough to have sex while Reverend Pat was in the house.

But now they had all gone back to Nowhere. The puppies, who had all been to the vet including Mr. Fluffy, had all gone to good homes. Apparently, they were part Leonburger. He was so glad they'd gotten them away from the Devil's Sinners. The vet thought they'd probably intended to use them as drug mules.

Apparently, it was a thing some gangs did, using dogs to carry liquid bags of heroin inside them. Luther must have bought them from somewhere out of the city and had been transporting them to the gang headquarters when he stopped to track down Regan and lost one. God knows how Mr. Fluffy escaped since he was rarely awake. But he somehow had.

Millie had been relieved when the vet said that it was fine for Mr. Fluffy to be that sleepy. But they'd both been shocked to learn he'd likely to grow to well over two feet tall and would probably weigh around a hundred and forty pounds.

He moved down her tummy and then knelt up, pushing the blankets apart.

"Legs spread wide and stay very still. I don't want you hurting yourself."

Luther hadn't done any further damage to her shoulder, thank fuck. But she was still unable to use that arm and he knew it frustrated her. There had been a few tantrums thrown over it, out of sight of their guests of course. This week, the ticks were going to be firmly on the punishment side of her chart.

He'd need to be imaginative with her punishment since he still wasn't comfortable spanking her with her injured shoulder.

Lying on his stomach between her legs, he spread her lower lips, licking at her clit with long, firm swipes of his tongue. She let out a satisfied cry. Yeah, his baby was loud during sex.

And he fucking loved it.

He twirled his tongue around her clit then dropped it lower, running it over her folds, lapping up all her juices.

She tasted fucking delicious.

He played with her, teased her, brought her up to the edge over and over.

"Please, please, Daddy. I need to come."

"Not sure you're ready yet." Her thighs were quivering, her whole body tense with the need to orgasm.

Poor baby.

Fuck, if his balls weren't already tight with need, he might have stayed down here all day, playing with her, drinking from her.

But he took pity on her and this time when she reached that peak, he pushed her over, her cries of ecstasy making him grin. Placing a final kiss on her clit he moved up beside her, lying on his side.

"My pretty pussy. My plump nipple. My sexy baby doll." Leaning in and took her nipple into his mouth, suckling on it.

"Oh. Ohh, please. I need you inside me. Don't tell me no."

He huffed out a laugh, and let her nipple go. "Baby doll, believe me, I don't want to. Not to mention I find it very hard to say no to you."

"That's nice."

He snorted. "Roll over towards me, onto your good side."

He got out of bed and climbed in behind her. Hack had suggested she try going on birth control for her migraines so there was no need for condoms anymore.

"Oh God, did you research the best way to have sex with me while I'm injured?" she asked as he grabbed her leg and pulled it back so it rested on his thigh. Then he slid himself deep inside her.

"Sure did. Fucking hell, you feel like heaven."

SHE FELT LIKE HEAVEN? He felt even better. He was stretching her, filling her. She wanted more but he kept his thrusts shallow.

"Please, Spike. More. I need more."

"Don't want to hurt you."

"You won't. Please. Please."

"Fuck. Christ. I'm so close." His movements became harder,

faster and she groaned in relief. He reached around to play with her nipples, careful not to jolt her arm. He toyed with them, pulled on them. The slight pain just pushed her arousal higher.

"Oh. Oh."

Reaching down, he slid his finger against her clit. His movements became more erratic. She could hear his breath coming in faster pants.

"Come for me, baby doll. Come for Daddy."

"Yes, oh yes," she screamed as she came, clenching down around his hard dick. He gave his own roar of satisfaction. No less quiet and a smug smile crossed her face.

Definitely heaven.

∼

"You ready to get dressed, baby doll?" Spike called out from the bedroom.

"Yep, just doing my make-up. I'll only be a second. I have it all laid out."

It felt like it had been forever since she'd overheard that conversation in a dark alleyway. Since her life changed forever. So much had happened.

Some of it hadn't been good, of course. She was still worried about Tabby, she hadn't heard from her at all. Spike promised he'd keep trying to find out what he could about her. So she guessed that would have to suffice. For the moment.

Even though she was sad that her friends had to leave, she was happy to have Spike to herself once more. Her body was still humming from the way he'd woken her up this morning.

Today, she was going to her first ever barbeque at Sunny and Duke's place. Apparently, Duke and Sunny had these barbecues at least once a month and everyone would be there. She couldn't wait to get to know Sunny and Betsy better. But she was also nervous as hell. About making a good impression, about what they might think about her, if she'd fit in.

"Millie, what is this?" Spike pointed at the clothes she'd laid out on the bed.

He didn't like her dressing herself. He told her it was because she might strain her shoulder, but she had a feeling that even once she was healed, she still wouldn't be allowed to put her own clothes on.

"It's the clothes I chose, why?" She looked at the plain, black dress she'd bought online.

"You're not wearing this."

"Why not? Is it too casual? Not casual enough?" She chewed her lip. "What's wrong with it?"

"It's not you. That's what is wrong with it. Now, go choose something else. Something you would really wear. With color. While I go put this in the trash." He picked it up and walked towards the door.

"You can't throw it away."

"Why not? You're not ever going to wear it."

"But . . . but . . ."

He strode back to her, his eyebrows drawn down and then leaned in and kissed her fiercely. "What did I tell you? That you don't ever change you, understand me? No. Matter. What."

Tears filled her eyes. How had she been so lucky to find him?

"Now, find a new dress," he commanded as he walked away. "And that's two ticks on the naughty side of the chart."

What? Well, that sucked.

∼

MILLIE GIGGLED as she watched all the puppies playing together. Royal and Baron each threw a ball and the excited fur balls practically fell over their big paws, trying to chase them. Well, all the puppies except for her boy who had found a patch of sunlight and promptly fell asleep.

Baron lay on the ground, laughing as the puppies crawled over him.

"Gonna have some tired puppies tonight," Sunny said as she came and sat on a chair beside Millie. Betsy had taken a seat on the other side. They'd just eaten lunch and now the guys were up on the porch, having a drink and talking, while she'd come down here to watch the twins play with the puppies.

"Bandit has been sleeping in with the boys at night," Betsy told them, sipping on a pink lemonade. "He alternates between their beds."

"Spike won't let Mr. Fluffy sleep in bed with me." Millie pushed the skirt of her red dress down. She didn't know why she'd been so worried about what she wore or fitting in. Everyone here was so nice.

"Razor is so sweet with his puppy, Luna and she adores him," Sunny whispered, looking back at the large, dark-skinned man.

"I wish Hack was here with his puppy," Millie said.

"I'm glad he took one, I worry he gets lonely," Betsy said.

So did she.

"Hatter keeps chewing Duke's boxers, at this rate he's not going to have any left," Sunny said with a grin. "I'm not complaining."

"All of your friends have returned home?" Betsy asked.

"Yes, I miss them. But Spike said we can visit. I think he was pleased to see them go. Not that I can blame him, he's used to having that big house to himself and they're pretty loud. Plus, Reverend Pat kept grilling him on his intentions towards me."

Sunny grinned. "Does that mean there's going to be a wedding soon?"

She felt herself growing red. "I don't know."

But maybe.

∼

She yawned as Spike carefully lifted her out of his truck.

"Someone's tired."

She scowled. "Am not."

He raised his eyebrows at her as he grabbed hold of Mr. Fluffy in one arm. "And grouchy."

"I'm not tired and I'm not grouchy."

"Uh-huh."

"Urgh. Daddy, I'm not tired."

"Right."

Oh, he could be so infuriating sometimes. Taking her hand in his, he led her inside. He set Mr. Fluffy down on the floor then helped her remove her shoes.

"You missed your nap."

"I don't needs a nap. I'm a big girl," she complained. Only, she wasn't right now. It had been a long time since she'd been able to let her Little side free. But finally, the house was free of people.

"Nope, you're my baby doll. You need some Little time."

Yeah. She really did.

He glanced at his watch. "Too late for a nap now, though."

Yes!

"But if you're too grouchy, Daddy will just have to put you to bed straight after dinner."

Her lower lip dropped. He wouldn't. "But Daddy we were gonna sit out and watch the fairy lights twinkle tonight."

"Hmm, well you better be on your best behavior."

"I will. I promise."

Leaning in, he kissed her gently. "Such a beautiful girl. Got a present for you."

He was always buying her gifts. "Daddy, you didn't have to get me something."

"Course not. I wanted to."

They walked into her playroom. Instantly, she felt more relaxed. She loved it in here. Maybe she couldn't really play with a lot of the stuff yet, sitting on the floor was a problem, but it still fed her Little's soul with happiness.

Her gaze was immediately drawn to the big wooden desk and pink velvet chair set against the opposite wall.

"Daddy, when did you get this?"

"Ordered it last week. It arrived one day while you were busy with your friends. Snuck it in here as a surprise. Thought you could sit at it and craft."

"It's amazing."

"Also thought you could sit at it and write lines when you were naughty."

Not so amazing.

"I's never naughty, Daddy."

"Uh-huh." He turned away and if she thought she could get away with it, she'd have poked her tongue out at him.

Spike moved towards a big cane basket, that sat next to the stage. That was new too.

"What's in there, Daddy?"

"Play outfits." He opened the lid and started pulling things out. There was a sparkly pink cape and a princess tiara. A bright orange feather boa. A pair of oversized glasses.

"Here it is." He held up a lavender tutu.

"Daddy! That's so cool!"

"Figured it might be easier to wear than your ballerina outfit with your shoulder."

Yeah, her ballerina outfit would be hard to get on and off, but this would be perfect.

"I wanna wear it now. I needs tights and a top though." She glanced down at her own outfit.

"I'll get you something to wear. First, though." He drew out her behavior chart, adding two ticks to the naughty side.

"What's that for?" she cried.

"For earlier. Trying to wear that awful outfit."

"I thought you were joking about that!"

"Since when do I joke?"

He grasped hold of her hand and led her to the desk and chair. On top of the desk, he'd set out paper and her coloring pens already.

"Sit."

When she was seated, he handed her a ballpoint pen and pointed to the bit of paper. "Fifty lines. I am perfect just the way I am."

"I love you, Daddy," she whispered.

"Not as much as I love you."

～

Later on that evening, they sat outside on the rocking chairs. She still wore her tutu, although she had plenty of other layers on too. And she was bundled up under a blanket. She finished her hot chocolate as she stared out at the twinkling lights.

Spike stood and grabbed her empty mug, placing it down. He held out a hand to her. "Dance with me."

Her mouth parted. "Really? I thought you didn't like to dance?"

He shrugged. "Will be more like swaying back and forth than dancing."

With a smile she put her small hand in his much larger one and he gently helped her up, holding her hand and leading her down the steps onto the lawn. Under the fairy lights, he drew her close against his wide chest. Placing both hands on her lower back, he was careful not to place any pressure on her injured shoulder.

She snuggled in close, breathing him in. She felt so safe. Loved.

"Promise me something," he murmured.

"Anything."

"Never leave me. No matter what."

Her heart filled with love. She didn't think it possible, but somehow, she fell in love with him just a bit more every day.

"Pinky promise."

"Pinky promise," he repeated, leaning in he kissed her forehead before pulling back.

And then he smiled.

LET'S KEEP IN TOUCH!

Don't miss a new release, sign up to my newsletter for sneak peeks, deleted scenes and giveaways: https://landing.mailerlite.com/webforms/landing/p7l6g0

You can also join my Facebook readers group here: https://www.facebook.com/groups/386830425069911/

Printed in Great Britain
by Amazon